Written
on the
Wind

Books by Elizabeth Camden

THE BLACKSTONE LEGACY

Carved in Stone
Written on the Wind

HOPE AND GLORY SERIES

The Spice King
A Gilded Lady
The Prince of Spies

The Lady of Bolton Hill
The Rose of Winslow Street
Against the Tide
Into the Whirlwind
With Every Breath
Beyond All Dreams
Toward the Sunrise: An Until the Dawn *Novella*
Until the Dawn
Summer of Dreams: A From This Moment *Novella*
From This Moment
To the Farthest Shores
A Dangerous Legacy
A Daring Venture
A Desperate Hope

Written on the Wind

ELIZABETH CAMDEN

BETHANYHOUSE
a division of Baker Publishing Group
Minneapolis, Minnesota

© 2022 by Dorothy Mays

Published by Bethany House Publishers
11400 Hampshire Avenue South
Minneapolis, Minnesota 55438
www.bethanyhouse.com

Bethany House Publishers is a division of
Baker Publishing Group, Grand Rapids, Michigan

Printed in the United States of America

Library of Congress Cataloging-in-Publication Data
Names: Camden, Elizabeth, 1965– author.
Title: Written on the wind / Elizabeth Camden.
Description: Minneapolis, Minnesota : Bethany House, a division of Baker
    Publishing Group, [2022] | Series: Blackstone legacy, the ; 2
Identifiers: LCCN 2021048403 | ISBN 9780764238444 (paperback) | ISBN
    9780764240133 (casebound) | ISBN 9781493437306 (ebook)
Subjects: GSAFD: Historical fiction.
Classification: LCC PS3553.A429 W75 2022 | DDC 813/.54—dc23
LC record available at https://lccn.loc.gov/2021048403

Cover design by Jennifer Parker

Baker Publishing Group publications use paper produced from sustainable forestry practices and post-consumer waste whenever possible.

22 23 24 25 26 27 28   7 6 5 4 3 2 1

1

*N*atalia Blackstone always considered the third floor of her family's bank the most fascinating five thousand square feet in the entire United States. This was where the research used to fuel the industrial revolution was produced on a daily basis. It was filled with maps and blueprints and stacks of financial reports.

Unfortunately, her cousin Liam disliked it for the same reason.

"Too many books," he growled as she gave him a tour of the Blackstone Bank's library. "It's like being in school again."

"True," she said, but that was why she loved it. As the bank's leading analyst for Russian investment, Natalia needed access to vast amounts of research, and the bank was the only place she truly felt at home. The society events that most ladies of her class enjoyed were tedious affairs that made her itch, but the chance to learn more about the Russian timber market? Or help finance the construction of the Trans-Siberian Railway? These challenges sparked her curiosity, and she wanted to share that love of business with Liam.

Her cousin was thirty-three years old and recently arrived in New York after working as a welder in the shipyards of

Philadelphia for most of his life. He needed a hard and fast education in high finance to succeed on Wall Street.

She gestured to a map of Russia on the library wall. A red line stretching across the country marked the route of the Trans-Siberian Railway, a monumental endeavor that would someday be the longest railway in the world.

"This is where the Trans-Siberian starts," she said, pointing to Moscow. "Building the railroad was easy in the well-developed part of Russia, but everything is harder now." She pointed to the blank part of the map east of the Ural Mountains, where the land was so sparsely populated that a person could ride for days on horseback without seeing a single village. "This is where our construction team is currently working. They need to build hundreds of bridges to cross all those rivers, and it's slowing them down."

"How does this affect the bank?" Liam asked.

"It makes planning my finance schedule a nightmare." She laughed. "That's why communication with the Russian manager is so important. He usually sends me daily updates to track the railway's progress."

Usually. Lately those telegram communications had veered badly off-kilter, and it worried her. The bank had invested gigantic sums in the Trans-Siberian, all on her recommendation. Anything that endangered the account could upend Natalia's entire world.

"Let me show you the communication room and how we monitor our overseas investments," she said.

They crossed through a room where a dozen junior analysts were stationed at individual desks, busily compiling data. Like worker bees deep within a hive, the analysts on the third floor produced steady streams of research reports on potential new investments. These men—and all of them were men—looked so ordinary in their business suits and paper-strewn desks, but their appearance belied the extraordinary endeavors that occurred on this floor. It was here that Rockefeller, Vanderbilt, and other business tycoons obtained loans to build the infrastructure for the nation. This was where cities and states applied for bonds to build railroads and bridges. The White House controlled the political fate of the nation, but Wall Street had more impact on the daily life of Americans.

Natalia spent six days a week on the bank's third floor, the only kingdom she ever wanted to rule. Her father was president of the bank, which was how she'd attained such influence here. It was the dawn of the twentieth century, and although women had made strides in science and the arts, the world of finance was still closed to them. It was no secret that Natalia worked at the bank, but society would have a heart attack if they knew exactly how much power a twenty-eight-year-old woman had in managing the bank's largest investment in Russia.

"This is the communication room," she said to Liam, who ducked through the ornate wooden doorway. Men as tall as Liam probably had to duck a lot. She and Liam shared the same black hair and green eyes, but that was where their resemblance ended. She had the willowy figure of her ballerina mother, while Liam towered well over six feet and had the broad shoulders and brawny build of someone who grew up laboring in the shipyards.

Telegraph machines rattled a stream of intermittent clicks as messages arrived from as far away as London or Japan, or as close as the New York Stock Exchange two blocks down the street.

Aaron Jones, the supervisor of the communication room, munched on a bagel while monitoring the tape coming in off the London ticker. With his rolled-up shirtsleeves, full beard, and colorful suspenders, he looked like a younger version of Santa Claus.

"Good morning, Aaron," Natalia said as she entered the room.

Aaron flushed and shot to his feet, brushing crumbs from his hands and then reaching for his jacket. "Yes, Miss Blackstone," he said, shrugging into his jacket. "How can I help you this morning?"

She wished he wouldn't be so formal, but some of the employees never felt comfortable around the boss's daughter. Her father was powerful, intimidating, and ran the bank with an iron fist, but he allowed her the freedom to set the tone among the third-floor employees.

"First names, please," she reminded Aaron, then winced as Aaron reached for a tie to wrap around his collar. "And there is certainly no need for a tie."

Aaron continued hastily knotting his tie. "When I dined with the senior Blackstones last week, Mrs. Blackstone said everyone should wear a tie, even in the back office."

Natalia's smile froze. Her stepmother might reign supreme at home, but Natalia refused to let Poppy bully her coworkers on the third floor.

"Mrs. Blackstone rarely visits the bank, and I would prefer to keep a more relaxed atmosphere here," she said, trying to conceal her dislike for her father's new wife. It was galling to think of Poppy as her stepmother. After all, she and Poppy were the same age.

She pushed the disagreeable thoughts aside to continue Liam's tour. "I'm showing my cousin how we communicate with our overseas accounts. Has there been any news from Count Sokolov?"

"Not a thing, ma'am."

Her spirit dimmed. Count Dimitri Sokolov was her point of contact for the railway, and his continued silence was worrisome. For the past three years, they had exchanged regular telegrams as she wired him funds to supply tons of coal and steel to his remote Siberian outpost. What began as a business arrangement had soon morphed into a friendship. The count's telegrams were long, chatty, and fascinating. After their initial formality, he soon addressed her simply as "Dearest Natalia." Then he would fire off all manner of questions and observations. He had opinions on everything from the proper way to brew tea to the merits of classical music. He was a bit of a hypochondriac, frequently bemoaning the state of his health in the desolate Siberian wilderness.

Dearest Natalia, he had written last week. *I am glad to report that the sun has been shining, but this morning I noticed a rash on my hands. I fear it is sun poisoning and I am likely to catch my death. It can happen to even the strongest of men.*

It was typical of Dimitri's melodramatic suffering, but she would send him words of teasing comfort, which he thrived upon. She didn't know if he was handsome or homely, but she knew his favorite ballet was *Swan Lake,* and that he crossbred apple trees at his summer estate. He was a bit of a snob, always praising the pomp and formality of Russian feudalism, and he teased her mercilessly over American informality. *Why do Americans shake hands instead of bowing like the rest of the civilized world? It is unsanitary, Natalia. One day I shall learn of your death by a pestilence contracted from your obsessive handshaking.*

When Natalia saw the world through Count Sokolov's eyes, everything became more vivid. Sunsets were not the end of the day, they were blazing fires of a dying sun as it reclined in exhaustion. The chocolates she sent him for Christmas weren't a simple gift, but quite possibly the finest culinary creation since God himself sent manna to the Hebrews wandering in the desert.

"Let me show you how we communicate," she said to Liam, taking a seat beside Aaron at the telegraph machine. Her message notified Count Sokolov of the incoming loan installment and projections for the next month. Even though the wire was going to Russia, they were always sent in English.

Natalia was fluent in Russian, of course. Her Russian mother had raised her from birth on Russian language, folklore, and customs. It was Natalia's ease with Russian culture that gave her father the confidence to assign her to the Russian account. Soon Natalia had a better understanding of the Russian economy than anyone else in the bank, and she was promoted to lead the Trans-Siberian project.

While Aaron tapped the brass sounder to send the message, she continued explaining to Liam how the Trans-Siberian would soon reach the Pacific Ocean. It meant that Americans could start exporting their goods from California to the huge Russian market. It was a privilege to be a part of something that was going to change the world. Dreaming about the Trans-Siberian captured her imagination, even though she needed to keep this exuberant part of her soul hidden. It was essential to project the same logical formality as all the other soberly suited businessmen of Wall Street.

A cascade of clicks from the telegraph sounder came to life with an incoming message. Its brevity made it obvious it did not come from Count Sokolov, who would have berated Natalia for such a terse message without a salutation or an inquiry about his health.

Aaron passed her the message:

Confirmation received. Payroll next month anticipated to hold steady.

"That's all?" she asked in dismay.

"That's all," Aaron confirmed.

She wouldn't tolerate it. Dimitri's continuing absence worried her. "Send a message asking for the whereabouts of Count Sokolov," she ordered. The miracle of modern telegraphy meant that messages arrived at their destination after only a few minutes, but her growing unease made her impatient. When the answer to her message arrived five minutes later, the news was not good:

Count Sokolov has been reassigned.

"I don't believe it," she insisted. Dimitri would love to be transferred back to Saint Petersburg, but he would *not* have left his post without telling her goodbye. If Count Sokolov no longer worked on the railroad, she had no idea how to contact him.

But she knew who could help.

───── ∽ ─────

The police department of New York City served the most diverse community in America. Immigrants from all over the world clustered into ethnic enclaves, where their native languages continued to thrive for generations. Many of those bilingual immigrants found work in the police department, and Boris Kozlov was just such a man.

Boris arrived from the Ukraine twelve years ago and patrolled a Russian-speaking section of the city informally known as Little Odessa. He strolled the two-mile loop through the neighborhood and often stopped in at The Samovar, a Russian market and tea shop that catered to the Slavic community. If Natalia waited at the tea shop long enough, Boris would eventually make an appearance.

As always, customers filled the stools at the service counter of the crowded shop. Tightly packed shelves covered the walls, weighed down with jars of pickles, herring, and sauerkraut. Ropes of garlic and dried sausages hung from hooks near the ceiling, and barrels of imported spices filled the remaining floor space.

"Has Officer Kozlov been through recently?" Natalia asked the young waitress in Russian.

"Not yet," the woman replied, also in Russian. "He'll probably come by soon."

It was a rough neighborhood, and the owners of The Samovar usually slipped Officer Kozlov a pastry or a mug of something hot in exchange for regularly stopping in.

Natalia took a seat at the counter and ordered a pirozhki, a fried yeasty bun filled with cabbage and onions. This sort of peasant food would never be served at her father's Fifth Avenue mansion, but when Natalia's mother was alive, they came here often, and Galina delighted in sharing the comforting food of her youth and filling Natalia with tales of her faraway homeland.

Natalia had just finished her pirozhki when Officer Kozlov entered the shop. The police officer's uniform did little to disguise his rough edges. Everything from Boris's bulldog expression and thick mustache to his barrel chest made him seem tough and intimidating. He'd been walking the beat for years but aspired to become a detective and thus sought investigative work on the side to prove himself to the police hierarchy.

Natalia waved for him to join her at the last remaining seat at the counter and ordered him a pirozhki. "I need information about a man in Russia," she said.

"Name?" Boris asked.

"Dimitri Sokolov. *Count* Dimitri Sokolov."

Boris looked surprised by the lofty title, but only for a moment. "I've never heard of him. Where does he live?"

"He's originally from Saint Petersburg but has been posted to the far eastern provinces for the past three years, working on the railroad. He left his post a few weeks ago. He may have returned to Saint Petersburg, but I can't be sure."

"This one is going to cost you," he said.

Anything Boris did for her always cost plenty. She slipped him a few bills, which was probably more than he earned in a week.

"That should get you started," she said. "There may be fees for wires or informants in Russia. I'll pay for those too. And if you find him, there will be a nice reward."

"How nice?" Boris asked, his eyes gleaming.

"*Very* nice," she said simply. Coming from one of the wealthiest families in America meant Natalia never had to scrimp. She would give almost anything to learn what had happened to Dimitri, because his abrupt disappearance did not bode well.

2

SAINT PETERSBURG, RUSSIA

*C*ount Dimitri Sokolov drew a sobering breath as he adjusted the high stand collar of his dress coat, examining his image in the mirror. There was no visible sign of the gold coins he had stitched into the lapels of his coat, but the lump of three diamonds hidden beneath the lining of his shoe could be felt with every step he took. The authorities might seize his clothing and thus his hidden treasures, but they would never find his last diamond.

His light brown hair was long enough to cover the scar he had cut into the back of his head, where he had inserted a diamond beneath his scalp. The scab still throbbed, but that last, precious diamond was beyond detection. With luck he'd never have to dig it back out, but knowing it was there kept a spark of defiance smoldering within him.

He was a son of Russia, the last of a proud and noble line, and he would present himself with dignity when he faced the judge in the courtroom. He straightened the braided tassels hanging from the epaulettes on his shoulders. It was time to face his sentencing, even though his fate was a foregone conclusion.

He was going to lose everything. His fortune, his lands, his title. But losing Mirosa would hurt most of all. The estate had been in his family for three centuries. During his years in Siberia, it was dreams of Mirosa that kept him going. Memories of long summer evenings on the porch overlooking his valley had sustained him for years. That dream was gone. Mirosa and everything he owned had already been seized by the state, a harsh lesson to other aristocrats who dared to defy the czar. He had no lawyer or defense counsel. There was no longer any need after yesterday's brief show trial. His entire life was going to change because of the split-second decision he'd made three weeks earlier.

Dimitri looked straight ahead as he entered the courtroom, wishing his mother wasn't here to witness his humiliation. He'd begged her to stay away, but Anna Sokolova was a stubborn woman, and she sat in the front row, her face a mask of stone. To make it worse, Olga was here too, triggering another dart of sorrow. Olga wore her widow's weeds, a painful reminder that at last he and Olga were free to marry. Everyone assumed they would, but it could never happen now.

At least he was spared the humiliation of wearing irons and fetters, but those might come soon. The skirt of his mother's sunny yellow gown caught his eye as he headed toward the front of the courtroom, but he couldn't look at her. She was about to lose everything too.

"Count Dimitri Mikhailovich Sokolov," the judge said in a slow, ominous tone. "Having been found guilty of cowardice and dereliction of duty, you are hereby stripped of your title and all your estates. Any bank accounts in your name are now forfeited to the state. Upon leaving this courtroom, you will be transported to the town of Tobolsk."

Dimitri flinched. Tobolsk was where they sent all convicts destined for exile in the Siberian penal colonies. A pillar of stuccoed brick stood in Tobolsk, and convicts were allowed to lay their hands on it, press their faces to the ground, and say farewell to civilization before being funneled to one of the dozens of penal colonies scattered across the vast wasteland. Prisoners were encouraged to take a handful of soil with them, a reminder of the land they left behind as they headed into exile. No other spot in Russia had witnessed as much human misery as the pillar in Tobolsk.

Panic clouded the edges of his vision, and it was hard to comprehend anything the judge said in that awful, droning voice. All he could hear was his mother, who began weeping in terrible, keening sobs.

The judge's censorious voice continued. "You are hereby sentenced to the penal colony on Sakhalin Island, where you will serve seven years in the iron mines of the czar."

Dimitri should have expected it. Sakhalin Island was where most political prisoners were exiled, since it was the farthest outpost within the empire. Still, it was hard to keep standing upright as realization of his fate sank in.

If he could go back in time, would he have done anything differently that terrible morning three weeks ago? His refusal to participate in the massacre had saved no lives. All it did was destroy his own.

The lowering of the gavel sounded like a gunshot. Dimitri turned to walk down the aisle of the courtroom, maintaining a ramrod-straight posture but feeling the world crumble around him.

There was only one thing of which he could be certain: He was not going to Sakhalin Island. The icy, windswept island made escape impossible. Work in the iron mines was brutal, and few people survived their sentence.

God would not have sent Dimitri to witness the massacre of innocent people if he was meant to meekly accept his punishment. The world needed to know what he had seen. He had been silenced from the moment he was taken into custody, but he was not completely without resources. He had one bank account left to his name. It was in New York City, controlled by his last remaining friend in the world.

He must now find a way to reach Natalia Blackstone or die in the attempt.

3

It was no secret that Natalia and her stepmother did not like each other, but that didn't stop Natalia from doting on the child Poppy had given birth to last month. Alexander was a tiny infant for such a weighty name. He occupied the center of his princely crib, wearing handmade gowns stitched by nuns in Corsica and clutching a sterling silver baby rattle. Natalia loved the way he opened his huge, dark eyes and stared at the world around him, slowly blinking in baffled wonder. Then he'd let out a terrific yawn that seemed to consume his entire body until he released it with a look of contented exhaustion. How she adored this little scrap of humanity!

Nevertheless, the gossip columns loved claiming that Natalia was jealous of her baby brother, and that after twenty-eight years as Oscar Blackstone's only child, she resented the arrival of the long-hoped-for male heir who would oust Natalia from the bank and her father's inheritance.

It was all rubbish.

Well, mostly rubbish. The bylaws of the bank precluded women from having voting shares in the management of the bank's investments, meaning that Alexander would someday inherit her father's control of the bank while Natalia would forever remain a business analyst on the third floor. But that was all right. She was paid a generous salary for her work and had nothing but love for little Alexander.

Her stepmother was another story. Her father had long craved a male heir and married Poppy shortly after his first wife died. Poppy saw the close relationship between Oscar and Natalia as a threat and never missed an opportunity to subtly belittle Natalia.

The morning of Alexander's christening was turning into a classic example. Poppy wore a pale pink gown that perfectly off-set her golden-blond hair. Her father was also formally attired in a black frock coat, white satin waistcoat, and gray trousers.

"Natalia, I can't believe you're wearing that gown," Poppy said, frowning at the lavender moiré silk that clung to Natalia's figure as she descended into the foyer of their home. The gown featured a slight bustle and a frothy spill of ivory lace from the neckline.

"I love this dress," she defended. It was custom-made in Paris, and unlike the typical suits she wore to the bank each day, it was highly feminine and entirely appropriate for a society christening. She even had a cluster of violets pinned into her upswept black hair.

"It looks like you are in half-mourning, and that is bound to delight the journalists eager to see your disdain for my child."

"You're being ridiculous," Natalia said. "No one could mistake this for a mourning gown."

Her father adjusted his cufflinks and frowned at his wife. "No backbiting, ladies," he said. "My son is being introduced to the world today, and I won't have the two most important women in my life caterwauling at each other."

Natalia itched to point out that Poppy's attack was entirely unprovoked, but Oscar was right. This wasn't the day to let Poppy's barbs annoy her. A police escort had already arrived to lead their carriage to the church, where prominent socialites, politicians, and businessmen would be attending the celebrated christening.

But not quite *all* of high society. The Blackstones were among the richest families in America, but the stink of new money still trailed in their wake, and it infuriated Poppy. The success of the Blackstone banking empire lacked the heritage and prestige of old-world money, which was why Poppy bent over backward to host lavish parties and imitate the trappings of European aristocracy. The fortune spent on today's christening and reception was an excuse for Poppy to flaunt her wealth before the old-money matriarchs she envied.

So was the strategic selection of Alexander's godparents. The former secretary of the U.S. Treasury would stand as godfather for little Alexander. Religious considerations were not a factor. Natalia's own godfather, Admiral George McNally, had been chosen because the bank needed better ties with the military. Nothing happened inside the Blackstone family unless it was designed to advance the power, connections, or wealth of the Blackstone Bank.

As anticipated, the street in front of the church was crowded with onlookers, and photographers tried to capture the moment as Oscar escorted Poppy into the church. Poppy obligingly slowed her pace, turned slightly toward the photographers, and tipped the baby up to allow a fleeting glimpse of Alexander.

The ceremony was over in a mere twenty minutes, and then the entourage returned to their home, where an extravagant reception would last for most of the day. Natalia mingled with ease among the gracious company, welcoming every visitor as they entered the mansion. She refused to give the gossips any ammunition in their quest for her phantom resentment of her brother. Oscar beamed with pride as he stood behind Poppy, who sat enthroned in a chair with the baby's crib beside her. Oscar had a protective hand on Poppy's shoulder, looking as happy as Natalia had ever seen him as guests admired the baby.

As the afternoon wore on, the reception spilled into the courtyard garden, a green oasis in the middle of Fifth Avenue. Surrounded on three sides by their marble mausoleum of a house, it was lush with greenery and a splashing fountain. Talk soon drifted away from the baby and toward normal gossip about sports, politics, and the social scene in New York. Natalia joined her cousin Liam, who was with Darla Kingston, the dazzling woman he was courting. Darla had a profusion of corkscrew red curls and ran with a bohemian crowd, but she and Liam rubbed along remarkably well.

The talk soon turned to steel. Liam's recent appointment to the board of directors for U.S. Steel was still controversial, but he had an excellent grasp of the industry.

"You should come see our new electric arc furnace," Liam said to Natalia. "It's going to revolutionize the steel business."

"It's fabulous," Darla said. "That three-ton cauldron brimming with molten steel was simultaneously the most terrifying and awe-inspiring thing I've ever seen."

"You actually saw it?" Natalia asked in surprise.

Darla nodded. "I felt like Persephone wandering into the underworld. Such a huge, cavernous space with cauldrons of orange metal as fluid as any river. And the men! They were like dark, shadowy shapes, absolutely fearless as they handled the equipment. I was dazzled."

Darla was beginning to make a name for herself as a sculptress, so perhaps florid language was to be expected from an artist.

Liam certainly seemed impressed as he beamed at Darla. "She was a champ! The foundry floor is no place for a woman, but she suited up and went in with me. You should come too."

Natalia was already familiar with the new arc furnace. "I've read our analyst's reports on it, and I agree with you. It's very impressive."

"Natalia." Liam cocked a brow at her. "There's only so much you can learn about life from reading. You can't understand the steel workers until you step into their world to see it, smell it, and feel the heat. Sometimes you need to leave the third floor of the bank and get your hands dirty in the real world."

Ouch. The comment stung a bit because it was true. If Darla could walk into a steel mill, so could Natalia. She agreed to let Liam give her a tour, but she had just caught sight of Admiral

McNally shrouded in clouds of cigar smoke in the corner of the garden, which meant she had business to conduct.

Admiral McNally was a frightfully intimidating figure who'd been selected to be her godfather for political connections, not spiritual reasons. Whenever he visited their home, he recounted exotic war stories and foreign exploits. As a child, she'd been partly terrified, partly intrigued by him.

He currently stood clustered with a few other men in uniform, talking about the ongoing Boxer Rebellion in China, and Natalia knew exactly what her father expected of her. She needed to welcome him, feign a warm relationship, then ask about the new Virginia-class battleship featuring mixed-caliber gun turrets that would revolutionize the navy. Construction had just gotten underway at the Brooklyn Navy Yard, and her father wanted the bank to finance them.

She put on a gracious smile and ignored the pungent stink of tobacco as she greeted Admiral McNally. "Welcome to this side of the river," she said, and he offered her a terse nod in return. "Can I offer you something more satisfying than Turkish cigars?"

Admiral McNally's eyes narrowed as he scrutinized her. "I don't know. Can you?"

"My father's wine cellar features an eighteenth-century riesling from the Mosel Valley, and his alliance with U.S. Steel would provide a better caliber of steel alloy than the German company you interviewed last week. I *know* we can offer you better."

The admiral clapped his hands with a hefty grin. "Ha! I've always said you were the sharpest knife in the Blackstone family. When are Oscar's people going to start hectoring me for a new contract?"

Before she could reply, the family's butler rushed to her side. "Ma'am, there is a man to see you in the front hall," Mr. Tyson said in a tense voice. "It would be best if you came right away."

Natalia excused herself and followed Tyson into the house.

"What's wrong?" she asked as soon as they were out of earshot of the guests.

"The man is not an invited guest," the butler said tersely. "He was very forceful and flashed the badge of a policeman, so we dared not throw him out. He insists on seeing you."

Natalia hurried through the main hall, the vestibule, and the banquet hall, where Poppy still sat on her throne, showing off the baby. Natalia dared not slow down to chat but couldn't miss her stepmother's poisonous glare as she hurried after Tyson toward the billiard room, where the insistent police officer awaited her. The only person who fit Tyson's description was Boris Kozlov, but it was too early to expect news of Dimitri yet. She'd only spoken with Boris three days ago.

Sure enough, Boris was pacing in the billiard room in a rumpled suit. His rugged face was swathed in amazement as he gaped at the room's mahogany paneling and garnet drapes of crushed velvet that pooled on the floor.

"I always figured you lived fancy, but I never expected any-thing like this," he said. "I'll bet people like you probably stuff your mattresses with hundred-dollar bills."

"Have you learned anything?" she asked, eager to get him out of the house before Poppy discovered him and had palpita-tions. She spoke in Russian, because her request for information about Count Sokolov wasn't something she wanted overheard by others in the house.

Boris nodded. "It wasn't a hard case," he said. "Your count has landed himself in a world of trouble."

"How so?"

"He's been convicted of cowardice and dereliction of duty. They stripped him of his title and everything he owns."

Natalia braced a hand against the cool wood of the bil-liard table and listened in growing dismay as Boris outlined how he'd wired an old friend in Saint Petersburg, where the scandal of Count Sokolov's disgrace was trumpeted across the newspapers. Count Sokolov had refused to assist the army in defending the river that marked the dividing line between Russia and China. His title had been revoked, and he had been exiled to a penal colony.

Natalia shook her head in confusion. Russia wasn't at war with China, and Dimitri wasn't in the army, but whatever he did must have been awful if he'd been condemned to a penal colony. A chill raced through her, and she gaped at Boris.

"Are you certain?" she asked.

Boris smirked in satisfaction. "Your fancy aristocrat is about to get a swift lesson in how the rest of the world lives."

"Don't be so disrespectful," she instinctively lashed out.

Boris looked insulted, straightening to his formidable full height as he adjusted his coat. "We're all equals in America, and I can be disrespectful if I want," he said, loud enough for his voice to carry. "It's why I got out from under the czar's boot, but it looks like you've still got a toffee nose. Your mother wasn't like that. She was one of the richest women in the country, but she never forgot that she was a woman of the Russian heartland."

"Don't talk about my mother," she snapped. Thinking about her gentle mother threatened to weaken her resolve when all Natalia wanted was to understand what Dimitri had done to cause this catastrophe. "Which penal colony has he been sent to?"

"Sakhalin Island," Boris said. "They must really hate him. That's where they send the people who personally offended the czar. Most are never seen again."

The double doors to the billiard room banged open, and Poppy filled the entrance, her face white with anger.

"Natalia, must you consort with Russian riffraff?" she asked stiffly.

Natalia stepped in front of Boris, fearing the tough cop might lash out at Poppy, and that would be a disaster. "Officer Kozlov kindly brought me news of a friend in Russia."

"And I need to be paid for it," Boris said in English. "I didn't come across town to be spit on by the likes of you toplofty snobs. I want my money, and I want it now."

To Natalia's dread, her father appeared behind Poppy, glaring at Boris through his one good eye. With his other eye covered by a black patch, her father was a master at projecting a coldly sinister appearance.

"What's all this?" Oscar asked in a steely voice. That voice could make robber barons wilt, and Boris must have sensed the danger. He immediately corrected his posture and lowered his voice.

"I carried out an errand for Miss Blackstone, sir. I came across town as soon as I could to deliver the results personally." He gave her father a slight bow, but Oscar's icy demeanor did not thaw.

"Then accept my daughter's payment, and don't ever come to this house again. Is that understood?"

"Yes, sir."

Most men feared her father, and Boris proved true to form. Someday it might be nice to meet a man who could stand up to her father, but Natalia doubted it would ever happen.

Natalia was too upset about Dimitri's fate to return to the reception. The cream pastries she'd eaten felt sickeningly sweet in her stomach. While she'd been sampling champagne and pastries, Dimitri was suffering torments she could not begin to imagine.

What had he done to deserve such a fate? She headed upstairs, then down the corridor to her mother's private chapel on the second floor. The sanctuary was covered in Russian icons and looked nothing like the rest of the house. She quickly lit a dozen votive candles, then sank onto the kneeler to pray for the man she cared for but did not truly know.

Could he be guilty of the charges? Dimitri was always so melodramatic, bemoaning his misery and discomfort in "the frozen wasteland that is my life." She always suspected he was a bit of a hypochondriac, for how could a man be "practically on his deathbed," as he often complained, and then moments later send her messages overflowing with lyrical prose sparkling with humor? He had the soul of a poet as he paid homage to stars that glittered like diamonds on the velvety night sky or the joy at seeing the first violets of spring peeking out of the wet snow to defy the harsh climate. His observations were keen, sharp, and humorous. He wrote better English than most native speakers.

She rested her forehead in her hands. It was impossible to know the circumstances of his dereliction of duty, but she would not be his judge. Dimitri had enough loyalty to his country to accept an appointment in the middle of Siberia for the past three years. He'd once told her he took the dreadful assignment because he wished to prove himself worthy of his title.

For hundreds of years my family has dined on the nectar of privilege. I wish to venture out of our halcyon valley and into the frozen wasteland, building an iron rail to conquer time and distance.

Over the years, Dimitri moved from outpost to outpost, following the newly constructed railway as it tracked toward the Pacific. He negotiated for provisions, kept the supply lines operating, and worked with the local population to ensure rights of way. In recent months, he'd expressed concern over the Boxer Rebellion, which raged across the border in China, where insurgents had turned violent. Dimitri worked less than five miles from the border with China. Could he have gotten caught up in the violent rebellion? It seemed unlikely, but so did his arrest and conviction.

Someday she might learn more, but no matter what happened, she would always consider him a friend. Dimitri was a man born into unimaginable wealth and privilege, and yet he set out for Siberia to prove himself to his czar and his country. And if he balked in the face of battle . . . well, he wouldn't be the first man to do so.

After saying prayers for Dimitri, Natalia extinguished the candles and retreated to her bedroom, where she set her favorite Brahms record on the turntable of her phonograph. What a miracle of modern technology that the thin disc coated with a layer of wax could contain the majesty of a Brahms symphony.

She cranked the handle, set the stylus onto the record, and let the moody music fill her bedroom.

Then she indulged in a unique sort of torture by rereading the telegrams she and Dimitri had exchanged over the years.

Dimitri's initial messages to her were short and businesslike until the day he alerted her of a slowdown on the construction of a bridge. Natalia asked for a revised timetable and an explanation behind the slowdown.

It should have been a simple question. All she wanted to know was how long the delay would last and if there was anything she could do to get the schedule back on track, but little did she know that she had pricked a sore point that unleashed centuries of ingrained European resentments.

Count Sokolov complained that his German bridge engineer refused to work with French-supplied concrete mix. The engineer insisted on waiting for a costlier mix from Berlin because it was allegedly superior to what the French could produce, which prompted Count Sokolov to rant about German pedantry.

Heaven save us from the German love of rules. The only good thing ever to have come out of Germany is the incomparable music of Johannes Brahms, and this is a verifiable fact.

Natalia telegraphed a one-word reply: *Beethoven?*

She feared she might have offended the count with her blunt reply. She didn't know if he had a sense of humor, and communication through a telegraph wire could be so easily misinterpreted. It took a while for his reply to come through, but when it finally arrived, it contained a keen analysis of the difference between Brahms and Beethoven and why he appreciated Brahms's ability to incorporate the folk traditions of eastern Europe into his symphonies. Of Beethoven, the count was dismissive:

Beethoven's compositions are generic romanticism. They sound like they could have been composed anywhere: Berlin, London, Paris, or heaven help us all . . . New York.

Natalia had burst into laughter. Count Sokolov *did* have a sense of humor, and that day changed the nature of their correspondence forever. The count confessed that he was bored and lonely in Siberia, where most of the workers on the railroad spoke Belarusian, Chinese, or any one of a dozen Mongolian dialects he did not understand. There were a few Russian workers, but most of them were convicts. Those men were glad of the opportunity to knock a few years off their sentences by laboring on the railroad, but their goodwill did not extend to befriending the managers of the construction site, whom they instinctively regarded with hostility.

Count Sokolov's isolation made him wax poetic over his home not far from Saint Petersburg, and his profound love for the estate was endearing.

> I long for the comfort I can find only at Mirosa. The creak of the waterwheel, the fragrance of the apple blossoms on the damp morning air, the golden light over the valley on long summer nights when the sun never fully sets. My grandfather planted a ring of birch trees around the estate because in Russian folklore, birch trees protect against evil. I am a Christian, but still believe those trees have protected Mirosa because the valley seems wondrously suspended in time and preserved like a castle in a snow globe.

She loved Dimitri's lyrical ramblings, even when they veered into politics. Although love for his homeland came through in almost every message, he was concerned about the continuing decay of the Russian economy, which was mired in natural resources rather than pursuing the opportunities of industrialization. Tensions among the classes grew worse by the year, and he feared for the long-term stability of his family's investments.

> I want to invest outside the country. What do you recommend? Your father is universally famous for his business acumen.

Natalia had been reluctant to suggest any single company for Dimitri to invest his savings and simply said she would trust her father's bank for its diversified investments.

He took her advice, and over the next few months, Count Sokolov's secretary in Saint Petersburg began transferring huge sums of money to the Blackstone Bank for investment. Eventually, Count Sokolov acquired a four-percent stake in the bank, which Natalia was pleased to see earned a healthy profit with each quarterly dividend.

Their curious friendship made working with Dimitri a joy. Over time they began calling each other by their first names and engaged in good-natured debates. They both had passionate opinions but could rarely sway the other. The perfect example was Dimitri's insistence that she read *War and Peace*. The novel did not sit well with her, and she unleashed her feelings on Dimitri.

Why did you make me read War and Peace? I foolishly began to love and care for those characters, but Tolstoy seems to enjoy making them suffer and inflicting miserable deaths upon them. I shall never forgive you.

His response was not long in coming.

Dearest Natalia. The history of Russia is a litany of grief and sorrow woven into the fabric of our nation. A Russian novelist must dip his pen in his own blood to write his story. You may avert your American eyes if you choose, but there is glory and valor in suffering that transcends our paltry physical lives. I practice it daily.

That dreary message prompted her to ship a copy of *Little Women* to Dimitri, pronouncing it a faithful representation of real life in all its tragedies, but mostly filled with hope and optimism.

That was last month. She didn't even know if he'd received it, and now she would never learn what her lonely Russian count thought of *Little Women*.

On the phonograph, the needle had reached the end of the moody Brahms symphony, but the record kept rotating on its turntable, the needle making a rhythmic clicking sound with each rotation. She plodded over to lift off the needle, her spirit heavy. It looked like Dimitri had found his tragic Russian fate, but she could see no glory or valor in it.

4

*D*imitri found a sad irony in riding to a penal colony on the same railroad he helped build. The rhythmic clicking of the train wheels had become the background noise of his world as he was transported farther east with each passing day.

At least he was not uncomfortable. Unlike ordinary criminals, political prisoners were afforded a certain amount of respect by the guards, and Dimitri's title made this especially true. He had been granted the courtesy of "free command," a status that allowed him to wear his own clothes, move about without shackles, and mingle with whomever he chose. Security was lax because escape meant almost certain death in the vast wilderness.

The guards loved socializing with him. Each night they played poker, drank vodka, and sang bawdy songs. It had always been easy for Dimitri to make friends, and never had that skill been more important than now. He carefully cultivated the image of a bon vivant, carousing with the guards as though indulging in a last great hurrah before his grim imprisonment. The guards peppered him with endless questions. How big was his estate? Had he met the czar? Was the czarina as beautiful as reported? He was able to truthfully report that he'd seen the czar at the Winter Palace. They hadn't been introduced, but yes, the czarina was as lovely as reported. The guards also wanted to know about Mirosa, Dimitri's ancestral home.

It was the only topic he was reluctant to discuss. Mirosa was carved on his soul, a two-thousand-acre estate of unspoiled wilderness alive with birch groves, cedar trees, and of course, the apple orchard that perfumed the air. Summers at Mirosa were tragically short, but while they lasted, it was an earthly paradise. As a boy, he used to explore the woods, sometimes stumbling across sunlit clearings where he would lie on the grass to stare up at the cloudless sky and imagine he was speaking directly to God. He only left Mirosa to prove himself by helping build the czar's ambitious railroad that was supposed to be Russia's salvation.

Instead, it had been Dimitri's undoing.

What was it about Siberia that turned minor aristocrats into major revolutionaries? Prince Kropotkin, Fyodor Dostoevsky, and countless others had been transformed into radicals by the vast Russian landscape. Dimitri didn't want to be a radical. He only wanted to return to Mirosa, where he could be a guardian of the land, the orchards, and the lake.

He could never return to Mirosa, but he would not meet his end in a prison camp. God had sent him to witness that atrocity for a reason, and Dimitri needed to escape so he could proclaim it to the world.

The train would soon turn north, after which the climate would make escape impossible. That meant he needed to make his bid for freedom soon.

He affected a casual pose as he joined a group of guards for poker. They played hand after hand late into the night. Dimitri didn't have anything to barter with, but the guards didn't mind. He was good company, and they had a grand time.

By ten o'clock, Dimitri was examining the cards a young guard had tossed on the table before him. Dimitri's three-of-a-kind beat Mikhail's two pair, but he tossed his cards facedown and grinned in good-natured defeat.

"You've won again, Mikhail," Dimitri said with a jaunty salute. "Let's have another round, shall we?"

"Not unless you and Oleg do the Hopak dance," Mikhail said, and Dimitri groaned.

The Hopak squat dance hurt his knees, and he wasn't as young as he used to be. The speed and energy required in the classic folk dance was something few men could master, but the guards loved it, and they were drunk enough to want a show. Oleg was ten years younger than Dimitri's thirty-four years and could trounce him in the fast and furious squat kicks.

It didn't matter. The more resigned to his fate that Dimitri seemed, the better. He and Oleg stood back-to-back in the aisle. They held their arms straight out for balance, then sank down into a squat. The others stomped and chanted a rousing accompaniment as Dimitri began the rhythmic kicks.

The ache in his thighs turned to a burn, making his legs feel like weights. Dimitri toppled over within a minute, but Oleg kept at it. Dimitri lay where he fell and shouted his support to Oleg. Other men funneled into the aisle to give it a try, and Dimitri staggered back to a bench to look out the window while the others caroused.

The moonlight cast thin illumination over the endless pine forest. It would be good cover for his escape. He grabbed a shot glass of vodka, stood, and raised it over his head.

"Let us eat, drink, and be merry, for tomorrow we may die!"

The guards cheered, stamped their feet, and drank. Dimitri deliberately sloshed his onto the ground, then grabbed a bottle to refill everyone's glass but his own. The drunker they were, the better his odds.

Tonight was the night, and fear mingled with elation. One way or the other, he would meet his fate soon.

Dimitri waited until everyone in the compartment had fallen into a stupor, but the train kept barreling eastward. He held his breath as he rolled off the bench and studied the guards. Their snoring and wheezing did not alter as he crept to the doorway, holding his hand over the mechanism as he twisted the handle.

If anyone caught him, he would claim he needed to relieve himself, but he got through the door with no one stirring.

Wind tugged his hair as he stood on the open-air platform between the railcars. The train moved at only thirty miles an hour, but the railroad bed was covered with stones, and it would be a hard landing. Would this be the end? The weeks and months ahead were going to be hard, but it was time to act.

Dearest God above, you know what I saw. You know that it can happen again if someone does not put a stop to it. Let me be that man. Let me escape and find my way to freedom. In your name I pray.

He crossed himself, drew a deep breath, and leapt into the darkness.

He landed on his heels but toppled forward, smashing his face against the gravel. But there was no time to waste. He scrambled down the gravel embankment and into the cover of the spindly trees ahead. Pain throbbed in the side of his head, and blood trickled down his face.

The next hours were nothing but a blur of fear as he staggered through the forest, twigs and saplings whipping at his face. Guilt gnawed at him. The guards had been decent men, but once he was discovered missing, things would be hard for them.

He couldn't afford to worry about them. He was hungry, thirsty, and had four thousand miles to travel before he reached the safety of the Pacific Ocean.

Four thousand miles.

If he obsessed over the magnitude of the journey ahead, he would never make it. With each step he was a tiny bit closer to Port Arthur and salvation. He had nothing in the world but the clothes on his back, a tin cup he'd stolen from the guards, a bit of flint, and the will to survive. There were gold coins sewn into his coat, three diamonds hidden in his shoe, and the single diamond buried in his scalp. They were useless in the middle of the forest, but he would pass villages along the way. Eventually he would reach Port Arthur, board a ship, and seek out his only friend and last remaining asset in the world. Both were in New York. Natalia Blackstone would help him.

Natalia! Had there ever been a more beautiful name? He repeated her name like a talisman as he trekked through the hideous wilderness. Natalia held the keys to the one investment the czar had not been able to seize: a four-percent share in the Blackstone Bank.

It was worth millions. If he could get to New York, he could use that money to shine a spotlight on the atrocity he'd witnessed, but first he had to evade pursuit and survive the immensity of the Russian taiga, the seemingly endless expanse of cedar, spruce, and hemlock trees.

It was October. His breath wasn't coming out in white puffs, so the temperature wasn't freezing yet, but that would change as winter deepened. Could he get to Mongolia before the weather made it impossible? The pain from the wounds on his face was savage but wouldn't kill him. Neither would the stitch in his side or the blisters forming on his feet.

But the cold could kill him, so he had to get to Mongolia ahead of the winter. From there he could use his assets to ride on river barges or buy a horse to take him to Port Arthur.

It felt like forever before the first hint of dawn cut through the forest. Only tiny patches of sky were visible through the canopy of pine needles above him. It was time to find a place to hide while he tried to sleep, but everything looked the same in all directions. There *wasn't* any place to hide. Just tall, spindly tree trunks that left him exposed to the sight of any man or beast wandering in the wood.

The best he could do was make a bed of pine needles. He dragged a smattering of broken tree limbs to his makeshift bed to screen him from prying eyes. Dry bark scratched his face and the needles itched. Cold, clawing fear tensed his muscles, but he closed his eyes and tried to pray.

Dear Lord, please let me live long enough to reach Natalia Blackstone.

5

It was the middle of October before Natalia made good
on her promise to tour a steel mill with Liam. She had
been prepared for the heat. She had been prepared
for the harsh orange glare of molten metal. But she hadn't
been prepared for the wall of noise that hit her the moment
she stepped inside the mill. The deafening roar of machines
and motors was nonstop. Chains clanked, boilers hissed, and
hammers forged liquefied metal into finished steel. By the end
of the tour, her eyes hurt from the glare, and her clothes were
damp with sweat.

Liam had been right about the need to see the workforce in
action instead of trying to learn about their working conditions from an industry report. She hadn't even been doing any
manual labor and she felt limp from the heat as she followed
Liam outside. They sat at a picnic table in the blessed cool of
the mill yard while Liam explained how the newly invented arc
furnace meant the workers deserved a pay raise.

"I can see that the job is challenging, but is it different?" she
asked. "Harder? More exhausting?"

"No," he reluctantly admitted. "It's not any harder than it
was before, but the new furnace is making the company richer.
Why should all that money go to the guys in the offices?"

Natalia desperately wanted Liam to succeed on Wall Street,

but it was going to be tough. He was completely uneducated but smart in the ways of the world. Liam had been a Blackstone until he was three years old, but then he was kidnapped and held for ransom. Her uncle paid the ransom, but Liam was never returned and had been presumed dead long ago.

The people who kidnapped Liam despised robber barons like the Blackstones and took grim satisfaction in raising him in the gritty world of steel mills and street gangs. He'd been taken out of school at thirteen to work shoveling coal into furnaces, which was why he could barely read. He'd worked as a welder all his adult life until last summer, when he'd been identified as the missing Blackstone heir. After inheriting a fortune in stock from his long-dead father, Liam now sat on the board of directors of U.S. Steel. It was the nation's largest steel company, but Liam was floundering as he tried to make the leap from being a steelworker to a man sitting in the boardroom. He wanted to revamp how the company's labor force was paid, and she feared he would make a fool of himself. His heart was in the right place, but he lacked the ability to express it in any but the most inflammatory terms. Natalia didn't need Liam to persuade her that the work was hard. Her ears still hurt after the two-hour assault inside the mill, and the workers endured that cacophony every day.

"You've convinced me," she said. "Now you need to convince the members on the board, and they are a stern lot. You will need long-term financial projections to win your case. It will be your most powerful weapon in a war with the board of directors, and I'm good at that sort of thing. We can write the proposal together."

"Why don't you write it, and I'll present it?"

She shook her head. "You can't present it unless you understand it, and that means math class. I'll tutor you. It will be fun."

"We have different ideas about what is fun. I'm taking Darla to Coney Island tomorrow. Want to come with us?"

Natalia recoiled at the prospect of carnival rides and sticky candy. "Or you could spend Saturday at the bank with me and fight for the men we just saw sweating it out on the floor. Take your pick."

Liam grimaced but gave her a good-natured grin anyway. "I respect you for coming here today, even though you hated every second of it. I'll probably hate your math class just as much, but you've got a deal."

The difference was that Natalia wasn't expected to actually learn how to make steel. Liam was going to have to do more than "come to math class." He had to master advanced finance and long-term planning, and she feared he didn't have it in him.

Natalia's visit to the steel mill was more upsetting than she cared to admit. Her life seemed so easy compared to the heat, noise, and danger the mill workers faced every day. On nights like these, she retreated to her bedroom, where music helped soothe her soul.

Her prized phonograph rested on a table beneath the window, and its flare-shaped horn pointed into the bedroom. She'd been playing her favorite Brahms symphony for almost an hour, wallowing in the wonderfully moody music.

She leaned against the window of her room, which overlooked Fifth Avenue. It had been raining most of the evening, but as the temperature dropped, bits of sleet pelted the window. Streetlamps reflected off the wet pavement, and well-heeled people huddled beneath umbrellas as they scurried along the sidewalks. It was October, and women were already wearing their sealskin furs.

Was it cold where Dimitri was? It had been a month since she'd gotten word about his terrible fate. Given the size of Siberia, he probably hadn't arrived in the penal colony yet and was still trapped on a slow-moving cargo train lumbering across the wilderness at thirty miles an hour.

She closed her eyes and let the languid Brahms melody slowly mount with a swelling sense of urgency. She loved this part.

The soaring majesty made her want to become a better person. Stronger. More valiant—

Her bedroom door banged against the wall. "How many times are you going to play that wretched song?" Poppy demanded. She strode to the phonograph and yanked the arm off the record.

Natalia gasped and picked up the fragile record. "You scratched it!"

"My son is sleeping," Poppy said stiffly. "I suggest you do the same. It's nine thirty, for pity's sake."

"Alexander can't hear my phonograph on the other side of the house."

"You don't know that," Poppy snapped. "You've played this record at least five times in a row."

"Because it's my favorite symphony."

What was the point of living in a mansion if she couldn't even listen to her own music? Poppy's bedroom was in a separate wing of the house, but she must have heard the music while climbing the main staircase. This was one of the largest private homes in the state of New York, yet it wasn't big enough for Poppy and Natalia to live beneath the same roof.

Her father heard the commotion and came into the room. "What now?" he asked in exasperation.

Poppy pointed to the record Natalia held. "If I have to hear that song one more time, I swear to high heaven I will leap out a window."

"There are children laboring in coal mines," Natalia said, "but yes, Poppy, your life is very difficult."

Poppy's eyes narrowed, and Oscar tried to play peacemaker. "I believe you have played that recording somewhat obsessively," he said, because he usually sided with Poppy whenever she and Natalia locked horns.

"That's why this house has doors," Natalia said. "I had mine closed. I suggest you do the same, and then my music won't bother you."

Poppy grabbed the shellac disc out of Natalia's hands, lifted it high, and then slammed it against her upraised knee, snapping it in two. "There," she said, flinging both halves into the corner of the room. "Now we won't have to hear it at all."

Natalia's palms itched to wipe the smirk off Poppy's face. Either that or to go out and buy another copy of the record and set up the phonograph right outside Poppy's door. She glared at her father and waited for a reaction.

"Poppy," her father gently scolded, but his cautious tone made it clear he wouldn't do anything to offend his beloved wife. "I think the two of you need to try a little harder to get along. Natalia, it would be helpful if you could limit playing the phonograph to hours when Poppy is not in residence. And Poppy—"

Natalia didn't want to hear what else he had to say. She picked up the two halves of the record and hugged them to her chest. If she had to choose between Brahms or Poppy, Johannes Brahms won every time.

"No need," she said primly. "I think I have overstayed my welcome in this house." She could move into a hotel tonight and buy a home of her own somewhere else. She probably should have done it long ago, but she'd worried it would stoke the rumors of a feud between her and Poppy.

Why should she care? There *was* a feud between her and Poppy.

"Now, Natalia," her father cautioned.

"Too late. I'm leaving tonight, and then we can all be happier." She said it breezily, but her sense of triumph didn't last long in the face of Poppy's triumphant gloat.

6

At first Dimitri thought the forest was deserted, but by his second night, he started seeing all manner of nocturnal wildlife. There were owls, raccoons, minks, and wolves. His first sight of a wolf terrified him until he threw a tree limb at it and the mangy animal fled.

But it worried him. Where there was one wolf there were others, but there was nothing he could do except pray that God would keep him safe. He couldn't afford to get lost, so he followed the railroad east. Fear of being spotted by a passing train meant he traveled only under cover of darkness, and then before dawn he slipped a few hundred yards into the forest to sleep during the day. His entire body hurt, the blisters on his feet were bleeding, and he shivered with cold, but he wasn't hungry.

The peasants of Russia had long survived on cedar nuts, and now so did Dimitri. Pine cones littered the forest floor, and it was easy enough to bash them open and pick out the tiny nuts. His pockets were stuffed with them.

On the fifth day he saw the first sign of bandits. Most of the bandits in the forest were either escaped prisoners from penal colonies, soldiers who had deserted the army, or men who abandoned their agreements to work on the railroad.

All were dangerous.

His first glimpse of them came an hour before sunset as he

scavenged for cedar nuts. They were a rowdy group of at least a dozen men, and some of them were drunk. From his hiding place behind a tree, he heard them arguing over how to divide the money from a soldier they had robbed.

Trying to join them would be dangerous. Given his fine coat and custom boots, they might rob him blind rather than share their food or supplies. It also looked like they were heading south, and Dimitri needed to go east. He hid until they were well out of sight before continuing his journey.

Over time, he learned the sounds and smells of the forest. The creak of tree trunks, the rustle of wind, and the thud of his footsteps on the peaty forest floor. He became accustomed to the scent of moldering leaves and damp earth, all mingled with the smell of his own sweat and fear. It was that fear that kept him walking through the endless hours of darkness and solitude.

Forward, forward, forward.

How much longer could he go on? At this rate it would take months to reach the Mongolian border, and then what? With luck he could find a village where his gold coins could be bartered for passage on a river barge, but his feet were in dangerously bad shape. The blisters had broken open and leaked a combination of pus and blood. He could only hope his feet would toughen, and until then, he would suffer. How could three small blisters cause such misery?

He laughed in the darkness. Natalia Blackstone used to tease him about his hypochondria. It started when he complained of a mosquito bite on the side of his lip. He told her how annoying it was when he spoke or ate, and she could not let such whining go unnoticed.

> Sir. You are the descendant of proud Russian Cossacks, the people who battled the Golden Horde and defeated Napoleon. I expect you to triumph over a mosquito bite.

Natalia didn't understand the prowess of the Siberian mosquito. With the greening of springtime came formidable swarms of mosquitos that descended with blood-sucking enthusiasm on any warm-blooded creature. Each spring his entire body was spotted with their bites, but he only complained to Natalia about that single bite on the corner of his lip that hurt every time he opened his mouth. She spared him no sympathy.

The world will survive if you don't speak for a few days. It is only a mosquito bite, Dimitri.

He loved that. Crisp. Witty. He started regularly sharing his various maladies, whether it was chapped skin from the blustery climate or muscle aches from the poor mattress, but he wasn't a hypochondriac.

Well, his mother sometimes accused him of exaggerating his illnesses, but that mosquito bite on the corner of his lip really hurt.

Undeserved charges of hypochondria aside, he adored Natalia's teasing messages. For three years they were a rare bright spot during his lonely isolation. She was the most obsessively organized person he'd ever met. She routinely wanted his financial projections well before he had completed them. Unbelievably, she wanted him to predict the weather so she could adjust shipments of supplies. He would reply: *Natalia, where is your spontaneity? If the weather stops us for a few weeks, in a hundred years no one will remember, so we must batten down the hatches and make the best of it. A little suffering is good for the soul.*

He had a long view of history, but like most Americans, Natalia could be impatient. She wanted things done *now*. Russians weren't like that. He was not worried about this week or this year. He thought in terms of this decade or this generation.

Over time he saw beneath Natalia's prim fustiness to the deeply passionate nature she kept carefully concealed. Her irrational outrage over the tragic outcome in *War and Peace* was proof of that. She still hadn't forgiven him for Prince Andrei's death, even though it was Tolstoy's fault, not his. For weeks she criticized gloomy Russian authors who killed off fictional characters and caused her to mourn for days. He finally shut her up with seven perfectly chosen words:

It is only a mosquito bite, Natalia.

She immediately understood and quit nattering about Tolstoy's cruelty. After that, the term *mosquito bite* became their code word. Whether he whined about bad food or she complained about her stepmother, the answer was the same. It was only a mosquito bite.

At the moment he wished he could send her a long, rambling telegram describing his current misery. He would bemoan his thirst and his difficulty sleeping during daylight hours. She would tease him that it was only a mosquito bite, and he'd feel better.

He tried to imagine what Natalia's voice sounded like. Would it be soft and feminine, or throaty and strong? Not that it mattered. In his imagination he tried them all. Whenever exhaustion tempted him to sit down, lie back, and give up, it was Natalia's voice he heard urging him onward.

Dimitri, it's only a mosquito bite. Keep going. Keep walking. Get to the coast, send me a telegram, and I will help you.

"I'm coming, Natalia," he said into the darkness and continued onward into the east.

Natalia had always known she lived a sheltered life. From the moment she left the crib, there had been people to help her bathe, dress, and tend her hair. Someone else cleaned her room and prepared her food. Natalia didn't peel an orange until she was sixteen years old, and she was taken aback by the buildup of sticky white pith beneath her fingernails.

Her helplessness was embarrassing, and it would stop now. She was going to establish her own household and look after it herself. Most women lived without servants waiting on them, and Natalia would too. It would prove her independence.

And her superiority over Poppy, who scoffed at Natalia's determination to live independently. "You won't even know how to make toast!" she mocked, but Natalia ignored her and set off to meet Liam, who accompanied her on the thrilling adventure of buying her own home.

They met with a real estate agent named Mr. Leighton. At first the realtor was reluctant to show her properties in the neighborhood she chose, insisting that she could find much nicer homes uptown.

"I want to be close enough to walk to the bank," Natalia insisted, which limited her options. Most of the area surrounding the bank was filled with commercial buildings, and the apartments above the businesses were all for lease, not to own.

Mr. Leighton reluctantly told her about a row of older townhomes three blocks from the bank. The six units were all attached, but each had a short walkup of steps and a charming bow-fronted window facing the sidewalk. The only one for sale had been owned by a German immigrant who'd lived in it for thirty years before he died last month. It had running water but no electricity.

"I think you will do much better farther uptown," Mr. Leighton cautioned as he unlocked the front door. "A woman of your position will need modern amenities and more space for entertaining visitors. This house has only a single parlor."

"She said she wants to be able to walk to work," Liam said. "Stand aside and let us look around."

Mr. Leighton pursed his lips. "As you can see, the previous owner was overly fond of the craftsmanship of his native country."

Natalia stepped inside, a little dismayed at how dim it was, but after Liam jerked the heavy draperies from the front window, it was easier to appreciate the splendid woodworking in the parlor. The fine craftsmanship was evident in the crown molding and the casing around the doors and windows.

"The unfortunate choice of wallpaper would need to be changed," the realtor said. "The old-fashioned crown molding should also go, and the plaster is going to make adding electricity a challenge. Surely you would be happier—"

"You know what?" Liam interrupted. "Why don't you wait outside? Natalia can make up her own mind about the place."

She ought to say something to soften Liam's blunt order, but she was too intrigued by the mantel over the fireplace. It was a massive piece of wood, ornately carved with ivy vines across the entire length. Hidden among the carving were nesting birds, a few clusters of berries—oh, and a little raccoon!

"I think I like this place," she said.

"Let's go see the kitchen and the washroom before you fall in love," Liam cautioned, which was good advice because the kitchen was unlike any she'd ever seen. It wasn't even a room. It was only a few pieces of equipment on the wall of the dining area. It had nothing but a sink, an icebox, and a single-burner kerosene stove.

She lifted the latch on the wooden icebox. The frame was heavy with a thick lining of metal inside and iron grates at the bottom.

"Where would I get ice for it?" she asked Liam.

"You can hire an iceman to bring a block over a couple times a week. You'll need to keep an eye on that pan and empty it. It will fill up pretty fast, and you don't want water running all over the floor."

It seemed easy enough, but her biggest concern was in the washroom upstairs. It had a claw-foot tub, but the only source of water was a single spigot on the pedestal sink.

"Why isn't there a tap for hot water?" she asked Liam.

"Because this house doesn't have a water heater," he said. "You'll have to heat water on the stove downstairs."

Her eyes grew wide. "And carry it up?"

"And carry it up," Liam confirmed with amusement. "You'll grow muscles you never knew you had." He must have noticed her concern, because his face softened and he spoke kindly. "It's not so bad. Look, you've got a sink right here. You can use it to fill the tub with cold water while heating the rest downstairs.

And when you're done with the bath, you can dump everything down the sink instead of lugging it back down to the kitchen."

This all seemed a little more daunting than she'd anticipated, but it was time to learn how to be an ordinary adult, and she could manage without the servants Poppy needed to get dressed each morning.

The bedroom seemed terribly plain, just four walls with a single window overlooking the alley. The clicking of her heels sounded loud as she walked into the room, entirely empty except for an accordion-shaped radiator beneath the window. It was cast iron with knobs and pipes, but once again, she was ignorant of how to operate it.

She set her fingers on the cold iron. "I feel so stupid," she said, and Liam immediately understood.

"Don't let it worry you. If you buy this place, I'll come over and show you how it's done. You'll get the hang of it. Trust me. I've run into at least one thing that makes me feel stupid every day since I walked back into this family."

She smiled at him. Liam was uneducated but street-smart, while she was the opposite. She could analyze business proposals worth millions of dollars but couldn't turn on a radiator.

Mr. Leighton showed her two more properties farther north, but none of them sparked an immediate sense of home like the cozy German townhouse with the hand-carved mantel and lovely wooden moldings.

She insisted on returning to the townhouse later that afternoon for another look. This time, Liam asked Darla to join them because she had the critical eye of an artist to help evaluate the house. Once again, he made the estate agent wait outside while they toured the home.

"You can't trust those guys," he said. "If they sense you like the place, they'll tell the owner, who will start jacking the price way up."

He was probably right, but this place might be worth it.

Darla seemed equally impressed with the craftsmanship as she admired the hand-carved mantel. "This is rare black walnut. And look! Here's a turaco bird nestled among the ivy. I'm beginning to suspect your German homeowner was really Swiss, not German."

"Why?" Natalia asked, leaning in closer to admire the curious bird hidden in the vines.

"The turaco bird is the national bird of Switzerland."

"I've heard of Switzerland," Liam said. "That's where the pope lives, right?"

The odd statement hung in the air.

"What makes you say that?" Darla asked.

"Everyone knows about the pope and the Swiss guard. I saw a picture of those guys once. Crazy outfits."

Darla's eyes sparkled with amusement. "The pope lives in Rome. He has the Swiss guard because in the Renaissance, the Swiss mercenaries were the best fighters in Europe. Plus, since they're from a neutral country, they aren't perpetually jockeying for position inside the Vatican."

"Oh." A flush stained his cheekbones. "I guess that was a dumb thing to say."

Darla flashed him a wink and pressed a kiss to his cheek. "Don't worry. You're handsome enough to make up for it."

Natalia paid no more attention to them as she continued walking the perimeter of the room. Everywhere she looked, the house brimmed with hidden treasures. The nook created by the bay window would be a perfect place to read on long winter nights. Amber light from the late afternoon sun cast a comforting glow into the room. This place felt like it could be a home. She set her hand on the mantel and surveyed the cozy parlor.

"I'm ready to buy it."

Darla hugged her in excitement, but Liam was appalled that she was willing to pay full price instead of haggling. She disagreed.

"Haggling will draw things out, and I'm afraid I might lose it."

Liam covered his eyes and groaned. "You're an idiot if you pay asking price. You *always* haggle over a purchase this big. They won't respect you if you don't."

He was probably right. Emotions must never enter into a business decision.

It took three days of negotiation, but in the end, Natalia had her townhouse for an excellent price and was ready to step into the next chapter of her life.

7

*D*imitri saw no other people for the next two weeks, and with each passing day, he doubted his ability to survive the winter alone. As much as he feared the roving gangs of bandits, finding a group to join might be his only way to stay alive. It was almost November, and his need for human contact was almost as strong as his painful cravings for real food and decent rest.

One night the scent of woodsmoke and cooked meat penetrated his fog of exhaustion. All senses on alert, he crept toward the scent of a campfire. The nickering of a horse sounded in the forest ahead, and Dimitri snuck closer, taking cover behind a tree to squint at the group.

There were six of them, a ragtag lot. Their garments were a mishmash of western and tribal clothing. Some wore traditional sashes tied around their middle like the nomadic people of the region, but others wore the striped tunics of a penal colony. Flickering light from the campfire illuminated two of the men's faces. They had the look of many of the nomadic peoples from this part of the world.

It would be hard to join them if he couldn't communicate. He hunkered behind a spruce tree, blowing into his hands to keep them warm as he considered the risk.

A shout sounded from the camp.

He'd been spotted. His heart surged, and his mouth went dry. He wasn't strong enough to flee and had no choice but to fall on their mercy. *Dear Lord, please be with me.*

He came out from behind the tree holding his hands up, the universal sign of surrender.

"I mean you no harm," he said in Russian.

No one responded. There were six of them, and three held rifles pointed directly at him.

"I mean you no harm," he said in English, then tried German, his only other language. There was no response. He scrambled for what few words in Chinese he knew, but he couldn't remember them, and the men with weapons drew closer.

He kept his hands up while stepping backward. "Please," he said. "I am a wealthy man. My family will pay well for my safety."

The man in front unleashed a stream of foreign words directed at him, but Dimitri shook his head, still retreating.

"I don't understand."

The diamonds in his boot were hard lumps beneath his foot. If he could offer them a diamond, it might help. How could he get it out? Reaching toward his boot would alarm them, but if he could figure out how to offer them a diamond, he might have a chance.

He kept talking as he retreated. "Please. I want to join you."

A man with his hair pulled into a topknot smiled. Perhaps he understood Russian after all, because he let the rifle drop from his hand and carried it by the barrel as he approached Dimitri, a taunting hint of a smile on his face.

Like lightning, the stranger swung the rifle, slamming it behind Dimitri's knees and knocking him to the ground. A punch to the side of his head almost knocked him out. His vision whirled, but before he could rise, someone hauled him up from behind, and another fist slammed into his jaw.

Down again. Voices shouting, men surrounding him. Kicks, shoves, fists. He braced a knee beneath him and tried to stand, but a boot between his shoulders forced him back down.

"Please," he choked out. "I am a—"

A fist shut him up. He couldn't die out here in this godforsaken wilderness. His mother would never learn what happened to him. But maybe that was for the best.

Someone jerked one of his boots off. They tried to get his coat off, but he clenched his arms tight. If he lost this coat, he would freeze to death.

"Back away," he roared, but it was hopeless.

The stitching on his lapel ripped open, and the gold coins rolled out. Now the men descended like jackals as they tore at his clothing and pulled the other boot from him.

More blows to his head, then nothing but black.

The cold woke him. Everything hurt. He tried to move, but the pain in his head was brutal. The groan in his ears sounded like an animal, but it came from his own throat. Blood was crusted on his face and down his neck. He tried to open his eyes, but they were swollen shut.

A crackle and a pop sounded. Fire.

Panic raced through him, and he managed to get an eye open. A small campfire was only a few yards away.

He was alone in the forest except for a lone figure on the other side of the fire. It was the man with the topknot, and he wore Dimitri's coat. With its epaulets and gold braid, it looked strange on the man with long hair and dark eyes that glinted in the firelight.

"Are you awake?" the topknotted man asked in Russian. Good Russian too.

"Awake," Dimitri croaked.

The topknotted man held a lump of meat over the fire with a skewer, and the tantalizing aroma of hot, seared meat made Dimitri dizzy. The tiny carcass looked like a squirrel, but he'd never craved anything so desperately as that chunk of meat.

"We found eight gold coins in this coat," the man said casually. "Do you have anything else on you?"

Dimitri rolled onto his elbow and took stock of his situation.

The only items of clothing he had left were his trousers, socks, and broadcloth shirt. A blanket was draped over his shoulders. There was no sign of his boots. The diamonds hidden in them were gone.

"Nothing," he said. "Where are my boots?"

The other man shrugged. "Everything you had got split up. My share was the coat and a gold coin. Someone else got your boots." He casually tossed a pair of filthy moccasins toward Dimitri. "You can wear those."

Dimitri sagged. "Those shoes are completely inadequate."

"That's what the guy who was wearing them thought. Be grateful he left them for you."

Dimitri wasn't grateful for anything at his point. The campsite was abandoned except for the topknotted man, who sat with a rifle across his lap as he watched Dimitri.

"Where is everyone else?" Dimitri asked.

"Gone. We were getting too big to feed. They are headed for Abakan, but I need to go farther east."

Abakan sounded good to Dimitri. It was still in Russia but remote enough that nobody would be looking for Count Sokolov there.

"What's wrong with Abakan?" he asked.

"I am a wanted man in Abakan," the other said. "Horse theft. I need more distance before I settle somewhere, and I'll move faster without them. The two of us can help each other."

Everything hurt as Dimitri pushed himself into a sitting position. "You've stolen my coat and one of my gold coins. You attacked me. Why should I help you?"

"Because I have half a squirrel and a cup of water. I am willing to share. Are you interested?"

Dimitri's mouth salivated. Were he able, he'd be willing to kill for that squirrel and cup of water. All he could manage was a weak nod.

"My name is Temujin," the man said as he extended the skewer with the lump of squirrel meat on it, and Dimitri had never been so grateful for a mouthful of food in his life.

8

Natalia moved into her new townhouse in mid-November. It was only three blocks from the bank and four blocks from the New York Stock Exchange. She was in the heart of the Financial District, so she could walk to work each morning instead of spending half an hour in a lumbering carriage on jammed city streets.

Why hadn't she done this years ago? She loved this compact townhouse even though it lacked electricity and the plumbing was rudimentary. It was *hers*. The kitchen was inadequate, but there was an Italian delicatessen on the street corner and plenty of pushcart venders offering a huge array of hot pasties, sausages, and sandwiches.

She bought a sofa, a wingback chair, and two bookshelves, which filled most of the parlor. The flaring bell of her phonograph stuck out from its corner table, and she purchased a special rack for her records. Instead of crystal, she bought charming stoneware mugs and plates. This part of the city had peddlers selling flowers on almost every street corner, and she treated herself to a bouquet at least once a week. She loved nothing more than walking home from work, buying her own flowers, and arranging them in one of her new stoneware jugs.

Each evening she slipped into a sarafan like her mother used to wear. The loose gowns with their wild tribal patterns were a staple of the Russian countryside, and there was no garment on earth that made Natalia feel more feminine. Poppy always mocked Natalia's sarafans, calling them peasant garb, but Natalia was now her own woman and could wear whatever she pleased.

Despite the joy she took in her new home, it wasn't without difficulty. Her first attempt at making a hard-boiled egg resulted in a rubbery mess with bits of shell stuck to the whites, prompting her to buy a cookbook to learn the trick for slipping the shell from a cooled hard-boiled egg. It only took a few tries, but she beamed with pride as she enjoyed her first hard-boiled egg made on her tiny stove. She sprinkled it with salt and pepper and felt like a genuine chef.

Washing her hair was a challenge, but she soon figured out a system. Heating and lugging water was tedious, but she played the phonograph loud enough to be heard throughout the house, and she loved the charm of Mozart while performing the humble chore.

Her only truly disastrous mistake came when she tried to light her first fire. She'd never laid a fire before, but she'd seen servants do it, and she knelt before the compact fireplace in the parlor, mimicking the way she'd seen servants lay the wood with plenty of open space for air circulation, then set some smaller kindling at the bottom. She did everything right . . . except she forgot to open the damper before lighting the fire, and billowing clouds of smoke poured into the parlor. She flung a bucket of water on the fire, which splattered wet bits of charred ash all over the hearth and her gown. Clearing the stench of smoke from the room took forever, since the windows were so old that they'd been painted shut long ago.

Minor disasters aside, she was learning how to be independent, and her relationship with her father had never been better. Now that he no longer had to perform peacekeeping duties between his feuding wife and daughter, they hummed along in perfect harmony at the bank. Her third-quarter report on the profitability of the Trans-Siberian Railway almost had him levitating.

"Are these numbers right?" he asked as he stood in the open doorway of her office.

She nodded. "Enough of the railroad has been completed that it can now be used for transporting supplies, which has slashed our transportation costs to one third what they were before."

Her father still scrutinized the report. "Very good, but that still can't account for this level of profit."

"We're also charging the British and the Germans to use the line," she said with pride. "Anyone who wants to do business in central Russia is now paying us a surcharge."

Oscar straightened, his face still expressionless, but his voice vibrated with pride. "That's my girl," he said before leaving her office.

The interchange took less than sixty seconds, but it filled her with satisfaction. Half the robber barons in New York lived in fear of Oscar Blackstone. He never gave praise without cause, and she had just exceeded their third-quarter expectations. The railroad would ultimately belong to Russia, but until the bank's loan had been repaid, a portion of the profits went directly into the Blackstone coffers.

That night she hurried home a little early because the weather was taking a turn for the worse. Tiny bits of sleet pricked her face by the time she arrived home. It was early for a cold snap like this, but Liam had already taught her how to use the cast-iron radiator on each floor. She turned them on, but it seemed to take forever for the steam to build up and begin heating the house.

By nightfall, snow had crusted along the panes of the windows, and chilly drafts snaked through the rooms. She made a pot of hot apple tea, wrapped a heavy shawl around her shoulders, and leaned against her bedroom window to watch the snow flurries fly.

Did an early winter in New York mean an early winter in Russia too? She doubted Dimitri had access to a radiator or hot tea. By now he was probably becoming used to a gloomy prison camp in the middle of nowhere. All the money in the world could not buy him a warm blanket or a bowl of hot, nourishing soup. She had no understanding of what he'd done to earn such a harsh punishment, but she ached for him.

A chill rushed through her at the thought of what his life had become. She snuggled deeper into her shawl and said a prayer on behalf of the friend she would probably never hear from again.

Dimitri never expected to develop a genuine friendship with the Mongolian horse thief he met in the middle of the Russian taiga, but something about mutually saving each other's lives tended to bring men together. Temujin once shot a wolf that had been creeping up on Dimitri while he'd been hunkered over an icy stream to fill the waterskin jug. Another time Dimitri woke to find a lone bandit about to slit Temujin's throat. The bandit had been frightened away by Dimitri's well-thrown rock. Over the following weeks, Dimitri and Temujin leaned on each other while foraging for nuts or tramping through the woods at night.

Their journey through the taiga of south-central Siberia took almost a month, but Temujin had the ability to blend in during the rare times they came to a village. He was a Buryat who didn't know if he'd been born in Russia or Mongolia but moved easily in both. No one looked askance at Temujin as he haggled for rides on the back of a wagon, and once he bartered for a ten-day journey on a river barge, which transported them nine hundred miles.

Over time, they learned each other's life stories. Temujin had once been a nomadic herder who moved with the seasons and lived in a yurt made of animal hides stretched over a lightweight frame. That came to an end after he married.

"Tania wanted a real house made of wood," Temujin said, and he had built her one with his own hands. It was only a single room, but it had a real wooden floor and a doorway through which they watched their goats grazing on the land. They had

Written on the Wind

lived happily for three years before Tania died giving birth to a stillborn son, and that was when Temujin, by his own admission, "went a little crazy."

"I couldn't live in the place that had been built for a woman no longer on this earth. I left and never looked back."

He embarked on a life of stealing horses. He was eventually caught and condemned to a penal colony near Iskitim. For the next two years, he mined copper before escaping and joining the gang of outlaws.

"I am a nomad again," Temujin said one night as they trudged through the first dusting of snow. "I was foolish to try to be otherwise."

"Will you go back to stealing horses once we make it out of the forest?"

Temujin shrugged, but Dimitri had learned to see the good in this thief.

"I don't believe God would have sent you a good woman like Tania and then taken her away for no reason. She proved you can be more than a thief."

He expected Temujin to scoff, but he merely stared into the distance in speculation. "You have often spoken of this god who comes in three parts," he said. "The Father, and the Son, and the one I still don't understand."

"The Holy Spirit," Dimitri said. "Out here in the wilderness I feel the Holy Spirit everywhere. Whispering in my ear, urging me to survive long enough to deliver my message. It was the Holy Spirit that gave me the courage to leap from the train. Somehow, I believe we are both going to survive, Temujin."

Their friendship did not come without arguments, and as November turned into December, those arguments became more urgent. The climate was worsening, and they could not survive the winter on their own. Each time they stopped to make a camp, they argued.

"We should turn south," Temujin insisted, squinting against the sideways-falling sleet as he kicked aside pine needles in search of kindling dry enough to burn. "We can find shelter in Mongolia for the worst of the winter."

Dimitri shook his head. "I can't afford to stay in one place for months on end. I must get to Port Arthur before the worst of the winter arrives." It was the only way he would be able to reach Natalia and begin righting the terrible atrocity he had witnessed.

Temujin dumped a jumble of twigs into a mound. "I can't believe you really intend to sail to America. What about that house of yours? The one with too many rooms and a name?"

"Mirosa."

"Yes, Mirosa. And the woman with the blond hair and hot eyes?"

"Olga." Dimitri smiled a bit at Temujin's characterization of *hot eyes*. It was no secret that Olga hoped they could finally marry now that she was a widow, but his exile meant Olga was lost forever. So was Mirosa and his apple orchards and picnics in the dappled sunlight with friends from across the valley. It was all gone, and when he was this cold and miserable, he didn't have the strength to discuss it.

In the end, Temujin agreed it would be easier to suffer the cold heading toward Port Arthur than risk the mountains to the south, but their troubles soon got worse. Snow gathered and deepened, soaking the thin leather of Dimitri's moccasins. He was in danger of frostbite until they came across a dead Russian soldier in the snow. A deserter? The wolves had already gotten to him, but his boots were still in good shape. Dimitri tried not to look as he stripped the body of the boots, gloves, and a hunting knife. Temujin took the scarf and belt, and then they headed onward.

The weather got so bad that Dimitri risked approaching a village nestled beside a frozen lake. One of the villagers had a pony and sledge used by hunters to haul animal carcasses. It was only a five-foot slab of wood with two runners at the bottom and a bar for the driver to hold while steering the pony, but it could travel quickly across the snow.

The only thing of value they had to barter was the gold coin. It was worth ten times what the pony and sledge cost, but they had no choice. They were both wanted men, and that sledge could be the key to their salvation.

They harnessed the pony, boarded the sledge, and set off toward the east and freedom.

9

On Friday morning, Natalia tried to tutor Liam on the impact of tariffs on exchange rates. They sat at the worktable in her office but hadn't made much progress because Liam's attention kept wandering to the family gathering at her cousin Gwen's lake house that weekend. It would be his last chance to row on the lake before winter, and he wanted to leave work early to enjoy a full three-day weekend. Natalia hadn't had a three-day weekend since . . . well, not since becoming an adult.

"All work and no play makes for a dull young lady," Liam teased.

"Then I'm dull," she replied with a shrug. Her salary reports were due on Monday, and she planned to finalize them this afternoon. She didn't mind. Working for the bank was what gave shape and meaning to her life, and she loved it.

"I'll make a deal with you," Liam said. "If I prove that I can make sense of fluctuating exchange rates before lunch, we take off for the lake this afternoon."

"Deal!" she said. It would be worth it if Liam could finally buckle down and start making progress on mastering finance.

Their deal worked. By two o'clock they were aboard a carriage heading north for the lake house, but Natalia still brought along a book on economic philosophy to read over the weekend.

It wasn't that she disliked gatherings at the lake, but at least she could put her evenings to good use learning something important.

She and her cousin Gwen were the same age but had nothing in common. Gwen loved hosting soirees that lasted into the early morning hours, while Natalia usually wanted to retreat to her bedroom with a good book.

Gwen was Liam's sister, and she'd recently scandalized New York society by becoming engaged to Patrick O'Neill, a lawyer from the Lower East Side. Patrick had a number of strikes against him. He was an Irish immigrant who refused to mask his humble origins, which annoyed Poppy to no end, and he wasn't a comfortable fit for their family. But all that was pushed aside because it was Patrick who solved the mystery of what happened to the missing Blackstone heir. He risked his life to bring Liam back into the family, and the two men had forged a tight friendship.

Gwen's lake house was an hour north of the city and nestled in a stretch of thickly wooded land. The rustic home looked like a sprawling Swiss chalet and was large enough for the entire Blackstone clan to gather for weekend reunions.

"You're late," Poppy said as they walked into the great hall of the house. Woven rugs covered the slate floor, and a stacked-stone fireplace dominated the wall of the gathering room. "You missed lunch, and the food went to waste."

"Some of us have a job," Natalia said, refusing to let her stepmother get the better of her this early in the weekend.

"Motherhood is a job," Poppy defended.

"Of course it is," Natalia said. "Where's the baby? I've been looking forward to seeing him again."

The answer was as she expected. "Alexander is with his nanny back home. I'm not going to risk my child's health in this drafty house."

Natalia itched to point out that Poppy rarely spent more than an hour a day with her baby, but a trio of her elderly great-aunts came drifting in to greet them. Her grandfather and his sisters were all in their seventies and eighties, and the tone of the gathering immediately turned respectful as the elder generation funneled into the great room.

During the evening meal, the conversation veered to Liam and his growing fascination with Darla Kingston, whose daring art was beginning to make waves in the city.

"She's teaching me how to sculpt," Liam said. "Darla does her stuff in clay, but I'm doing mine with a blowtorch." He beamed in pride as he described how he welded thin strips of metal together, sometimes pounding them into shape with a hammer, other times twisting the strips with clamps.

"It doesn't sound very pretty," Poppy said.

Liam shrugged. "It's not. Darla says it looks strong and tough. Manly. That's good enough for me."

"Are you blushing?" Aunt Martha said. "Good heavens! He is."

The flush on Liam's face deepened, and everyone in the room was amazed to see the strong, brawny Liam in the throes of infatuation.

But Natalia worried. Liam was a newcomer both to the city and to vast wealth. Women had been swarming around him, but he showed no particular interest in any of them until Darla, and now things were progressing at an alarming speed.

The older generation turned in for the night early, and Gwen made hot mulled cider for the people who wished to stay up late. Poppy and Gwen worked on a jigsaw puzzle in the corner while Patrick and Liam discussed politics. Natalia's book about economic philosophy lay neglected on her lap while she listened in on the conversation. This evening had been more enjoyable than she anticipated.

When the conversation turned to Gwen and Patrick's upcoming wedding, a little of her happiness faded. Was there anything more dispiriting for a woman on the precipice of spinsterhood than to help plan another woman's wedding? Nevertheless, when Gwen began discussing musical selections, Natalia perked up. Music was one thing she probably enjoyed more than anyone else here.

Gwen wanted Maxim Tachenko, the world-famous Russian violinist, to play at the ceremony, and Poppy was over the moon at the prospect.

"Mrs. Astor tried to get him to play at her spring reception, and he refused," Poppy gushed. "He called her 'a useless plutocrat,' whatever that means, but most people would give their eyeteeth to land him for a private event. How on earth did you persuade him to play for you?"

"He owes me a favor," Gwen replied. "He lives on the other side of the lake, and I saved the ailing lilac bushes he had shipped over from Moscow. He is ridiculously fond of them and said he would gladly play for my wedding."

"Marriage is a sacred rite, not a music concert," Patrick said. "Any hymns or songs we want can be played on the church organ."

Gwen sighed. "Organ music is so stodgy, and Maxim can make a violin sing in a way that is practically a sacred rite in itself."

"Perhaps instead of the ceremony, he can play during the reception?" Natalia suggested, but Gwen dismissed the possibility.

"Maxim Tachenko isn't the sort of man who would tolerate being asked to play background music at a reception. He's notoriously vain and would consider it an insult."

"He's also a notorious revolutionary," Natalia pointed out. "Rumor has it he won't sign a contract to appear with an orchestra unless he is allowed to play 'The Internationale.'" The socialist workers' anthem had been banned in several European countries, and it would be a scandal if the famous violinist broke into a rousing rendition of "The Internationale" during Gwen's wedding.

"Let him play it," Liam said with a snicker. "The Russkies are nuts, but I love them. The next great workers' revolution will come out of Russia, and it will make the French Revolution look like a tea party."

"I won't have my wedding become a political rally," Patrick

insisted. "I'm sorry, Gwen. I know Mr. Tachenko is a friend of yours, but I want a traditional ceremony. You can have Tachenko whip up a musical storm any other time, but not while you and I are taking holy vows."

Patrick's voice was gentle but firm, and Natalia loved that about him. He was a confident man who could assert himself without bullying or backing down. Too many of the men she'd known over the years were completely cowed by her father, but Patrick never had been. The admiration in Gwen's eyes as she gazed at Patrick let the whole world know how much she adored him.

It made Natalia lonely.

Wasn't that odd? She was never lonely when she was curled up at home with a good book, but witnessing the love between Gwen and Patrick was like shining a spotlight on a howling void in her life.

Soon the discussion turned to clothes and the fact that Gwen intended to wear Aunt Martha's silk wedding gown, which had been in the family for generations.

"Are you allowed to wear white?" Poppy asked skeptically.

"I'm a widow, not a fallen woman," Gwen replied.

"Yes, but white connotes purity, and people will talk."

Poppy's comment was ridiculous, but Patrick took it in stride, his Irish accent teasingly affectionate.

"Gwen could walk down the aisle in bare feet and a potato sack, and she would still be the most beautiful woman in the church."

Natalia kept her tone practical as she said, "If you opt for a potato sack, please let me know in advance so I can invest in potato futures. A dress like that will make prices soar."

Silence hung in the air for a moment before everyone broke into peals of laughter. Sometimes people didn't know when she was joking. True, she tended to keep to herself, but maybe it was time for that to change. Tonight had been wonderful. For too long, her only real friend was a man who lived six thousand miles away and whose face she didn't even know.

Liam wasn't the first person to accuse her of having no life outside of the bank. Perhaps it was time she learned to relax and have a bit of frivolous fun.

The next morning, Natalia sat with her father on the enclosed back porch overlooking the lake. With its wall of windows and rustic décor, it was the most casual room in the house. The wicker furniture, mismatched pillows, and an old cuckoo clock made it feel a thousand miles away from New York City.

A pair of her elderly great-aunts joined them for tea and reading, but everyone else was down on the shore, watching the battle between Patrick and Liam in a rowing contest. Each were in their own canoe and charged with rowing a lady of their choice to the opposite shore and back. Patrick was paired with Gwen, and Liam had wanted to row Natalia, but she declined, so he'd been stuck with Poppy instead.

It looked fun, but reading the morning newspapers was essential for keeping abreast of the business world. Natalia tried to concentrate on an article about inflation rates, but dull cheers from outside distracted her. It looked like both canoes had reached the other side of the lake and were on the way back. Patrick was a few boat lengths ahead of Liam, but that could change.

A smile tugged at her mouth as she watched. Maybe she should have joined them after all.

Her father tipped the edge of his newspaper down to look at Aunt Martha. "It says here a developer has bought the old schooner yard. Isn't that where you worked during the war?"

Aunt Martha nodded. "It was a terrible place, but I don't regret my time there."

Natalia had grown up hearing about Great-Aunt Martha's volunteer work during the Civil War. Thousands of Confederate prisoners had been shipped north despite the lack of adequate housing, and men fell sick with all manner of diseases. Martha wasn't a nurse, but she could write letters and bathe

the sick. She eventually caught cholera and might have died, but once she recovered, she went straight back to tending the soldiers.

"I still can't believe you squandered so many years in that awful place," Aunt Helen said, her palsied hands trembling as she poured another cup of tea.

"Everyone warned me against it," Martha admitted. "When I got cholera, I wondered if they were right. It was awful, but I survived, and so did countless men I tended." She brightened. "Did you know I had a letter from one of them a few years back? He built a pencil factory in Atlanta and has twelve employees."

Aunt Helen rolled her eyes, but Natalia beamed. A woman *could* make a difference in the world. A pencil factory didn't sound very glamorous, but twelve people owed their livelihood to the man whose life Aunt Martha helped save.

Aunt Martha deserved to be proud of her service during the war, just as Natalia was proud of her work on the Trans-Siberian Railway. Millions of people would benefit from the railroad, but she liked to imagine a young girl on some isolated farm in central Russia whose life was confined to the wind-swept plains. The railroad was going to change that young girl's world. Natalia would never see that girl or know her name, but it didn't matter. She knew that girl existed. Hundreds—no, thousands of girls like that would benefit from the railroad.

A round of cheers came from outside, where Liam and Patrick had arrived back at shore. Gwen and Poppy were now setting up a game of pin the tail on the donkey.

The trip here had been fun, but like Aunt Martha, Natalia wanted a life of accomplishment, not rowing contests or party games. A mound of unfinished work awaited her at the office, and she stood to give her father a kiss on the cheek.

"I'm heading back to town early," she said. "Construction problems in Russia need me to reevaluate some schedules."

Oscar looked surprised but not disapproving. "Best get on it, then."

"All work and no play makes for a dull young lady." Liam's teasing voice taunted her during the ride back to the city. Was there a middle ground between a life of single-minded purpose and one of pointless leisure like Poppy embraced? If so, Natalia hadn't found it yet.

10

The blades of the sledge made a whispery rasp as they cut across the ice-encrusted snow. That and the clomping of the pony's hooves were the only sounds Dimitri had heard for hours because he and Temujin were both too miserable to talk. It took too much energy.

Dimitri's hands and feet were numb, but he shifted from side to side, gently stamping his feet, praying it would be enough to keep his circulation moving and frostbite at bay. He'd been standing on this sledge for ten hours, but the nights were long now, lasting almost fifteen hours. The pony couldn't pull a sledge that long, and it was time to head into the forest for a rest.

"I'm going to find a place to stop," he called over his shoulder.

Temujin didn't answer. He was either asleep or dead. The frostbite on his feet made it impossible for him to stand anymore, and he lay curled on the flatbed of the sledge.

Dimitri gently slowed the pony and got off the sledge.

"What's for breakfast?" Temujin asked.

Dimitri smiled, relieved Temujin was alive and still had his sense of humor. The only thing they had eaten for weeks was cedar nuts, and they had plenty of them, but the first order of business was to tend the pony. If the pony died, he and Temujin died too.

After feeding the pony, Dimitri lit a fire to melt snow and get them all water. After that came finding more pine cones and smashing them on a rock to release the seeds. Only then could he eat.

By the time Dimitri returned from scavenging in the forest, Temujin had rolled upright to huddle near the small fire. Their only pot balanced on a few rocks above the flame, and Temujin had managed to refill it with snow.

"My feet are worse," he said.

Dimitri looked away. Once frostbite set in, there was little that could be done.

When Temujin's feet first started showing the telltale signs of waxy, yellowed skin, they tried dunking them in a pot of warmed water. It had been a mistake. Immediately after they removed his feet, the water that had absorbed into his skin froze, causing excruciating pain and worsening the frostbite. Now his toes had turned black, and it was spreading.

"I think it's time for you to leave me here," Temujin said. "Drive the sledge away and don't look back."

"Don't even think it," Dimitri said.

Temujin acted like he hadn't heard. "I can walk into a snow-drift and put an end to it. You have a chance of making it out alive. I don't."

Dimitri jostled the pot over the flame, mentally urging the lump of snow to melt faster. The hot water would taste good. There was a time when he drank only the finest tea imported from Ceylon to London, where teamakers infused the leaves with the oil from bergamot orange. It was then packaged and shipped to Saint Petersburg, where his mother served it in Limoges china teacups with cream and lemon.

Now he drank hot water and was grateful for it.

"No one is going to die," Dimitri said. "I'll figure something out."

The skin on the back of his head throbbed. The incision

where he'd hidden the diamond had completely sealed over, but it could pay for a doctor. They were only a few days outside of Chita, the last Russian city before they reached Mongolia. There would be a doctor in Chita. They could buy better clothes and nourishing food.

"Try to get some sleep," he said to Temujin, who burrowed deeper into his coat and curled up on the sledge.

There was no more talk of walking into snowdrifts, so Dimitri went to scavenge for more cedar nuts, praying to God for the courage to lead him through the coming days. He needed to survive. God willing, Temujin would too, but first they needed to reach Chita.

The first sign of civilization on the outskirts of Chita was clusters of men on the lake, fishing through holes in the ice. Soon there were scatterings of wooden homesteads and barns. Dimitri followed the Chitinka River toward the town, where almost ten thousand people made their home.

He no longer feared recognition. Wearing tattered clothes obtained through bartering with live bandits and stripping clothes off of dead ones, he looked nothing like the aristocratic man he'd once been. His face was chapped by the relentless wind, his beard scruffy, his clothes caked with mud. He looked like any other peasant, lugging a bulging sack of cedar nuts over his shoulder.

He used half the nuts to barter for stabling the pony and the sledge. It was done entirely through gestures since the stable-master spoke a language neither he nor Temujin understood. The people in this city were a conglomeration of Russians, Chinese, Buryats, and Dukhas, but it was anyone's guess what this stablemaster spoke.

Temujin hobbled to a bench outside the stable and collapsed. "I can't walk any farther," he choked out.

"I'll bring a doctor to you," Dimitri said with more confidence than he felt.

"How are we going to pay for a doctor?"

Dimitri clapped Temujin on the shoulder. "Let me worry about that."

He headed down a muddy street toward the town square, where pastel-colored buildings framed an empty fountain. An Orthodox church stood beside a mosque, and signage was in every language imaginable. He made note of a German jeweler where he could sell the diamond, and finally found a doctor whose features indicated he was probably a Buryat but who spoke enough Russian for them to agree on a price to treat Temujin.

"Let me get the money," Dimitri said. "I'll be back in an hour."

He walked into a bar on the main street. It was crowded, dirty, and smelled of wet leather, but he made his way to the counter and gestured to the Chinese bartender for a shot of whiskey. After paying for the shot with cedar nuts, he carried it to a shadowy corner and turned his back to the crowd. This was going to look odd, and he didn't want to attract attention.

The stubby knife Temujin used to skin squirrels was only a few inches long. Dimitri dunked the blade into the whiskey, hoping the old wives' tale that hard liquor was a disinfectant was true. After holding the blade in the whiskey for several seconds, he took it out, shook off the excess liquid, then drank the whiskey in one searing gulp.

It fortified him enough to walk behind the saloon, where he leaned against the back wall and drew a steadying breath. This was going to be hard, but he'd done it before and survived. He could do it again. He sank to his knees.

Dear Lord, he silently prayed, *this tiny piece of stone might save my friend. Both of us are unworthy, but if I live through this, I will forever fight in your name to honor your son and your will. In Jesus' name I pray.*

He stayed on his knees as he reached up behind his head, knife at the ready. The lumpy scar was easy to find, and he braced himself as he set the blade against it.

His yells echoed down the alleyway as he dug out the diamond.

Temujin's days as a bandit were over. The doctor had amputated his right foot and three toes on his left. He would hobble on a cane for the rest of his life, but he was alive.

Dimitri stood at the foot of his friend's cot in the rudimentary clinic. "Chita would be a good place to live," he said. "Settle down. Find another wife."

After paying the doctor, Dimitri still had money from the sale of the diamond, and he'd given half of it to Temujin. It would be enough for Temujin to start a new life, but it was time for them to part ways. Port Arthur was nine hundred miles to the east, and the worst months of winter loomed ahead. Dimitri needed to move quickly, but these few days in Chita had been a welcome respite.

"Here," he said, laying a beaded red sash on the bed. These sashes were used to tie traditional Mongolian clothing, and Dimitri had bought one for each of them. He wouldn't have survived the last two months without Temujin, and the red sashes would commemorate their friendship.

"Must you leave so soon?" Temujin asked.

For a few minutes this morning, Dimitri had toyed with the idea of staying here. He could change his name and start his life anew in Chita. He and Temujin could buy a farm and never look back.

But if he did, the massacre he witnessed would be lost to history, a tragedy written on the wind, soon to fade away. He needed to capture its memory and carry it to the world.

That meant he needed to get to New York. Even thinking about continuing his journey to the other side of the world was exhausting, but he would face it one day at a time.

"I can't stop until I reach my friend in New York. Natalia will help me."

Temujin's eyes crinkled in amusement. "If this woman is as rich as you say and is still unmarried, I'll bet she has the face of a donkey."

Temujin was probably correct, but it did not put a dent in Dimitri's regard for Natalia. "She is a good woman with the head of a strategist and the heart of a poet. A homely face does not matter, my friend."

That night he shared a farewell meal with Temujin. They drank long into the night while he piled log after log into the cast-iron stove to keep the room warm. It was one last evening of joyful companionship before heading off into the harsh Russian winter.

In the months after leaving Temujin, Dimitri traveled eight hundred miles by a combination of sledge, river barge, and foot. He crossed into the highlands of Mongolia and then the eastern region of China. He battled icy wind as January morphed into February, but the climate eased in March as he neared his destination. Five miles outside of Port Arthur, Dimitri bartered for a ride on the back of a chicken wagon headed toward the city. The clucking chickens made it crowded and stinky, but an unexpected surge of emotion welled in him as the rickety wagon entered the outskirts of the town.

For the past seven months, Dimitri had battled fear, hunger, and exhaustion, but he was so close to the ocean that he could smell salt in the air. When the chicken farmer arrived at his destination, Dimitri hopped off the back of the wagon to walk the final mile.

Twenty minutes later he rounded a bend in the road and caught his first glimpse of the ocean. Had there ever been a more beautiful sight? He fell to his knees and crossed himself as a sheen of tears blurred his vision. The ocean represented hope and freedom and escape. After four thousand miles, he had finally arrived, and the ocean looked like paradise.

But it was a dangerous paradise. Port Arthur was in Chinese territory, but the port itself was administered by the Russians, and they might still be looking for him.

Dimitri no longer looked anything like a Russian aristocrat.

He was dirty and emaciated, with a shaggy beard and his hair pulled into a topknot like Temujin wore. His fur-lined boots had come off a dead soldier, and his baggy pants had been bartered from a Dukha peddler. His coat was a leather deel, a traditional overcoat worn among the Mongolians, that reached past his knees. The flaps were tied shut with the red sash he'd bought in Chita, and a gunnysack bulging with cedar nuts was slung over his back.

He leaned against the side of a warehouse and looked down into the port below. Storefront signs in Chinese characters stood side-by-side with Russian Cyrillic, French, and a smattering of English. He couldn't communicate in Chinese, and a Russian outpost could mean the kiss of death, but at last he spotted an American ship. The USS *Pacific Star* was docked in the harbor, low in the water and with room for passengers in the hold.

He headed toward the American shipping office, where a lump settled in his stomach at the hefty ticket prices. A steerage berth to San Francisco would cost the remainder of his money. But the USS *Pacific Star* sailed tomorrow, and he needed to be on that ship. The moment he sailed out of Russian-controlled territory, he would be a free man. A broke, hungry, and sick man, but free.

Free. He had never appreciated that concept until it was taken away from him.

After paying the cost of the ticket, Dimitri was down to his last few pennies, and he still needed to contact Natalia. San Francisco was nowhere close to New York, and he'd need more money as soon as he arrived in California. Natalia could get it to him.

The telegraph office inside the American shipping terminal only took cash, and a wire to New York would be expensive. He calculated the costs, carefully figuring the charges for the telegraph fee.

It was going to cost more than he had.

His boots were worth something. They were the finest thing in his possession, even though they'd been taken off a dead soldier. He wandered toward a street of market stalls and food vendors. The aromas of fried fish and baked dumplings made him weak with hunger, but he ignored them and headed toward a tinker's cart to sell his boots.

The haggling took a while, but in the end, Dimitri walked away with twenty rubles and the cheapest pair of shoes on the tinker's cart. They were a tattered pair of lapti, a traditional shoe worn by peasants and made of woven birch bark. They were neither sturdy nor warm, but it didn't matter. Soon he would be in California, and Natalia would be able to help him.

He took his remaining funds to the shipping office. Telegrams cost by the letter, so he parsed his words carefully. The only thing on which he could not afford to scrimp was the salutation. *Dearest Natalia.* If he opened the wire with those two words, she would know it came from him.

Dearest Natalia. Arriving on Pacific Star, March 25. Wire a thousand dollars to port of San Fran. Dimitri

He bowed his head and prayed that she would come through for him, for he was going to need Natalia desperately in the months ahead.

11

*N*atalia sat in the bank's conference room for the monthly review of their investments. A mahogany table with space for eighteen people dominated the center of the room, her father on one end and her grandfather on the other. Bank executives sat on the sides according to rank, and the remaining chairs were filled by managers reporting on the state of their projects.

Natalia was the only woman in the room. Even the stenographers and secretaries taking notes were men, but Natalia had been invited to these meetings since the day she turned sixteen. At that point, her father had become resigned to never having a male heir and began grooming her for a significant role at the bank. At first she sat with the stenographers in the chairs that hugged the wall. After earning her college degree, she was entrusted with her first account, a modest plan for road-paving, and she was invited to sit at the table. Over the years, her seat at the table moved to increasingly more prominent positions, and now she sat next to her father.

The topic of this morning's review was an investment to deepen the harbor in Seattle so it could accommodate the new freighter-class ships the navy was building. The bank had loaned the Hammond Construction firm a fortune to perform the task, but this was the third month in a row they'd missed their target. Silas Conner was the bank's executive handling the account.

"The Hammonds have a new excuse each month about why the project is lagging," Silas reported. "They claim that persistent fog is interfering with the dredging operations."

Her grandfather was skeptical. "The Hammonds just built a warehouse for the Union Pacific, who will be introducing refrigerated railroad cars next month. I think the Hammonds are using our money to expand their railroad investment instead of the port."

Trust was the most important commodity in any banking relationship, and it was hard to monitor how the Hammonds spent the bank's money from the opposite side of the country. It was one of the reasons Natalia valued her relationship with Count Sokolov. Not that she had any reason to doubt his replacement, but trust could take years to build. The Hammonds dutifully reported how they'd been investing funds in the harbor, but how could the bank be certain it was truthful?

"Let's set this aside for now," her grandfather said. "We'll take a break, then move on to the discussion of bonds for the Boston subway." He looked pointedly at Silas Conner. "I will expect a more definitive report from you next month."

The break gave Natalia an opportunity to move her stiff muscles as she headed into the lobby and helped herself to tea from the elaborate service set up outside the conference room. Silas stood before a bank of windows overlooking Wall Street, his face stormy as he glared at the street below.

She empathized, since it wasn't easy bringing bad news before her grandfather. She joined him at the window.

"Have you thought of going to Seattle to see the harbor for yourself?" she asked.

He looked surprised. "What for?"

"It's harder to pull off a shell game with our money if the Hammonds know a bank executive might suddenly appear for an inspection."

His brows lowered. "Forgive me, Natalia, but I don't recall you going out to inspect the Trans-Siberian Railway in person."

"That's different," she defended.

"How so?"

"The Russian project is ahead of schedule, and the port of Seattle is lagging." Plus, for three years she had an agent in Russia she implicitly trusted, while Silas relied on accountants in Seattle he'd never met. She was about to point that out when an office clerk handed her a folded card.

"Excuse me, ma'am, a telegram has arrived for you."

"Thank you." She tucked the card into her leather portfolio before turning back to Silas, but he had a raft of excuses.

"I'm not a port engineer," he said. "How would I know if the Hammonds were even telling me the truth?"

She tamped down her frustration. A skilled investment banker ought to be fluent in all manner of ventures, whether it was a steel mill, a railroad, or a construction project. If a topic was beyond her experience, she knew where to go for help.

"We have consultants here in New York," she said. "Take one with you. I guarantee if you arrive in Seattle to inspect that project, their behavior will improve."

His eyes narrowed. "You may be the most smug, egotistical woman in the entire state of New York."

Her jaw dropped at the unprovoked attack. "What did you just say?"

"You heard me. I have a college degree and had to claw my way through low-level clerkships while you bounced on daddy's knee and waltzed into a corner office."

She itched to point out that she had also gone to college and served in entry-level clerkships, but she wouldn't let him put her on the defensive. "I'm sorry you find my presence here so intimidating."

Tension crackled between them as they headed back into the conference room. Resentment still pulsed in her veins as she took a seat at the table, but she swallowed it back as their analyst handling the Boston subway began speaking.

"Good news," he said as he flipped open a file. "The geologists report that the ground composition beneath Boston is going to allow the drilling of the subway tunnels to proceed faster than anticipated."

The discussion was actually quite interesting, but the rim of the telegram peeking from beneath her stack of papers distracted her. She slid it out and flipped it open.

Dearest Natalia. Arriving on Pacific Star, March 25. Wire a thousand dollars to port of San Fran. Dimitri

The breath left her in a rush. Dimitri was the only person in the world who addressed her as "Dearest Natalia," but this message made no sense. It didn't sound like Dimitri. It was probably a fraud, and a cruel one at that.

She slid the card back under her stack of papers. She wouldn't let herself be distracted from the discussion about the subway because of a nonsensical telegram. Soon there were questions from the other bankers, and she tried to put the odd message out of her mind.

But it was hard to concentrate, and she slid the telegram out to read it again. Someone was clearly trying to defraud her. Boris Kozlov, the hard-bitten policeman she'd hired to find news of Dimitri, was the most likely suspect. She'd never quite trusted Boris. He took bribes from the owners of local stores to stop by several times a day. He probably assumed that a rich woman like Natalia wouldn't hesitate to wire money to a friend in need.

But how would Boris know about the "Dearest Natalia" greeting?

She thrummed her fingers against the card, one ear listening to the subway discussion while her mind was halfway around the world. Plenty of people knew that was how Dimitri addressed her. It was an open joke among the telegraph operators on the third floor, and Boris could have easily learned that detail.

Why would he ask her to wire money to San Francisco, though? If he was trying to impersonate Dimitri to trick her out of a thousand dollars, why send the money to the other side of the country? Granted, it would be harder to trap a fraudster in San Francisco than if Boris asked for the money to be wired someplace like Boston or Philadelphia, but still. . . .

"Natalia!" her father said, jerking her back to the present. "I asked about your plans for structuring the loan."

She cleared her throat and supplied the answers, heat flushing her face. On the other side of the table, Silas Conner gloated at the way she'd been caught woolgathering.

She needed to concentrate on getting this loan finalized and waste no more time worrying about the unknown scoundrel trying to swindle her out of a thousand dollars.

12

Dimitri stepped off the ship and into the port of San Francisco, looking around in appalled amazement. It was huge! Dozens of piers crowded the port, where steamships unloaded people and cargo. Other ships waited offshore, ready to dock as soon as a pier was open. His own ship had been forced to wait six hours before it could claim a space on a wharf, all while Dimitri cooled his heels on deck, eager to get ashore and claim the payment Natalia had sent. The moment he had his hands on it, he'd buy a meal, a bath, and some decent clothing.

Except now that he was on land, the experience was overwhelming. Piers, wagons, warehouses, and drays cluttered the shore as far as his eye could see. To the south, dredging equipment widened the harbor, while on the north, dozens of railroads funneled into warehouses. And the noise! It made the chaos even more unnerving.

How would he find the telegraph office where Natalia had sent his money? He hadn't expected San Francisco to be so big, and he kept walking down the harbor path, looking for sign of a telegraph station. It had rained this morning, and the damp soaked through his tattered lapti shoes, which had outlived their usefulness. The woven strips of birch bark began to fray during the voyage, but he had tied pieces of string around each shoe to hold them together.

The port stretched for miles in each direction, but the largest and fanciest building was straight ahead. It was a white, neoclassical building with two long wings on either side and a clocktower in the center. It seemed a logical place to start looking for a telegraph station.

A long arcade stretched down the interior of the building, its high ceiling framed by exposed ironwork arches. It was a feast for the eyes. Cheese shops, flower stalls, casks of wine, and merchants selling all manner of imported goods filled the arcade. The scent of hot coffee mingled with baking bread made him weak with hunger.

People looked at him oddly, probably because of the conglomeration of clothes he wore. The flaps of his Mongolian deel were loosely held together with the red sash, and his shoes were falling apart, but he didn't care, especially after spotting the Western Union telegraph office straight ahead.

A grumpy clerk with wire-framed glasses stood behind the front counter as he haggled with a woman who didn't want to pay for the telegram she'd just sent. Behind the clerk was a wall with hundreds of tiny slots filled with telegrams either waiting to be picked up or delivered. Dimitri's heart pounded so hard it made him dizzy, but at last he arrived at the front of the line.

"Please," he said. "My friend has wired a message for Dimitri Sokolov. Please see if it has arrived."

The clerk looked taken aback. "What?" he asked. "You need to speak English."

Dimitri hadn't even realized he'd spoken in Russian. He repeated the request in English as the clerk's suspicious gaze flicked to Dimitri's hair, tied up in a topknot. He frowned in disdain but turned to scan the mail slots. It didn't take long.

"There is nothing here for you," he said. "You'll have to move along. There's a line behind you."

Dimitri clenched his fists. "It was scheduled to be here today. Can you consult the arrivals again?"

The clerk shook his head. "I don't need to look again. I've been here all day, and nothing like that has come in. Move along. There's a line behind you."

Dimitri stood, poleaxed. It could not be! There was no way Natalia would have failed to respond to his plea for help. If she knew of his desperation, she would have moved heaven and earth to help him.

A headache began to pound, and he battled a wave of anxiety as terrible thoughts descended. What if Natalia learned he'd been condemned for cowardice and wanted nothing to do with him? Knowing she might think badly of him scorched. He would have to find her and explain. If it took the rest of his life, he would clear the stain of dishonor from his name.

What was he going to do now? No clothes, no food, no money. Strange land. He wasn't too proud to work, but who would hire a sickly man whose shoes were held together by string?

He could not accept this. He'd traveled too far to be discouraged this easily.

He headed to the other side of the telegraph station where an older man was sorting messages in a back office. Dimitri raised his voice to get the clerk's attention.

"Sir," he called out, "can you check for a message? Please! It will be coming from New York, from Natalia Blackstone."

The older clerk looked taken aback, but Dimitri didn't care. Then a voice came from behind his shoulder.

"Dimitri?"

He whirled around. A lovely young woman stood a few yards away, looking at him in a combination of hope and curiosity. She was a vision. Black hair, green eyes. Beautiful.

He dared not hope but couldn't help himself. "Are you Natalia?"

She beamed a radiant smile. "I am Natalia," she said, then stepped forward to kiss him on the cheek. "Welcome to America."

Relief washed through him, and he grabbed her in a mighty hug. She smelled like lemon and sunshine and hope. Tears stung his eyes.

"I think this is the happiest moment in my life," he choked out, still clutching her, but her voice was lighthearted in response.

"Oh, Dimitri, must we begin with your typical exaggerations?"

He wasn't exaggerating. Eight months of fear and deprivation had just come to a swift end, but he had forgotten his manners. He released her and stepped back a pace.

"Forgive me for being so forward," he said, adjusting the flap of his jacket to its proper position. "You have taken me by surprise. I did not expect you to be here."

Her smile was sympathetic. "The telegram didn't sound like you, but I couldn't be sure it *wasn't* you either, so I came to see for myself."

"I'm very glad you did. I finally know what you look like. Natalia, you are beautiful! And you can finally see me, a little ragged and worse for wear, but alive."

She took a step back, her eyes traveling up and down the mishmash of clothing he'd collected. "You look like a Cossack," she said, nodding toward the red sash tied around his middle.

He shook his head. "Cossacks live on the other side of Russia. This is a Buryat sash and a Mongolian coat, with trousers from a Dukha peddler. The shoes are pure Russian peasant."

He smiled at her like an idiot, and she smiled back. "I didn't realize you had a beard."

"It comes and goes with the seasons." Right now, it was itching. He probably wouldn't keep it much longer. San Francisco wasn't as warm as he expected, but it was no Siberia, and he didn't like looking anything less than respectably groomed.

"Are you hungry?" she asked.

"Starving."

"Then follow me," she said with a charming smile, and at that moment Dimitri would gladly follow her anywhere.

Natalia led Dimitri to a shop that sold warm bread and hot soup inside the Ferry Building. He didn't look like she'd expected. His messages were always so genteel and well-spoken, but the man before her looked like a mangy skeleton wearing filthy rags.

And yet he displayed the exquisite manners of a gentleman. He held a chair out for her at the café and unfolded his napkin with long, elegant fingers before draping it over his lap. The way his eyes widened as the soup was delivered made her suspect he was famished, but he still bowed his head in prayer before eating.

He might not look like Dimitri, but he *sounded* like her old friend. He praised the chowder as being like ambrosia kissed with sunshine. His observations of traveling in steerage were pure Dimitri.

"What a spectacular horror. They served us rice that tasted like sawdust seasoned with wallpaper paste, but I made friends with a man from Shanghai who shared his sack of gingerroot with me. He ground it into the rice, spoke some sort of spell, and then voila! It was as though kissed by the gods. Life will never again be so grim now that I have discovered the miracle of gingerroot."

Natalia was grateful for his talkative rambling, since it gave her time to study him. The grubby clothes and shaggy hair couldn't disguise the strong line of his features. He had high cheekbones and a long blade of a nose. His hair was so grimy that it was hard to know what color it was, but probably some sort of chestnut shade.

He needed a bath, a haircut, and a shave. There were public bathhouses on Market Street, and she could buy him a change of clothes while he bathed. His dingy shirt stank and was smeared with old bloodstains. His shoes were strips of woven birch bark held together by a few pieces of dirty string. All of it should be burned.

When she suggested as much, his hand went to the red sash tied around his middle. "You may burn everything but this," he said. "This sash is sacred to me, a symbol of enduring friendship and struggle. I will keep it until my dying day. It shall be a part of my funeral shroud."

"Enough with the Russian fatalism," she teased. "I didn't come all the way across the country to plan your funeral."

"Then, why did you come?" he asked. All trace of humor was gone as he watched her.

She came because she couldn't stay away. If there was the slightest chance that Dimitri had managed to escape from a Siberian penal colony, she couldn't twiddle her thumbs in New York while he struggled to survive. She used trouble in the port of Seattle as an excuse to head out to the West Coast.

"I had business in a nearby city called Seattle," she said. "Our bank is financing a major expansion of their port. It hasn't been going well. I wanted to meet with the construction manager and report back to my father."

Dimitri put down his spoon. "Tell me about your manager in Seattle. Is he as interesting as me? As friendly?"

"I'm not going to stroke your ego," she said. "You're too conceited as it is."

He snorted. "I am confident, not conceited. There's a difference."

The way he held himself, with perfect posture and a proud gleam in his eyes despite his filthy clothes, made him ridiculously attractive. She knew he was smart and accomplished. That he had a deep love for music and literature. Most especially, she knew he had no difficulty expressing himself in extravagant language that made her laugh from six thousand miles away. She desperately wanted to know what had caused everything to collapse so badly in Russia, leading to that horrible conviction. Most of all, she wanted to know how he managed to free himself from captivity.

"What happened in Siberia?" she asked softly. "I read about the trial. It said that you refused to follow orders, but it didn't say what those orders were, and I don't understand."

He picked up his spoon and went back to his soup. "Not while I'm eating. It's a long and tedious story, and this soup is getting cold."

His knuckles were white, and he wouldn't meet her eyes.

She would learn what happened in good time, but for now she needed to get him cleaned up.

When she rose from the table, he immediately shot to his feet and offered his arm to escort her out of the Ferry Building. People looked at them oddly, because women wearing silk gowns tailored in Paris rarely allowed themselves to be escorted by men who looked like vagabonds, but her smile was so wide it hurt. She *loved* Dimitri's courtly manners and didn't give a fig if people gaped at them. As they walked up Market Street, Dimitri craned his neck to look all around the city, commenting on the grandeur of the buildings with typical exaggeration.

"The architect must have been in a joyous mood when he designed that building," he said, gesturing to the Palace Hotel with its nine stories, colonnaded balconies, and elegant mansard roof.

"We can stay there if you wish, but the doormen won't let you cross the threshold looking as you do."

A nearby barbershop boasted of hot baths in the back of the establishment, though it might not be up to Count Sokolov's typical standards. She'd always known Dimitri was shamelessly vain. Even while stationed in Siberia, he imported special soap from France and rosehip oil from the Caspian Sea to keep his skin smooth.

Dimitri stood in the doorway of the barbershop, gazing with rapt longing at the shelves laden with bottles of ointments and tins of shaving balm. "I have just stepped into paradise."

"There will be time to shop after you're clean," she said. Dimitri didn't have a single American dime to his name, so she pressed a few bills into his hand. "Buy yourself a haircut and a bath. I'll head to the emporium next door and bring back clean clothes."

Thirty minutes later, she returned to the barbershop with a charcoal-gray suit, a shirt, socks, undergarments, and a pair of new shoes. She sent the clothes to the back of the shop because Dimitri was still in the bath.

Ten minutes later, he finally emerged from behind a paisley

curtain, and she gasped at his transformation. The beard was completely gone. The long hair was gone too, cut short to reveal light brown hair with rich chestnut highlights. His facial features were finely molded, with high cheekbones and a long, aristocratic nose.

"You look like a new man!" she enthused even though the suit she'd bought for him was a little too big. Dimitri was very slim, but he'd tied the exotic red sash around his waist because she'd forgotten to buy a belt, and it made him look even more dashing.

But something was wrong. Instead of looking pleased, he was tense as he strode to her side, leaning in close to speak in a low voice. "I need three dollars."

She blinked. "What for?"

Dimitri glared at a man standing behind a register. Several large, dark bottles sat on the counter before him.

The barber pushed one bottle across the counter. "This is the oil I recommend. The others are cheaper, but eucalyptus oil is the most effective."

Dimitri looked back at her. "Please say nothing. Just buy the eucalyptus oil, and let us be on our way."

It wasn't the money that concerned her but the fact that Dimitri was coldly furious. Had someone said something unkind to him?

She instinctively wanted to protect him, but he was already drifting toward the door, eager to leave. She gave the clerk a bill and didn't even wait for her change, just grabbed the bottle and followed Dimitri outside into the bright sun.

"What happened?" she asked, struggling to catch up to his long-legged stride. He pulled her into an alcove behind a newsstand. It was quieter back here, sheltered from the view of the bustling street.

"The barber informed me that I have . . . I have already forgotten the English word he used, but it is bad. A humiliation."

Her eyes widened, not understanding what could have upset him so. "Tell it to me in Russian," she prompted.

He said a short, blunt word, spitting out the harsh syllable like a curse. He repeated it for her twice, getting angrier each time he said it, but she didn't know that word.

"Describe it for me," she said.

"The barber says I have little things in my hair." He held up his fingers, pinched together. " Tiny animals. In my hair."

She gasped. "Lice?"

"Yes! That is the word he used. Lice! It must have happened on the ship because it was too cold for it to have happened in Russia. Natalia, I assure you, I am not a man who normally has lice in my hair."

This explained the eucalyptus oil. Dimitri looked mortified as he explained the procedure the barber recommended to treat the infestation and why he had to cut his hair so short and shave his beard as well.

"Let's get checked into a hotel, and I'll help you," she said. "It doesn't sound like this is something you can do alone."

Natalia made arrangements for two rooms in the Palace Hotel, then went to Dimitri's room to begin the long, exacting procedure for treating a lice infestation. Dimitri sat on the floor while she perched on a chair behind him. He'd already soaked his hair in the eucalyptus oil, and she pulled a fine-toothed comb through sections of his hair, leaning in to search for the tiny lice. The menthol made her eyes water, nose run, and skin tingle, but it was working. The pungent oil stunned the lice into immobility, making it easier to drag them from his hair.

Dimitri was in a better frame of mind, casually sitting with a towel draped over his shoulders while submitting to the treatment.

"Once this is over, we will never speak of it again."

"You think?" she teased, scraping out a few more nits and dunking the comb in a mug of hot water. He was so lordly, but she felt no compunction to fall into obedience.

"Have you issued the quarterly dividend from my investment in the bank?" he asked.

Normally the bank issued a huge check to their investors on the fifteenth of March, but Natalia had put a hold on it, not sure how it should be handled after Dimitri's bank account in Saint Petersburg had been seized. There had been no demands from the Russian government for Blackstone Bank to surrender Dimitri's American assets, and she doubted they even knew about them.

"We've been keeping your funds in an escrow account," she said. "They are yours whenever you wish."

The tension visibly drained from his shoulders and neck. "Good," he said simply.

She waited, hoping he would offer more details about what drove him out of his position at the railroad, but he added nothing. Dimitri clearly had no wish to discuss whatever happened in Russia, and for the first time since she met him in the telegraph office, an awkward pause filled the air. She blotted her eyes against the watering from the eucalyptus oil, then moved to another section of his hair.

"Did you get the copy of *Little Women* I sent you?" she asked.

"I got it."

"And?"

He released an exaggerated sigh. "I do not understand why you thought I would enjoy that novel. The only good part is when Beth dies."

She threw the comb at him, but he caught it, laughing raucously as he shot to his feet and whirled to face her. "Did you think I was serious?"

"I *know* you're serious, and that's why I want to strangle you!"

Dimitri slanted her a chiding grin. "Come, we both know it is a maudlin and sentimental novel. You must forgive me for not wishing to drown in sugary syrup."

"I haven't forgiven you for making me read *War and Peace*, and I never shall."

"It is an honest portrayal of the human condition," he retorted.

"So is *Little Women*."

He looked heavenward as though pained. "It is a boring portrayal of mundane domesticity. Novels should be written on an epic scale to explore and celebrate the depth of human suffering. Don't subject me to women chatting beside the fireplace. *Little Women* is nothing more than a sleeping draught. That is not the purpose of literature."

She stood up to face him. "You arrogant Russian snob! What gives you the right to decide the purpose of literature?"

A wickedly taunting grin lit his face. "Centuries of literary tradition agree that tragedy is more worthy than cozy domestic stories. Even though you are wrong about Tolstoy, I find your defense of sappy literature strangely appealing. Please continue."

She smothered a laugh. It was fun being able to tease him without fear of offense, and it appeared he felt equally at ease returning fire. She really ought to defend her favorite novel more, but her eyes were still watering, and they had work to do.

"Sit back down and let me finish your hair."

He complied and continued finding fault with *Little Women*, but she quit listening when she came across something odd on Dimitri's scalp. Near the base of his neck, a lump of raised skin. She ran her thumb across it.

"Be careful of that spot, please."

His hair was short enough to see a scar about the size and shape of a nickel. "What is it?"

"A memento of my time in Chita," he said. "Perhaps the only wise move I made before my trial was to hide things of value on my person. Sadly, the items I sewed into my clothes were stolen before I could use them, but I hid a diamond beneath that scar you have just discovered. It survived long enough for it to be useful."

She pulled her fingers away, aghast. "You hid a diamond beneath your own skin?"

"A good hiding place, yes?"

She felt dizzy as she absorbed the news. "Does it still hurt?"

"Not usually, but please be gentle with the comb on that spot. The eucalyptus oil will not be kind if the skin breaks open again."

She leaned in closer, no longer caring about the eye-watering sting of the oil. She needed to inspect his scalp without hurting the scar tissue. "I sense there is quite a story behind this scar," she said, hoping he would share it with her.

Fortunately, he was in a chatty mood. "I spent many months with a friend who needed to escape as badly as I did." He went on to describe his improbable friendship with a Buryat outlaw who had escaped from a penal colony. Together, they traveled thousands of miles before going their separate ways in a remote city called Chita.

What sort of man cut a diamond out of his own skin for an outlaw? Who navigated for months on end through a brutal wilderness in his quest for freedom? All her life she had admired brave, daring men who weren't afraid of a challenge.

It looked like she had found one, but Dimitri was hiding something from her, and she feared it did not bode well.

13

Dimitri was beginning to feel like a man again, restored both in body and spirit. His first few hours in San Francisco had been a hectic experience. The sudden onslaught of noise and crowds, the fear of being alone and penniless, then the joy of falling into Natalia's welcoming friendship. The mortification of telling her about the lice faded when she rolled up her sleeves to help him with the disagreeable problem.

After the lice treatment, Natalia noticed the disastrous shape of his hands and insisted on soaking them in warmed oil to soften the calluses he'd earned driving the sledge for months on end. He would probably go to his grave with those calluses, but he gladly accepted her ministrations.

Now they dined at a rooftop restaurant called the Oyster House, situated on a terrace overlooking the harbor on one side and the glittering lights of the city on the other. Few people chose to dine outside on such a chilly night, but it didn't feel cold to him, and Natalia wore an elegantly tailored wool coat with a charming hat cocked at a saucy angle. She looked like a Russian princess in the clear, cold night.

He rotated a crystal goblet, staring at the remnants of a steak dinner and the votive candles that lit their table with a warm glow. Once again, he was on top of the world, dining with a beautiful woman, his belly full.

And somewhere in the cold, windswept land not far from the Trans-Siberian railroad lay thousands of people in unmarked graves. They called out to him for justice. The czar and his allies had done their best to silence him, but now he was in America, and the tables had just turned. It was time to embark on his next mission.

"I need to tell you what I witnessed in Siberia," he said.

Natalia met his gaze across the candlelit table, pained sympathy in her face. "I'm ready to hear it."

Dimitri drew a deep breath, bracing himself to relive the memory.

Natalia already understood his role along the southern route of the Trans-Siberian that skirted the Amur River. He did not need to tell her how the land was remote and isolated, nor how the border between Russia and China had repeatedly shifted over the past century. Many Chinese people had settled north of the Amur River in Russian territory even though it put them in a precarious legal situation. When the border was finally defined in 1858 by the Treaty of Aigun, those Chinese settlers living in Russia were guaranteed the right to keep their property in perpetuity.

The agreement worked well until the Boxer Rebellion of last year, when riots against European settlers broke out in China. It eventually spread toward the Russian border, potentially endangering the railroad.

"There was an incident in which Chinese insurgents launched shells across the river at the Russian town of Blagoveshchensk," he told Natalia. "I was twenty miles away at the construction outpost, but the attack infuriated the Russian army. They used it as an excuse to expel the Chinese people living north of the river. It was too big a job for the local military, and I was ordered to appear along with workers from the railroad to help secure the border."

He braced his elbows on the table, clenching his hands and

looking away as dark memories came to the fore. He'd arrived at Blagoveshchensk with a hundred workers. At first he didn't understand what was being asked of him, but soon it was apparent that he was to help expel the Chinese villagers by any means necessary. Some villagers went peaceably, but others resisted. Then the army moved in, and it became a stampede, with Chinese people racing to get across the river. The barges and ferries were soon overwhelmed.

"By the time I arrived, dozens of men had already been killed," he said. "They had fought the expulsion from their homes, and the retaliation was brutal. Thousands of others, mostly women and children with a few possessions carried on their backs, begged for mercy, but they received none. They were driven at the point of a rifle toward the river."

Natalia's eyes were wide with horror. He wished he didn't have to share these details with her, but they were at the crux of the charges against him.

"I was ordered to command my men to guard the flanks and prevent anyone from escaping as the army drove the Chinese toward the river. It wasn't an expulsion; it was an extermination. There were thousands of people, and they were helpless as the soldiers closed in. Then the shooting began."

Dimitri swallowed back his revulsion. "I shouted at my men, ordering them to break ranks. We couldn't step in front of the bullets to save those people, but we could give them the chance to escape. A Russian colonel ordered me back to the line, but I refused. I reminded him of the Treaty of Aigun. I said *he* was the one in violation of the law, not me. It was useless. I was arrested on the spot and taken to the governor's mansion in chains. They sent me to Saint Petersburg to face trial on charges of refusing to obey orders, for which I was guilty, and of cowardice, for which I was not."

His intransigence hadn't done much good for the people of Blagoveshchensk. He later heard that over three thousand people had been killed. They had either been shot, axed, trampled, or drowned in the river.

"I have asked myself a thousand times if I could have done anything differently," he said. "I wish I had never been put in that situation, but I cannot regret my decision. Had I participated in forcing those people into the river, it would have been murder."

Natalia reached across the table, laying her hand over his clenched fist. How smooth and unblemished her hand looked against his weather-beaten one. He opened his hand, turning his palm up to clasp hers. She looked at him with no contempt, only sympathy, and he was grateful for it.

"The Russians do not wish this story to be known to the world," he said. "I was not allowed to speak of the incident at my trial because the authorities needed to make an example of me. They publicly humiliated me so that others who witnessed the massacre would remain silent."

And so far, it appeared the tactic had been successful. Certainly, no one came forward to protest at his trial.

"What can I do to help?" Natalia asked.

He scrutinized her across the table. Just how brave was she? Natalia wasn't going to like what he wanted of her. She would argue with him, fight him, maybe even work against him . . . but he hadn't come this far to back down now.

It was too early to risk their friendship by revealing his plans. He broke the tension by reaching for his wine glass and raising it in a toast.

"There will be time to discuss it later," he said. "For tonight, we must celebrate our friendship. I am very glad to have finally met you, my dearest Natalia."

The challenge ahead of them was daunting. He had survived the ordeal of the Siberian wilderness and crossing the Pacific, but what lay ahead would test Natalia in a manner she never expected, and he didn't know if she could deliver.

He and Natalia would board a train to New York the following afternoon, where the showdown would begin.

95

The following morning Dimitri ordered an atrociously large breakfast in the hotel's dining room, only to be dismayed at how little he could eat. After months of surviving on little besides cedar nuts, he ordered scrambled eggs, toast smothered with cheese, and raspberry tarts. He dove into the eggs first, but after a few bites he felt stuffed to the point that even looking at the raspberry tarts made him nauseous. He pushed the plates away while listening to Natalia chat about her new townhouse. Their train did not depart for New York until five o'clock, so he intended to spend the day shopping and sightseeing with her.

"Are you finished?" she asked with a glance at his mostly untouched plate. It seemed a crime to walk away from it. What would Temujin say? It was a shame, but he couldn't eat any more without becoming ill.

"I'm finished," he confirmed.

Natalia took him to the city's largest emporium, where he shopped in the gentleman's section. They had a six-day train ride ahead of them, so he picked two more ready-made suits, a proper overcoat, and a gold satin vest embroidered with swirls of ivy. Vanity had always been his greatest personal failing, and he was in the mood to indulge it. At the tie counter he practically wept at the feel of the silks on his chapped skin and proceeded to buy patterned cravats, ascots, and bow ties in every imaginable shade. At the jeweler's counter he purchased garnet cuff links, a timepiece on a fine watch chain, and an opal stickpin. The packages were shipped directly to the train station so he and Natalia remained unencumbered during his voracious quest to keep shopping.

They rode a cable car up Market Street, where he persuaded Natalia to stop at the perfumery so he could buy a bottle of something pretty for her. They laughed while sampling over a dozen bottles, and he persuaded her to buy the most expensive blend of rose and night-blooming jasmine in the store, a charming perfume improbably bottled in Kentucky. Then they sampled cologne for him.

"Any scent other than cedar," he said as they headed to the

gentlemen's counter. Dimitri could happily live the rest of his life without the scent or taste of cedar nuts. In the end they found a nice sandalwood with a hint of citrus, and Natalia opened her purse to pay for it.

"Once we are in New York and I have access to my funds, I shall repay every dime for this lavish excursion," he said. "I am not certain, but given my four-percent investment in your family's bank, I think that I am wealthier than you. True?"

"True," she laughed, but it was getting tiresome, having her pay for everything, so they visited a bank, where she withdrew an advance from his quarterly payment and gave him a fat roll of bills to sustain him until they reached New York. The bank also had a telegraph office, and he was anxious to send a wire to his mother.

"She will be pleased to learn I am not festering in a Siberian iron mine."

It was a challenge to find the proper telegraph location code. After Mirosa was seized, his mother had been forced to move in with his sister and her husband in a village south of Saint Petersburg, and he did not know the correct station code. The clerk had to consult a Russian directory of telegraph codes, and it was lunchtime before the message was sent.

Dimitri breathed easier once the message was on its way. His mother would not spend another night fearing for his well-being.

"Worrying about her was one of the worst parts of this ordeal," he said once he and Natalia were seated at a café on Market Street. "I know she fears for me, and living with my sister probably has not been easy for her. Sometimes mothers and daughters do not live in perfect harmony."

"I can understand."

He peered at her in curiosity. Natalia's love for her mother was the reason she learned so much about Russia, but Galina had died several years ago, and Natalia had a frosty relationship with her father's new wife.

"I sense you do not care for your stepmother," he said. "Your messages often praise your father, but you have little good to say about the woman he married."

Natalia shrugged. "There's nothing specifically wrong with Poppy, aside from the fact that she's a terrific snob."

"What is her best quality?" he asked, and Natalia looked taken aback by the question.

She glanced all around the interior of the restaurant, taking an undue amount of time to come up with an answer. "Poppy is remarkably good at playing golf," she finally said.

"That's it? That's the best thing you can say about this woman your father adores and who has given birth to your only brother? Come. Tell me why you dislike her."

"I'll need a fresh cup of coffee for that."

14

*N*atalia wasn't proud of her relationship with her stepmother. Many people thought her disapproval of Poppy was rooted in jealousy over her father's affections, but it wasn't.

"My father has an unhealthy dependence on Poppy," she finally said. "I don't like it."

"How so?" Dimitri asked.

Natalia began by describing an attempted assassination that took place seven years earlier, when an anarchist lobbed a bomb at Oscar as he left the bank. The bomb destroyed the façade of the bank and killed three bystanders. Her father was badly injured, losing an eye and the use of one leg, but he survived.

"I think it was the first time he realized he wasn't invincible," Natalia said. "My mother was still alive then, but she couldn't help him. She tried to tidy the bedsheets in his sickroom and bring him meals, but he was so angry. He barked at her to leave him alone, and my mother was too soft-hearted to stand up to him. She always felt inadequate because she hadn't been able to give him a son, and she tried to make up for it by catering to him, but it just made him feel like an invalid."

Oscar's leg refused to heal, and he relied on a wheelchair for years before he met Poppy Galpin, a young, athletic woman whose father managed the country club where Oscar once played golf. Oscar's days as a sportsman ended after the bombing, but he still visited the dining room at the club for business meetings. When Poppy saw him being wheeled across the lobby of the clubhouse, she boldly approached and asked when he intended to take up golf again. The people accompanying Oscar glared in disapproval, but her father was curious, challenging her to suggest how a half-blind cripple dragging a useless leg could play golf.

"Easy," she tossed off. "You'll have to get out of that chair and start working on developing your strength and balance, but it can be done."

Her father scowled, but Poppy shrugged and tossed a parting quip over her shoulder. "It takes a strong man, but if you think you can handle it, tell my father. He can arrange some lessons."

Oscar took the bait. Instead of handling him with kid gloves, Poppy bullied him into standing on his own and ordered him to the gymnasium to develop the muscles that had atrophied after years of disuse. Soon her father abandoned his wheelchair in favor of a walker, and then a cane. At first he could only manage a few steps, but exercise helped build his strength. Then Poppy got him out on the golf course. His initial attempts to swing a club were feeble, but he grew stronger and more confident by the month. He and Poppy played incessantly. It got to the point that junior businessmen joined him on the golf course to brief him on bank developments, because when the weather was good, there was no way Oscar would miss a chance to squeeze in a round of golf with Poppy. It was as if his life depended on those rounds of golf, and in a way, it did.

As Oscar regained his physical strength, his passion for the bank came roaring back stronger than ever before. He earned money hand over fist. He engineered million-dollar deals and extended the bank's influence to all corners of the world. He brokered funding for the Trans-Siberian Railway, their greatest overseas investment, solidifying the Blackstone reputation in the international arena.

Then, four years ago, Natalia's mother died while delivering a stillborn baby boy. Her father had mourned. Of course he did. But five months later he married Poppy Galpin.

Or Poppy Blackstone, as she was now called. They still played golf, and her father's dependence on Poppy still annoyed Natalia.

Natalia stirred cream into her coffee and looked up at Dimitri. "I'm grateful for what she did for my father, I merely wish she wasn't a howling, self-centered snob in all other areas of her life. But she is indeed an excellent golfer." She set the spoon on a dish with a clink. "And *that* is the nicest thing I can say about Poppy."

Dimitri seemed amused. "You may cringe in horror, but what you just said about your reviled stepmother was actually quite flattering. I am looking forward to meeting her."

Natalia raised her teacup. "And I am looking forward to seeing you regret those words."

He flashed an engaging look of challenge, and she could sit here for hours wallowing in his charm, but she needed to watch out. Dimitri had been starved not only of food and shelter, but for the past four years, he had also been devoid of female companionship. He would probably flirt with a doorpost.

And yet there were plenty of appealing women in the café, and the waitress was especially pretty, with red hair and a sweet disposition, but Dimitri seemed oblivious to them all. The way he focused entirely on Natalia felt enthralling. She could drown in this sensation, even though opening her heart to him would be risky.

For the first time in her life, she didn't want to do the sensible, logical thing. She wanted to let Dimitri swoop her up in a joyous embrace like he had at the Ferry Building. She wanted to argue over *War and Peace* with him. She wanted to laugh about those stupid lice, because even though he'd initially been mortified, by the end of last night, they had found the humor in it.

She drained the last bit of her coffee and set the cup down. "Come, we should head toward the station. Our train doesn't leave for two more hours, but I need to send a message to my associate at the bank who has been handling the railroad account while I've been gone."

Dimitri clamped a hand over her wrist, holding it immobile against the table. "Not yet."

She stilled. The intensity in his voice was odd. "What's wrong?"

"I think you should delay sending that message to your associate at the bank." He removed his hand and folded his arms across his chest, looking at her with a dark, brooding frown. It alarmed her.

"What are you talking about?"

Dimitri was suddenly at a loss for words. He opened his mouth several times, but nothing came out. He blotted his forehead because he'd started perspiring even though it wasn't warm in here.

"Natalia, there are many things to consider," he finally said. "At my trial in Russia, I was ritually humiliated. My lands and title were stripped from me, and then the court branded me a coward before the entire nation."

He looked at the floor as he spoke, the pain obvious in his voice. It hurt to see.

"I understand," she said softly. "We can hire a lawyer for you in New York. Pay him to fight your battle in Russia and perhaps get your title back."

He blanched. "Do you think it is *my title* I care about?"

He looked wounded. Oh dear. She'd always known Dimitri's feelings could be easily hurt, and perhaps it was too early to discuss this. In all likelihood, he was going to live the rest of his life in exile, and it would take time to become accustomed to this reality.

Dimitri leaned across the table, his face dark and earnest. "Natalia, you must understand. Although I would like my title and lands restored, it is not a priority. I witnessed thousands of innocent people driven to their deaths, and this will haunt me until justice has been served."

"Yes, I'm sorry about that. It must have been terrible for you." What else did he want her to say?

Dimitri's eyes softened in pained sympathy, and a hint of

misgiving took root. He wanted something from her . . . something he knew she would be reluctant to provide. Suddenly, she felt very cold.

"Dearest Natalia," Dimitri said, a world of grief and regret on his face, "I'm afraid you don't understand. My mission in life is to correct the wrong I saw that day at the Amur River. The only way I can do that is to stop the Trans-Siberian Railway."

It was as if he'd slapped her. She must have misheard, but when she asked him to repeat himself, the words were the same.

"I intend to stop the Trans-Siberian Railway," he said simply. "It is the only way I can get the czar's attention and force him to act."

He must have lost his mind. The Trans-Siberian was the largest civil engineering project in the world. It would invigorate the Russian economy and improve the lives of countless millions. Her heart pounded so hard she felt dizzy, but she needed to stay calm and reel Dimitri back from the precipice he was about to fling himself over.

"How on earth will stopping the railroad solve anything?"

"Thousands of innocent civilians were slaughtered to secure passage for that railroad, and you ask me why I want it stopped?" He sounded appalled, as though *she* were the one who was being irrational.

"Stopping the railroad won't bring those people back."

He folded his arms across his chest. "The Russians are still driving eastward. They won't hesitate to commit more atrocities if the local population gives them resistance. More lives are in danger as we sit here, and it is the Blackstone Bank that is paying for it all."

His voice cut through the din of the restaurant. People at neighboring tables had swiveled to gawk at them.

Natalia switched languages. "If you are going to say my family's name in that tone of voice, please speak in Russian."

The last thing she needed was bad publicity for the bank, but Dimitri conceded to her request and spoke in Russian.

"I know this will be difficult for you, but the railroad must be stopped. It has a stain on it that can only be scrubbed away by the czar himself. I want nothing to do with the railroad other than to halt its construction until the czar does penance for what happened and ensures it does not happen again."

Natalia clasped her hands together so he wouldn't see her trembling. Everything about this conversation felt unreal and disorienting, like the world had suddenly flipped upside-down. Her father had invested a fortune in that railroad on *her* recommendation. Pulling out now would be a financial and political disaster. Nations from all over Europe were helping build this railroad. The czar wanted it done. Dimitri might as well lay his head on the chopping block and invite the state to hack it off.

Dimitri continued bombarding her with questions and strategies for stopping the railroad. "Have you authorized this month's payment for railroad supplies yet? Is that what you were going to contact your associate about?"

It was, but suddenly she no longer felt comfortable discussing railroad business with Dimitri. She folded her arms across her chest and glared at him.

"Natalia, I asked you a simple question."

"Since you are no longer affiliated with the railroad, it wouldn't be appropriate to discuss it with you."

He didn't let her frosty tone dissuade him. "I know very well that the payments are released on the first of the month, so please wire someone at the bank to stop it. The sooner we starve the project of money and supplies, the sooner the czar will pay attention."

She clenched her fists. The bank was contractually obligated to deliver that payment, and failing to send it was unthinkable. "Do you know what breaking the contract would do to the bank's reputation?"

"Do you know what a thousand bodies floating in a river look like?"

She took a fortifying breath and fought to rein in her temper. Dimitri had always let passion rule his life, but there had to be a way to make him see logic.

"Dimitri, you must draw a distinction between the railroad and the actions of the Russian government. The bankers and engineers behind the railroad had nothing to do with that massacre. It was the fault of the army."

"But it was done to secure the railroad. I want it stopped. You can wire your father and bring construction to a standstill."

"There are other banks in the world. If we don't fund it, there are plenty who will."

Dimitri was not deterred. "That will take months to arrange, giving me time to force the czar to the negotiation table. Wire your father to stop the funds."

She stood so quickly that her chair bumped into the gentleman behind her, but she was too angry to slow down. "I won't wire my father, and I won't let your overblown emotionalism destroy us both. Whatever you think you saw—"

"Do you think I'm lying?" He was shouting, and everyone was staring at them.

She fumbled in her purse to set payment on the table, then stormed out of the restaurant. Dimitri could follow or he could stay inside and sulk, but she wasn't going to continue this insane conversation. A wall of chilly air hit her as she stepped outdoors, and the clanging of a bell heralded a cable car heading her way. She intended to board it.

Dimitri drew up alongside her, his expression mutinous. She couldn't bear to look at him and turned her attention to the cable car as it drew near. Their luggage had already been delivered to the depot, but she had the train tickets. "This car will take me to the depot. You are welcome to accompany me, or you can meet me there for its departure at five o'clock. Or you can stay in San Francisco and lob your bombs at me and the railroad from here. I don't care."

His eyes glinted with intensity, but when he spoke, his voice was cool. "We have two hours before the train departs. I would like to continue exploring the city, for I doubt I will pass this way again."

She fumbled inside her attaché case and produced his ticket, handing it to him without a word. He took it, and she turned to board the cable car, grasping the hold bar and hoisting herself aboard.

They locked steely glares, but he made no move to follow her on board, and with a jerk, the trolley continued on its way, leaving Dimitri behind.

She watched as he faded into the distance, still facing her as she quietly seethed. Let him get lost in a strange city if he thought she was being unreasonable. She'd come all the way across the country to meet him, and he couldn't even go twenty-four hours without letting his overly emotional temperament upend her life.

She'd always wanted a fearless man, but now that she had invited one into her world, it was turning into a disaster.

15

imitri watched the cable car pull away, the clang of its bell blending with other noise on the busy street. Was she really going to abandon him in the middle of a strange city? He swallowed back a momentary rush of panic. He'd made it this far from the wilds of Siberia with little more than the clothes on his back. He could get to the train station before his train departed.

Besides, he'd seen a Russian shop a few blocks away, and perhaps they would have newspapers from home. It would be good to know what had transpired in the months since he'd fled. He headed back up Market Street until he found the storefront with its familiar Cyrillic lettering painted across the top of the window.

A pang of homesickness hit as he entered the shop, which was redolent with the scent of tobacco and spicy sausages. It had been years since he'd set foot in a Russian store like this, with ropes of sausages dangling from hooks and barrels of dry goods on the floor. Kettles of soup, salads, and delicatessen meats were behind the front counter.

"Good afternoon," he greeted the shopkeeper in Russian. Sadly, the store did not carry Russian newspapers, but his attention was quickly diverted by the group of men gathered in a tiny dining area, wolfing down hearty bowls of stolichny salad.

107

Dimitri wasn't hungry, but the traditional salad made from potatoes, capers, onions, and peas, all covered in sour cream, was a familiar touchstone with home.

He ordered a bowl, then reached into his pocket to study the American currency. He had a wad of ten-dollar bills and several fives and ones. How much was that? He had no understanding of American money, but the bowl of salad was less than a dollar, so he bought an almond cake and sweet rolls to share with the men at the back table.

They gladly made space for him when he approached with the huge platter of food. They clapped him on the back and welcomed him like an old friend. He felt an instant comradery with these men, whose humor he shared and who had no complicated loyalties to banks or international investments. The men were soon engaged in a fierce debate about a shipment of timber that was late, and since they cared so passionately, Dimitri did too.

One of the men provided a shot of vodka for their coffee, and soon they were singing songs from the old country. They smoked cigars and gave one another long and complicated toasts, falling over themselves to pay compliments. It would have been nice to linger among this newfound comradery of the people who spoke his language and welcomed him with such ease, but Natalia and the train would not wait.

He wanted to take a piece of Russia with him on the train, and he selected a box of cream cigars because the familiar scent of vanilla, tobacco, and dark coffee was like the most precious perfume known to man. He didn't even enjoy smoking, but he wanted to get drunk on their heady fragrance.

He should buy something for Natalia. He scanned the shelf of trinkets, nesting dolls, and cheap hair combs with paste jewels. The only thing that truly caught his eye was a little figurine of a firebird. It was brightly painted in the colors of a blazing sunset, and he wanted to share the bit of whimsy with her.

He bought the cigars and the firebird, then flagged down a streetcar in the same manner that he'd seen Natalia do and rode it to the train station.

American train depots were not terribly different from those in Saint Petersburg, except here the porters were black men in uniforms of the Pullman company instead of former serfs from the countryside. He saw a passenger tip a porter with a few coins. Tipping was another difference here, but Dimitri had always been generous, and the roll of bills Natalia had given him was fat.

He approached a porter and showed him his ticket. "Can you tell me where I should board this train?"

The porter studied the ticket, which indicated Dimitri had a sleeping berth for night travel but was sharing a first-class compartment during the day. "I'll escort you to both, sir."

The porter showed him to a men's sleeper car, where his newly purchased clothes had already been delivered. The sleeping berths were stacked on top of each other three high, but each had an accordion screen for privacy. Facilities were in a neighboring car and would be shared by all the men slotted into these odd, coffin-like sleeping berths. Then the porter walked him through a series of cars joined together by pass-throughs until they came to the first-class compartments.

Dimitri had no idea what sort of tip was the norm, so he peeled off a few bills.

"Thank you, sir!" the porter said with a huge grin, and a surge of benevolence overcame Dimitri. He was alive and had made it to America. He was on his way to New York in a first-class compartment. He peeled off a few more bills and tipped the porter again, grateful for another broad smile because Natalia would probably still be angry and this might be the last friendly face he would see today.

Natalia was already seated in the first-class compartment. The booth had polished wood paneling, a table in the center, and benches on either side. Velvet draperies framed a large portrait window with a view of the train depot.

"Where have you been?" she burst out the moment he opened the door.

"Shopping. I needed a few things."

"The train is leaving in ten minutes!"

He raised a brow. "Then I had five more minutes to shop. A pity."

He immediately regretted the acerbic response. He needed to lower the tension between them, and Natalia had a right to be angry. Her friendship had been his lifeline, and she deserved more than what he had done for her.

A wave of sadness descended as he slid onto the bench opposite her. The porter closed the door, and they were alone.

She wouldn't look at him. Her jaw was clenched, and she stared out the window. He wanted to lay the world at her feet, not argue with her.

"The Hebrews gave burnt offerings when they wished to restore a relationship," he said. "Napoleon gave Josephine a palace after he annoyed her." He set the firebird on the table. The painted tin figurine looked cheap in this lavish private compartment, but he hoped she might appreciate the gesture. "I saw this and thought of you. In Slavic folklore, the firebird is a harbinger of either great blessing or dark catastrophe. Natalia, I hope that we are at the beginning of a long and wonderful friendship. After all that you have meant to me, I cannot bear the thought of disappointing you."

There was no thaw in her expression. She swiveled her head enough to look at him. "Are you truly going to try to block the railroad?" Icicles dripped from her words.

"I truly am."

She batted the firebird aside, and it clattered to the floor. "I won't let you meet my father."

He stiffened. "You won't 'let' me? I own four percent of his bank and can demand a meeting without your help."

"Let me restate that. I won't let you make a fool of yourself. I don't know what you saw at that river, but news of it hasn't reached America, and trying to stop the world's largest engineering project is pure idiocy. My father has invested a fortune in that railroad, and you have no idea what you are wandering into if you try to challenge him on this."

Dimitri leaned down to collect the firebird from the floor. A bit of paint from its fiery red wing had chipped off, exposing the cheap tin beneath. He set the firebird carefully on the table, struggling to find the words to express what Natalia meant to him, for he had never told her. It was time.

"After two years in Siberia, I was offered the chance to return home. I refused, because of you."

That got her attention. She locked eyes with him and waited.

"I remembered you had said the Trans-Siberian was your chance to leave a mark on the world. That long after you were dead and in your grave, the railroad would be your legacy to the world. I wanted to join you on that quest. I also want to leave a mark on the world, so I stayed because you inspired me."

"Then why are you seeking to destroy it?" she demanded.

"It is the only way I can get the czar's attention. He has staked his reputation on completing that railroad, and when he ran into trouble with the Chinese settlers, the army slaughtered them. They will do it again if they get away with it."

He stood. They both needed to calm down, and she needed time to absorb what he was telling her.

"I shall leave you in peace," he said with a little bow before setting off to explore the train.

Natalia battled surges of guilt after Dimitri left, but he could cool his heels in the parlor car until it was time for dinner. Perhaps then they could speak logically and without threats to destroy her life's work.

An hour after leaving San Francisco, a porter arrived to convert her first-class compartment into the place where she would sleep for the next five nights. The table slid to the side, and sheets spread over the upholstered bench made it a snug sleeping berth. She would close the drapes across the window in her door, and the compartment would be as cozy as a hotel room.

By the time she arrived at the dining car, she was surprised to see Dimitri already seated at a table with a large family. He had them all spellbound as he described the glories of the

Winter Palace in Saint Petersburg, but he raised his arm when he spotted her at the entrance of the dining car.

"Natalia, come join us. You can listen to Mr. Cipolletti talk about his olive groves in California."

How could he sound so cheerful, as if their afternoon spat meant nothing? She lifted her chin a little. "No, thank you," she said, and asked the steward to seat her at another table.

That evening set the tone for the next two days. Each time she ventured out of her private compartment, she found Dimitri chumming about with strangers. At breakfast he was gently scolding a pretty young woman for drowning her waffle in too much syrup.

"The delicate texture of a waffle cannot be appreciated once smothered in syrup. Must I teach you everything?" he teased.

The young lady basked in Dimitri's attention even though it was perfectly awful for him to criticize how a stranger ate her breakfast. Natalia joined a nearby table of diners but surreptitiously eavesdropped on the ongoing flirtation as the young lady asked where Dimitri was staying in New York and if he had a special lady waiting for him.

"Sadly, no," Dimitri replied. "I have been alone since the tragic loss of my fiancée many years ago."

The girl oozed empathy and begged for the story. Natalia held her breath as Dimitri spoke of Olga, a woman as lovely as the moon to whom he was engaged to marry since childhood. Tragic fate separated them many years ago, but after she became widowed last year, he believed they might marry at last.

"Alas!" Dimitri said with typical flair. "I am now in exile, and fate has separated me from Olga yet again."

"Can't she join you here in America?" the girl asked.

Natalia leaned forward to listen in, but the blast of the train whistle as they approached another town completely obscured Dimitri's response.

Who was Olga? Why had he never spoken of her during their years of correspondence? Not that she cared, of course. Dimitri probably had dozens of women scattered across the mighty Russian empire, all of whom deluded themselves into thinking they were special to him.

Dimitri charmed every female he met on the train, but it wasn't only women he befriended. At dinner she saw him chatting with a group of traveling salesmen by the bar. He dined like a king and flirted like a reprobate. He drank with fellow passengers in the dining car and played card games with ladies in the parlor car.

One evening she saw him indulging in foul-scented cigars with a group of men. He wore a navy pinstripe suit with the gold waistcoat. To her annoyance, the impractical garment looked like the epitome of elegance on him.

"I thought you didn't smoke?" she said.

He blew out a stream of sickeningly sweet tobacco. "These are imported from Vladivostok. I felt compelled to share my good fortune with my new friends. Join us! I shall even extinguish my cigar on your behalf."

She declined and retreated to the parlor car to read a report on the timber industry, but she couldn't stop thinking about how easy it was for Dimitri to make friends. She needed to stop feeling special for the unique relationship she'd cultivated with him during all those telegram messages, because she was obviously just one of the multitudes he befriended wherever he went. It didn't matter that he invited her to join him each time he spotted her on the train. He certainly hadn't fought very hard for her when she refused.

The only time he insisted on her company was during the railway stops, when passengers could disembark for an hour while the train refueled. The stations always had a retail area offering trinkets, a café, and a Western Union telegraph window.

At each stop he nagged Natalia to wire her father about canceling the upcoming infusion of funds to the railroad, and each time she refused.

"Time is growing short," he said. "If the April payment is halted, it will cause a crisis when the steel deliveries fail to arrive. That is exactly what we need to get the czar's attention."

"Which is why I will be sure the payment is delivered on time," she said primly and pretended not to notice the burning look of disappointment on Dimitri's face as she returned to the train.

The impasse with Natalia was driving Dimitri insane. Her reluctance to disrupt the railroad was understandable, but didn't she realize that he was compelled to act? Each day the Trans-Siberian laid additional miles of track, driving farther eastward toward rural villages that might trigger more bloodshed if the 1858 treaty with China was not honored. He could force the czar to affirm that treaty, but not without Natalia's help.

On the third day, the train arrived at the inappropriately named town of Springville, Utah. It was a bleak, windswept place with a light dusting of snow blowing down the barren main street. Refueling would take an hour, giving Dimitri time to explore these different places in America. Although San Francisco had been a chaotic shock to his system, Utah felt familiar. High, windy, and frozen. He liked it.

Natalia burrowed into her coat, a sour expression on her face as they headed toward the station shop. Their boots made hollow thuds on the plank walkway, and as expected, a signpost indicated a telegraph station was inside the shop. He had given up hope that Natalia would wire her father to halt the payment due at the end of the week, so he took a bold stance.

"Let me wire him," he said. "I shall instruct him on what needs to be done to stop the railroad."

She rolled her eyes. "Dimitri, everyone in my family already thinks you are insane. Please don't provide them with additional confirmation by suggesting my father destroy the Trans-Siberian Railway."

She continued scanning the assortment of goods for sale behind a storefront window, but he considered her words, not sure he understood her correctly.

"What do you mean, they think I am insane?"

"They've seen the telegrams you send me, going on for hours about the color of the sunset or the howling of the wind. They think you've lost your mind."

Dimitri looked away. All these years he had poured out his soul to Natalia because they were kindred spirits. He wanted to share the terrible beauty of the Russian winter and the frustrated dreams he nurtured in his lonely isolation.

He tried to sound as if he didn't care. "You don't think that about me, do you?"

"Don't be ridiculous," she said dismissively. "I've got better things to do than tend your wounded ego. Would you like some cedar nuts?"

He blanched at the sight of the barrel brimming with the nuts that sustained him for months in the wilderness. He doubted he could choke down another cedar nut to save his life.

"No, thank you," he said with admirable restraint. "I would rather discuss why you have told your family that I am insane. Please correct that. Tell them we joke and tease each other, but that I am not crazy."

"No, you're not, but you're the most vain and melodramatic man I've ever met."

"I am a rational man without a hint of insanity. I confess to being vain, but I am not crazy and would prefer if you corrected that impression with your family."

She sighed in frustration. "Why does it matter? It isn't as if you will meet any of them. When we get to New York, I will give you access to your money, and then we will go our separate ways."

That Natalia might abandon him in New York was something he had never considered, and it panicked him. "You can't," he sputtered. "I must get the czar's attention, and causing a disruption on the railroad is the best way."

"Don't you understand?" she said, her self-control beginning to slip. "If I cause a scandal at the bank, I lose *everything*. My father's approval. My career. The bank is my only chance to prove myself by helping build something great."

He understood. He had also been born into wealth and privilege but felt the same compulsion to challenge himself on the railroad. He and Natalia had worked in tandem on that quest, and they shouldn't abandon each other now. If the railroad could not be built in an honorable fashion, they should join forces to stop it.

"Your father would not banish you for acting on your beliefs. You said he is a great man."

"He *is* a great man, but a hard one too. From the day I began work at the bank, he warned me to stay in the background. He never touts me in the press or has me represent the bank in public. It's too risky. People don't have faith in a woman managing their investments. And yes—he would cut me out if I ever attract bad publicity to the bank. I've always understood that."

Dimitri frowned. "That seems rather cruel."

"It's why I double- and triple-check everything I do. It's why I over-prepare and burn the midnight oil. If something goes wrong on a project I oversee, blame will be laid at my doorstep no matter how it happened. If I get cut out of the bank, my life would be nothing but tea parties and dress fittings."

He shook his head. "Natalia, I know you better than that. Your world is Beethoven and Shakespeare. You have a baby brother you love and will help raise to manhood. You must not reduce yourself to what you do within the four walls of a bank."

"Don't change the subject. As long as you persist in trying to damage the railroad, we can have nothing to do with each other. It would be best if we part ways once we reach New York."

He couldn't let that happen. He spoke the language of Americans but didn't understand their customs or business environment. He had no allies here. Somehow, between now and the time they reached New York, he must find a way to get through to her.

"Don't abandon me," he said. "We can find an answer to this dilemma, but I am a stranger here, and I need your help."

His plea was carried away on the wind. Natalia turned to head back to the boarding area without looking back.

16

*D*imitri's plea disturbed Natalia more than she cared to admit, because she would never consider doing anything to hurt the railroad.

Would she?

Her refusal to take action hurt Dimitri's feelings, but couldn't he understand that he'd hurt her as well? His obsessive nagging left her feeling used and dismissed, as though she meant nothing to him aside from her influence at the bank.

She pondered the problem all night and into the next day. The train passed through northern Colorado and into Kansas while she worried. She believed what Dimitri said about the atrocity and the possibility that it could occur again. That meant she had to think of a solution short of destroying the railway and the bank's reputation all in one poisonous swoop.

That evening it was particularly crowded in the dining car, but she spotted Dimitri immediately. He sat across from an older man with a long beard and a yarmulke on his head.

Dimitri stood and gestured her over. "This is Yitzhak Menshikov," he said when she arrived at the table. "He is from Russia, but look! Here we are, two Russians who have met each other in the middle of a Kansas cornfield. Is not the world a grand place?"

Dimitri's enthusiasm cracked through her gloomy mood,

and she joined them. The three of them spoke in Russian because Mr. Menshikov confessed that even after twenty years in America, he still struggled with the language. He insisted she call him Yitzhak, and soon she learned his story of leaving his tiny village in search of more freedom in America. He found it as a clothmaker, and now he was wealthy enough to pay for passage for other members of his family to come to America. He was heading to New York, where he would meet his nephews as they arrived at Ellis Island.

"They will breathe free air here," Yitzhak said, his voice trembling with emotion.

Natalia listened in fascination as Yitzhak explained how he funded his textile business by collecting investments from members in his synagogue. It was different from how the bank loaned money, but it had paid huge dividends for both Yitzhak and his investors. Now he shipped bolts of fabric all over the country.

"None of this could have happened back home," he said. "A Jew could have his property seized and his children turned out of school. Life is better here."

Dimitri became unusually serious as he met Yitzhak's gaze. "My friend, I am sorry Russia treated you badly. I wish you could have seen it through my eyes, where the streets of Saint Petersburg rival Paris for charm and Rome for majesty. The cathedrals are a celebration of grandeur, but just outside the city are the rustic churches of the countryside. You can walk through endless fields of grain, feeling like you are the only person in the world, when suddenly the crown of an old wooden church will rise on the horizon. Centuries of people have found solace in those lonely, humble churches. Peasants, soldiers, mothers praying for their children. They are the heartbeat of Russia, and it is in the quiet of a church that I sense their memory."

Dimitri looked away, and a pain unlike anything she'd ever witnessed darkened his face. "I yearn for home," he whispered. "My wild, beautiful Russia. It lives in every beat of my heart. When I close my eyes, I see the apple orchards of Mirosa and hear the people of the valley singing on the wind. I remember the lilacs growing in joyful abandon during their brief moment of summer glory."

He spoke with loving anguish but still smiled through the pain. "Come, Yitzhak," he said in a chiding tone. "Even you must admit to missing the scent of Russian lilacs."

The creases in Yitzhak's face pulled into a sad smile, and he clamped a hand over his chest. "You have stirred a longing for home I never thought to feel again." He laughed. "Which is ridiculous. No one on earth is more accustomed to wandering than the Jew. As said in the psalms, *By the rivers of Babylon we sat and wept when we remembered Zion.*"

"Russia is my Zion," Dimitri said in a fervent voice. "I can never go back, but it is carved on my soul, and I will hear its echoes forever."

His wistful expression reminded Natalia of her mother, who never truly felt at home in America. Until her dying day, Galina mourned the loss of her homeland. It was the same expression on Dimitri's face.

How could she help him get the czar's attention without destroying the railroad? It was going to be hard, but she had position, wealth, and connections. It was time to use them and help Dimitri navigate this audacious quest, but she still didn't know how to pull it off without ruining her world.

The following morning they stopped to refuel in Quincy, Illinois. Natalia was reluctant to leave the train because of the driving rain, but Dimitri wanted a postcard of the town to send to his mother. They scurried through the downpour and darted around puddles to reach the depot shop a block away.

Natalia blotted the damp from her hat with a handkerchief while gaping at the curious collection of military arms blanketing the walls. The rifles, swords, and flags made it seem like a military museum. An old Union uniform was displayed in one corner, and a mounted cannon pointed into the center of the shop. It gave Natalia the uncomfortable sensation of being in the line of fire.

The elderly shopkeeper must have noticed her distaste. "It's not loaded and it can't hurt you," he teased from behind the front counter.

"Did you serve in the Civil War?" she asked politely.

"First Regiment, Illinois Light Artillery," he said with pride. "You see that rifle on the wall? I carried that through three years of service until I got wounded at the Chattahoochee River and was shipped home."

The old veteran grabbed Natalia's elbow to draw her toward a map on the wall, where red dots marked each battle he'd fought in. Dimitri stood in the far corner twirling a wire rack of postcards and couldn't rescue her from the shopkeeper's rambling, but she smiled politely and let him talk. He proceeded to show off his old medals and military insignia.

The profusion of war memorabilia reminded Natalia of her godfather. Admiral McNally's office also featured mementos from his military service, mostly collected during his years in the Ottoman Empire and the Far East. Instead of carrying a rifle, her godfather was a military attaché, traveling the world to study how other nations organized their defenses and gathered intelligence.

She sucked in a quick gasp. Admiral McNally had been at Alexander's christening, where he'd been talking to a group of men about the Boxer Rebellion. As a former military attaché, he was well-connected to the hundreds of American officers scattered all over the world, quietly gathering military intelligence and funneling it back to Washington. He might be the key to solving her problem.

She raced over to Dimitri, who still perused the postcards. "We need to go!" She grabbed a handful of postcards and shoved a few dollars at the baffled shopkeeper. She dragged Dimitri onto the tiny porch outside.

"I just thought of something," she said breathlessly. "About the massacre at the river. If there was a military attaché anywhere in the region, he probably heard about it."

Dimitri's brows lowered. "What are you talking about?"

"A military attaché. I don't know what they call them in Russia or if they even use them, but the American government sends people to observe foreign armies. My godfather used to be just such a man. They collect information and send it home. Sometimes they are very up-front about it, other times less so."

"Like a spy?"

She shook her head. "Not a spy, just someone who watches and gathers information. Sometimes they are historians trying to document a war, or a doctor observing how an army handles medical issues. Usually they are military officers studying how foreign armies carry out business."

"And you think there may have been such a man near the Amur River?" Dimitri looked skeptical, and she had to admit it seemed improbable. The southern area of Russia was remote, rural, and at peace before this incident. It would not have been a region of interest to military observers, but what about the Chinese side of the border?

"The Boxer Rebellion is one of the most turbulent upheavals in a decade," she said. "My godfather used to be up to his neck in foreign intrigue, and he will know how to sniff out allies. If you break the story on your own, people might think you have a grudge against the czar because of losing your title. We need an impartial witness who can confirm your account."

Then they could go on the offense and trumpet news of what happened to the world. She could frame the bank's role as trying to solve the problem rather than being complicit in it.

But first they needed to seek out her godfather.

A hint of a smile tugged at Dimitri's mouth. "I am willing to join you in seeking out this man," he said, and for the first time since hearing of the catastrophe, Natalia felt a seed of hope take root.

17

*D*imitri remained mildly skeptical of Natalia's plan to sniff out witnesses of the massacre along the Amur River, but he readily embraced the thaw in her temper, delighted to have his dearest friend back.

That evening he tipped a porter an outrageous sum so he and Natalia could enjoy a private table in the dining car. It let him pelt her with all sorts of questions about her life, and she freely answered. He loved listening to Natalia speak of her mother and how Galina grew up in the tenements of Moscow but was saved from a life of drudgery when she earned a spot in the Bolshoi ballet. The ballet took Galina to London, where her beauty brought her to the attention of Oscar Blackstone. Galina gladly left the world of ballet to marry the man who took her to America.

"My mother wasn't able to stand up to my father," Natalia said. "He treated her well, of course. He bought her whatever she wished for, but all they really wanted was a son. She miscarried over and over, and it took a toll on her. So did her longing for Russia, because she never truly felt at ease in New York. When we were alone, she used to wear the most beautiful sarafans. I'm embarrassed to admit it, but my interest in Russia started because I wanted to wear a sarafan too."

He beamed at her over his mug of hot tea. "And did you?"

Imagining the prim Natalia in one of those riotously patterned folk gowns that blended Nordic and tribal patterns was delightful.

"Oh yes! I still wear them when I'm alone at home. Stop laughing! You have no idea how uncomfortable a corset can be, and in a sarafan I feel like I can float."

He would love to see Natalia wearing a sarafan at Mirosa. He lived informally out at the lake, and she would look entrancing in a traditional sarafan, gazing out over the water on a long summer evening.

But that vision could never happen, and the longing for home became a physical ache in the center of his chest. He forced himself to think brighter thoughts.

"Enough about Russia. Where do you suggest I live once we arrive in New York?"

"My stepmother would be over the moon if an actual aristocrat stayed at her house. Poppy knows the old-money society matrons look down their nose at her, so she will want to show you off like a prize pony."

"But I am no longer an aristocrat," he pointed out. "The czar took my title away."

"What's he going to do, come over here and arrest you?" Natalia assured him there had been no news of Count Sokolov's disgrace in the American newspapers, probably because it wasn't in the czar's interest to publicize the incident overseas. That would change if Natalia's plan to expose the massacre succeeded, but until they had collected allies supplied by Admiral McNally, they would keep quiet about Dimitri's humiliation.

The water in their glasses sloshed. He and Natalia both listed as the train abruptly began slowing down.

Dimitri looked outside. The silhouettes of passing trees outside the window slowed, then stopped altogether. A hiss of steam and the clicking of metal sounded as the train settled into place on the tracks. Bewildered diners glanced at one another, and he rose to put a protective arm around Natalia.

Within moments a porter arrived with news. "No cause for concern," he announced. "There's a washout on the tracks a mile ahead. We need to wait a few minutes until it is cleared."

There was no such thing as a washout that could be cleared in "a few minutes." It would more likely be hours, but Dimitri and Natalia were finished with their meal, and others were waiting for a table. With the train at a standstill, they could take advantage of the opportunity for some fresh air.

He offered Natalia his arm. "Shall we go outside to enjoy the night sky?"

They fetched their coats and soon stood on the platform on the back of the caboose, alone except for the stars and a sliver of moon. The train had come to a standstill in a field of winter wheat. The cold air was invigorating, but Natalia shivered and shrank deeper into her coat.

"What sort of gentleman would I be if I let you suffer in the cold?" Dimitri slid behind her and wrapped the edges of his coat around her, sharing his warmth. They both faced the field lit by the silvery moon. Satisfaction coursed through him, for he had been wanting for days to savor a full-bodied embrace with Natalia. It was a shocking intimacy, but he didn't care. It had been four years since he'd held a woman like this. "Better?"

She folded her hands over his forearms and squeezed. "Better."

Her head fit just below his chin, and he liked her there. They fit together perfectly. He lowered his head to whisper in her ear. "Now that we have met in person, am I as you expected?"

He could feel her smile against the side of his face. "You are better."

He drew her closer. "Tell me how. I can never hear enough of such things."

"You're a lot tougher than I realized," she said with an embarrassed laugh. "I'm sorry I teased you over that mosquito bite. Your incessant moaning over such tiny things gave me the wrong impression."

"It was an exceptionally painful mosquito bite."

She rotated in his arms, still nestled within his coat, and looked up at him. "Where was it?"

He pointed to the corner of his mouth, and she touched the spot with the tip of her finger. The intimacy sent a shiver through him, and he turned to kiss her fingertip, never breaking eye contact with her.

Now would be the perfect moment to kiss her properly. She looked as if she would welcome it . . . but there were things she did not yet know about him. It would not be fair to mislead her.

He strove for a lighthearted tone. "My life has been plagued with illness and misery. I suffer when there is not enough sunlight, but I can get sun poisoning too. I get clobbered with the flu every winter. It is a problem."

Her eyes danced as she battled laughter, which was always the best remedy for sad subjects. He held both her hands and smiled down into her eyes as if this discussion didn't hurt.

"Then there are the mumps," he said. "I contracted a near-fatal case when I was nineteen. For weeks I was a swollen bag of human misery. My mother had the nuns at three different convents praying around the clock for me. I recovered, but things were never quite the same."

He held her gaze, his heart hammering so hard it threatened to burst. Olga had rejected him after his crisis with the mumps.

Mumps rarely had lingering complications if caught in childhood, but if it struck after puberty, the disease could make it impossible for a man to father children. Although the damage was rarely permanent, Dimitri was not so lucky. For two years he consulted physicians to learn if the fever had rendered him sterile. Specialists from Moscow, Berlin, and Saint Petersburg were all in agreement. Although Dimitri could enjoy normal marital relations, there would never be children as a result of them.

"You were nineteen when it happened?" Natalia asked cautiously, apparently aware of the dangers for men who caught this disease.

He nodded. "It was a bad case. I can see by your expression

that you understand what that means. I had been engaged to a woman named Olga since childhood. We waited to see if my condition would improve, but over time it became obvious that it would not. There could never be any children, so I could not blame her."

Olga's father and a series of lawyers extricated her from the engagement. There were legal agreements to terminate, rings to be returned, wounded hearts to mend. Dimitri never blamed Olga. They were still friendly. He had even attended Olga's wedding to an upstanding baron from Moscow and always wished her well.

Olga was a widow now, with two children from her first husband. Had Dimitri not been forced into exile, he could have returned to Mirosa, married Olga, and adopted her children as his own. Their life could have been exactly as they always planned.

It could never happen now. Russia was his past, and there was no going back. Now that Natalia knew everything, could she accept him as he was? Although he would never stop mourning Russia, the prospect of staying in America with Natalia had an exciting allure.

He had been attracted to Natalia before they ever met. Now the air fairly crackled with electricity whenever they were together, but he needed to be patient with her. It would be hard for any woman to accept him with this terrible flaw. She needed time, but he could not resist pulling her forward to kiss her forehead. She did not pull away, but after a few moments, she swiveled in his arms to continue looking out over the darkened fields, still nestled within his coat but somehow a little further away.

"Most women want children," she said softly.

"And are you like most women?"

"I am."

It was as he expected, but he ignored the familiar shaft of pain that came from acknowledging the truth. He looked up, where the moonlight cast a curious glow across the wispy clouds and illuminated the wheatfield with silvery light and shadow. Darkness and light. It felt suitable for this fleeting moment of pain and honesty.

"Maybe we should go back inside," she whispered, regret heavy in her voice.

He tightened his embrace. "Maybe. But I have never seen the moon light up a field of winter wheat in Illinois before. It would be a shame to waste it."

Again, she burrowed against him and gave a contented sigh. "Oh yes. I think you are entirely correct."

He wrapped the flaps of his coat closer around her. This might be the last time she would ever permit him to hold her. Tomorrow they would go back to their old friendship. It would be fun. Intellectually stimulating and exciting because they shared a common mission.

Maybe in time Natalia would come to a different decision about him, but he would never pressure her. This was not a trivial topic he could badger her about like the merits of *War and Peace* over *Little Women*. This was something that would be entirely in Natalia's hands to decide.

But for a few more enchanted minutes this evening, they could linger beneath the waning moon and dream of a world that might have been.

Natalia wrestled with a strange sort of grief after her evening on the caboose with Dimitri. How did one mourn a child that had never even been conceived? Logically, it was far too early to even begin considering marriage and a family with Dimitri, but there had never been anything logical about her feelings for Dimitri, and yes, her mind had already started exploring the possibility of a future together.

The following morning, she and Dimitri reverted back to their usual banter while dining at breakfast. He flirted outrageously with every female, from the toddlers on up to the grey-haired ladies leaning on canes. He flirted with Natalia too, but it was a different sort of flirting. More personal. It carried their history and shared interests. It was laden with respect and admiration, even as he freely insulted the way she put too much sugar in her coffee and criticized her love of German composers.

Though they did not discuss it again, Dimitri's story about the mumps made her want to protect and pamper him even more. His color was better than when she met him in San Francisco. He no longer looked so weather-beaten, but his fingernails were still in bad shape, with ragged cuticles and grime embedded beneath his nails. She sent for a bowl of warmed oil and proceeded to give him a manicure. In the privacy of her compartment, Dimitri gladly presented both his hands for her to fuss over. After soaking his nails in the warmed oil, she massaged it into his cuticles while recounting her recent trip to Seattle.

"The bank is spending a fortune to deepen the harbor," she said, then explained how she met with construction analysts and three bank auditors to confirm that the Hammonds had been directing a portion of the bank's loan to a railroad project instead of the harbor.

"Silas would have known that if he'd been paying closer attention." She dried Dimitri's hands and began using an orange-wood stick to work out the last of the dirt embedded beneath his nails. "I've already wired the report to my father, which will make Silas hate me more. He's always disliked me. He once told me that while he was toiling away in college and low-level clerkships, I was being bounced on my daddy's knee."

Dimitri bristled. "How dare he? He must never utter such a personal attack on you in my presence."

"Pistols at dawn?" she teased. Dimitri's gallantry on her behalf secretly pleased her, but the incident with Silas was still troubling. "I know my father opened doors for me. I know I wouldn't have risen so far without—"

"Shh," Dimitri said. "I do not like that this Silas fellow insulted your accomplishments. I like it even less when I hear you echo his sentiments. Here, you missed a spot beneath my thumbnail."

She hid a smile as she tended his neglected thumb. Dimitri reveled in her ministrations, especially when she proceeded to file and buff his nails. He only complained when she began applying the cuticle pusher.

"That hurts," he complained.

"Oh hush, you can barely feel a thing."

"I know, and yet the thought of what you are doing hurts."

She stifled a smile but wouldn't let him dissuade her. Now that she had committed to giving him a manicure, she would execute it with finesse. Besides, she liked indulging him. His abused hands were evidence of the trials he'd endured while driving the sledge for months on end, foraging in the woods, and smashing pine cones for scraps to eat. No wonder his hands looked bad.

On their final night before arriving in New York, Dimitri tipped the waiters so they could once again have dinner at their own candlelit table.

He lifted his goblet in a toast. "In case I have not adequately expressed it, I will be forever grateful that you came to meet me in San Francisco. Thank you, Natalia."

She tapped her glass to his with a gentle *ping*. The candle-light illuminated the fine molding of his features and made his eyes twinkle. She loved looking at him. She loved flirting and dreaming and arguing with him. Were it not for . . .

Well. She and Dimitri could never have children, and it was foolish to continue toying with the idea of *forever* where he was concerned.

"This time tomorrow we will be in New York," she said. Maybe it would be easier to ignore the ache in her heart once they embarked on the next stage of their mission. This magical interlude on the train had been exquisitely painful and pleasurable at the same time. She adored Dimitri but could never have him unless she abandoned the dream of someday having a child. And she did not know if that would ever happen.

Either way, soon they would be in New York, where their real test would begin.

18

*D*imitri battled a strange sense of unease as he
walked beside Natalia down Wall Street toward
the Blackstone Bank.

New York was different from Saint Petersburg and not what
he expected. The streets were narrow and clogged by horses,
wagons, and trolleys all jumbled together. The buildings were
too big to be on such small plots of land, smothering the narrow streets and blocking out the sun.

"Careful," Natalia cautioned as a young man on a bicycle
whooshed past, almost knocking into them.

"Are they allowed to ride on the footpaths like that?" he
asked. People in Russia were more mannerly.

"Not really," she replied but didn't seem overly concerned.

They'd arrived only an hour ago, and their luggage had been
sent directly to Oscar Blackstone's mansion, where they were
expected for dinner. Natalia would escort him there after they
paid the necessary visit to her bank, where she would transfer
his funds and he could send some to his mother.

He craned his neck to look all around. Horns honked, and
a boy selling newspapers shouted at pedestrians. The buildings were impressive, even if they were crammed too closely
together. All the windows had ornate moldings, and each floor
was demarcated by elegant entablatures. Straight ahead was a

graceful four-story building of granite with arching windows and a mansard roof. Dozens of men were clustered outside, shouting and jostling to get closer.

"What are those people lined up for?" he asked.

"That's the New York Stock Exchange," Natalia said. "Those are traders waiting to get inside. It's going to be torn down later this year and replaced with something much grander."

"But it looks brand-new."

"It's almost fifty years old," she replied as though that explained everything. "Come, the bank is just around the corner."

He quickened his steps to follow. He needed to quit worrying about the traffic or the waste of a perfectly good building and get his finances in order.

Soon they arrived at the intersection of Devon and Wall Street, where the Blackstone Bank's stately building dominated the corner. Columns across the front soared all five stories high, and uniformed men stood guard at the front door. Walking up the marble steps felt like entering a temple.

"Welcome back, Miss Blackstone," one of the guards said as he opened a brass-studded door, and they stepped into another world.

Street noise faded as they entered a spacious lobby with Persian carpets, arched colonnades, and tapestries warming the cold stone walls. As Natalia had once told him, this wasn't the sort of bank that had tellers standing behind counters to deal with individual customers. It was the sort of bank that funded the development of cities and states, the kind that paid for harbors in Seattle and railroads across Russia.

"Would you like to see where the analysts work?" Natalia asked as they stepped inside the elevator. "They're near my office, which has a splendid view of the city."

Dimitri shook his head. "I'd like to conclude the transaction with my mother as quickly as possible."

"Of course." She gave instructions to the elevator's attendant to take them to the third floor.

Unlike the grandeur of the first floor, the third floor had a mail room, clerical offices, and an oversized room with a telephone switchboard and two telegraph machines. Clerks shuffled paperwork, but a heavyset man with a full beard and bright red suspenders stood as they entered the communication room. Natalia performed the introductions.

"Aaron, this is Count Sokolov, all the way from Saint Petersburg."

It felt odd to be referred to by his title. For the last eight months, Dimitri had been a vagabond scrambling for food and shelter. Now this portly telegraph operator stood at attention and sent him a slight bow, as if uncertain how to address a man with a title.

"It is an honor to finally meet you," Aaron said.

Natalia stepped in to explain the odd comment. "Aaron is the operator who has decoded most of our messages over the years."

Dimitri sent him a polite smile. "Thank you for your patience. Natalia often says that my messages were long-winded. I shall be more concise with the message to my mother. Can we start that now?"

Natalia seemed a little taken aback by his abruptness, but he was anxious for this task to be concluded. While she and the operator discussed how to wire a large sum of money to his mother, he studied the room. It was a bustling office crammed with people and technical equipment. The windows were closed, but noise from the street still trickled inside.

This was nothing like where he'd imagined Natalia when she received the heartfelt messages he sent. His rural outposts were so different. Sometimes he had been stationed deep in the pine forests, other times in the barren steppes, but always out in nature. In his mind, he pictured Natalia alone in some cozy, book-lined room as they exchanged messages. He never imagined this congested office or the chaotic city that was unlike anything he'd ever seen, and it felt strange. He drifted to the window, where he had a better view of the urban streets below. It was almost hypnotizing. So many people moving so quickly. Where were they all going?

Behind him, the clicking of the telegraph sounder came to life as the operator established contact with a bank in Russia. It took a while to complete, but Dimitri remained transfixed at the window, wondering at this strange malaise that had blanketed him ever since their train entered the city this afternoon.

Natalia joined him. "You can see the townhouse where I live," she said brightly. "It's the third brownstone building just past the church. You see it?"

"I do." The street was cluttered with traffic and telegraph lines and electrical wires. It was ugly.

"Dimitri? What's wrong?"

He didn't know. He should be elated. After months of fear and deprivation, he had arrived at his destination, but a strange exhaustion had come from nowhere and clobbered him.

"I miss home. I don't belong here."

She blanched, and her wounded expression cut through his self-pity. He shook off the malaise and forced himself to stand upright.

"Forgive my foolishness. I must immediately see your townhouse since I cannot properly admire it from here. After all, you have a very special mantelpiece that I have wanted to see from the moment you described it to me. I want to see the daunting steam radiators you learned to operate and where you taught yourself to boil an egg." He leaned over to whisper in her ear. "And I would like to see you wear one of your Russian sarafans."

A gorgeous flush bloomed on her cheeks. A spark of attraction flared to life, but he tamped it down. He wanted much more than to see Natalia in a sarafan. He wanted her alone back on the train, huddled in their compartment together, indulging in an embrace. . . . But he'd vowed he would not pressure her into any form of intimacy until she was ready, and he forced his hands into his pockets.

Natalia smiled up at him. "We'll have to hurry. My father is expecting us for cocktails before dinner, and it will take at least twenty minutes to get there. The sarafan will have to wait."

It took a while to receive confirmation regarding the transfer of his funds, but within the hour they were ready to go, and he was in a better frame of mind. He could become accustomed to this. He *could*.

"We can walk to my townhouse," Natalia said as they stepped out onto the street. "I feel quite proud of myself, walking to and from work each day, just like every other normal New Yorker."

He grabbed her hand and tucked it into the crook of his arm. "You must show me how to be a normal New Yorker. I want to see the Statue of Liberty and shop at the grand emporium you talked about."

"Macy's?"

"Yes! I want to go shopping at Macy's and ride in a trolley, even though they appear to be a horse-drawn deathtrap to me. I must experience all things New York. I want to walk across the Brooklyn Bridge and climb to the top of the Washington Monument."

"The Washington Monument isn't here. It's in Washington, DC."

"So? I still wish to see it." When she cautioned him that Washington, DC, was far away, he scoffed. "Don't try to tell me about long distances." He then launched into an ode about the mightiness of the Russian taiga.

He was still waxing poetic as they mounted the steps leading to Natalia's townhouse. "Don't be too critical," she said. "It's nothing grand, but I am ridiculously proud of it."

She turned the key in the lock. The interior was dim because the drapes had been drawn across the window. The wooden floors creaked when she stepped inside, and she stopped, blocking his entrance so he could not follow. Even from the porch, the house smelled odd.

Natalia darted into the front room to yank the drapes open and gasped when sunlight filled the space.

It was chaos. The ceiling had caved in, and water dribbled through the ruined plaster. Strips of wet wallpaper curled away from the wall. The fireplace mantel had fallen down, lying at a haphazard angle in the middle of the floor. It was split in half.

"Oh no," Natalia moaned, staring in horror at the ceiling. Everything looked and smelled wet. Water gurgled through a pipe overhead.

"I will go upstairs and find the problem," Dimitri said, then vaulted up the steps two at a time. He followed the sound of water to a washroom, where water gushed from an old pipe beneath the pedestal sink. He squatted down to examine a corroded joint on the copper pipe. Water had pooled on the wood floor and seeped into the plaster ceiling below, probably for days. Maybe even weeks.

He was no plumber and couldn't fix this, but downstairs Natalia was heartbroken. He returned to her quickly. She knelt on the floor beside the fireplace, looking at the hand-carved mantel that lay split down the center.

"It's ruined," she said, her voice bewildered and despairing. "Everything I've done is ruined. The wallpaper, the mantel-piece. Did I leave the water running upstairs? How could I have been so stupid?"

"Shh," he soothed. "There was corrosion on the pipe beneath the sink, and it cracked open. This can happen with old pipes."

She glanced up at the ceiling, where water still dribbled, soaking the walls. It had damaged the plaster and caused the mantel to fall away from the wall. "I don't know what to do."

"Stay here. I will go outside and find a way to turn off the water to your house. It is going to be all right, Natalia." After the horrors he'd seen and endured in Russia, a leaky pipe was not a problem, but it had destroyed something Natalia valued, and that meant he cared too.

She drew a ragged breath and nodded. He hurried to the alley behind the house, where a pipe and a valve were low to the ground. He cranked the iron lever, which took a few twists before he was confident it had been turned off. He entered the house and hurried back upstairs, relieved to see the jet of water was dribbling to a halt. He turned the knobs on the sink faucet, which caused a short spurt, and then all the water stopped.

"The water is turned off," he said, rejoining Natalia where she still knelt with slumped shoulders amidst the damp plaster and sodden floorboards.

It was his fault this had happened, for if she had not spent weeks traveling to San Francisco and back, she could have stopped the leak before the damage got this bad. He ran his hands across the cracked mantel, seeing the carved ivy patterns she had told him about. The floor and the plaster could be repaired. New wallpaper could be bought and hung. But he did not know what could be done for this mantel. How proud she had been about this humble house, but it was not fit for habitation in its present state.

"Perhaps you would like to stay with your father as well?" he suggested.

She shook her head. "I can't bear the thought of what Poppy will say if I have to move back because I destroyed my own home only a few months after I bought it."

"You will have no water here," he said gently.

She swiped a lock of hair from her face, leaving a trail of plaster dust in the dark strands. "I'll be all right. I'll figure something out." She pushed herself to her feet. The skirt of her gown was smeared with grit and water stains. "I need to change before we go to my father's. Please say nothing about this. I'm simply not up to Poppy's derision today."

He nodded and watched as she trudged up the stairs, her usual spritely manner vanquished and defeated. The wet, smelly catastrophe of her house would be dispiriting for anyone, but it could all be repaired.

She emerged a few minutes later wearing another of the prim suits she'd worn since he met her. This one was moss green with a tailored vest, a wasp-waisted jacket, and a slim skirt. She sent him an apologetic glance.

"I hoped to take you on a trolley so you could feel like a real New Yorker, but we need to go by cab. We're already late, and Poppy is going to throw a fit."

"Whatever you think best," he said.

Impressing Poppy Blackstone was of little interest to him. Of far more importance was establishing a rapport with Oscar Blackstone. Natalia had put her faith in Admiral McNally's ability to find someone who could verify what happened at the Amur River, but that was an uncertain prospect. In the meantime, Dimitri still needed to be prepared to scuttle the ongoing construction of the Trans-Siberian Railway.

That meant finding the best way to maneuver around Oscar Blackstone.

19

Natalia could tell Poppy was annoyed the moment she and Dimitri arrived in the foyer of her former Fifth Avenue home.

"We expected you hours ago," Poppy said with ill-concealed annoyance. "Couldn't you have at least worn something appropriate? Everyone else is dressed for a formal dinner, and you show up looking like a day at the office."

Natalia silently groaned. She had hoped to introduce Dimitri with as little fuss as possible, then leave to survey the disaster of her home, but a glance down the long marble corridor showed a dozen relatives already gathered for a black-tie affair to welcome Count Sokolov to the city. The men wore starched collars and formal black tailcoats, while Poppy dripped with diamonds and pearls.

"I thought we agreed on a small family dinner," Natalia said, wondering why each encounter with Poppy had to be so contentious. Couldn't Poppy understand that Dimitri was a stranger in New York? That after traveling halfway around the world, a man might want a few hours to relax?

Actually, Poppy *couldn't* understand. None of the people gathered here tonight knew anything about Dimitri's disgrace in Russia or his flight through the wilderness to reach freedom. Natalia had already advised him to keep quiet about his trial until she had the opportunity to speak privately with her father about what happened at the Amur River.

Despite her worries, Dimitri immediately slipped into fine form as he greeted Poppy. "You have a beautiful home," he said, giving a courtly bow as he kissed the back of Poppy's hand. "Its splendor is surpassed only by the beauty of its hostess."

"Count Sokolov!" Poppy flushed beautifully at the ridiculous flattery, but it appeared Dimitri was in a mood to lay it on thick.

"You are as lovely as Helen of Troy," he said with a nod to Poppy's enameled brooch liberally studded with opals, diamonds, and pearls.

"You recognize it?" Poppy asked in surprise.

"But of course. Helen is always portrayed with the white roses of Aphrodite and the doves of peace. You have both in your brooch. Is it Fabergé?"

"It is!" Poppy enthused. "Oscar bought it for me when he was in Paris. The jeweler said no one would understand the symbolism, but it looks like he never met you!"

They headed deeper into the house, where Poppy made the introductions to the rest of the family. The newly married Gwen and Patrick were here, as were Liam and some of her father's elderly aunts.

All throughout dinner, Poppy was in her element. She continued nattering about the quality of Fabergé versus Tiffany, and Dimitri indulged her by adding insightful commentary in his elegant accent during the soup and fish courses. To Natalia's astonishment, Gwen and her father seemed to find the conversation engaging. Patrick mercifully managed to change the topic after the turtle soup was cleared to make way for the gouda cheese soufflé.

"What brings you to America after all these years?" Patrick asked in his lilting Irish accent. Patrick was the kindest man ever to walk the earth. It was an innocent question, but Dimitri paused for a fraction of a second before answering.

"I wanted to meet Natalia in person," he said, raising his goblet to her.

"Well, well," Poppy fairly purred. "We must arrange for you and Natalia to do something more interesting than fritter away time at the bank."

Natalia could see the wheels turning behind Poppy's calculating gaze. Getting an aristocratic title in the family would be the ultimate coup for her status-hungry stepmother, who continued jabbering on about all the places she intended to take Count Sokolov, as though he were her newest fashion accessory.

"I'd like to arrange for us all to see the opera," Poppy said. "We have the best box seats at the hall. Or perhaps Liam could host a party aboard the *Black Rose*? We can invite people of consequence for a lovely afternoon sail."

Liam winked. "I'm not sure you'd approve of the kind of parties I like to have on the *Black Rose*, Pops."

Poppy's smile stiffened. First of all, she hated being called *Pops*. Secondly, the *Black Rose* had been Oscar's yacht until last year, when Liam managed to finagle it out of her father's hands in a quick-thinking business negotiation. The deal had been brokered by Patrick and was a rare victory for the younger men over her father.

"An afternoon sail would be the perfect way to introduce Count Sokolov to all the right kind of people," Poppy insisted. "You could invite Senator Lansing and his daughter. Millicent Lansing is a lovely young lady, and I think she might be perfect for you, Liam."

Liam snorted. "Milly Lansing wouldn't be caught dead with a lug like me."

"Nonsense," Poppy said. "For all his power, Senator Lansing doesn't have deep financial pockets. We do. I should think Senator Lansing would find your courtship of his daughter very appealing. And it would be nice to have a senator in the family."

"What is a senator?" Dimitri asked, bringing the conversation to a dead halt. Dimitri spoke such beautiful English that it was easy to forget he was a complete stranger to the United States.

"It's an elected position," her father replied. "Each state

only gets two, and they are very powerful men. Senator Lansing controls the committee on foreign relations, so his status is even higher than that of most senators."

It was as if a jolt of electricity brought Dimitri alive. "Tell me more about Senator Lansing," he asked Poppy in a honeyed voice, and Poppy happily obliged, describing the senator's charm and his reputation for hosting the best badminton games in the city. Dimitri was coolly elegant as he bantered with Poppy, but Natalia knew he had no genuine interest in Senator Lansing's badminton court, only the senator's position on the foreign relations committee.

Dimitri continued to lavish charm on Poppy, who wallowed in it like a pig in mud. Actually, he was charming everyone at the table, but Natalia was distracted when Alexander's nanny entered the dining room to whisper to Poppy. It was impossible to overhear what Miss Felicity said, but she looked frazzled, and Poppy's displeasure was evident as she rolled her eyes and quickly dismissed the nanny.

Was the baby ill? He'd started cutting a new tooth shortly before Natalia left for San Francisco, and he suffered terribly during the process. It wasn't normal for the nanny to interrupt dinner unless it was urgent, and Poppy couldn't be trusted to care. After all, Poppy had already returned to fawning over Dimitri, pretending to admire his opal stickpin as she ran a finger down his tie.

Natalia abruptly stood, causing all eyes to swivel toward her. "I haven't seen Alexander in three weeks," she said, setting her cloth napkin beside her plate. "I'd like to go check on him."

She ignored their surprised glances as she headed upstairs. Let them be surprised. Dimitri didn't need any help from her in winning her family's affections.

When she arrived at Alexander's nursery, Miss Felicity had the baby on her lap as he happily sucked on a bottle. Alexander was nine months old, with dark hair and a dimple in his chin when he smiled, but at the moment he was entirely engrossed with the bottle clutched in his pudgy fists.

"Is everything all right?" Natalia asked.

"I think so," the nanny replied. "Mrs. Blackstone wants him trained not to need a bottle before bed, but he suffers so. He's been crying for over an hour, and I couldn't deny him any longer."

Alexander's eyelashes were still wet and spiky, but he looked calm and happy in the dim light of the nursery. Natalia approached, loving the way he rotated his head to look up at her and the quick flash of a smile when he recognized her.

"Can I feed him?"

Miss Felicity carefully stood, and the transfer was managed with ease. Soon Natalia was settled in the rocking chair, admiring the way Alexander was able to hold his own bottle in place. She assured the nanny that she would properly burp the baby and lay him down once he'd had his fill.

Then the nanny left, and Natalia had the baby all to herself. These moments were so rare, and a calming, simple joy settled over her. It didn't take long before Alexander started dropping off to sleep even before he had finished the bottle. She set it aside and draped him over her shoulder, gently rocking as she patted his back, waiting for a burp or two before laying him down.

She wanted this someday. She turned her head to breathe deeply of his soft baby scent. It was a dangerous game, but she closed her eyes and dared to pretend that he was hers.

Dimitri got lost twice trying to follow Natalia through the winding corridors. At first he feared she was storming out of the house over the way Poppy had been fussing over him, but then he found the nanny, who directed him to the nursery where Natalia was visiting with the baby.

The mansion had the finest of everything, including electric sconces made to look like candles adorning the hallways. No expense had been spared in the acres of fine carpets in the hallways or the sculptures gracing the wall niches every few yards.

When he finally found the nursery, he stood silently in the

open doorway, rendered breathless by the aching love on Natalia's face as she stroked the baby slumbering over her shoulder.

"This is your brother?" he asked quietly.

Natalia beamed, gently shifting so he could admire the child. The tender pride on her face was laden with adoration, and he sank down onto his haunches to be on the same level as she and the baby. He set a hand on her knee.

"I feared you were leaving," he whispered. "I couldn't let you escape without saying good night. And to thank you for bringing me here."

He loved looking at her with the baby even though it was exquisitely painful. He would never see a woman cradle his own child with the look of contentment on Natalia's face. Her maternal pride looked like a da Vinci masterpiece. Her allure was like a Botticelli. Her fusty sense of humor was pure Natalia Blackstone. The compulsion to claim her as his own was growing stronger each day he was with her.

"Put the baby down," he said softly.

She met his eyes in surprise. "Why?"

"Put the baby down."

She didn't say anything else; she simply rose and carried the boy to the crib. He held his breath as she lowered the sleeping child, settling a blanket over him with infinite care. Her motions were timeless. For millennia, mothers had performed such motions with breathtaking grace, and he felt privileged to witness it.

They tiptoed out of the room, and he held his hand over the doorknob to muffle the sound as he closed the door. He reached out to catch Natalia's elbow when she turned to head down the hall. He wasn't ready to let her go yet.

"Why did you leave the table so abruptly?" he asked quietly.

A hint of mutiny appeared in her expression. "I needed to see Alexander. And I was tired of watching you flirt with Poppy."

It was as he suspected. "Were you jealous?" He braced an arm on the wall above her, enclosing her within the shelter of his body.

"Of Poppy? Don't be ridiculous."

She *was* jealous, and it pleased him. His vow not to pressure Natalia unless she decided to pursue a courtship with him was becoming increasingly difficult. She was everything he wanted in a woman. Smart. Principled. She was deeply passionate but masked it beneath a veneer of cool logic, and he adored that about her. Nevertheless, he'd come to New York on a mission, and he couldn't forget it no matter how badly he wanted her. He needed more allies, and Poppy could help.

"Poppy knows people who may be able to open doors for me," he said. "Senator Lansing sounds like the sort of man—"

"He's not. And quit talking so loudly. The baby is sleeping."

He lowered his voice and tried again. "Senator Lansing seems well positioned to communicate with the czar. We can use him—"

"Dimitri, please," she quietly implored. She cupped his face between her palms, looking up at him in appeal. "We already have a plan. Don't let Poppy sway you from it."

The touch of her palms sent a thrill through him. Every nerve tingled, made worse by the longing he saw in her face as she locked gazes with him. He remained motionless as he fought to control his breathing.

"Dearest Natalia, I would prefer if you did not lay hands on me unless you wish for a far greater intimacy, because I am dangerously close to pressing you up against this wall and kissing you until we are both mindless."

She sucked in a breath and jerked her hands from his face. "You wouldn't."

"I most certainly would. I wish I could do so morning, noon, and night, but you already know of my miserable failings as a man. I won't make any sort of advance unless you ask me." He leaned down, close enough that the tip of his nose brushed against her soft hair, and whispered in her ear. "Ask me."

She tilted her face toward his, her mouth only an inch from his own. Time felt suspended as she said nothing. He kept his arm braced on the wall above her, but true to his word, he did not touch her. The sound of their breathing was the only thing that could be heard in the marble emptiness of the hallway.

Then she stepped away. "I need to get back to my family."

She did not look back as she hurried down the hallway, the gentle swish of her skirts sounding fainter as she departed. His heart thudded in disappointment, but he'd suffered worse. He could be patient.

"Good night, my dearest Natalia," he whispered after her.

20

After the cramped and rackety sleeping berth on the train, the massive four-poster bed in the Blackstone guest room made Dimitri feel like a visiting potentate. He awoke on his first morning after arriving in New York enveloped in such grandeur that he simply lay flat on his back to savor the opulence. Velvet draperies framed the windows, an Aubusson rug warmed the floor, and crystal teardrops dangled from the chandelier. Each corner of the room featured marble Corinthian columns made to look like they were holding the carved plaster ceiling aloft.

The bedroom was gaudy, but he loved it. No more shivering on a bed of pine needles or wearing boots taken off dead soldiers. No more cedar nuts washed down with hot water for breakfast. He now had silken sheets, running water in the adjoining washroom, and servants to assist him with whatever he needed.

He eventually rose and pulled on a robe, then pressed the call button to summon a servant. He had no idea where or when breakfast would be served, but a footman wearing a cutaway black jacket arrived two minutes later with an invitation to join Mrs. Blackstone in the breakfast room. Dimitri thanked him and offered a five-dollar bill, but the man seemed taken aback and made no move to accept it.

"Is tipping not done here?" Dimitri asked.

The footman was visibly embarrassed. "Sometimes guests leave an envelope on the dressing table after an extended visit, but it is certainly not expected, sir."

Dimitri slid the bill back into his billfold. "My pardon. I was premature."

There would surely be other missteps as he adjusted to New York, but his first order of business would be to restock his wardrobe with a complete set of tailor-made clothes. Persuading men of consequence to support him could not be done while wearing ready-made suits purchased off the rack in San Francisco.

Natalia had told him last night that she would be at the bank all day, but he suspected Poppy knew where the best tailors could be found. Now that he had access to his funds, he was eager to begin looking like a gentleman again.

He indulged in a ridiculously long and hot steamy bath, then groomed his beard. He had shaved his beard entirely in San Francisco because of the lice fiasco, but it had grown back over the past week, and he shaped it into a sleek, tightly clipped style. A slick of Macassar oil on the sides of his hair, a dash of cologne, and a quick buffing of his nails with a chamois cloth, and he was ready to face the world.

He headed down a curving marble staircase and navigated through mirrored hallways until he arrived at the blindingly white breakfast room, where a bank of windows overlooked a courtyard garden. The early spring greenery was the only relief from the white walls, white table linens, and white roses. Silver food warmers weighted down a sideboard, where even the candlesticks were white and hard.

This was the setting for his opening battle with Mrs. Poppy Blackstone.

Poppy wore a slim-fitting gown of ice-blue silk embroidered with pearls and crystal. Her golden-blond hair was elegantly styled atop her head, and she brightened when he entered.

"Count Sokolov," she purred, setting down her teacup. "Did you sleep well?"

Noise from clattering horses' hooves and the rumble of street trolleys had awakened him repeatedly. He'd never liked cities, and New York was exceptionally rife with all the qualities he found disturbing, but these were trifling things.

"It was the most comfortable night I have enjoyed in more than four years," he replied truthfully. "You have a lovely home, Mrs. Blackstone."

"Please, you must call me Poppy."

A woman of her standing had no business initiating such an intimacy with an aristocrat, but Dimitri didn't mind. The closer he could bring her under his wing, the better. Poppy was his key to New York society, and he was happy to begin fostering the relationship.

"And you must call me Dimitri," he said as he surveyed the offerings on the sideboard. Broiled smelts with tartar sauce, curried eggs, baked apples with sweet cream, raspberry tartlets—all of it exquisitely prepared and presented.

"There are so many things I must show you," she said once he joined her at the table. "We can take a carriage ride in Central Park. The mild weather means we should be able to take the open carriage so you can see the park properly."

Or so she can show me off, he thought.

"Naturally you will want to see a performance at Carnegie Hall. Perhaps later today we can have tea at the Waldorf. All of society takes tea there after a day of shopping, and I suspect we may see Mrs. Astor herself."

Ah, Mrs. Astor. Natalia had warned him that Mrs. Astor was the social arbiter of the New York elite and the one remaining battlement Poppy had yet to conquer. Hosting a European aristocrat at her home would surely make inroads with Mrs. Astor's set.

Unless they learned of his denunciation for cowardice in Russia. He had to move quickly before this house of cards collapsed around him. He would gladly help Poppy with Mrs. Astor, but not until she helped him make inroads of his own.

"Last night you mentioned Senator Lansing is in town and how much you enjoy his wife's skill at the piano," he said.

Poppy's nose wrinkled. "I was being polite. Mrs. Lansing never misses an opportunity to inflict her music upon her guests, but it's best to be appreciative in order to stay in her good graces."

"I would like to be in Mrs. Lansing's good graces, and her husband's as well. Could you arrange an introduction?"

Poppy's cool blond eyebrows arched as she stirred a cube of sugar into her tea. "There are others I think you would rather meet. The Vanderbilts are in town, and they always host such splendid dinner parties."

"I would prefer to meet the Lansings. Can you arrange it?"

Poppy hesitated. "I just had tea with Mrs. Lansing last week, and it's best not to wear out one's welcome. How about we go for tea at the Waldorf today, and then a ride in Central Park tomorrow? Between the two outings, you will have a wonderful introduction to the city."

"I will visit the park with you," he conceded. "I will escort you for tea at the Waldorf and make polite conversation with the ladies. And in exchange, before two o'clock this afternoon, I will need you to arrange for me to meet Senator Lansing."

Poppy rocked back in her chair at the note of command in his voice, but she recovered quickly.

"Not good enough," she said. "I will need you to *praise* me in front of the ladies at the Waldorf, and then we will share a box seat at Carnegie Hall, where we will be seen enjoying each other's company."

Dimitri's respect for her gamesmanship inched up a notch, and he smiled. "My dear, you are a monster of predatory ambition."

She raised her teacup in a toast. "I see we understand each other."

They did indeed.

Natalia had a literal tower of paperwork awaiting her at the bank. She'd never been out of the office for more than a few days, and business had continued at a brisk pace during her three-week venture to the West Coast.

Despite the size of her large office, Natalia had furnished it with the dainty rolltop desk that once belonged to her mother. The memento from Galina was comforting, and when she lowered the top over her paperwork at the end of each day, the entire office looked sleek and tidy for the next morning.

Not today. Natalia returned to a mound of accumulated paperwork almost a foot thick on her desk chair. Soon she would sort it all into orderly stacks on the worktable: those needing an immediate response, those that could be delegated to her clerk, and reports to read later.

But the first order of business was to see her father about Dimitri, and Natalia dreaded the meeting. Dimitri was a wild card who couldn't be controlled, and she needed to alert her father. When she left for the West Coast, she'd told Oscar it was to tour their investment at the port of Seattle, which she accomplished quickly. She'd made no mention of Count Sokolov until she wired him of their pending arrival, and he wasn't pleased about it. He made that clear the moment she sat down across from him at the baronial splendor of his desk.

"Riding with a bachelor across the country without a chaperone can lead to unseemly gossip," he said.

"We have more to worry about than unseemly gossip."

Her father quirked a brow at her ominous tone but didn't show the slightest hint of anger. When they discussed business, he was her employer, not her father.

"Continue," he said.

Where to begin? Her father didn't know about Dimitri's trial or condemnation to a penal colony. He knew nothing about Dimitri's heroic escape or the desperate circumstances behind his arrival in America. Most importantly, her father didn't know anything about what had happened at the Amur River. She pared the story down to the relevant details of the massacre, Dimitri's refusal to participate in the extermination of the villagers, and his subsequent trial, condemnation to a penal colony, and escape.

"What he saw haunts him," she said. "He fears there could be more violence along the river as the southern leg of the railroad draws closer to the Pacific, and he is upset about it."

Her father thrummed his fingers on his desk, his face grim. "I suppose anyone with a conscience would be. Dreadful business."

"Dimitri isn't the sort of man who keeps his emotions under wraps. His first inclination for how to prevent future atrocities associated with the railroad was to halt operations until he could be sure it won't happen again."

"He'd better not," Oscar snapped, and Natalia hurried to placate him.

"Dimitri doesn't understand business or politics in America. He doesn't know how to navigate here. He is driven by emotion and doesn't care what the personal cost is."

"Then you'd better *make* him care," Oscar said. "It's not the railroad he'll damage with his actions, it's our reputation. The press will smear us for being complicit in that atrocity. They will blame us for funding a venture that put profit ahead of human decency. It will take a wrecking ball to our reputation."

She wilted beneath her father's blistering tirade. She had witnessed his carefully controlled rages for years. His voice would lash out like a whip to slice underperforming executives to shreds, but he'd never turned that rage on her before. All her life she had been the daughter he doted on. He protected and promoted her within the bank and shot down anyone who dared look askance at her. It was a foregone conclusion that he would be upset about Dimitri, but she hadn't expected this torrent of anger.

He continued ranting for several minutes before stopping to catch his breath, a single tic pulsing in his cheek. The silence lengthened, broken only by the steady ticking of a clock on the desk.

When Oscar spoke again, his voice was drained of anger and carried only concern.

"If this gets out, people will learn you are the manager of

the railroad investment. They will assume you got your position through nepotism and then lacked the insight to anticipate problems. We both know that isn't true, but if blame for that massacre blows back on the bank, the public will be merciless toward you. A man might receive the benefit of the doubt, but they'll never do the same for you, and I won't be able to protect you. Do you understand what I'm saying?"

He was saying that she would become the scapegoat if they couldn't contain this news.

"I understand," she said. "I won't let Dimitri do anything to hurt the bank."

Oscar pushed to his feet, leaning heavily on his cane as he limped to the window. Normally he was so forceful that it was easy to overlook the infirmities he battled with every step he took. When he finally spoke, his voice sounded old and tired.

"You have other problems to worry about," he said. "I fired Silas Conner based on his poor performance at the Seattle harbor."

It wasn't a surprise, but it made her uncomfortable because the report she wired from Seattle had surely been the nail in Silas's coffin.

Oscar continued talking as he stared out the window. "He used to be a sharp man of business, but he's been getting sloppy, and it can no longer be ignored. He blamed you, of course. He started shooting off his mouth to anyone who would listen and refused to take responsibility for his slipshod handling of the account."

"What did he say?"

Oscar waved a dismissive hand. "Nothing but rubbish that no sane person would believe. I've already threatened a slander suit if he persists, but you need to understand that you are not without enemies. I've put a muzzle on Silas Conner, but be on the lookout for anyone who will pounce if you dare set a foot wrong. Understood?"

She did, but figuring out how to influence events in Russia without causing a scandal to break out in America was going to be a high-wire act that might be impossible to accomplish.

Natalia shared a carriage with her father back to Fifth Avenue. Tension still simmered between them, but they both pretended a calmness they did not feel. She looked out the window and Oscar read a report as they bumped and jostled over the cobblestones on their way uptown. How she despised this traffic, but she couldn't abandon Dimitri when her father was in a temper.

An overturned bread wagon at Canal Street caused no end of headaches, and they were late getting home. Natalia hurried inside, hoping Dimitri had not expired from boredom after enduring Poppy's shallow company all day.

She rushed to the butler and handed him her wrap. "Where is Count Sokolov?"

"He and Mrs. Blackstone left early this morning," Mr. Tyson replied. "They have not yet returned."

That was odd. She and her father were almost an hour late, and Poppy had planned a lavish private dinner to impress Dimitri tonight.

Natalia joined her father in the parlor outside the dining room, where he settled into a deep leather chair and snapped open a newspaper. Perhaps she could talk him out of his mood by engaging in a business conversation.

"I've been working with Liam on his plan to restructure wages in the steel business," she said. "Has he discussed any of this with you?"

Her father grunted behind the newspaper. "It's a pipe dream."

She initially thought so too, but Liam had been surprisingly effective in persuading a few other men on the board of directors to entertain his proposal.

"He's putting his heart and soul into it. Of course, it would be better if he could put some convincing financial projections behind it, but you know Liam. He struggles when it comes to math."

She was babbling, which sometimes happened when she was

exhausted, but at last voices came from down the hall. For once in her life, she was relieved to see Poppy, who flung both doors open with abandon as she sashayed into the room, Dimitri close behind.

Dimitri looked spectacular in a new suit Natalia had never seen before, and the sight of his sartorial splendor reminded her of the gulf between them. Dimitri was a European aristocrat whose bank account dwarfed hers. It had been easy to forget when he wore birchbark shoes and she picked lice from his hair.

"You had a successful day?" her father asked, peering over the rim of the newspaper.

"Sir, your wife is spectacular," Dimitri said. "She moves through the city like a Valkyrie, scanning the terrain, then swooping in to claim her next target with unerring accuracy. Tailors, butlers, old-guard society matrons at the Waldorf—all of them fell victim to her unerring instinct. I followed in her wake, watching with awe as she charmed or slayed lesser mortals, depending on her whim."

Poppy would explode if Natalia ever spoke of her that way, but Poppy beamed and took Dimitri's arm. "We made quite a pair, storming the gates at Senator Lansing's townhouse, didn't we?"

"Senator Lansing?" Natalia asked, mildly appalled. Such a man needed to be handled as carefully as a pipe bomb, not with Poppy's frivolous social airs.

Poppy gave her a smug look. "Dimitri wanted to meet the senator, and I can deny him nothing. We had a splendid afternoon admiring the senator's collection of antique revolvers."

"Can I offer you a drink before dinner?" her father asked, but Dimitri declined with a good-natured grin.

"We've been imbibing at Senator Lansing's house all afternoon. Probably over-imbibing," he added with a wink at Poppy.

"Senator Lansing served the most delicious cocktail called a Flash of Lightning," Poppy said. "I loved it, but what was that awful drink you were so enamored of, Dimitri?"

Natalia bristled at hearing Poppy so casually call Dimitri by his given name, but no one noticed as he laughingly relayed the ingredients of a revolting drink called a Flip, with brandy, sugar, and a raw egg all mixed together. It certainly sounded like he and Poppy had a marvelous time with Senator Lansing.

She called a halt to their hilarity. "Dinner is already overdue. The cook went out of her way to prepare roasted duck, and it will dry out if we linger much longer."

Inside the dining room, the candles had been burning for a while, leaving drips trailing down the ivory columns. They used the smaller, more intimate table that was set with Wedgewood china and crystal goblets. Silverware clinked, and servants moved about silently as they filled glasses and set out warm bread. Her father waited until the watercress soup had been served before homing in on Dimitri.

"What exactly was your business with Senator Lansing?" he asked, his voice cool.

"Senator Lansing has an interest in Russia," Dimitri said. "He told me of the time he was in Moscow and saw Saint Basil's Cathedral. He got lost in the old galleries!"

Poppy laughed. "We'll be meeting him at tonight's midnight performance of a string quartet in Central Park. It's to kick off his reelection campaign and should be smashing fun, since all the best people will be there. I'm assuming the two of you won't join us, since you get up so oppressively early in the morning."

"Would you like to come, Natalia?" Dimitri asked courteously, almost like an afterthought.

The prospect of battling to stay awake until midnight made Natalia sag. Her first appointment was at nine o'clock tomorrow morning, and she still needed to prepare.

"I'm not up for it tonight," she said.

"You see?" Poppy said with a look of triumph at Dimitri. "Natalia never likes doing anything fun, but I shall hold you to your promise to escort me on a gondola ride. There will be torches lining the shore and servants handing out warmed blankets."

Poppy and Dimitri continued to carry the bulk of the conversation while Natalia met her father's eyes across the table. Was he going to raise the topic of the Trans-Siberian? There had been plenty of opportunity, but still he said nothing.

By the cheese course, Natalia was struggling to keep her eyes open, and she still had a thirty-minute carriage ride to get home. She'd forgotten how rich the meals at her father's house could be and begged off before the final course of brandied cherries served over ice cream, but she wouldn't leave Dimitri entirely in Poppy's clutches.

"Dimitri, will you escort me to the coach house?"

He looked surprised but obligingly rose and followed her. She felt her father's eyes boring into her back the entire way down the hall.

Dimitri followed Natalia down a corridor and through a back door to the stable yard behind the house. The stiff way she moved indicated her ire over something, although its cause was a mystery. He liked the chilly air outside, but Natalia burrowed down into a coat she'd snatched from the hook outside the door.

"Natalia, I can see your displeasure. Tell me what has annoyed you."

She met him with equal frankness. "I think you need to watch out for Poppy."

"Do you? I found her to be splendid company." Poppy was a snob but also frank and funny and smart.

Natalia did not reply as she knocked on a door of the coach house. It was answered by a sleepy young man shrugging into a coachman's jacket, and Natalia requested a carriage to deliver her back to her townhouse. It would take at least ten minutes to harness the horses, and they headed to a walled garden beside the coach house to wait. The air smelled like damp earth mingled with the scent of leather and horses. Light from the stable lanterns made it easy to see the frustration on Natalia's face in the cold night air.

"Dimitri, Senator Lansing is using you," she said. "He is up for reelection soon and is looking to polish his image."

"What is a reelection?"

He must have said something stupid because Natalia rolled her eyes in frustrated wonder. She supplied an answer, explaining how every six years men in the Senate needed to submit to the will of the voters, which Dimitri had heard about but never seen in action. In the year leading up to an election, men jockeyed for position, shoring up their weaknesses and pandering to people who might be able to help.

"Senator Lansing likes the glamour of having a Russian count at his midnight party," she said. "He will string you along and tell you what he thinks you need to hear, but you mustn't put your hopes in it."

Dimitri sobered. "Things are very different in Russia. We are more honest and have no need of these troublesome 're-elections.'"

"Senator Lansing wants the president to strengthen our ties with Japan. The Amur River cuts straight through Manchuria, and Japan thinks they can get a piece of it because China is weak. If the Japanese get a foothold in Manchuria, do you think they'll be any kinder to the villagers than the Russians were?"

He shifted his weight, trying to process what she said. "And you think Senator Lansing has influence on this? If so, then it is essential I establish connections with him."

Once again, she seemed frustrated. "Dimitri, you don't know what you're doing. I don't have much experience in politics either, but I can assure you that relying on Poppy's guidance would be a catastrophe. I am asking you to swallow back three hundred years of inbred, aristocratic arrogance and trust me to lead you to the right people."

He frowned. Poppy was much smarter than Natalia had

implied to him, but Natalia knew his heart, and he trusted she would act in his interest.

"What do you think I should do?"

"I think you should stick with the plan I told you about on the train. Admiral McNally has wide experience in foreign affairs," she said. "Neither one of us knows what to do, but he can guide us."

"Very well, let's meet with Admiral McNally. Can you accompany me to meet him tomorrow?"

Apparently he had once again offended Natalia, because she looked thunderstruck. "I've been gone from the bank for three weeks. I have meetings all day tomorrow, a report due to my father by five o'clock, plus a stack of papers a foot high that need my attention."

"Must I repeat myself?" he demanded. "I need your help finding this Admiral McNally person, and I would like to do so tomorrow."

"Don't pull your antiquated loftiness with me. I invested forty thousand dollars in a line of music boxes that must be completed before Easter, and I'm meeting with the manufacturer tomorrow morning to discuss it."

Natalia's passion for business was one of her most appealing qualities, but she ought to put the railroad ahead of music boxes. He moved closer to her, drawn by an invisible force that always hummed just below the surface when she was near.

"You want me to wait because of music boxes?" he asked in disbelief.

"I want you to act like a normal human being who understands that the sun and the stars and the planets don't rotate around his whims."

Her wickedly pointed insults shot a bolt of pure desire into him, and she seemed just as aroused. He ripped off the starched collar that was choking him and threw it in the dirt. Now that he'd made up his mind to meet with Admiral McNally, it should be done immediately, not after she looked at pretty music boxes.

"Tomorrow, Natalia."

She sputtered in anger. "I know this may come as a surprise to you, Dimitri, but I actually have an entire life outside of your demands to go shopping or wire money to your mother. Ever since I met you, I've done nothing but cater to your every whim. I gave you a manicure, for pity's sake!"

"Will you take me to meet Admiral McNally tomorrow?"

"Yes!" she shouted, anger snapping. "Yes, I'll take you despite how arrogant and horrible you are." Her eyes flashed in the lamplight, furious and magnificent. "You owe me, Dimitri. You owe me a lot for catering to you like this."

"I will never deny it. I'll lay the world at your feet if you let me."

"I don't want the world," she said. "I just want *you*, which annoys me to no end."

Her words nearly felled him. "You know that I adore you, don't you?"

"Prove it."

It was the invitation he'd been waiting for. He swooped down like a Cossack and swept her into his arms, kissing her like there was no tomorrow. She didn't resist, and at last—*at last*—he was kissing his dearest Natalia. She kissed him back with equal fervor. He lifted her off the ground but didn't break their kiss.

"Ma'am?" The carriage driver stood a few yards away in uncertainty.

Dimitri drew on some of those three hundred years of arrogance to dismiss him. "Go away," he ordered.

He tried to kiss Natalia again, but she overruled him.

"Stay, Archer." Her hair had tumbled down her back, and she was still peeved, but she was also alive and vibrant and real. He didn't want this moment to end, and it didn't look like she did either. She stayed within his arms, her eyes fastened on him even as she spoke to the driver. "I'm ready to go home and have no more interest in pursuing this line of discourse."

"I don't know what *discourse* means," Dimitri said, scrambling for an excuse to prolong this moment.

"It means speaking. Debate. Arguing."

"I like this type of discourse. Don't ever back away from normal human discourse, Natalia." He loved it when she threw caution to the wind. It rarely happened, but tonight she was full of fire, and for once she let it burn without restraint.

"You're asking me to back away from my entire life," she said. "The bank. My father."

"Yes, in a noble cause. More noble than music boxes."

Apparently those were fighting words, for she straightened her spine and her voice rang with conviction. "This country was made great on the strength of *business*, and my calling is to help it flourish. Maybe it's only a music box to you, but it's also jobs and security for every artist or shopkeeper involved in their sale. I'm proud of my work. It takes two kinds of people to make businesses thrive. It takes dreamers and doers like you, and sensible people behind the scenes to make the dreams happen. That's who we are. Romance and reason. Fire and ice."

Dimitri struggled to keep his breathing under control. "That may be the most alluring statement since Cleopatra tempted Marc Antony to world domination."

"They both ended up dead," she pointed out.

"As befits all good heroes."

She finally laughed. He loved the sound because Natalia's laughter was a hard-won prize, and he hauled her back into his arms.

The odds were stacked against them, but there was no one else he'd rather walk into battle with than Natalia Blackstone. The future ahead was daunting. His title was worth something, but when news of its revocation reached American shores, it was anyone's guess how the public would respond, which meant he needed to collect allies quickly.

He leaned down, touching his forehead to hers. "Please, Natalia," he said in a rough voice, all hint of teasing gone. "I need your help."

She sighed, then pulled back a few inches to look up at him. "All right," she said. "Tomorrow morning we'll go see Admiral McNally and pray he can lead us to the right people."

21

The following morning, Natalia was still baffled by her own behavior outside the carriage house. She had never been so furious and entranced at the same time. Dimitri had kissed her as if his life depended on it, all in view of the carriage driver, but it had been the most alive moment of her life. Embarrassment rained down at the memory, but she needed to ignore it and get down to business.

She postponed her original meeting and instead arranged for a ten o'clock appointment with Admiral McNally at the Brooklyn Navy Yard. She met Dimitri at the porte cochere behind her father's house, where he paced impatiently.

"Why are you dressed like that?" he asked as she descended from the cab she'd hired. He seemed annoyed, but she looked exactly as she always did. Her slim-fitting suit was of the finest indigo wool, trimmed with velvet piping and completed with an ivory lace jabot at her throat. Her hat was trimmed with a matching ribbon band.

"I am dressed in a clean and respectful manner to meet an officer at the navy yard." There would be no rending of garments or tearing hair free or passionate kisses in the dark. A shame, but today was about business.

Without warning, Dimitri leaned over and lifted the hem of

her skirt, then tutted. "Those boots are completely inadequate for walking across the Brooklyn Bridge."

She yanked her skirt free and took a step back. "Why would we do that?"

"I told you my first day here that this was important to me." His eyes glinted with challenge while looking down his long, aristocratic nose at her. His ridiculous assumption that she had nothing better to do than take him sightseeing was exasperating and charming at the same time. They needed to cross the bridge anyway, but they didn't have much time before the meeting.

"We can walk over the bridge after our meeting with Admiral McNally," she said. She was proud of that awe-inspiring bridge and wanted to see it through his eyes.

It took almost an hour to get to the navy yard, a sprawling complex of dry docks, warehouses, and assembly yards facing the East River. Two tiers of cannons lined the riverbank, a memento of a time when the city's greatest danger was a naval invasion.

Admiral McNally's office had a commanding view of the shipyard, but the other three walls were blanketed by world maps and military accolades. A Turkish carpet covered the floor, and the bookshelf featured Greek pottery and jade carvings she suspected came from his many years as a military attaché at various postings throughout the Ottoman Empire.

Although the admiral was her godfather, he was her father's friend, not hers. After she introduced Dimitri and explained his role on the Trans-Siberian project, Admiral McNally tersely consulted his pocket watch before gesturing for them to sit.

"I'm glad my secretary was able to squeeze you in," he said after taking a seat behind his desk. "This week is dense with budget meetings, but I can spare a few minutes for my favorite goddaughter."

It was a polite order to get directly to the point, and she complied. "I remember listening to your tales of when you were a military attaché during the Ottoman wars. You said the military still has men all over the world, watching and gathering information about other countries. Dimitri saw some terrible things along the Russian border with China, but it does not appear that news of this atrocity has reached American shores."

Admiral McNally quirked a brow and turned his attention to Dimitri. All hint of impatience vanished as he listened to Dimitri describe the expulsion of the ethnic Chinese across the river and how an exodus turned into a stampede and then a slaughter.

Natalia clenched her fists beneath the table and asked the all-important question. "Did the Americans have any military observers in that part of the world last year?"

Admiral McNally shook his head. "Not that I am aware of. Your best bet is to hunt down a fellow named Dr. Louis Seaman. He works as a medical observer on behalf of the surgeon general. Last year he was stationed in Japan to study how they handle sanitation issues. He reported rumors of atrocities he'd heard from Russian soldiers who deserted the army, and yes, they were near the Amur River."

"What sort of atrocities?" Dimitri demanded.

Admiral McNally held up his hands. "I don't know the details, but I witnessed Dr. Seaman arguing with the Russian ambassador at a State Department reception, and it got heated. Dr. Seaman wanted the ambassador to answer for the rumors, and the ambassador accused Dr. Seaman of being a mouthpiece for Japan. He threatened retaliation against Dr. Seaman if he continued carrying tales. That's the last I heard of it."

Dimitri shifted uncomfortably. "It does not surprise me that the ambassador is hostile to Japan. There is no love lost between the two nations."

"Apparently Count Cassini feels the same," Admiral McNally said. "He warned Dr. Seaman against—"

"Count Cassini?" Dimitri interrupted, his voice full of appalled wonder. "Arthur Cassini is the Russian ambassador?"

"Indeed," Admiral McNally said. "Do you know him? He seems a rather imperious sort."

Dimitri shook his head. "I don't know him personally, but

I know who he is. I thought he was the ambassador to China, but now he has turned up in the United States?" His expression darkened. "This can't be good."

"Why?" she asked.

Dimitri shot off the bench and began pacing. "Count Cassini is uncomfortably close to the czar and wickedly clever. He speaks half a dozen languages. People in Moscow consider him a wizard for how far and how fast he has risen at court. His family is Italian, but they have made their home in Russia for generations. Somehow he wrangled a title out of the czar, but he is not to be trusted."

Natalia glanced at Admiral McNally. "What do you know about Count Cassini?"

A flush darkened the older man's face. "It is not a proper topic to discuss in front of ladies."

"Don't be absurd," she said, batting his concerns away. "Piles of dead bodies in the Amur River aren't proper either, so this isn't the time to worry about delicate sensibilities."

"Very well," the admiral said. "Count Cassini is an unmarried gentleman and has brought his niece to Washington to serve as his official hostess. She is a teenaged girl barely out of the schoolhouse but has acquired a rather notorious reputation. He insists that she be referred to as Countess Cassini, although it is rumored she is neither a countess nor a Cassini."

Natalia raised a brow at the unsavory implications, but of more concern was what Admiral McNally relayed about the ambassador's activities in Washington.

"Dr. Seaman despises Count Cassini. He suspects the Russian ambassador is trying to drive a wedge between America and Japan. A constant stream of diplomats and businessmen come and go from the Russian embassy. Ever since Count Cassini arrived in Washington, parties at the Russian embassy have become one of the most sought-after invitations in the city."

"He's gathering allies," Dimitri said, his tone dark. "My guess is that Count Cassini will do everything possible to discredit Dr. Seaman's report about what happened at the Amur."

It sounded like Count Cassini had a head start in shaping opinions in Washington, but if they could find Dr. Seaman, they might have their first powerful ally.

At long last, Dimitri had his chance to walk across the Brooklyn Bridge, but he'd lost his interest in the engineering marvel. Instead of admiring the towering pillars or the webbing of steel wire that stretched for more than a mile across the East River, he argued with Natalia.

"We must go to Washington immediately," he said. "We cannot underestimate Count Cassini. Even as we walk, I can feel him cozying up to the Americans and discrediting anyone who dares to come forward with the truth. He is months ahead of me. I must find this Dr. Seaman and tell him what I witnessed."

He had to raise his voice to be heard over the stiff breeze coming off the river. Perhaps Natalia mistook his shouting for anger, because she was certainly digging in her heels.

"I just got back to the city," she said. "I can't leave again so quickly. I have responsibilities here."

It had been nine months since he witnessed the massacre, and for most of that time, he'd been helpless and wandering like a nomad. Meanwhile, the czar and his allies were burying whatever evidence was left of the atrocity, and Dimitri needed to sound the alarm immediately.

"Natalia, you must come with me to Washington, and it must happen quickly. If word of my supposed cowardice hits American shores before I get my story out, all the doors will slam in my face. You are correct. I do not understand American politics and need your help. I realize I am asking a great deal of you, but it is like in the beginning of *War and Peace*. Prince Andrei didn't want to go to war, but it was his duty. His sacred—"

"I told you that's a horrible novel, and it won't persuade me to do anything." She twitched as she strode along the bridge. It was crowded today, requiring them to angle around others walking and riding bicycles on the boardwalk.

"*War and Peace* is a timeless masterpiece of love and sacrifice. Now is your opportunity to fight for a valiant cause." He grabbed her shoulders and turned her toward him. "Natalia, I know you better than anyone, and you will regret it forever if you do not come with me because of some mundane meetings at a bank."

She wilted a little. "It's more than the bank. I need to repair my house. The plaster, the water. I'll probably need a new floor in the washroom."

"Shh," he said, laying a fingertip on her lips. "Let me hire someone to do the repairs. You are not a plumber or a carpenter. You are one of the few people in the world who knows both the situation along the Trans-Siberian route *and* how to navigate American high society. I am a stranger here. I need your help. My three hundred years of aristocratic entitlement are begging you to come with me."

She looked up at him with wistful resignation. "I wish you didn't know how to get the better of me."

"It is a gift," he said, relief trickling through him. She would come. His darling Natalia would always come through for him.

They stood in the pedestrian walkway, and unmannerly people were giving them sidelong looks, so he pulled her to the metal railing where they could be out of the way. The city of Manhattan was straight ahead of them, an impressive view of towering buildings huddled on a narrow strip of land. Natalia was a woman of that city. She loved it, just as he loved Russia. He clasped her hand while they looked toward the Manhattan skyline.

"I wish you could love New York as much as I do," she said, and he looked at her in surprise.

"Did I say that I don't?"

She smiled and leaned against him. "You don't have to say anything. I can tell."

He closed his arms around her and looked over her shoulder toward the city. She was right. He didn't belong here. In a perfect world, he could sweep her away to Russia, where she could be Countess Sokolova and they would rule at Mirosa, his wild, rustic kingdom.

But for today, they needed to plan how to conquer Washington, DC.

~~~ ⌒⌒ ~~~

Natalia had been blessed with a forward-thinking father who opened doors for her in the world of banking, but even Oscar was going to resist letting her travel with Dimitri to Washington.

After returning to Manhattan, she went straight to his office. It would be better to make her appeal at the bank rather than at home, where Poppy eavesdropped whenever Natalia tried to be alone with her father.

After making an appointment with his secretary, she retreated to the ladies' washroom to splash cool water on her face and tidy her hair. This washroom had been built for her alone. When she started working here nine years ago, she was the only female on the entire staff, and her father had spared no expense to ensure her comfort. Other women soon joined the bank in clerical roles, but to this day, she was the only female business analyst in all of New York City.

At three o'clock on the nose, she was shown into her father's office for their meeting. To her surprise, he had her baby brother propped up on his desk, wearing a navy-blue suit complete with a checkered vest and a red bow tie. The spiffy look was marred by the baggy trousers cut to accommodate a diaper, but he certainly looked dandy.

She laughed. "Isn't he a little young for a clerkship?"

The baby squealed when he recognized her and nearly toppled over in delight as he waved a toy duck at her.

"Never," Oscar insisted with pride. "I've decided to bring him to the office for a few hours each week so he can feel at home here. Come inside and say hello to him. It looks like he wants you to pick him up."

Alexander's nanny and a footman were in the sitting area

of the office, but there was no sign of Poppy, which wasn't a surprise. Poppy rarely showed much interest in the baby except when there was an audience, but Oscar couldn't get enough of the boy.

Natalia wasn't jealous. She remembered coming to the bank when she was a child too, although she was eight or nine before Oscar began bringing her. She used to sit in the corner of his office, reading her schoolbooks while he met with his clerks and secretaries. Hopefully Alexander would grow to love the bank as much as she always had.

Alexander lifted his arms as she approached. He was a hefty baby, and it took some jostling to get him situated over her shoulder. Would she ever have a child of her own? It could never happen with Dimitri, but she pushed the disagreeable thought away as she patted Alexander's back, loving the way he babbled in happy contentment. It was a brief respite, and this conversation was about to get awkward.

"Can we speak alone?" she asked, and with a brisk nod, Oscar directed the servants to step outside. Natalia kept pacing, nervously patting the baby as she walked. This was not going to be an easy request.

"Well?" Oscar asked once the door closed behind the nanny and footman.

"There is a man in Washington, DC, who might be able to verify Dimitri's story about what happened at the Amur River. He's a doctor who was stationed in Japan and has spoken with credible witnesses to the event. The Russian ambassador is trying to discredit Dr. Seaman. Dimitri is heading to Washington in hopes of supporting the doctor's cause before it's too late."

Oscar shrugged. "By all means, I think he should go."

"I want to go with him."

"Absolutely not!" Oscar's voice cracked across the office like a shot, and Alexander began to cry.

She rocked the boy a little more vigorously and met her father's gaze squarely. "Dimitri doesn't understand American politics."

"Then I'll send someone down with him. It seems to me you are already too deeply entangled with this man. Are you?"

Lying to her father was impossible, so she kept pacing with the baby. She was more than entangled with Dimitri. He had a piece of her heart she could never get back. Her longing for a child might someday drive them apart, but for now she needed to see this mission through.

"I feel compelled to go," she said. "For three years I have considered the Trans-Siberian to be my finest accomplishment, and now it is in danger. Not because of finance or engineering problems, but because an evil incident has stained what should be a monumental accomplishment. We need to expose that evil so it can't happen again."

Oscar shook his head. "If you call attention to the massacre, it will embarrass not only the Russians but the bank as well."

"I understand. That's why it is important for us to be part of solving the problem. It will prove we haven't turned a blind eye to the massacre."

Oscar's hands clenched, and his face turned pensive. He took an unusually long time to ponder before finally speaking. "You may go, provided Poppy accompanies you as chaperone."

Natalia almost dropped the baby. "Poppy?" Having that woman latched to her side during this difficult trip would be unbearable. "The only place Poppy would like to escort me is over the side of a cliff."

Oscar heard the veiled contempt and narrowed his eyes. "Poppy may not be the kindest of women or the best mother. She isn't an interesting conversationalist or a skilled hostess, but by all that's holy, she has been an excellent wife to me, and you need to sheathe your claws."

"This isn't about Poppy," she retorted. "The Russian ambassador is as canny as a wizard, and she will embarrass us."

Oscar pushed himself to his feet in growing annoyance. "You are about to walk a tightrope while trying to pull off a diplomatic coup. You! An unmarried, twenty-eight-year-old woman traveling with a single man who is an outrageous flirt.

You *need* Poppy. We are fortunate news of your cross-country travel from San Francisco has not leaked out, but you can't roll the dice again, so Poppy is going with you, and that's the end of the discussion. My bigger concern is the railroad. I took a risk by letting you manage the project, and for three years I have defended you against critics who think I lost my mind. If scandal from this massacre taints the railroad, it will taint us as well, and I will have no choice but to remove you from all duties in the bank. Is that clear?"

The words landed like a fist in her gut. No other bank in the world would hire a female business analyst, especially one with a tainted reputation.

"I understand." No matter how uncomfortable, she would swallow her pride and make peace with Poppy for as long as the trip to Washington lasted.

22

Once the decision had been made to go to Washington, Natalia's plans fell into place quickly. Admiral McNally contacted the U.S. surgeon general's office and arranged for a meeting with Dr. Seaman, a man with deep connections in both the military and the government. Dr. Seaman was a popular speaker on the lecture circuit and had a knack for explaining complicated issues to a skeptical audience. The press and the public loved him. If they could get the daring army doctor on their side, Natalia hoped he would use his connections to pressure the czar into paying heed to Dimitri.

Oscar insisted on the best for Poppy, so he arranged for his private railcar to take them to Washington. Once in the city, they were booked into the grand suite at the sumptuous Willard Hotel, located only two blocks from the White House.

"This feels like a palace," Dimitri said as they entered the lobby of the hotel. The coffered ceiling was held aloft by towering columns of coral-colored marble. Potted palms and clusters of upholstered furniture in shades of garnet and sage green softened the grandeur.

"A letter has arrived for you, ma'am," the clerk at the hotel's front counter said as Natalia checked in.

She accepted the envelope, engraved with a return address

from the Office of the U.S. Surgeon General, and read the enclosed message quickly. Her heart sank. "Dr. Seaman has been called away to deal with an emergency in Philadelphia. A cholera outbreak."

Dimitri looked stricken, but Poppy was offended. "I think it's very rude for Dr. Seaman to have waltzed away when he knew we wanted to meet with him. Couldn't they have sent another doctor?"

Leave it to Poppy to feel like the aggrieved party. Dr. Seaman specialized in waterborne contagion and was the natural person for the government to send for such an outbreak, but his absence was a blow.

"What are we going to do now?" Dimitri's whisper was harsh, but his eyes were panicked. According to the note, Dr. Seaman wouldn't return to Washington for three days, and with each passing hour, the scandal of Dimitri's humiliation might reach American shores.

Natalia shoved the note back into its envelope. "Let's head to our suite and discuss it in private."

It took three bellhops to wheel their luggage to the suite. Poppy had brought two steamer trunks for her day and evening gowns, plus ten hat boxes so that each gown had a coordinating hat.

Their suite was lavishly appointed with a parlor, a formal dining area, and a separate alcove for a tea table. They each had their own bedroom, but Natalia forced herself to sit with Poppy in the tea alcove while the bellhops and two ladies' maids unpacked their clothing. Poppy chattered about the frumpy gown worn by a matron in the lobby while Natalia kept a worried eye trained on Dimitri as he paced before the windows. He wore a suit with a satin waistcoat and gold watch chain, looking every inch the European aristocrat, but she saw the vulnerability beneath the fine tailoring. He looked anxious as he rubbed his hands and adjusted the sleeves of his coat. His face twisted in disgust as he examined his wrists.

"Natalia, I don't know the word in English for this, but I

get them when I am nervous," he said, pulling back his cuffs to expose red, inflamed skin.

"It looks like hives," she replied. Dimitri was usually so flagrantly charming that it hurt to see him this anxious. "Try to quit scratching."

"It hurts when I scratch, but it hurts more when I don't."

"Let me send for a bowl of warm milk," she said. "Soaking might help."

He brightened. "Excellent idea! I always feel better when you take care of me." He shucked his jacket and rolled up his sleeves, revealing the red splotches tracking up his arm. In short order, a bellhop arrived with a pitcher of warmed milk, and Natalia dipped handkerchiefs in it to lay across Dimitri's forearms.

"I worry that news of my disgrace will leak before Dr. Seaman returns," Dimitri said. "It will be hard to claim an upper hand from such a position. Natalia, you missed a spot on my elbow."

"I can do a better job," Poppy said.

"No, no. It feels better when Natalia does it. I think I need a manicure, as well. My cuticles are bad again."

Natalia fixed the handkerchief and rubbed oil into his nails while she thought. Dr. Seaman's absence was a problem, but she was clever and could adjust their plan of attack. Dimitri was right. It would be harder to make progress if his reputation was in tatters.

"What if *we* released news of your disgrace to the press?" she suggested. "If we get ahead of the story, we can claim the moral high ground by revealing what happened."

"Oh, please don't!" Poppy gasped. "That would be a disaster. An embarrassment of epic proportions."

Dimitri looked sick. "Look, my hives are getting worse even thinking about such a thing."

It was true. Before her eyes, the red patches on Dimitri's forearms darkened and grew larger. She sighed and dipped another handkerchief into the warmed milk to exchange it with a cooled cloth. She wouldn't expose Dimitri without his consent, but she had to do something. She was a woman of status and connections. Surely she could use them to get the upper hand.

By the time the next batch of milk had cooled, she had a plan.

"I think we should go directly to Count Cassini at the Russian embassy," she said. "Today, if possible."

"Without Dr. Scaman?" Dimitri asked in surprise.

She nodded. "If I suggest the bank has misgivings about continued funding of the Trans-Siberian, he will fall over himself to accept an appointment with me."

Dimitri shifted uneasily. "Count Cassini probably knows of my trial and public humiliation. I need more allies before he learns of my presence here."

"He doesn't need to know who you are," she said. "I can introduce you by your patronym." Like all Russian aristocrats, Dimitri had an impressively long name, a combination of his given name, his father's name, and a collection of saint names, but there was no need to introduce him by that mouthful.

"My mother calls me Dimitri Mikhailovich when she is angry with me. It could work, but I still don't like it."

"Does Count Cassini speak English?" Poppy asked.

The innocent question seemed to make Dimitri wilt. He threw off the wet handkerchiefs and began pacing, flinging droplets of milk as he gestured.

"Count Cassini speaks English, French, German, Italian, and Chinese," he said. "He is brilliant. It is said he has so many medals that when he stands beneath a chandelier, he glitters like the Milky Way. We don't stand a chance of getting the better of him without more allies on our side."

"We have the *truth* on our side," Natalia said. She tossed him a towel to dry his arms. It was time to prepare for battle. "If Count Cassini is so intelligent, he will fear you more than you fear him. The czar and his imperial forces silenced you once, but you have come six thousand miles, most of it alone, hungry, and driven by nothing but your need to survive long enough to shout your story to the world. You had nothing and nobody on your side, but not anymore. You have powerful friends behind you, and today we begin backing Count Cassini into a corner and using him to turn the tide in our favor."

Dimitri's eyes gleamed with barely leashed energy. "Natalia, you are magnificent."

The air felt electric. She beamed at him across the expanse of the hotel suite, breathless simply from looking at him.

"The two of you need to strive for a little decorum," Poppy said, throwing ice water on them. "It's embarrassing even to be in the same room with you."

Natalia cleared her throat. It was mortifying to admit, but Poppy was right. Today wasn't the time to indulge her infatuation with Dimitri. Today they needed to begin shifting the balance of power to Dimitri's side in his battle against the czar.

Once again, Dimitri was impressed with Natalia's instinct for business. Her prediction about Count Cassini's willingness to accept her blunt demand for a meeting had been correct. They were told to arrive at the embassy at three o'clock for a private appointment with the ambassador to discuss funding for the Trans-Siberian Railway.

Poppy announced she was exhausted from the travel and refused to accompany them to the embassy, which was a relief. Dimitri didn't want Poppy underfoot and happily agreed that she was entitled to a nap after the long journey.

It was an unusually balmy day for mid-April. They rode with the carriage top rolled down so he could see Washington, which looked much nicer than New York. The tree-lined avenues, the monuments, and the open public squares all reminded him of Saint Petersburg. The Russian embassy was in a palatial building set back from the street by a wide lawn. The front doors were lavishly embellished, and everything carried a whiff of typical Russian grandeur.

What wasn't typical was their hostess. Countess Cassini was only eighteen years old. The coldly beautiful girl wore a loose gown of green silk that barely clung to respectability, but her jewels were appalling. A thick choker of Byzantine gold encircled her neck, and matching chandelier earrings dangled on each side of her gamine face.

"My uncle will be with us shortly," she said in heavily accented English as she led them to a tea table in the parlor. The girl waited for a footman to pull out a chair before she lowered herself onto it, her back as straight as a yardstick. A copper samovar heavily embellished with gemstones graced the center of the table. "Count Cassini likes for me to meet his visitors first. He believes everyone should have a nice tea before enduring diplomatic toil."

So the rumors were true. Count Cassini had elevated this brassy child to be his hostess. The American secretary of state claimed that despite the Cassini family's Italian origin, they were as Russian as borscht and lied with fabulous virtuosity. So far, Dimitri concurred. Titles in Russia were sometimes loosely distributed, but even so, it was odd to have a girl this young serve as a hostess. Nevertheless, he played along. He wasn't here to judge the count's strange relationship with this young woman but to force acknowledgment of what happened at the Amur River.

The countess poured the tea with a perfect display of grace, but she cast furtive glances at Natalia throughout. The two women could not be more different. While the countess dressed with theatrical abandon, Natalia wore one of her painfully restrictive business suits, cinched in at the waist and sporting a slim necktie tucked into a silk vest.

"You have business with my uncle?" the countess asked as she handed a teacup to Natalia.

Natalia nodded as she accepted the cup. "I handle the Russian investments for the Blackstone Bank. There are several issues the ambassador should know about."

"Ladies do not interfere with such things in Russia," the girl replied with a hint of disdain, but she brightened when a little white spaniel came bounding into the room, yapping with fervor. She lifted the dog to cuddle on her lap. Dimitri wanted to toss the ill-mannered beast outside, but he was supposed to be nothing more than Natalia's assistant, so he sat by obediently.

Count Cassini soon joined them. Dimitri and Natalia rose, but the girl remained in her seat, proud as a queen.

The count was a middle-aged man who wore his steel-gray hair ruthlessly groomed. A collection of medals glittered on his chest, and he greeted them with the utmost formality. He went directly to Natalia.

"Miss Blackstone?" he asked, and she held out her hand. The count took it and gave her a little bow.

"Thank you for meeting with us," Natalia said with admirable ease, although it shouldn't surprise Dimitri. Natalia had been raised since birth to be comfortable around robber barons, politicians, and dignitaries. "I have brought my consultant on Russian business, Mr. Dimitri Mikhailovich. We both have an interest in ensuring the success of the Trans-Siberian Railway, so I am grateful for the opportunity to discuss our concerns with you."

The count's face cooled a fraction. He gave a brusque nod to the countess, who prepared a cup of tea for him. He looked carefully at Dimitri but gave no sign of recognition as he accepted a teacup from the countess.

"The Blackstones should have no worries about the progress of the railroad," Count Cassini said. "I gather its construction is surpassing all expectations."

Natalia nodded. "So far, but I am concerned that there may be repercussions from the Boxer Rebellion in China."

Count Cassini turned his attention to Dimitri. "Have you been telling her tales?" he asked in Russian.

Shifting into Russian in the middle of a conversation was astonishingly rude and surprising for a diplomat, but Dimitri answered in the same language. "Miss Blackstone is well read in international affairs, so I did not need to inform her of the Boxer Rebellion."

"Tell her it had no impact on the railroad and we are progressing according to plan. I shall contact her father to seek reassurance that there will be no delay in his payments to the builders."

"It is actually Miss Blackstone who is managing the railroad account. You should know that she is fluent in Russian and can understand everything we are saying."

Count Cassini blanched but recovered quickly, sending a conciliatory glance toward Natalia. "My pardon, ma'am. The Russian people are grateful for our long and productive partnership with your father's bank."

"Thank you," Natalia replied, continuing to speak in Russian. "I am concerned with the southern leg of the railroad that cuts through Manchuria. The treaty negotiated in 1858 grants the Chinese people who settled north of the river the right to live in peace."

Count Cassini bristled. "Ma'am, having served as the ambassador to China for five years, I don't need a tutorial from you on the Treaty of Aigun."

Dimitri clenched his fists beneath the table. It was hard to calmly accept Count Cassini's insulting tone, but he had to remember that for today he was not an aristocrat, only Natalia's consultant. He swallowed back his ire as Natalia spoke.

"I cannot force you to acknowledge the massacre at the Amur River, but I can withdraw financial support for the railroad if we think more atrocities are likely to occur."

"There were no atrocities," Count Cassini insisted. "If your bank decides to withdraw from one of the most profitable investments in the world, we can go to the Rothschilds or J.P. Morgan."

Natalia did not soften. "Yes, but my father is known for his voracious desire to make money. If he pulls out of the Trans-Siberian amidst rumors of atrocities, it will send a clarion call to the world that *something* happened out there in those remote territories. Banks will be reluctant to dive in where others have pulled out."

Count Cassini's eyes crackled with fire. "I do not conduct business with women," he said tightly. "Come, Mr. Mikhailovich.

Let us go to my study where we may discuss the railway in cooler tones and leave the ladies to their tea."

Natalia blanched, but Dimitri sent her a warning shake of his head, praying she would understand. Count Cassini's chauvinism was too ingrained to permit a reprimand from a woman.

"I will join you when our business is concluded," he told Natalia, hating the need to cave in to the count's boorishness. Today they needed to play by Russian rules.

Natalia understood and had the dignity of a saint as she nodded her consent. Dimitri paused for a moment, locking eyes with her. How easily they understood each other, and he couldn't be prouder of how gracefully she stepped aside to let him take the lead.

Dimitri followed the ambassador through marble corridors until they reached a private office. Count Cassini ushered Dimitri inside the book-lined study, where an enormous standing globe dominated one corner of the room and the other featured a telescope pointing out a window.

The door closed behind them, and the count took his seat behind a desk that was as wide and impressive as the prow of a ship. He opened the lid on a box of cigars and offered Dimitri one. "I admire your patience, Mr. Mikhailovich. It must be maddening to report to a woman."

Dimitri declined the cigar but answered the count's question. "I have found Miss Blackstone to be a woman of remarkable good sense in the years I have worked with her."

Count Cassini clipped the end of his cigar and leaned forward to light it from a jeweled table lighter that looked like it had come from the Fabergé studio. He took a series of rapid puffs on the cigar to ensure a proper light before leaning back in his chair to peer at Dimitri through the cloud of smoke.

"She may be a woman of good sense, but she is mistaken about what happened in Manchuria. The Russian army is entitled to maintain peace along the route of the Trans-Siberian. There were no atrocities or broken treaties."

"We both know there were witnesses," Dimitri said. "Russian witnesses who are willing to come forward. Dr. Seaman gave you one such report that you have already dismissed, but there will be others."

Count Cassini drew a long pull on his cigar and blew a stream directly into Dimitri's face. "And will that come from you, Count Sokolov?"

Dimitri tried not to let his surprise show but failed. Count Cassini was matter-of-fact as he continued speaking.

"I knew that Count Sokolov had escaped his prison sentence and assumed he'd try to find his way to the Blackstones if he made it out of the wilderness. Your instinct for survival is commendable. Given the way Miss Blackstone looks at you with her heart in her face, it appears you have her in the palm of your hand."

Dimitri ignored the implied insult and went on the offensive. "It must be an embarrassment that the treaty you were honor-bound to enforce was so wantonly ignored by the army."

Count Cassini shrugged. "I was on the other side of the world when it happened. *If* it happened," he amended quickly.

"We both know it did."

"If it did, there is nothing you or I can do about it now."

Anger began to simmer, but Dimitri restrained it. "I lost everything by refusing to ignore what happened that day. Everything except my honor."

His words did not cause a flicker of regret on the count's face. "And I intend to save *my* honor by protecting the czar. No one will know what treaties might have been violated unless Russian officials acknowledge it, and I can assure you that will never happen."

"I've only just arrived in America. The Blackstones know about the massacre and will support my allegation."

"Ah yes, the Blackstones. Tell me, is Natalia your mistress?" The count spoke casually, and Dimitri bristled as he replied.

"Miss Blackstone is a woman of impeccable character, both in public and in private."

"I saw the way you looked at each other. The unspoken communication you share is generally something that takes years to develop."

"It is true that we have worked together for years. We were on opposite sides of the world, but we have always been of one mind. One heart."

"Then marry her," Count Cassini said. "Build a new life here. America is a wonderful country, and you can never go back to Russia, can you?"

The statement felt like the slash of a saber, all the more painful because it was true. Dimitri would never see Mirosa or his mother again. The unquenchable longing for home welled up inside him, but he wouldn't indulge it while locked in battle with a man determined to defend the czar.

He spoke with the steely determination forged during thousands of miles of deprivation. "You are correct that the past cannot be changed, but I will fight to ensure it never happens again. Will you honor the 1858 treaty that guarantees the rights of the Chinese settlers north of the river?"

"Myself? Of course I shall! It is already in the books, and I would never do anything to tarnish its sterling reputation."

That meant the count intended to do nothing. Dimitri's lip curled. "I don't know how you can sleep at night."

"I have no difficulty sleeping, and neither should you. You survived an ordeal few men could endure. You should count your blessings and celebrate. Marry that woman and resign yourself to a life of everlasting luxury here in America. You could do worse."

"Thousands of villagers are dead, and you want me to look the other way."

The count carefully set down his cigar, adjusted his vest, and leaned across the desk, piercing Dimitri with a cold glare. "I will destroy your ability to find a new life in America if you fight me on this. I can incinerate your reputation with a few carefully placed rumors."

"I've already had my reputation torn to shreds in my homeland. I survived it once. I can do it again."

"Then I'll go after *her*," the ambassador said. "Women's reputations are far more fragile, and the damage will last forever."

Dimitri froze. Natalia was his greatest vulnerability. He'd already resigned himself to losing everything in Russia, but the prospect of Natalia's ruination because of her association with him was unthinkable. "You must be a very small man if you need to wage war on women to achieve your ends."

"I am a *smart* man," Count Cassini asserted. "History is written by the winners. You can cooperate with the winning side and live a comfortable life in America . . . or not. Your decision."

Dimitri could not bargain while Natalia's reputation was on the line, which meant that unless he devised a way to get the better of Count Cassini, the ambassador had him pinned.

23

Natalia didn't like being separated from Dimitri. When Count Cassini lured him away to a private meeting, she initially feared for him but soon thought better of it. She had come to Washington because Dimitri needed guidance navigating the American government, but in dealing with a fellow aristocrat from Russia, he was the expert, not she.

Besides, perhaps she could take this opportunity to glean something from Count Cassini's "niece." At this point, it was impossible to tell if the young woman's rudeness was calculated or simply stupid.

"Come meet my other dogs," the girl said the moment they finished their tea. "They're French spaniels, and I love them more than anything on earth."

Natalia followed the countess through several twisting corridors, all of them lavishly decorated. Unsmiling Russian icons in gilt frames blanketed the wall of one hallway. Another was laden with antique firearms, battle-axes, and swords raised to form an archway down the hall. At last they entered a room at the back of the embassy covered entirely in blue-delft tiles where a cluster of yapping dogs climbed over each other in their eagerness for attention.

"My darlings!" the countess exclaimed as she dropped to

her knees, letting the dogs swarm around her. They were small, each less than a foot high, and covered in long, silky white fur. Natalia slid toward the nearest wall. She didn't mind dogs but had little experience with them.

The countess scooped one into her arms, kissed its snout, then rose to show it to Natalia. "Isn't he precious? I find dogs so much more interesting than people, don't you?"

Natalia silently wondered if the girl was meeting the right sort of people, but she smiled anyway. "They certainly seem to adore you."

"Yes, they do!" the girl enthused. "They need to be taken outside for a walk. Let's go."

She opened a door leading to a walled courtyard, and the dogs bounded for freedom. A profusion of roses and viburnum shrubs lined the enclosed garden, but the ground was littered with dog waste and spots where they'd dug up the soil. Even now, one of them was joyously scratching at the ground and flinging sprays of dirt in Natalia's direction.

"Stop that, Apollo." Countess Cassini laughed but made no move to restrain the dog. She scooped up another dog to jostle like a child as she paced in the garden.

Natalia tried to initiate a discussion about life at the embassy, but the girl wouldn't even look at her as she coddled her dogs.

"Ahem."

Natalia turned to see an attractive middle-aged woman standing in the doorway. She wore a fine gown of indigo bombazine, but the apron tied around her waist indicated she was probably a servant.

"Yes, Mrs. Betz?" the countess asked.

"You are needed to approve the menu for the reception honoring the wives of the diplomatic corps."

The countess sighed and set down her dog. "Must I? Those women are so tedious." She turned to Natalia. "You should see the wife of the French ambassador. Last week she wore a gown so small it made the rolls of her neck look like a stack of sausages." She proceeded to describe the rest of the woman's appearance with savage delight. It took the intervention of the housekeeper to call the malicious commentary to a halt.

"Ma'am, the menu needs to be approved before we submit a list to the grocer."

"Oh, very well," the girl said in exasperation. She turned to look Natalia in the face for the first time since they'd left the tea table. "Not all the dogs are finished with their business, so you'll stay and watch them, won't you?"

She didn't wait for a reply before following Mrs. Betz inside, the door slamming behind her.

Natalia was left alone with the dogs. She plopped onto a garden chair. Never had she been so thoroughly disrespected by two different people, all within the space of a few minutes. Although Natalia had been born into a similar level of opulence, her mother raised her to be respectful toward everybody. Galina was a gentle soul who had been born into poverty, and perhaps that was why she took such care to insist that Natalia see humanity in everyone, no matter their station in life. In the coming years, Natalia intended to do the same for little Alexander because she doubted Poppy would.

A light mist began falling, and it soon turned into a drizzle. The dogs were done with their business, and Natalia didn't intend to let the rain ruin her perfectly styled chignon. She opened the door and gestured for the dogs to come inside. They didn't like the rain either and scrambled back into the blue-tiled room, their yips and scrabbling claws sounding harsh in the otherwise empty room.

What now? She let herself out of the blue-tiled room and into the dim silence of the embassy, following the same route of decorated corridors so she could wait for Dimitri in the front lobby.

She paused in the hall filled with antique weaponry to admire a heavily embellished battle-ax. All was quiet, but from down the hall came the muffled voice of the countess speaking to the older servant.

Natalia wandered closer to hear. The door was open, and

Mrs. Betz sat at a modest desk. Was it the housekeeper's office? Natalia was about to continue to the main room when she overheard her name and came to a halt.

"They say she is the daughter of some rich banker," the girl said, and the housekeeper replied too faintly for Natalia to hear.

She ought to feel guilty for eavesdropping, but she leaned in closer, taking cover behind a suit of armor.

"I don't care how rich she is," Countess Cassini continued. "She speaks Russian like a peasant. She has a gutter accent, like she belongs pulling potatoes out of the dirt instead of visiting embassies."

"Shh," the housekeeper scolded. "It is said her mother was a famous ballerina from Moscow."

"A ballerina? Little better than a prostitute, then."

Anger began roiling inside Natalia at hearing her mother slandered by that hideous girl. Galina Blackstone had more poise in her pinky finger than Countess Cassini possessed in her entire body. Galina was a gentle person who was kind to everyone, and Natalia seethed at the insult.

Did her mother really have a peasant's accent? And did Natalia? It shouldn't matter, but she'd always been so proud of her ability to speak Russian, and no one had ever commented on her accent before. How dare that entitled brat speak so disrespectfully of people who'd never done her any harm.

But eavesdroppers had no right to complain if they heard something offensive. Natalia swallowed back her indignation and continued listening . . . and what she heard over the next five minutes made her eyes grow wide with astonishment.

Natalia still smarted over what had been said about her accent, but she tried to set it aside as she saw Dimitri heading toward her down the corridor. His face looked like a thundercloud, dark and furious. There was no sign of Count Cassini.

"Well?" she asked as he approached.

Dimitri shook his head. "It was not a profitable meeting."

A weight settled on her chest. She wanted to escape from this dim, oppressively decorated building. Outside, the drizzle had turned into rain, and by the time Dimitri succeeded in hailing a cab, her chignon was sliding down the back of her neck. It started unrolling as she climbed inside the carriage and plopped into the corner. This day was becoming a disaster from beginning to end. She tugged the long fall of her hair free and began blotting it with a handkerchief.

"Tell me what happened," she asked Dimitri once the carriage began moving.

"He is a vile person," Dimitri said. "He knows what happened but has no intention of acknowledging it. He said that if I tried to announce it to the world, he wouldn't bother with my reputation until he first destroyed yours."

She caught her breath. "He wouldn't dare."

"He would," Dimitri said, his voice smoldering.

"How could he? I don't have any skeletons in my closet."

A tic throbbed in his jaw, and his eyes turned to flint. "He made it quite clear that he is prepared to manufacture such skeletons, and given that women's reputations are easily shattered, he knows he has us cornered."

Everything Dimitri said was true, and even her father, with all his worldly power, could not stop a carefully planted malicious rumor. It made her want to fight back. Count Cassini had his own vulnerabilities, as she learned while eavesdropping. Given the torrid gossip flying around Washington, nobody believed the countess was his niece, and now Natalia had proof.

"I overheard something interesting," she said. "Something that might insulate us from any threats wielded by the count."

Dimitri quirked a single eyebrow in question.

"I overheard Countess Cassini speaking with the housekeeper at the embassy. They thought they were alone, and she called the housekeeper 'Mother.' In the course of the conversation, it became quite clear that the count is her father."

Dimitri let out a low whistle as a look of grim satisfaction came over him. "It is not unusual for a man in his position to dally with the servants, but rarely do they take the children under their wing and elevate them to such a position."

Natalia stared at the rain dribbling down the window. Speaking about that horrible young woman reawakened the insecurity planted by her vindictive chatter. From the moment Natalia met Dimitri in the port of San Francisco, he had made her feel dazzling. "*Natalia, you are beautiful,*" he said only seconds after meeting her, and she felt beautiful whenever he was near.

She never knew that all that time she had a gutter accent.

"What is bothering you?" Dimitri asked, and she shifted her attention to him. He would not lie to her.

"When I speak Russian, do I have an accent?"

A spark of amusement flashed across his face. "Of course you do."

"But I learned Russian at the same time I learned English, and my mother said I sounded as fluent as a native. So what kind of accent do I have?"

He shrugged and glanced around the carriage as though searching for an answer. "You sound like someone from Moscow," he finally said. "Like your mother, I suppose."

The carriage jostled and swayed over cobblestones, and the rain picked up speed, spattering against the windows. It sounded like he didn't intend to say anything else, which meant she had to pry it out of him.

"I overheard that awful girl say I have a gutter accent. Do I?"

Dimitri's eyes softened. "Dearest Natalia, you sound like the woman I adore. What else do you want me to say?"

"You can tell me the truth."

"The truth is that yours is the dearest voice in the world to me," he replied.

"Even with a gutter accent."

He nodded, the hint of amusement back. "Yes, even with a gutter accent."

She folded her arms and glared out the window, unaccountably upset. It shouldn't matter, but she'd always been proud of her ability to speak Russian. That awful girl had spat on it. Spat on her mother too. Natalia liked to think of herself as a prim and efficient business analyst whose knowledge of Russia was a priceless asset to her father . . . when in truth she showed her peasant heritage with every word she spoke.

Dimitri set a hand on her knee, but she couldn't bring herself to look at him. When he spoke, his voice was gentle with affection.

"Natalia, it is only a mosquito bite."

It felt like a ray of sunshine pierced the clouds. Why had she been letting the opinion of a vain, spoiled girl matter so much?

She beamed at Dimitri. "Thank you for that."

He slid off his bench and rotated to fill the space beside her. With a thumb and forefinger, he tipped her chin to look at him.

"You do not have an elegant accent," he said. "You sound like a woman of Russia, a strong woman who can be depended on to endure the longest winter and shoulder any burden. You traveled across the country because you feared someone was trying to impersonate me. You are strength and valor and compassion. If I was a composer, I would write a symphony to express how grand you are."

His kiss both thrilled and reassured her, and she sank into it with abandon. Maybe they didn't have a future, but they had today, and it was precious. When the carriage arrived at their hotel, Dimitri instructed the cabbie to drive around the block a few times, and they went back to kissing. Natalia settled into his arms and smiled against his mouth.

Could Dimitri be the one? Perhaps being a part of Alexander's life would be enough for her. Or they could adopt a child of their own. Dimitri's condition didn't have to dictate her life. Over the past few years, she had wondered if she would ever find the right man. It would be the ultimate irony if she was already being courted by the love of her life from the other side of the world. Dimitri would forever miss his homeland, but perhaps the two of them could find a way to create a wonderful life for themselves here in America.

24

Natalia awoke the following morning in a fog of happiness, blissfully anticipating showing Dimitri the sights of Washington over the next few days while awaiting Dr. Seaman's return. Today they would climb the Washington Monument so Dimitri could enjoy the panoramic view of the city, then visit the Smithsonian.

But, of course, Poppy had to ruin it all.

"You're not to go sightseeing without a chaperone, young lady," Poppy said from the breakfast table in their hotel suite.

"Poppy, you're three months older than me," Natalia pointed out. "I don't think you're in a position to wag your finger and call me a 'young lady.'"

"You are both young ladies," Dimitri said. "The three of us shall see the Washington Monument together, and all of society shall marvel at how I have managed to acquire a charming young lady for each arm."

"Not because of Natalia," Poppy said. "She was born old and stodgy. Natalia, sit down and stop making everyone nervous with that wretched pacing. The Washington Monument doesn't even open to visitors for another hour."

A copy of *Rand McNally and Co.'s Handy Guide to Washington* lay open on the table, and Natalia reluctantly joined them to skim the guidebook while Poppy continued to complain.

"Why must we go to the top of the monument anyway? It's too much of a climb."

Dimitri saved Natalia from answering. "It is imperative that I go to the top. I have walked across the Brooklyn Bridge and traversed the country from coast to coast. I must now scale the Washington Monument, or my life will never be complete."

Natalia continued flipping through the guidebook, searching for a way to dispose of Poppy so she could have Dimitri all to herself. It wasn't that she intended to do anything salacious with him, but she didn't like sharing him with Poppy. It didn't take long to find her stepmother's Achilles heel. Even after three years of marriage to one of the nation's wealthiest men, Poppy's thirst for buying things remained unquenched.

Natalia spoke with studied indifference as she consulted the guidebook. "It looks like we'll pass the city's prime shopping district on our way to the monument. Antiques, jewels, furs, a gourmet chocolate shop—my goodness, the list goes on and on."

Poppy snatched the guidebook, a feral glint in her eyes as she scanned the offerings. As expected, she found a humanitarian justification to shop. "Your grandfather's birthday is coming up," she said. "Perhaps I should forgo the trip to the monument to be sure he is suitably honored."

Natalia silently rejoiced. "That would be very thoughtful."

It didn't take long to gather their belongings for a day of sightseeing and shopping. Natalia wore a new hat with a wide brim that made her feel like the most feminine woman in the world. The sun was shining, and she was in love. The day couldn't be more perfect.

After stepping out of the elevator, they headed to the concierge to request a carriage, but before they could reach the service desk, a trim man wearing an army uniform came striding toward them.

"Count Sokolov?" he asked.

Dimitri gave the other man a slight bow. "You have me at a disadvantage, sir."

"Dr. Louis Seaman." He introduced himself with a relieved smile. "I was called to Philadelphia on an emergency, but instead of a cholera outbreak, all they had was a case of tainted beef. I am eager to hear what you have to say about the incident at the Amur River. Come! We must confer right away."

Sightseeing would have to wait. Something far more important was about to unfold.

Dimitri led Dr. Seaman upstairs to their suite, where he and Natalia cleared the remnants of their breakfast from the table so they could speak. Poppy had no interest in meeting the adventurous physician and took herself off to go shopping. Once seated at the tea table, Dr. Seaman explained how he had been on a routine assignment to observe Japanese medical innovations when a trio of Russian soldiers arrived in Tokyo, carrying tales of a shocking atrocity.

"One of the soldiers told me he could have walked across the river on the bodies of the dead," Dr. Seaman said. "He took advantage of the chaos to desert the army. He said he would rather live a life in exile than carry out those orders. The other two soldiers witnessed the events as well."

Dimitri's breakfast curdled in his stomach as memories rose to the surface. The stench of that day and the drone of flies buzzing in the air would haunt him forever. Those three soldiers in Japan could confirm what he'd witnessed. He bowed his head. *Thank you, God, for the bravery of those soldiers.*

Dr. Seaman continued speaking. "I submitted a report of what I'd heard to the Department of State, but it didn't go far. The only evidence I had was the word of three deserters. But if a Russian aristocrat can confirm their account with an eyewitness testimony? This time the report will be taken more seriously."

"Will it be enough to pressure the czar into honoring the treaty with the Chinese?" Natalia asked.

"Count Cassini can answer that question better than I can," Dr. Seaman replied, then turned his attention to Dimitri. "Count Cassini is fiercely loyal to Czar Nicholas. They depend on each other to maintain an idealized image of Russian strength and stability. You can throw a wrench into their illusion by revealing how they tried to humiliate you for daring to speak the truth. Surprise them. Go on the offense by walking into the highest halls of government and proclaiming your experience with a megaphone. If Count Cassini senses the Americans are losing trust in the Russians, he will scramble to repair the damage and provide cover for the czar."

Dimitri met Natalia's eyes across the table. "Do you believe we can gather enough people in the government to pressure Count Cassini to use his influence on our behalf?"

"I know we can," she said in a voice brimming with confidence.

For the first time since his trial, Dimitri was no longer ashamed of what had happened to him, but was instead ready to turn the tables on the czar and go on the attack.

Natalia was amazed by the speed at which Dr. Seaman's plan gathered momentum. The doctor had connections in the military, the government, the press, and high society. He knew which reporter would write sympathetic newspaper articles and which Washington socialite could host a high-profile banquet in honor of a daring Russian aristocrat.

In short order, Dimitri was invited to testify before a congressional committee on Far Eastern affairs. Six congressmen sat on one side of the polished mahogany table while Dr. Seaman and Dimitri sat opposite them. The committee members appeared spellbound as Dimitri reported what he'd witnessed at the Amur River and the harsh retaliation he endured after refusing to participate.

Natalia had an excellent view of the proceedings from a seat in the gallery above the committee room. Dimitri was flawlessly groomed and attired, but that couldn't entirely mask his gaunt frame or the hollows beneath his cheekbones. For all his fine manners, he was less than a month past the harrowing ordeal of his escape, making his testimony all the more compelling.

After his congressional presentation, Dimitri left the committee room, and reporters swarmed around him in the hallway, pelting him with questions. They were far less mannerly than the congressmen. Instead of international treaties, they wanted to know what Dimitri ate in the wilderness, where he slept, and what it was like to live on the run from the czar. Natalia hugged the back wall, her heart bursting with pride as she watched Dimitri joke and banter with the journalists.

She wasn't able to accompany Dimitri to his private meeting with the secretary of state, but he recounted the entire meeting for her that evening as they dined in the Willard Hotel's impressive dining room.

"Secretary Hay is not an admirer of Count Cassini," Dimitri said, twirling a crystal goblet. "He claims Cassini is clever, crafty, and a master at manipulating affairs to produce whatever outcome he wants. The secretary assured me he will convey my story directly to President Roosevelt."

More meetings followed in the coming days. On Tuesday he met with ranking members in the army to discuss the border skirmishes between Russia and China, as well as his impressions of the Boxer Rebellion. That night he was invited to speak before the National Geographic Society, a gentleman's club of academics, explorers, and cartographers. They met at the Cosmos Club, where Natalia admired the walls of maps and standing floor globes. Unlike the army officers who wanted military insight, these men were most interested in Dimitri's trek across Siberia and his friendship with Temujin. They wanted to know about the various ethnic groups he encountered and how people managed to barter without a common language.

As news of Dimitri's heroic journey across Siberia gained circulation, so did his fame. Each group he visited seemed to have a different reason to be intrigued by his story. He was the guest speaker at a meeting of the Red Cross, who wanted to know if there were orphans who had escaped the massacre and how to send help to the survivors. Natalia also accompanied Dimitri to a luncheon hosted by a group of congressmen's wives, where the discussion quickly devolved into unsavory gossip about Count Cassini's "niece."

"Have you met her?" one of the wives asked.

"She served us tea," Natalia replied, reluctant to fuel the gossip. Her and Dimitri's objective was to force the count to act, not to disclose an affair with his housekeeper.

"If I have to kowtow to that wretched teenaged girl one more time, I shall be tempted to burn down the embassy," the congressman's wife said, and plenty of other women at the luncheon agreed.

After five days of engagements, Dimitri had become so popular that their calendar was filled with invitations from morning to night. A professor from Georgetown asked Dimitri to speak to his classes, and reporters from the AP and Reuters both wrote flattering profiles of him. Getting picked up by the AP wire meant Dimitri's story was now being published in newspapers all across America. Reuters was the British equivalent, so the story was being published in Europe too. It didn't matter that Dimitri's title had been revoked. He was consistently referred to as Count Sokolov, and his courage in the face of his trial and punishment only added to his heroism.

Dimitri was vain enough to love the attention. One evening he escorted Natalia and Poppy into the dining room at the Willard, and someone in the back of the room stood to raise a toast to him. All the other diners applauded, and a few came over to shake his hand. Poppy basked in Dimitri's fame, but Natalia no longer cared about her stepmother's embarrassing need to claim the limelight alongside Count Sokolov. Dimitri deserved every bit of acclaim being showered on him.

During the dessert course, a Russian officer wearing full regalia arrived in the dining room to hand-deliver a message to Dimitri.

"Count Cassini requests a private meeting," the officer said, clicking the heels of his polished boots together and proffering an engraved invitation with a formal bow.

"When?" Dimitri asked, caught off guard but not displeased.

"Now."

Dimitri arrived at the embassy alone, since bringing Natalia might be seen as a needless provocation. All he cared about was forcing Czar Nicholas to acknowledge that the 1858 treaty had been violated and to renew his commitment to honor the treaty in the future.

It was dark by the time Dimitri arrived at the embassy. This time he wasn't greeted by a belligerent teenaged girl but by the ambassador himself.

"Count Sokolov," Count Cassini said with the tiniest of bows as he met Dimitri in the sweeping front hall of the embassy.

Dimitri responded with a matching infinitesimal bow. Count Cassini escorted him down the meandering hallways and into his private office. The normal formalities of offering him a drink and a cigar were offered and accepted, and then Count Cassini took a seat behind his desk.

"I want you to know how shocked I am to learn the full details of the events in Manchuria," he began. "Such a tragedy."

"And yet you seemed to know all about it when I saw you last week."

Count Cassini gave him a thin smile, the smoke from the tip of his cigar spiraling upward as the pungent scent filled the dim office. "As a sophisticated man of the world, you understand how the public positions of the imperial government may sometimes differ from actual historical events. The wonderful thing about history is that it is so easy to rewrite. And perhaps it is time to rewrite what happened last summer."

So far, the Russians had billed the atrocity as a skirmish in which soldiers defended themselves against Chinese belligerents affiliated with the Boxer Rebellion. There was no mention of the thousands of civilians who met their death in the river.

"And how do you propose we rewrite history?" Dimitri asked.

"There was a miscommunication between Moscow and the eastern outposts. All a misunderstanding, but it won't happen again."

"No acknowledgment of guilt? No officers to be punished?"

"Correct." The ambassador's statement was emphatic.

"Not good enough," Dimitri said.

Count Cassini's face hardened. "It is time to make myself clear. You need me, and you need the czar if you want to see those treaties with China honored. I don't care if you paint yourself a hero in the United States. Go to the parties and speeches in your honor. Bask in the celebrity that easily impressed Americans wish to bestow upon you. But in the back of your mind, you know there are thousands of people living in rural isolation on the other side of the world. Those people wish only to tend their fields and raise their children in peace. Simple people with modest desires. Isn't it ironic that their ability to have that life will be decided right here in this room while we smoke cigars that cost more than they earn in a month?"

The ambassador took a long pull on his cigar, then blew it out with a laugh in an attempt to break the tension. "Come, Dimitri. It was a miscommunication, and what happened to you was a series of unfortunate events. Let us put it to right. The czar is more than willing to affirm the ongoing status of the 1858 treaty and will assign ownership of Mirosa back to you as a sign of goodwill. He is prepared to restore your title, as well."

Dimitri's heart skipped a beat. He hadn't expected this, and a wave of hope surged, but he held tightly to his impassive expression. There were untold millions of people in the world, most of whom had no control over their lives. Their safety was decided in palaces and embassies thousands of miles away. Today he was a hero, but his celebrity would soon fade, and his ability to demand change would deteriorate.

He couldn't afford to wait for the perfect deal. Labeling the atrocity as a miscommunication was acceptable, provided a renewed commitment to the 1858 treaty was honored.

"When can I have it in writing?" he asked.

Count Cassini gave a negligent shrug. "These niceties can take time. Provided we all get along, I would expect the official word to come from the czar's secretaries within a few weeks."

Dimitri set his cigar on the crystal tray and stood. "Then in a few weeks we will shake on the deal. Not before."

The ambassador was just as intransigent. "And in the meantime, you will publicly state that Czar Nicholas is entirely innocent of wrongdoing and had no knowledge of the incident."

Dimitri had yet to publicly attack the czar, but it was too soon to take anything off the table. "When I have everything in writing," he said again. "Not before."

Neither he nor the ambassador had exactly what they wanted, but the end was in sight. And most amazingly, Mirosa was going to be his again.

Knowing that Dimitri was meeting with Count Cassini filled Natalia with anxiety. Rather than twiddle her thumbs and worry, she agreed to accompany Poppy to a presentation at the Naval Observatory as they had originally planned for this evening.

The young astronomer hosting the demonstration ought to have kept her fascinated. He spoke of planets and stars and celestial comets that hurtled through space millions of miles away. And yet a vague uneasiness gripped her that she could not quite shake.

What was happening with Count Cassini? The next move in this epic chess match was happening as she sat here in a chilly, dome-shaped room while Professor Harkness described the solar system. A narrow panel in the observatory's ceiling was open to expose a sliver of the night sky. He moved a telescope the size of a cannon into position and turned dials and levers to focus lenses, then invited the guests to have a look at the moon in a way they'd never seen before.

Natalia lined her eye up before the lens. At first all she saw was a haze of white and gray, but as the professor rotated the dial, the features zoomed into sharp, crisp focus, revealing jagged craters and rocks.

"I had no idea," she whispered, her heart in her throat. What a huge and vast universe in which they lived. God showed them only a tiny fraction of it, but how wonderful that they were learning to see more.

She stood aside so Poppy could peer through the telescope lens. The sound of a door opening in the rear of the observatory caught her attention. Light from the hallway revealed the silhouette of a tall, slim man.

It was Dimitri. He probably couldn't see much in the dark room, so she closed the distance between them. He recognized her as she drew near, his face radiant.

"Natalia, I have good news," he said in a choked voice.

Her heart seized, and she squeezed his hands. "Tell me." Her voice echoed beneath the cavernous dome, but she didn't care.

"Count Cassini has yielded. He has promised to clear my name and return Mirosa. I can go home."

Her heart started breaking at the same time as she rejoiced. His arms closed around her, and she smiled against his neck. Was it possible to be happy and heartbroken at the same time? She was going to lose him, but oh, he deserved this. For the rest of his life, Dimitri deserved nothing but good things and happiness.

"Congratulations," she whispered. "Congratulations, my dearest, dearest Dimitri."

"A little decorum, please." Poppy's voice came from a few yards away, but Natalia wasn't going to let Poppy interfere with this moment.

"Let's go outside," she said.

"Are you sure?" Dimitri asked with a nod to the telescope and the cluster of people standing at its base. "You were watching the stars."

"We can watch them outside."

199

They escaped Poppy's surly glare and went up a staircase that led to the roof of the observatory and an unobstructed view of the sky. The air was crisp and cool, and a smattering of lights twinkled in the city below. Above them were millions of stars, but at the moment, all she could see was the tender affection on Dimitri's face as he smiled down at her.

"When will you go?" she asked him.

"As soon as I have official word from the czar."

The hopeful dream of a future for them began to die. That was all right. The sensible part of her always knew this day might come. She met his eyes bravely even though she wished she could cry.

"Good," she said, meaning it from the bottom of her heart. She laid her hand against his smooth, trim beard. "Why do you suddenly look so sad?" she asked.

He grabbed her hand and pressed a kiss to her palm. "Because it means I must leave you behind."

She could hardly breathe. "I'll be okay."

"Will you? I'm not sure I can say the same." He lowered their hands but kept gazing into her eyes. "Natalia, do you think you could ever be happy in Russia?"

He did not need to elaborate. She had often daydreamed about visiting Russia someday, but the thought of leaving everything behind forever wasn't an option. She would lose her family and her life's work. Russia was a highly traditional society, with no place for a woman in business.

"I don't think so," she finally said. "I belong here, just as you belong in Russia." She managed a smile, even though the combination of joy and sadness was almost too much to bear. "I've always thought there are some people who are destined to be happy while others are not. I don't mind."

His eyes gleamed. "Be careful, you are sounding very Russian."

She laughed. "I *am* part Russian. I don't entirely belong in America, but I certainly don't belong over there either. But *you*, Dimitri. You are Russian all the way down to that big, generous, and overly dramatic heart of yours. I want the world for you, and that means I want you to have Mirosa back."

He kissed her forehead, and they clung to each other, enjoying Dimitri's triumph even though it meant the beginning of the end for them.

25

Dimitri had been invited to a gala celebration at the Russian embassy for his final night in Washington. The coveted invitation was a clear sign that Count Cassini was making good on his promise to rewrite the incident in Russia as an unfortunate misunderstanding. The white-tie affair would have dozens of guests from the military, foreign embassies, and even a handful of celebrities. Archbishop Raphael, the highest-ranking patriarch of the Russian Orthodox Church, would be in attendance, as would a famed opera diva, who would sing after dinner.

Dimitri eyed himself in the mirror as he adjusted the center knot of his snow-white tie, flawlessly starched and pressed by the staff at the hotel. Opal studs and cufflinks flashed as he adjusted his black cutaway jacket. A barber had been in earlier to trim his beard, clip his hair, and apply a slight sheen of Macassar oil. Dimitri looked every inch the aristocrat, down to his buffed nails and the patent-leather dress oxfords on his feet.

And yet, while he had been indulging in the luxury of a shave and a manicure, he wondered what Temujin was doing at this exact moment. How was he coping after the amputation of his foot? Had he succeeded in buying a farm? Their friendship felt like it belonged to another lifetime, but Temujin was one of those faraway people whose life would be affected by the czar's reaffirmation of the treaty.

A knock sounded on his door. "Dimitri?" Natalia called from the other side. "The carriage is here."

He opened the door and was nearly struck mute at seeing Natalia in a watered-silk gown of ice blue that gleamed in the candlelight. The silk was gathered at the shoulders like the dress of a Grecian goddess, then swept into a slight bustle before draping in graceful folds to the floor. At last he was seeing her dressed as a real woman, all soft and elegant. Instead of a sleek chignon, her hair was amassed at her crown and tumbled down her back in a spiral of ebony curls.

"That dress would make Helen of Troy envious," he said.

A hint of color warmed her cheeks. "You exaggerate."

The way he felt for her was no exaggeration. Natalia was his opposite and equal at the same time, and the mix was enthralling. He had sensed it from the other side of the world, and now that she stood within feet of him, the sensation was overwhelming.

"Exaggerate my feelings for you? Never! You look like a goddess."

"Aren't you going to say anything nice about me?" Poppy demanded from the front room of the suite.

Poppy's nose had been out of joint ever since learning that Dimitri could only escort one lady to the Russian embassy and he'd chosen Natalia. Poppy still insisted on having her hair done and intended to treat herself to a five-course meal in the restaurant downstairs. Such behavior would be appalling for a woman in Russia's conservative society, but things were obviously different here.

"I am only sorry I cannot escort you both," he said gallantly. "With a beautiful lady on each arm, I would be the envy of the nation."

It was twilight by the time their carriage arrived at the embassy, where torches illuminated the front staircase and portico.

Guests mingled before the embassy, and to his amazement, Dimitri spotted a familiar young man with fair hair and a neatly groomed mustache. Johann Kuhn sported a few more lines around his eyes than the last time they'd been together, but his slim, athletic figure was the same.

"Johann!" Dimitri said as he lifted his hand in recognition.

His old school friend grinned. "Good to see you, Dimitri! When I heard you were the guest of honor, I finagled an invitation. How are you, my friend?"

He and Johann had attended boarding school in Zurich, where Dimitri had been sent to learn German and Johann was sent to keep him out of trouble. Their friendship flourished even though they couldn't have been more different. Dimitri wanted nothing more than to return to the rustic comfort of Mirosa, while Johann wanted to open a bottle of champagne and seek out the nearest opera house. Now Johann had become a respectable envoy from Switzerland, so perhaps miracles really did happen.

"I'm doing well," Dimitri said after returning a back-pounding hug. "Allow me to introduce Miss Natalia Blackstone. Natalia, my friend Johann is the man who helped me learn German and how to escape from a third-story dormitory room without detection."

Johann's eyes gleamed in masculine appreciation as he greeted Natalia. Dimitri watched her mingle easily with Johann and the other dignitaries on the portico. She socialized with ease, giving Dimitri confidence that she could flourish in Saint Petersburg as well. He was falling in love with her and refused to give up hope of a future for them in Russia.

"Let me introduce you to the king of Denmark," Johann said. "You'll like him. King Christian keeps ducks and pampers them like they are his children."

The middle-aged Danish king stood on the far end of the portico, facing the lush gardens while surrounded by a circle of guests who watched him in fascination. The king had his hands cupped around his mouth and made surprisingly realistic bird calls as he tried to coax a mockingbird nestled in a nearby tree to return his tweet.

Johann leaned in close to whisper in Dimitri's ear. "Let's wait to see if he can make that bird sing. He's been trying for the last ten minutes."

A dozen guests dressed in silks and glittering with diamonds watched the king try a variety of whistles and chirps while the mockingbird looked curiously at them. The bird flicked its tail feathers from side to side and finally let out a single warbling chirp.

The guests cheered in approval, causing the mockingbird to take flight, but the king was flushed with pride and accepted hearty congratulations from the onlookers. Dimitri proffered his arm to Natalia as they made their way toward the group. Johann performed the introductions, and Natalia was the epitome of elegance as she dropped into a gorgeous curtsy before the king.

King Christian nodded with approval, then turned his attention to Johann. "It looks like you've collected a few more medals since last we met."

Johann grinned and laid a hand over the bronze star dangling from a ribbon. "This one caused the gray hair you see at my temples."

He proceeded to tell how an avalanche in the Swiss alps crashed into a school, shoving the schoolhouse and the people inside down the mountain. Johann risked his life to rappel down a cliff three times to bring emergency supplies to the stranded survivors. Even the king was riveted as Johann recounted the tale.

"The teacher had two broken legs, and nightfall was nearly upon us, so it looked like she was going to have to endure the night down there. Luckily for her, I knew someone from a village downstream who had a sledge, and I thought we might be able to get her to a warmer place. I didn't have much time—"

Johann was interrupted by Countess Cassini, who boldly injected herself into the group with a brisk clap of her hands to command attention.

Her attire stunned them all into silence. She wore a Byzantine-inspired tunic in shimmering bronze fabric. It was a sleeveless gown with a plunging neckline, and she had added bands of golden snakes coiled around both her arms. A stole of leopard's fur was thrown over one shoulder.

"Welcome to the Russian embassy," she announced. "Please follow me to the back garden, where the evening will commence."

The eighteen-year-old girl's demeanor did not sit well with the older ladies gathered on the portico.

A German matron with a scarlet sash across her hefty bosom lifted her chin. "The Swiss envoy was telling us how he saved some villagers caught in an avalanche." She turned her attention back to Johann. "Please continue."

Countess Cassini would not permit it. "The hors d'oeuvres are getting cold, and the evening is planned to begin on the back terrace. If you will all follow me." Her smile was tight as she lifted her bangle-covered arm to gesture the guests toward the interior of the embassy.

Disapproval crackled in the air as the matrons and dignitaries followed the young hostess through the winding hallways until they arrived at the courtyard, where a splashing fountain sat amid potted trees and rosebushes. The evening air was fragrant with roses and wisteria. Tiny lights were strung through the trees, and uniformed footmen circulated with flutes of champagne. Most impressive was the collection of white doves nesting in the trees. Their wings must have been clipped to prevent them from flying off, but the effect was spectacular.

A handful of guests were already here, including the Russian orthodox bishop in full regalia. Bishop Raphael's cassock robes were trimmed with gold, and a black veil trailed from his towering, tube-shaped hat. With his bushy black beard and piercing eyes, the bishop was striking, but Natalia's attention was riveted by the older man chatting with the bishop.

"That's Mark Twain," she whispered, gesturing to the man with shaggy white hair and a full mustache. "I once sent you his novel *Huckleberry Finn*. Do you remember?"

206

"I remember." How could he forget? It was a good story but far too American for his taste.

Before he could say more, both the bishop and Mr. Twain noticed him staring and began heading their way. Bishop Raphael cut an imposing figure as he closed the distance between them, his robes swaying majestically as he walked.

"Count Sokolov, you are to be commended for your bravery in the face of an inhuman ordeal," the bishop said. "Your courage is a worthy example for us all."

The bishop then provided an introduction for Mr. Twain. Apparently, Twain and the bishop were old friends, having toured Sevastopol and Yalta together many years earlier. The two men reminisced about searching the rocky shores of the seaside town for relics of the Crimean War. They found nothing but had a marvelous time. They seemed an odd pair. Mr. Twain constantly smiled, while the bishop listened with a gloomy air. Then again, Dimitri and Natalia were an odd pair too.

Everyone breathed a sigh of relief when the bishop excused himself to speak with the Danish king on the far side of the courtyard. Mr. Twain launched into another rousing story of his travels in Russia. Any time a man as colorful as Mark Twain spun tales, he attracted a crowd, and soon the wives of the German diplomats congregated around them.

"I lost my passport somewhere along the way," Mr. Twain said. "For the rest of the trip I lived in a state of trembling anxiety, worried I was about to be found out and condemned to join the nameless hordes destined for oblivion in Siberia." Mr. Twain raised his glass to Dimitri. "And I would not have had the wily Count Sokolov to lead me out of perdition."

Dimitri flushed with pleasure. He was vain enough to enjoy the praise of America's leading novelist and was about to add some of his own insights about Siberia when Countess Cassini inserted herself, along with a footman carrying a tray of delicacies.

"Would anyone care for some vorschmack?" she offered.

Hannah Schreiber, the German matron wearing a scarlet

sash, looked with curiosity at the tiny crackers topped with a meat paste. "What is vorschmack?" she asked in her heavily accented voice.

Instead of answering, the countess glanced at the footman and spoke in Russian. "Frau Schreiber's husband used to be an accountant, so perhaps her ignorance is to be expected. It's a pity I didn't ask the cook to prepare boiled cabbage." Then she pasted an overly sweet smile on her face and reverted to English. "It is a delicacy made from minced lamb and caviar. It may not be to your taste."

Dimitri glared at the countess, and even the footman looked embarrassed, but Frau Schreiber gamely sampled a bit of vorschmack. Apparently she didn't appreciate the delicacy, because she excused herself to fetch a glass of water, and the countess soon left as well.

Mark Twain watched the interchange with ill-concealed delight. "What did the countess say?"

Dimitri thought carefully before responding. "She had some pointed observations about German cuisine."

"Ha!" the older man exclaimed. "That fiendish girl will be the font of literary inspiration for decades. I came tonight specifically to watch the matrons of Washington cringe in her wake. She is too outrageously fabulous not to be immortalized on the page."

Dimitri had no interest in that awful girl but wouldn't mind discussing literature. "I had a chance to read *The Adventures of Huckleberry Finn*. You are to be congratulated. The story was quite good, but I think it would have been better had the boy died in the end."

Natalia choked on a cracker, but Mr. Twain seemed intrigued. "You think so?" he asked. "Tell me why."

It ought to be obvious to any serious literary artist, but Dimitri explained anyway. "It would have solidified his heroism. He came through many challenges with wit and ingenuity, but in order to prove his heroic stature, he must be willing to die for a cause. This is true in all the great Russian stories."

"I'm not Russian," Mr. Twain said.

Dimitri raised his glass with a smile. "A pity. It is the only thing standing between you and literary greatness."

Mr. Twain warmed to the challenge. "According to your logic, you should be dead by now. Allow me to rewrite the ending of your adventure. You would have staggered into Port Arthur and then, with the last of your strength, sent a desperate telegram to the rest of the world announcing your findings. A lovely Russian maiden would have noticed your suffering and taken you under her wing to heal you, but alas! You were too far gone. With your last bit of strength, you would have proclaimed love for the girl, then let death claim you as the sun rises on another Russian morning."

"Ah, but my story isn't finished yet," Dimitri said. "I have yet to secure a full restoration of my honor from the czar, so perhaps all is not yet lost. I may still have the opportunity to enjoy a tragic fate."

Mr. Twain's laugh came from deep in his belly, and he asked to be seated opposite Dimitri and Natalia at dinner. It caused a ruckus with the seating arrangements, and the young countess fumed because the last-minute adjustment stuck her next to the grim Russian bishop.

The dinner lasted until midnight, followed by more drinks and conversation in the courtyard. Each course of the meal had been paired with its own wine, so like most of the other guests, Dimitri had sampled a Bordeaux from France, a fine German riesling that tasted like distilled sunlight, a hazelnut liqueur produced by Italian monks, and the finest Russian saperavi wine from the hills near the Black Sea. A haze of well-being enveloped him as he escorted Natalia to the courtyard. Goodwill and comradery abounded among the three dozen guests from across the world who gathered in this enchanted moonlit garden.

No wonder state dinners such as these were a staple of diplomacy. They were essential in building trust and friendship among the elites who ruled the nations of the world. The bonhomie was alive and vibrant tonight. The king of Denmark prodded Mark Twain to compose extemporaneous poetry, the German diplomatic corps played with the countess's French spaniels, and the Swiss delegation jested with the Canadians about when they would break free of the British Empire.

All Dimitri could see was Natalia, and his chest ached at the sight of her. Would this be all they had? A few fleeting weeks of joy before he returned home? Natalia was no country mouse, but perhaps she could find happiness at Mirosa. Without a doubt she had the ability to navigate the royal palaces of Saint Petersburg. Even now he enjoyed listening to her converse with guests on everything from Renaissance sculpture to the politics of the Suez Canal.

Bishop Raphael joined their little group beside the splashing fountain to ask Natalia about a rumored collection of religious icons owned by the Blackstones.

"My mother collected them," Natalia confirmed. "She built a private chapel in our house and lined it with the icons that reminded her of home."

Countess Cassini overheard and once again chose to speak in Russian. "I'm surprised she didn't decorate it with a stage curtain and greasepaint."

Natalia stiffened, and Dimitri was rendered speechless, but this time Frau Schreiber refused to overlook the breach of decorum. "I wish you would speak in English when you know most of us don't understand Russian."

The reprimand was obvious, but Countess Cassini's eyes danced with amusement as she looked at Natalia. "I don't think Miss Blackstone would be comfortable speaking about such things in public," she said in English.

"Then you should not have said them," Frau Schreiber scolded.

"I don't mind translating," Natalia said, and Dimitri held his breath, drawing closer to Natalia's side. "Countess Cassini pointed out that my mother was once a dancer," Natalia said calmly. "She danced with the Bolshoi Ballet, but after she came to New York, a part of her heart stayed in Russia. That's why she created her own private chapel that reflected her love of Christ and her longing for her homeland. Even dancing girls can be women of faith."

Dimitri lifted Natalia's hand and pressed a slow kiss to the back of it, lingering a fraction too long, but he wanted the world to see his devotion to Natalia. "One of my greatest regrets is that I never had a chance to meet Galina Danilova Blackstone," he said, gazing directly into Natalia's eyes. "She raised a daughter who loves her ancestral homeland but has the strength and ingenuity of America. It is an entrancing combination."

"My goodness," Countess Cassini said, "the way your eyes are devouring Miss Blackstone looks positively lascivious, and in front of the bishop too."

Dimitri would tolerate no more. He raised his chin and pierced the girl with a stare he inherited from centuries of aristocratic privilege. "You are only partially correct," he said, loud enough for everyone in the garden to hear. "Miss Blackstone is indeed lovely, but my eyes are not lascivious, they are full of reverence. I know the difference between crude physical needs and something more lasting. The heart of a man is wider, deeper, and stronger than anything that can be measured with the human eye. Natalia is my North Star. When I wandered in the wilds of Siberia, it was thoughts of Natalia that kept me alive."

By now all the conversation in the garden had thudded to a halt. A group of matrons silently cheered him on as he continued addressing Countess Cassini.

"After I witnessed the unspeakable evil committed in the czar's name, I lived with the shame of being affiliated with that corrupt regime. The shame deepened when the czar failed to denounce the act, but I clung to the wisdom and optimism I learned from Natalia to sustain me during those dark months. I love her beyond measure. When I was lost in the woods, it was Natalia who inspired me to fight when I wanted to give up. Memory of her humor made me laugh when I wanted to weep.

She is everything good in a woman, and if I die tonight, I will consider myself blessed for having found her against all odds."

Natalia looked flushed in pleased embarrassment, but everyone who witnessed his declaration smiled except the young countess.

He meant every word of it. Now he prayed that he could convince Natalia they belonged together for good and to make their home beneath the wild, glorious skies of Russia.

Dimitri felt heat building beneath his collar when he saw the unforgiving look on Count Cassini's face. It was the end of the evening, and the ambassador stood at the top of the embassy steps—seemingly to wish everyone farewell, but his displeasure was obvious.

Dimitri felt the older man's eyes boring into his back as he helped Natalia into a carriage. Natalia noticed the ambassador's odd behavior, her worried gaze glancing across the torchlit driveway.

"Wait here," Dimitri told her. "I'll be back in a moment."

He feigned a look of casual elegance as he strolled across the driveway toward the ambassador, but his hands itched. Hives, probably.

He stuck them in his pockets as he arrived at the top of the landing and met the ambassador's frank gaze. "Why are you staring at me? I am clearly the object of intense fascination, but I think you have something else on your mind."

The ambassador's face relaxed, which was mildly alarming. "I know it seems as if you have the world in the palm of your hand," he said in a low voice, "but it only *seems* that way."

Dimitri lifted his chin. "Don't play word games. Tell me exactly what you want of me."

"From you? Nothing. I welcomed you here tonight to demonstrate that the czar has nothing to fear from you, that the incident at the Amur was only the reckless behavior of a few rogue army officers. But tonight you included the czar in your attack, and that won't be tolerated."

Dimitri silently cringed as he realized his mistake. During those reckless moments while he lavished praise on Natalia, he'd accidentally let loose his true feelings about the czar. It wasn't intentional. It was a stupid, careless misstep, and possibly a costly one.

He bowed his head. "You are entirely correct," he conceded. "It will not happen again."

The ambassador's face did not soften. "If you persist in casting aspersions on the integrity of the imperial regime, I will make life uncomfortable for the woman you claim to love so ardently. We have already discussed this. I hope we don't need to revisit the conversation ever again."

Count Cassini turned on his heel and walked back inside the embassy, the doors slamming shut behind him, and Dimitri could only pray his carelessness would not carry greater repercussions.

26

*N*atalia existed in a haze of painful infatuation during the train ride back to New York. Dimitri had been closemouthed about whatever he said to the ambassador last night, but she already knew their trip to Washington had been a triumph.

They loved each other. Against all odds, they had found each other from opposite sides of the world, but Dimitri's bone-deep love for his homeland was going to pull them apart. She leaned her head against the window, the rhythmic clicking of the wheels keeping pace with her whirling thoughts as they sped across the countryside. Dimitri's mission would not be complete until they had the official word from the czar. They would continue whipping up publicity about the Amur River upon their return to New York until they had the czar's promise in writing.

And then?

She sighed. Then Dimitri would return to Russia. She would lose everything if she followed him. Alexander. Her ability to have a meaningful job. Her ability to carry a child. She would be isolated on a rural estate with little to occupy her mind and no children of her own.

She gazed fondly at Dimitri on the other side of the compartment where he played cards with Poppy. A report on the turpentine industry lay unread on her lap, but she'd rather admire Dimitri. Soon he would be gone forever, and she wanted to engrave this moment in her mind to remember in the years to come. She didn't want to miss a moment of it, even though Poppy chattered incessantly.

"If we arrive in the city before five o'clock, we must attend the symphony tonight," Poppy said.

"And why must we?" Dimitri asked, coolly laying out another hand of cards.

"Maxim Tachenko is the guest violinist. Gwen telegrammed me to report that he will be performing "Waves of the Amur" in your honor, and it is his last night in New York. I have box seats at Carnegie Hall, and it will be a grand opportunity for us to show you off."

Poppy was practically glowing at the prospect of the chance to sit beside Dimitri in the family's box seats. Emotions warred inside Natalia. This was precisely the sort of high-profile event Dimitri needed to solidify his celebrity in America, but their time together was growing short. Every hour seemed precious, and she didn't want to share him with Poppy.

Two hours later, the train approached Grand Central Station and slowed to a crawl while navigating the railway switches across six lanes of track. Dimitri sat on the bench beside Natalia as they watched the station come into view. She rotated to look up into his profile, and he met her eyes, a fond smile tugging at the corner of his mouth.

The train finally halted, its gears clicking and hissing as it settled into place. Natalia reluctantly stood to depart the car. Outside, iron girders arched over the huge terminal. It was always so loud in here, with the noise of engines and people echoing off the massive overhead tunnel. The open fretwork of steel frames was supposed to minimize noise, but it wasn't very effective.

A familiar figure stood on the crowded platform. Natalia hadn't expected Liam to meet them, but what a delight. Maybe he would even join them at the symphony tonight if he could refrain from throwing darts at Poppy. A porter came to open the door of their compartment, and Dimitri descended first, lifting his hand to help Natalia step down onto the platform.

"Natalia!" Liam called out as he pushed through the crowds to reach them, a grim look on his face.

Dimitri stayed to help Poppy down, but Natalia made her way toward Liam and pressed a quick kiss to his cheek. "Hello, Liam. Why so glum?"

"We need to talk," he said. "I don't think you want to go home. Come stay on the *Black Rose* with me."

Liam had been living on his splendid yacht ever since he moved to New York. His sudden urgency that she retreat to it made her worry.

"Why?" she asked. "What's going on?"

"I don't want to talk here, but you need to trust me. Let Poppy take Count Sokolov back to her house, but come with me to the *Black Rose*. You don't want to go home."

"Why not?"

"Trust me, Natalia."

Something was clearly going on, but Dimitri and Poppy had joined them, and aside from a quick greeting, Liam made no move to discuss what bothered him. She was going to have to trust him.

"Dimitri, you go along with Poppy back to Fifth Avenue. I'll be joining Liam on the *Black Rose*. My townhouse is still a mess."

"Are you sure?" Dimitri asked. "I thought we were all going to the symphony tonight."

He looked so dear, so tender as he frowned down at her in concern. She rushed to embrace him, grabbing both cheeks to kiss him directly on the mouth. She didn't care who saw. Something about the pity in Liam's eyes worried her.

"I'm sure," she said, even though uncertainty swamped her. "I'll meet you at Carnegie Hall tonight, but I want to join Liam for a meal."

Poppy looked typically annoyed at Natalia's abrupt change

of plans, complaining mightily as they summoned a porter to bring an additional pushcart to separate Natalia's trunks from the others. It took a while for them to navigate back up to Forty-Second Street, where it was so crowded that Natalia barely managed a wave of good-bye to Dimitri as he escorted Poppy to the Blackstone carriage. Liam already had a cab waiting to take them on the twenty-minute ride to the marina where he docked the *Black Rose*.

It was snug inside the carriage, with two benches facing each other and a stack of newspapers taking up part of the bench opposite her. Once Liam climbed aboard, she had to angle her knees to accommodate his long legs.

"Well?" she asked as soon as the cabbie closed the door on the compartment.

Liam looked apprehensive as he set his hand on the stack of newspapers beside him. Normally he was so easygoing, making his grim demeanor worrisome.

"The press is falling all over themselves to sing Count Sokolov's praises," he said as the carriage started moving.

"That was the idea," Natalia replied.

"Yeah, but it's getting out of hand. As they celebrate Dimitri like a hero, they're looking for someone to paint as the villain. Count Cassini is claiming all this happened without the czar's knowledge or consent, so the press is blaming the Russian army."

"Okay," Natalia said, still not sure how this could be construed as bad news.

"Your father's bank has never been popular, and the press loves an excuse to attack it." He handed her a copy of *The New York Times* folded open to a story. The headline was a slap in the face.

Blackstone Bank Complicit in Massacre along the Trans-Siberian Railway

She struggled to hold the paper still as the carriage bumped and jostled over the cobblestones, but she quickly gleaned the gist of the article. It was exactly as her father had feared. The Blackstone Bank had sunk its greedy tentacles into another nation's business to extract as much profit as possible. When the Russian army retaliated against a local uprising, the Blackstones averted their eyes rather than complain. Natalia was painted as a dilettante who was given a Russian investment as a present from a doting father.

"It gets worse," Liam said, his face pained. "The article at the bottom of the page interviewed someone who claims to work for the bank. He unloaded a ton of hogwash that makes you look pretty bad."

He pointed to a paragraph, and Natalia felt sick as she read the damning details, all of which were true but had been painted in the worst possible light. The article said that Oscar Blackstone built his pampered daughter a washroom for her exclusive use that had marble counters and perfumed hand towels. That she frittered time and money on expensive telegrams flirting with men in Russia. That even though she had one of the biggest and best offices in the bank, she used a tiny antique desk that was too small for anything except twiddling her thumbs.

Most damning, the article reported that insiders in the bank had been concerned with Natalia's mismanagement and had reported it to the Russian embassy in Washington, but Oscar refused to do anything to admonish his spoiled daughter.

"Oh no," she whispered, her teeth beginning to chatter. This was a disaster. She had to think fast. This sort of vitriol smacked of Silas Conner, but the damage had already been done.

The carriage was heading west to the marina, but she needed to go to the bank to see her father. She turned to jerk open the panel on the wall behind her, but Liam slammed it shut.

"What are you doing?" she stammered. "I need to see my father."

"Not until you've got your head screwed on straight," Liam ordered.

Her stomach soured as other implications sank in. How many times had her father warned that he couldn't protect her if she ever failed in the eyes of the public? It didn't matter what was true; it only mattered what the public believed.

She was dizzy and nauseated at the same time. "I think I'm going to be sick."

"Do you want to pull over and get out?"

Liam's voice was kind, his hand a reassuring weight on her shoulder. She still had allies. She could get through this.

"I'll be okay," she said. The worst thing would be giving in to panic and doing something foolish. Liam was right. She needed to retreat somewhere away from public view and plan a strategy out of this mess.

One thing she did know was that she couldn't go to Carnegie Hall tonight. Russia's famed violinist would be playing in Dimitri's honor, and she would be a distraction. She needed to stand aside and let Maxim Tachenko lend his talents in support of Dimitri's cause.

By the time they arrived at the marina, she had calmed herself. The briny scent from water sloshing against the pilings was oddly comforting. One of the crewmembers who lived aboard the yacht lowered the gangway for them to board, and Liam led her to the main living area belowdecks.

It was a long, narrow room with a low ceiling, but it was comfortably furnished with card tables, tufted lounging chairs, and brass portholes overlooking the marina. It was dim, and Liam turned up a little kerosene lamp to brighten the room. A lazy English bulldog slumbered in a large wicker basket at the foot of Liam's desk. Liam squatted down to give Frankie a good rubbing beneath its chin.

Books, manuals, and stacks of papers were mounded on the table closest to the light. She fingered the edge of a financial ledger. "How is the math coming?"

"Okay," he said, but his tone was dismissive as he petted his dog. It wasn't coming along okay, and she'd been useless to him while she'd been in San Francisco, Washington, and everywhere in between. The board meeting for raising the workers' pay was coming up soon, and she doubted he'd be ready.

"Let me see," she said, reaching toward a financial ledger, but he got there first.

"Natalia, this isn't the time for that. Tell me what I can do to help."

There was *nothing* Liam could do. Her reputation had been dragged into the mud, and in all likelihood her father was about to cut her out of the bank forever.

And without the bank, there was nothing left for her in New York.

Poppy was right, Dimitri thought as he escorted her into Carnegie Hall. There was a grandeur to the concert hall reminiscent of those in Europe. The exterior had a striking Italian Renaissance-style façade of terracotta brick, while the inside was a feast of color. He wore his finest evening attire, complete with white tie and a black cutaway jacket. He proudly wore his red Buryat sash instead of a cummerbund.

"That's the mayor of New York," Poppy whispered as he escorted her up the stairs to a private box on the second tier of the auditorium. "He hosted Maxim Tachenko at his home last week. It was scandalous, because everyone thinks the mayor's wife is infatuated with Tachenko."

She continued chattering about the exalted guests she spotted as they entered the Blackstone private box overlooking the auditorium. They had it to themselves because Oscar had stayed late at the bank and Natalia had sent a message that she could not come. Poppy arranged herself close to the banister to have a perfect view of the crowd below.

"This box is the best place to see and be seen anywhere in the city," she assured him as she scanned the audience below, where diamonds gleamed among the silk and satin. On the opposite side of the auditorium, a pair of matrons gawked at them while exchanging confidences behind their fans. Others on the main floor craned their necks to look up at them.

"Your celebrity precedes you, Count Sokolov," Poppy said

loudly enough for spectators in the nearby box to hear his title. "Oh look, there's Senator Lansing." She nodded to another private box.

Dimitri recognized the senator and tipped a nod of greeting. Senator Lansing returned it with an approving smile.

The lights in the auditorium dimmed, and the curtain rose to reveal the finest symphony orchestra in the nation. The conductor walked onto the stage to polite applause. A smattering of chatter and shifting in seats continued until the conductor's tap of his baton settled the crowd.

And then Maxim Tachenko strode onto the stage, and the audience erupted with unabashed fervor. He wore a formal black frock coat and tails, but his mane of golden-blond hair was ridiculously long, brushed back from a face handsome enough to make the angels envious. The violinist crossed the stage with the confidence of a matador, eyeing the crowd with his bow and violin dangling from his hands like weapons ready to be called into action. It took several attempts by the conductor to settle the audience back into respectful silence.

Mr. Tachenko took center stage, settling the violin beneath his chin and holding the bow suspended an inch above the strings. The conductor raised his arms, and for a single moment, silence reigned. Then the conductor's arm sliced downward, and the soaring majesty of a Berlioz symphony filled the hall.

Dimitri let himself be swept into the torment of *Symphonie fantastique* as it moved through the stages of grim, majestic, and joyous passages. He wished Natalia was here. She would love this. No phonograph could ever carry such resonance.

Beside him, Poppy whipped out her opera glasses to spy on the audience, occasionally elbowing him to point out notable individuals. Some of her acquaintances didn't wait for intermission to begin slipping into their box, begging an introduction. Poppy was in her element, sprinkling his title in every sentence while keeping a protective hand on his arm. He didn't mind. The adulation was flattering, but throughout it all he kept an eye on the program, for "Waves of the Amur" was the last song before intermission.

As a selection of Paganini favorites came to an end, it was time for the song. To Dimitri's surprise, the violinist introduced the selection with a political statement, his heavily accented voice ringing with conviction as he spoke.

"My friends, the Amur River travels through some of the most harshly beautiful lands in the world. It marks the dividing line between Russia and China and has long been a source of pride for us. Along its banks live the Tatar, the Mongol, the Buryat, and the Cossack. Tonight, I play a song of homage to our great river. The music embodies the Slavic soul, filled with majesty but with sorrow as well. I dedicate this song to Count Dimitri Sokolov, whose presence tonight honors us all."

Dimitri caught his breath as the violinist raised his bow, pointing it directly to his box. He hadn't expected this. Every eye in the auditorium swiveled to look at him, and he stood.

The crowd rose to their feet as well. The standing ovation was thunderous, and a wellspring of emotion threatened to swamp him. Was this real? Two months ago, he was a starving nomad stumbling through the forest and bartering for a mouthful of food. Now he was the toast of New York City. That season of hunger and fear seemed a distant memory as he basked in the gilded limelight, the applause, the glamor.

But there was danger to this glamor. Was he Icarus, flying too close to the sun? How much higher could he climb before the inevitable collapse arrived? He felt like an imposter as he bowed in gratitude to the adulation coming from the audience below.

The applause calmed, and Dimitri sat once again, holding his breath as the violinist positioned his bow to play "Waves of the Amur." The song was laden with familiar Slavic moodiness, and longing for his homeland swelled inside Dimitri, painful in its intensity. The music had a hypnotic effect, summoning memories of Russia even as he remained trapped in this gilded cage. It would be impossible ever to be truly happy until he returned home, the site of his greatest joy and sorrow.

The sense of incongruity continued at intermission as Poppy guided him toward a private club room behind the mezzanine. Rich hardwood paneling lined the walls, the chandelier dripped with crystals, and waiters circulated with libations.

Poppy worked her magic. She glided through the crowd like a figurehead on the prow of a ship, slicing through water with his hand clasped in hers as she introduced him to dozens of people. Dimitri smiled and nodded, but his soul longed to escape back to Natalia's townhouse and tell her about Tachenko's performance. She loved gloomy Russian music as much as he did and would understand its characteristic blend of melancholy and joy.

A stout woman who looked like a bulldog swathed in diamonds gestured to Poppy. "That's Mrs. Astor!" Poppy said, dazzled to be invited to join the famed socialite's corner.

Dimitri did not follow because he'd just spotted Senator Lansing angling through the crowd, reaching out to shake his hand.

"When we met last month, I had no idea of the hazards you'd endured," Senator Lansing said. "With a few more evenings such as this, you can have the whole nation eating out of your palm."

"I am not interested in anyone eating from my palm," Dimitri said. "I merely want to draw attention to the atrocity so that such a thing can never be hidden from the world again."

"I can help with that," Senator Lansing said. "People like seeing David trounce Goliath, and you've got all the makings of a David, while the czar is Goliath."

Dimitri held up his hand. "No, no. I do not believe the czar was personally involved in the atrocity. The army is to blame. It was all a miscommunication."

At all costs, Dimitri would not endanger Natalia by arousing Count Cassini's ire. The most important thing was to get the czar to reaffirm the Treaty of Aigun. Only then could Dimitri rest easy.

Senator Lansing amiably nodded his head, but then he said the strangest thing. "Have you given any thought to how you will handle the Blackstone affair? Especially the Natalia Blackstone issue."

Dimitri blinked. His understanding of English was not perfect, but he didn't consider Natalia to be an *issue*. Especially not in the distasteful way Senator Lansing spoke the word.

"I do not understand your meaning," he said.

"Well, Miss Blackstone's failure to spot trouble looming along the Amur is partly what caused this whole mess," he said. "I understand you are associated with the family, but you may want to distance yourself from that woman for a while."

"I will do no such thing," he sputtered. "Miss Blackstone is entirely blameless regarding what happened. Where did you get such a foul impression of her?"

His mind reeled as Senator Lansing recounted the flurry of newspaper articles that resurrected old resentment about callous Blackstone financial practices of the past and described an incompetent woman who had been given oversight of a massive investment by her indulgent father.

"Stay away from her," Senator Lansing warned. "No one understands the sort of long-distance financing she was doing, nor do they care. The press wants villains. You carry a shine of heroism, but don't risk it by associating with her."

Dimitri braced his hand on a column, his thoughts reeling. This was Natalia's worst fear, and once again, it was his doing.

"Count Sokolov?" the senator asked curiously. "Are you well?"

He forced himself to stand up straight. It wasn't the time to defend Natalia but to capitalize on this fleeting moment of fame to fight for the people of the Amur. They deserved nothing less.

He raised his champagne glass. "Quite well."

But inside, he despaired.

27

*N*ew York had three newspapers that came out each morning, and Liam sent a crewmember to collect all three. Natalia sat on the deck of the *Black Rose*, skimming them with a sinking spirit.

The news was bad. It was based on speculation rather than actual facts, and almost all of it centered squarely on her. Unlike Poppy, Natalia avoided society events, and few people knew her, giving journalists free rein to fill in the blanks of her life with their own speculation. They dwelled on her youth and lack of experience at other banks that would have given her a broader perspective to understand overseas investments.

One of the newspapers had a photograph of her taken at Alexander's christening last year.

"It's a good picture," Liam said.

It was flattering, but the photograph showed her in the worst possible light to be taken seriously as a businesswoman. The ultrafeminine gown was of expensive silk, and a cluster of violets had been artfully arranged in her hair. The amethyst drop earrings emphasized her wealth. She looked frilly, feminine, and pampered—not the sort of woman to be trusted with a major investment.

Today was going to be difficult. Normally she enjoyed working with her father, but he was an iron-hard man of business. His wrath was notorious. Tightly leashed fury was her father's normal reaction when angered, but when supremely provoked, he withdrew behind a wall of ice. On such occasions, he skewered the target of his ire through his one good eye, fist tightened on the top of his cane as he spoke with whisper-soft rage. Both versions of his anger were terrible, and she had no idea which one she would confront this morning.

She hired a carriage to drive her through the early morning drizzle to the bank, where she asked Mr. Asher, her father's long-time secretary, to make an appointment to see him.

"Your father is already expecting you," Mr. Asher said. "He said to go inside as soon as you arrive."

Mr. Asher's face was full of sympathy, and she took a sobering breath before crossing to her father's office door.

Oscar rose to his feet as she entered. To her surprise, he looked neither furious nor coldly angry . . . only tired and sad. Defeated. He leaned heavily on the desk, his shoulders sagging.

"You have seen the newspapers?" he asked.

"Yes."

His leaned even more heavily on the desk, looking up at her with pained eyes. "Natalia, you don't deserve this. I'm so sorry."

She hadn't expected kindness. The wall of armor she'd been preparing all morning slipped, and anguish bloomed inside her.

"I am too," she whispered.

Her father gestured to a chair. "Have a seat. We need to discuss how to handle this."

Despite his kindness, it didn't sway him from what needed to be done. She would be removed from the railroad account. Attempting to keep her on would undermine the bank's reputation. It wasn't fair, but society had never been fair toward women who tried to slip into a man's world.

Her father warned that reporters had been congregating outside the bank for two days, hoping to catch a glimpse of her. "It would be best if you could stay out of sight for a while. Is there somewhere you'd like to go? I still have the hunting lodge in Canada."

She glanced away, rebelling against the idea, but Oscar clearly wanted her as far away from New York as possible. It would probably be wise, but she couldn't do it. Her townhouse still needed to be repaired. At least now she would have the time to see it done properly.

"I'd rather stay here," she said. "Who will you assign to lead the Trans-Siberian?"

"Howard Shipley has agreed to take it on."

She flinched. It hurt to realize that she had already been replaced. There was nothing wrong with Howard Shipley. He had wide-ranging experience in the transportation industry and understood the requirements for financing large-scale engineering projects. She only wished . . .

Well, it didn't matter what she wished. She smoothed all emotion from her expression and faced her father squarely. "I would be happy to meet with him to go over the files and be sure he understands the timetables for the various segments."

Oscar looked uncomfortable. "We've already transferred those files from your office. Go ahead and see him today if you wish, but going forward, he won't need any assistance."

She shook her head. This was a massive project, and the timetables became erratic depending on the season. The scheduling demanded flexibility, and she needed to warn Howard about them—

"Natalia." Her father's voice interrupted the cascade of thoughts. His face was full of compassion, but she didn't want to see it. It was essential that Howard Shipley understand the project he was about to inherit. She wasn't in charge anymore, but she still loved that railroad.

She opened her mouth to make her case, but Oscar interrupted her.

"Natalia, go home," he said gently. "Figure out what you're going to do with the next phase of your life. There is no place for you at the bank anymore."

It would have been easier if he'd been angry, but every word he spoke ached with sorrow. If he'd been angry, it would have stoked her to fight against these unjust charges, but his pity meant that he already knew and understood. She was about to lose the work that gave her life meaning. On the day the Trans-Siberian Railway was completed, there would be someone else at the helm.

She had always known this could happen. Her father couldn't even help her get a position somewhere else, since no bank could risk their reputation by employing her.

A tap on the door interrupted her thoughts, and the secretary tipped his head inside. "Miss Felicity and your son are here."

Her father's expression momentarily brightened, but he quickly hid it. "Excellent. Send them in, please."

Alexander's nanny wheeled the baby buggy inside. Alexander was already sitting up, and he reached out his arms the moment he saw Oscar.

Her father leaned down to lift the boy. It was impossible not to smile at her brother's delight as he basked in Oscar's attention. The cuddling would continue for a few more minutes, and then the boy would be consigned to his playpen in the corner.

As he grew older, she hoped Alexander would come to love this place as much as she had. She hoped he would become her father's protégé, the sort Oscar had always wanted. She had once looked forward to helping Alexander learn the ropes at the bank, but that was just another foiled dream.

It was time to leave.

Dimitri read the morning newspapers with appalled confusion. The articles about the Amur praised him to the skies, but the same newspapers slaughtered Natalia. At best she was branded an indulged heiress whose ignorance of the world meant she couldn't spot a catastrophe that happened on her project. At worst they accused her of blithely disregarding the atrocity in the interest of profit.

He sat at the table in the breakfast room, thrumming his fingers on the table as he read the last of the newspapers. Oscar had departed for the bank before sunrise, but Poppy was still here, adding a stream of unhelpful commentary.

"I always warned Oscar that Natalia's interest in the bank was unnatural and would get her into trouble eventually," she said. "No one likes a woman who is too mannish."

"Really? I find myself in love with that mannish woman."

Poppy rolled her eyes. "You just feel sorry for her. Trust me, Natalia is unnatural, and it's going to take all my skills to fix her reputation."

The specter of how Poppy might foist herself on Natalia to "fix" her gave Dimitri the chills. He didn't know much about New York high society, but no man of honor would stand aside to let his woman be torn to pieces, whether it was metaphorically in the press or in person from the claws of Countess Cassini. This was no mosquito bite; this was the ruination of everything Natalia had hoped to achieve with her life.

And there was likely more to come. The bombshells in the New York press had been set in motion days ago, but the ambassador's threat the night of the reception indicated he had additional plans to attack Natalia should Dimitri prove difficult.

He dabbed the corners of his mouth with the napkin. "Is there a telephone in this house?" he asked Poppy.

Ten minutes later, he had been installed in Oscar Blackstone's private study. Unlike the rest of the marble splendor in the Blackstone home, the wood-paneled office was designed for business, not to impress. Beside the desk was a table set up with a telegraph machine and a stock ticker.

Dimitri stood beside the telephone mounted on the wall, listening through the telephone earpiece as his call was patched through a series of switchboards from Manhattan to Philadelphia, then Baltimore, then Washington, and finally to the Russian embassy. It took several more minutes for Count Cassini to be summoned to the telephone, but when he came on the line, it sounded like he had been expecting Dimitri's call.

"How are you finding the climate in New York?" the ambassador asked in a silky tone.

Dimitri would not pretend a cordial tone. "What other information do you intend to release about Miss Blackstone?"

"That depends on you," Count Cassini said. "When we came to our agreement, you indicated that you would proclaim the czar's complete innocence in the matter. You had every opportunity to do so at the gala I hosted in Washington, but you failed. It was disappointing."

Dimitri clenched his fists but kept his voice calm. "I repeat. What additional slander do you plan to release about Miss Blackstone?"

"Slander? That is an inflammatory word. Everything I have on Miss Blackstone was passed along by a knowledgeable source from *inside* the Blackstone Bank."

"Who?" Dimitri demanded.

"Mr. Silas Conner," the count replied. "He had some interesting observations about how Miss Blackstone purchased only a single first-class sleeping compartment for the two of you on a five-night journey from San Francisco to New York."

Heat began to build. It didn't matter that Dimitri spent five nights sleeping in a berth that was little better than a coffin. A woman's reputation could be shattered so easily, and he should have suspected this would be the tactic Count Cassini would use, since it was both true and carried a seedy undercurrent. What he didn't suspect was what came next.

"San Francisco is notorious for its opium dens," the ambassador continued. "Perhaps it is little wonder that the person overseeing the Trans-Siberian account was sloppy in her duties, since she was known to dabble in that terrible vice and just got back from several days in San Francisco."

It was a complete lie, but it *sounded* as if it could be true. Dimitri braced his hand on the wall, his gaze trailing out the window to the glamor of Fifth Avenue. It was a gloomy day, with storm clouds scuttling across the sky and well-heeled ladies scurrying to get inside ahead of the coming rain. Natalia would never be able to hold her head up among this fusty crowd once Count Cassini was done with her.

Dimitri waited the space of ten heartbeats before responding. Count Cassini was not without his own vulnerabilities.

"Sir, we are men of honor," Dimitri said. "We do not make war on women. You would not like to see Countess Cassini subjected to the same sort of slander Miss Blackstone is currently enduring."

Count Cassini's voice slashed out like a whip. "If you dare insult my niece, there will be consequences."

The violence of the ambassador's reaction confirmed what Natalia had reported about the likelihood of the young girl being the ambassador's illegitimate child with his housekeeper. This conversation was vile, but Dimitri was going to use everything in his arsenal to protect Natalia.

"I never threatened to denigrate the young countess," Dimitri replied. "I do not attack the young and blameless, but your housekeeper is neither. Countess Cassini would not like seeing her mother dragged through the muck of scandal, as is currently happening to Miss Blackstone. Can you assure me that no additional stories will emerge from Washington, DC?"

There was a long pause on the other end of the telephone. They had each other over a barrel, and the ambassador knew it. In the end, Dimitri agreed to leave the czar out of any additional discussion about the Amur, and the count would sheathe his claws regarding Natalia.

After concluding the distasteful telephone call, Dimitri took a carriage to the bank and headed up to Natalia's office. He was surprised to see several unfamiliar men boxing up papers from the delicate rolltop desk that once belonged to Galina.

"Where is Miss Blackstone?" he asked a man wearing coveralls.

"She doesn't work here anymore," the man replied. "She wants this desk sent to her house."

His spirit sagged, and he didn't even respond before racing back downstairs. When Natalia claimed she would be cut out of the bank should she ever visibly place a foot wrong, Dimitri hadn't believed her. Now the proof was before his eyes.

The drizzle from earlier in the day had turned into a steady rain, and there were no cabs in sight, but it didn't matter. Natalia lived only a few blocks away, and he strode toward her house. He darted around puddles and dashed across the street to stand on her tiny front porch, banging on the door as the rain poured down. There was no overhang, and soon water dribbled from the brim of his hat.

She didn't answer the door. Inside, music was blasting from the phonograph, and she probably couldn't hear. He pounded with the side of his fist hard enough to rattle the door.

"Natalia!" he yelled. "Natalia, open up, it's me."

At last he heard footsteps thudding down the stairs. The music stopped, and the door flung open.

"Dimitri!" Natalia gasped. "Heavens, get inside, I didn't know you were coming."

He took off his hat and held it outside to shake water from the brim.

"Let me take your coat," she fussed. "You poor dear, how long were you out there?" She looked tragic as she took his coat. He was dry underneath but didn't mind accepting her pity for his drenching.

"Too long," he said. "I'll probably get pneumonia."

She rolled her eyes. "Dimitri, you're healthy as an ox."

"A very sad ox," he said. "Natalia, I've seen the newspapers. And your empty office." He held his breath, hoping she might shrug this off with cocksure aplomb, but it didn't happen.

Her eyes were full of anguish as she looked up at him. "My father already appointed someone else to the railroad account."

It wasn't fair. There were no words to express his regret. All he could do was hold his arms wide, and she immediately stepped into them. He rocked her from side to side.

"There, there," he soothed, wishing he could say something to minimize the situation, but he would not belittle her anguish with empty platitudes.

"I've been ripping out the ruined floor upstairs," she said. "It gave me something to do, and it felt good to hit things."

Her entire townhouse was a dreary, depressing sight. Strips of wallpaper curled from the plaster, and the cracked mantel lay tucked against the wall. Not only had she lost her job because of him, but the state of this wretched townhouse was his fault too. The damage wouldn't have been so bad if she hadn't gone to San Francisco.

"It seems it is your fate to suffer on my behalf."

He held her as he recounted the telephone call with Count Cassini. Thanks to Natalia's insight into Cassini's relationship with his housekeeper, the ambassador had now been neutralized, but much of the damage to Natalia was already done.

"Everything is over," she said. "The life I thought I was going to have is gone."

He stroked her shoulders and her back, wishing he could solve this for her, but it was something she would have to do on her own. "The last chapter of your life hasn't been written. What do you want it to be? You have the freedom to choose almost anything, and that is a rare gift in this world."

"I know," she whispered. "I have been blessed beyond all reason, but I'm still mourning. I think this is going to hurt for a long time." She suddenly brightened and looked up at him with the eager, curious expression he knew so well. "How was the concert? Did Mr. Tachenko play the song?"

"He did, and received a standing ovation for it." He relayed how the violinist stood on the center of the stage and recognized Dimitri in the audience, which caused a thundering round of applause. He could still hear it echoing in his ears.

"I'm so proud of you," Natalia said. "You earned it."

Had he? The months following the disaster at the Amur had been harrowing, but now he garnered accolades and acclaim from it. As soon as he got official word from the embassy, he would return to Russia, but he didn't want to leave Natalia behind, especially not after her dreams had been stolen because of her association with him.

"Natalia, marry me. We could elope right now and start a new life together. I would gladly introduce you to the world as Countess Sokolova, and no one would dare cast aspersions on you."

She startled and looked at him with such hope in her eyes that it made his spirit soar. "Are you going to stay in America?"

He looked away. Staying in America was not a possibility. He was a misfit in New York and would never belong. With every beat of his heart, he longed for home.

"I can't stay," he said gently, hating the way disillusionment took root in her face again. They could be happy in Russia. *She* could be happy in Russia. He just had to make her believe it. "Natalia, you could come with me. As my wife, you could be whatever you wanted, and I would make it happen for you. If you want a bank, I will buy you a bank."

Her smile was sad. "No one in Russia would patronize a bank run by a woman."

It was probably true. Russia was even more conservative than America.

She continued to rattle off the reasons she couldn't move to Russia. "Dimitri, I love you, but my entire world is here. My father. Alexander. I want to be a part of his life as he grows up. I love that boy as if he were my own."

And he could never give her a child. The fever had robbed him of that possibility forever.

"We could adopt children," he said. "Natalia, I want us to walk into the future side-by-side. Come with me to Russia."

Her look was part hurt, part curiosity, and his heart ached because he suspected what she was about to say.

"Can't you stay here? Has it been that awful?"

Noise from the street leaked into her house. Even in her father's mansion, the noise was ever-present. The city felt tight and congested and, yes, awful. He could never be at home here, but he had other reasons for needing to go back to Russia.

"If the czar restores my land and titles, I can use my influence to make sure the treaties are honored. I will need to be in

Russia to ensure that happens. I shall stay in New York until I receive official word about the restoration of my title and estates, but then I must return home." He cupped her cheeks between his palms, trying to memorize every facet of her face. It didn't seem possible that this could be the end. "I don't know what is ahead for us."

"I don't either." Then she brightened and pulled away. "But I know what will happen for the next few minutes." She crossed the room to the table that held her bell-shaped phonograph and began cranking the lever. "Brahms," she said with satisfaction, and moments later, she placed the needle on the rotating disc, filling the dreary room with symphonic magic.

"Isn't it a miracle that so much joy can be immortalized on that little bit of pressed wax?"

"Indeed it is, dearest Natalia."

He moved to stand behind her, and they held each other, listening to Brahms in the rain.

Natalia snapped awake in the middle of the night with the perfect idea to capitalize on Dimitri's triumph at Carnegie Hall.

Music could move the human soul. The few moments while Maxim Tachenko serenaded the elite audience at Carnegie Hall had been powerful, but it was already fading from the collective imagination of sympathetic New Yorkers. That emotion could be stoked again. Why not commission a recording of the song and distribute it all over the city? All over the country?

She rolled from bed, yanked on a robe, and darted down the steps to her phonograph and the stack of records beside it.

Natalia understood how musical recordings were made because she once considered investing in a record company for the bank. She rejected the proposal because the process was expensive, risky, and had a slow rate of return.

She hugged herself in the chilly night air and smiled. What was the point of being born with a fortune if it couldn't be deployed to do something good? A shaft of bright hope pierced her veil of despondency. Commissioning a recording of "Waves of the Amur" would use her talents as a businesswoman and Dimitri's budding appeal with the public. It would keep the pressure on the czar to deliver on his promise to reaffirm the 1858 treaty.

All she had to do now was track down the notoriously fickle Maxim Tachenko and convince him to cooperate in the recording.

28

imitri was gratified at how quickly Natalia's mood lifted now that they had a mission. Her idea to make a recording of "Waves of the Amur" was excellent, provided they could get Tachenko's cooperation. The reclusive violinist had retreated to his lake house for the rest of the summer, where he lived like a hermit when he wasn't on tour. Luckily, Natalia's cousin had a summer cabin on the same lake and was friendly with the difficult violinist.

One week after the concert at Carnegie Hall, Natalia made arrangements to visit Gwen and her husband at their lake house. They used Oscar's carriage for the one-hour drive north of the city. The windows of the carriage were open, and the peaty, green scent of the deeply wooded forest permeated the air as they neared their destination.

"I like this place," Dimitri said. Sunlight filtered through the green canopy of foliage, and the twisty paths cutting through the woods reminded him of home. "I can see why your cousin would prefer to live here rather than in the city. The air smells good."

Natalia shook her head. "They live in downtown Manhattan," she said. "Gwen is working on a doctorate at New York University, and Patrick is a lawyer in one of the rougher parts of the city. They only come to their cabin for a few weeks a year."

The carriage lurched as it turned onto a graveled path so narrow that tree branches scraped the outside of the coach, but soon they arrived at a wide clearing before the cabin. Dimitri handed Natalia down from the carriage and marveled at the home. It was no humble cabin but was more like one of the chalets of Switzerland, a multistory home of wood with peaked rooflines, balconies, and stone chimneys.

The rustle of leaves mingled with the warble of birdsong, and a surge of well-being filled him. He propped his hands on his hips and looked up at a patch of shockingly blue sky overhead.

"What a glorious day the Lord has sent to us!" he boomed. "Look, the cherry plum trees have begun to bloom. Does anything smell more heavenly than the first cherry plum flowers of summer?"

"Good afternoon, Count Sokolov," a wry voice said, and he turned to greet Natalia's cousin Gwen, who wore a long braid of blond hair over her shoulder. She looked too delicate for her rugged husband, who towered well over six feet.

"I once promised you a bottle of perfume, didn't I, Gwendolyn?"

It seemed like another lifetime, but it had only been a year ago when he conversed with Natalia's cousin during one of their marathon wire exchanges. He had teased Gwen about her blunt, unappealing nickname and insisted on calling her Gwendolyn. She sent him a recipe to distill the fragrant juniper berries that grew near his outpost into a perfume, and he had managed to produce it during the long, dark Siberian nights. That bottle of perfume, along with everything else he'd owned, was abandoned after he was arrested at the Amur River.

She smiled at him. "I thought you had forgotten that."

"I have forgotten nothing of my conversations with Natalia," he said. "They were happier times."

"Happy?" Gwen asked in surprise. "We were given to understand that you were lonely and miserable in Siberia."

Had he been miserable? It was a more innocent time, when all he worried about was how to fill the hours while battling loneliness and cold, but pride in what he had accomplished during those years was a form of joy too.

"Sometimes our best memories are born during our harshest trials," he said. "They become happy only in hindsight."

Gwen sent him a smile of bittersweet understanding before gesturing him toward the house. "Come out to the back porch and tell us about it," Gwen said. "We're about to have lunch."

Dimitri followed her through the house to a porch overlooking the lake. A luncheon had been set out on the picnic table, but he had no interest in it. All he wanted to do was wrangle an introduction to Maxim Tachenko and persuade him to record "Waves of the Amur," but Gwen was adamant that it was impossible.

"He'll never agree to do it," she said as she poured lemonade into glasses. "Once he retreats to his lake house for the summer, he turns away all guests. He battens down the hatches, takes in his welcome mat, and lives like a monk. He is a complete recluse."

Her husband was equally adamant. "Old Mrs. Johnson learned that the hard way last summer when she put a cherry pie on his doorstep in honor of the Fourth of July, and he blasted it to pieces with a shotgun. He's a fussy artist with an insanely irrational streak."

"He is a *patriot*," Dimitri insisted. "That man was driven out of Russia because he couldn't resist stoking the revolutionary fire. A man like that might like to start a little conflagration over here as well. Which house is his?"

He scanned the opposite side of the lake and identified Tachenko's house even before Gwen pointed to the gabled roof peeking through the woods. It was a classic Russian dacha, painted pale blue with white gingerbread trim. A rickety wooden fence surrounded an overgrown garden and a profusion of wildflowers.

"We should go over there," he said. "We are accomplishing nothing sitting here, discussing why he will not cooperate. I shall go ask him."

Patrick stood. "Not without backup. I'm serious about that

man's irrationality." He looked at Gwen. "We'll need you to come with us to soothe his ire. Let's go."

Natalia was surprised by the shabby condition of the famous violinist's house and garden. The picket fence needed a coat of paint, and the eaves on one side of the porch listed at a dangerous angle. The garden was a mess, full of unkempt wildflowers and vines crawling along the fence. She hoisted her skirts to hop along the stepping-stones barely visible in the overgrown grass. Gwen pointed out the lilac shrubs she had saved last year, but it was impossible to pay attention because a violin solo coming from an open window held Natalia captivated. It was a Mendelssohn solo but heavily embellished with improvisational riffs and cadenzas that felt like joy itself shaking off its cocoon and coming to life.

She looked at Dimitri, who stilled and placed his hand over his heart, equally moved. They stood in wonder, for such music deserved complete reverence. Oh yes, she must convince Mr. Tachenko to record his music for posterity.

Gwen and Patrick had gone ahead to stand on the back porch, preparing to knock. "Are you coming?" Gwen called back to them.

The music screeched to a halt. "Go away!" a voice hollered from inside. It was followed by a string of curses in Russian, along with the sound of window sashes slamming down, one after another in rapid succession.

Dimitri raced to the one remaining window still open and leaned inside. "Mr. Tachenko, we have come to pay homage!" he announced in Russian.

Another string of curses came as the violinist stomped toward the final window, preparing to slam it down on Dimitri's outstretched arm. Good heavens, Tachenko was wielding a baseball bat!

"Wait!" Natalia implored. "This is Count Sokolov, the hero of the Amur River."

Tachenko reared back in surprise. He dropped the bat and held his arms wide. "Comrade!" he boomed. "Welcome to my home!"

He threw open the back door and beckoned them inside. Natalia craned her neck to admire the dacha. It wasn't a splendid craftsman's house like Gwen's but like her mother always described Russian country dachas. The cedar plank walls were unpainted except for some folk patterns along the edges. Carpets in tribal patterns covered the floors, and lacy curtains framed the windows. Jugs of wildflowers sat beside a priceless Meissen figurine; a chipped mirror hung beside an oil painting framed in gilt. It was a curious mix of grandiosity and humble folk art, and she loved it.

Tachenko insisted they call him Maxim and was apologetic as he set out a paltry tea served in mismatched china.

"All I can offer is cheese and apples," he said. "I dislike having servants underfoot and am too engrossed learning new music to bother with nonsense such as food." Nevertheless, he did not decline Gwen's offer to send over a few loaves of bread and a side of ham.

His jovial mood cooled when Natalia proposed a recording of "Waves of the Amur." He wasn't rude, but he wasn't polite either.

"I refuse to submit to the horror of a phonograph recording. They can never capture the depth and volume and vibrations of a live performance. My music must be heard live or not at all."

"What about people who don't have a chance to come to a big city?" Natalia asked, but Maxim shrugged.

"This is not my concern. I cannot be a hero to the entire world."

She was no poet, but she tried to describe the feeling she had just experienced in the overgrown garden when she caught a few passages of his music. "It was like stumbling into an enchanted glade. I felt like I didn't need air or water, just the chance to listen and let my mind follow where that violin led me."

He preened at her admiring words but remained adamantly

opposed to letting himself be recorded. "I won't let my music be reduced to an inferior recording. Those tinny records will never rival the sound of the real thing."

She persisted. "But if you won't let yourself be recorded, when you die, your music will die with you."

He shrugged again. "I have already been praised in newspapers around the world to commemorate my genius. It is enough."

For every inducement Natalia offered, Maxim had an excuse. Money was not tempting to him. He had no need of additional fame. He wanted nothing to do with the business aspect of music or promoting the nascent recording industry.

Dimitri joined the fight. "What about the people of Russia? You have lived a decade in exile, but shouldn't they have a chance to hear their country's greatest violinist?"

For the first time, Tachenko hesitated, but he quickly retrenched. "My countrymen know I play on their behalf. I won't let them hear an inferior recording. What if I make a mistake? It will be carved onto that wretched wax disc for all eternity."

Dimitri leaned forward, his voice earnest. "If you make a mistake, we stop, throw out the disc, and allow you to try again."

Natalia tried to stifle her surprise. It never occurred to her that Tachenko's reluctance was rooted in fear of capturing a poor performance. Recordings were shockingly expensive, and musicians were rarely given a chance for a second performance. Still, if Tachenko needed two or even three chances to play the song, she would pay for it.

"How many opportunities will you give me to capture it to my satisfaction?" Maxim asked, his voice cautious.

"As many as you need," Dimitri enthused. "Ten. Twenty. Fifty!"

She nearly choked but remained silent. Whatever it took. She was prepared to pay whatever it took to capture that song, pair it with Dimitri's story and Tachenko's renown, then send it out into the world.

Tachenko seemed on the verge of agreement when he upped the pressure. "If I record 'Waves of the Amur,' I insist on recording 'The Internationale' too."

Natalia's father would have a heart attack if she participated in recording the notorious communist anthem, but that was a worry for another day. She shot to her feet and extended her hand. "It's a deal!"

In light of Maxim's bare pantry, they rowed across the lake to celebrate their newfound alliance at Gwen's house. The cook brought out platters of roast beef and crusty French bread. They popped corks, swapped stories as though they were long-time friends, and Maxim treated them to delightful folk songs on his violin.

The music prompted Dimitri to show off in an impromptu squat dance, sinking down onto his haunches with a huge grin. Maxim played an energetic tempo as Dimitri spread his arms wide and kicked his legs in impressive rhythm. She and the others clapped along until Dimitri lost strength and staggered upright.

"Natalia, join me," he beckoned.

"I can't do that!" she laughed.

"Nonsense, your mother was a dancer. Gwen, you too. Time for a troika dance!"

They followed his lead. Soon she and Gwen had their elbows looped with Dimitri's, and he taught them the fast-moving circle dance. The cook and two maids joined in, and soon everyone was dancing as the world's most famed violinist provided a flurry of riffs to keep them moving.

Then came the sound of hoofbeats outside. The music scudded to a stop.

Gwen glanced at Patrick. "Are you expecting anyone?"

Patrick shook his head and strode to the front door. Moments later he returned with two men. One of them was Oscar Blackstone's butler.

"Mr. Tyson?" Natalia asked, still a little breathless. "What's going on?"

"A message for Count Sokolov arrived at your father's home," Tyson said. "It's from the Russian embassy in Washington. This fellow insisted on delivering it directly into Count Sokolov's hands."

An imposing envoy in uniform stood beside Mr. Tyson. "You are Count Sokolov?" he asked Dimitri.

"I am," Dimitri said, looking cautious and worried.

The envoy presented him with a thick envelope, sealed with a wax stamp and tied with elaborate ribbons. "I was charged by Count Cassini to deliver this message directly into your hands and to await your response."

Natalia's heart began to thud. Whatever was in that letter was important enough to be hand-delivered all the way from Washington.

Dimitri's face paled as he took the letter, then turned his back on everyone as he untied the ribbons. He spread the papers out on a table, bracing his hands on either side of the documents as he read.

His shoulders sagged, and his head dropped to his chest. Even from yards away, she heard his ragged breathing. She rushed to his side and stared down at the papers, but the calligraphy was so lavish that it was hard to read.

"What is it?" she asked.

"The czar has restored my title and my properties," he said in a choked voice. "Mirosa is mine again."

The breath left her in a rush. It was official? They had won? She met Dimitri's gaze in wonder because it felt like a dream.

Maxim Tachenko's voice brought it all crashing down. "And a reaffirmation of the treaty?" he demanded.

Dimitri looked back at the paper, skimming it quickly. "It is silent about what happened at the Amur. Nevertheless, I will return to Russia to continue my battle for the rights of the villagers from Saint Petersburg."

Maxim closed the distance between them, grabbing Dimitri

by the shoulders and kissing both his cheeks. "I wish you well, my friend. I will carry out my end of the bargain here, and together we shall be a force to be reckoned with."

Gwen and the others began to applaud and cheer, but Patrick's voice cut through the celebration. "Do you trust it? I wouldn't."

"Sir," the envoy sputtered, "Count Cassini had a wire from the czar himself. You are insulting the highest officials in our land."

Natalia glanced at Dimitri. "Could it be a trick? Just a ploy to get you back in Russia where you can be silenced?"

The celebratory atmosphere vanished. The envoy looked offended, but Dimitri sent her a tired, cynical smile of understanding.

"Anything is possible," he finally said. "I won't know until I go."

"And if you are arrested and disappear forever?"

"Then I die," he said with a simple note of fatalistic acceptance. "I have made my mark in America, and if the czar makes a quick end of me in Russia, my voice will become all the more powerful as my allies continue my quest."

And he would finally enjoy the tragic ending so important to all Russian novels.

Over the next two days, Dimitri spent every moment with Natalia. Their time together was growing short, and unless he succeeded in convincing her to come with him to Russia, this might be their last few days together.

She took him to a shabby tearoom called The Samovar, where she once came with her mother to soak in the sounds and taste of Russia. Sticky tables crammed close together weren't his idea of fine dining, but the aroma of fried herring and baked cabbage rolls felt like home. They sipped hot tea and quietly strategized how to ensure the czar honored his agreement to reaffirm the treaty.

"The first thing I must do is get back to ensure my mother is safely returned to Mirosa," he said. "Meanwhile, Tachenko will keep drumming up publicity about the Amur River here in America. It will make it harder for the czar to go back on his word. We must fight on all fronts, but especially with the American government."

"Senator Lansing can help with that," Natalia said. "During the summers he plays golf with Poppy every week. Poppy won't mind twisting his arm to be sure President Roosevelt is aware of the czar's promise."

Dimitri's mouth tilted in amusement. There was a time when Natalia would have moved heaven and earth to avoid Poppy, but now she did not hesitate to recruit all the allies at her disposal.

"Send me a wire the moment you know what the czar plans to do," Natalia continued. "If he balks, I'll sound the alarm in Washington. If he concedes, the moment you have the document in hand, I will rally the journalists to trumpet news across the land. It will lock the czar into position, and he will lose face if the army goes back on his word."

It felt like old times. They would be working in tandem on opposite sides of the earth, still joined together in a noble cause. Dimitri warmed with pride as he raised his teacup in a silent toast, and Natalia clicked her teacup with his.

But then her gaze strayed over his shoulder. He turned to see what captured her attention and spotted a woman who had just pulled the flap of her blouse aside to let a baby nurse.

Joy faded, and he turned back around, but Natalia still contemplated the woman, a wistful smile hovering on her mouth.

"You would like a baby," he stated needlessly.

She did not tear her gaze from the nursing child, but she gave a little nod of her head. As much as he loved her, he could never give her what she wanted most.

"We could adopt," he said abruptly. "Were you to come to Russia with me, we could adopt as many children as you wish."

"I know," she whispered. "But there's something about having a baby of one's own."

Without warning, she stood and began weaving through the densely packed tables to approach the woman.

"How old is he?" she asked the woman in Russian, but Dimitri turned away before he heard the answer. This was too painful to watch.

Behind him, the two women chatted, and Natalia's cooing over the infant felt like shards of glass. He could lay a fortune at her feet, but he could never give her a child, and that fact would hurt until his dying day.

Natalia's heart ached as she escorted Dimitri to the steamship that would take him back to Russia. She clasped his hand as they walked toward the embarkation point. All around her, life went on as usual. Water sloshed against boulders lining the harbor, seagulls wheeled overhead, and excited children pestered their parents to board the ship, but inside, her heart was breaking.

It was time to say good-bye. She was determined to do it with grace and good cheer. After all, Dimitri was going home to his beloved Mirosa, and she ought to be overjoyed for him.

"I will forever wish you well," she said, looking him in the face even though it mirrored the pain in her own.

"This doesn't have to be the end, does it?" he asked. "Even after we have secured the czar's agreement . . . you will still send me telegrams, won't you?"

She nodded. "Of course."

"I am not sure what will happen once I arrive back in Russia. The road ahead is not clear to me."

"Please don't die heroically," she said, trying to laugh a little. "I know that would be breaking with Russian tradition, but, Dimitri, I couldn't bear it."

"Shh. If the worst happens, we shall be like characters in one of those epic novels that hold the world spellbound by exploring the depth of human misery."

Natalia pulled back a few inches. "I never thought a man

would try to tempt me with the prospect of 'exploring the depth of human misery.' Is that the best you can do?"

He leaned down to touch his forehead to hers. The wistful smile on his face caused the corners of his eyes to crinkle with affection. "We have known great joy, have we not, Natalia?"

She nodded. It was the best she could do because of the lump in her throat.

"I don't think the worst will happen, but I am not afraid to die," he continued. "If God calls me home early, I will go, knowing I have done my best to carry out His will."

She loved that he had such faith. Everything he said was correct, but she wasn't as good and selfless as Dimitri.

"I still wish you wouldn't go. I love you and I'm afraid for you."

He tucked a few wayward strands of hair behind her ear. "Don't fear for me. Natalia . . . I will never stop hoping that you can join me at Mirosa. You can come with me right now. Walk up the gangplank with me. The captain of the ship can marry us today."

She couldn't take it anymore. She reached up to grab his cheeks and pull him down for a hard, fast kiss. "Go," she said. "Go and make the czar honor his agreement. Go get your title back and return to Mirosa in time for the apple harvest."

Mercifully, he didn't press her. He merely clasped her hand over the pounding of his heart. "I will carry you here always," he said, then turned, and she watched until his tall frame disappeared through the gates.

A better woman would wait for him to emerge on the deck of the ship to wave a final good-bye, but she couldn't. It would be awful if Dimitri's last sight of her on this earth was of her blubbering on the shore as he sailed away.

She straightened her shoulders and turned around, pushing through the throngs of people preparing to wave farewell to the ship. She hadn't cried. She'd comported herself like a sensible woman who was going to survive this heartbreak perfectly well. There wasn't even any need to retreat home. Instead, she would visit stores that sold phonographs to begin learning about the music industry.

Her good intentions lasted until she reached the street, where she was surprised to see Liam waiting beside a carriage. His face softened in sympathy when he spotted her, and he closed the distance between them.

"What are you doing here?" she asked, though she suspected the answer.

"I figured you could use a friend right now. Let me take you to the *Black Rose*. We can both play hooky from work and go for a sail."

"I'm fine," she said. "Truly. You don't need to help me pick up the pieces." She would have sounded more convincing if her voice hadn't cracked on that last bit, but her eyes started to prickle, and sometimes everything was just so hard.

"You're not fine," Liam said. "Come home with me."

She was glad he said it instead of her. Everything was falling apart. Nothing was left. Her face crumpled, and Liam's arms closed around her.

"You're going to be okay," he said. "It'll just take some time, but you're the toughest lady I know."

She wasn't tough. She was a weepy mess and had just lost the man she would probably love forever.

A heartbreak was something she could survive, and it was time to embark on a new life. The one she would have chosen for herself was gone, but a blank canvas lay ahead. It was up to her to decide what the rest of her life would look like.

Her first order of business was to make Tachenko's recording and mass-produce copies to distribute all over the country, because despite Dimitri's assurances, Natalia still didn't trust the czar.

29

An ominous sense of uncertainty tormented Dimitri throughout his voyage home. It took three weeks to make his way back to Saint Petersburg, all the while wondering if the czar's promise might somehow be a cruel trick that would be revoked the moment he set foot on Russian soil.

His fears came to nothing. As he stepped off the train in Saint Petersburg, he was greeted by the familiar face of Felix Lapikov, the clerk who had served the Sokolov family for the past thirty-five years. He had long sideburns, a bald head, and eyes as sharp as an eagle's, and he quickly set Dimitri's fears to rest.

"I have secured ownership for your townhouse in Saint Petersburg," Felix said. "It has been cleaned, aired, and prepared for occupancy. Same with Mirosa. Your mother has already moved back to Mirosa and has summoned people from all over the valley to a party to welcome you home."

The relief was dizzying. Dimitri arranged for Felix to deliver his trunk to Mirosa because he was too impatient to accompany the lumbering wagon that wouldn't arrive until after nightfall. He hired a horse to ride directly home and could arrive within two hours if he hurried.

Soon he was riding through the countryside, fields of grain stretching on either side of him. How desperately he had missed the sights of these expansive Russian skies. He nudged the horse into a canter once he was on Sokolov land, smiling at the groves of apple trees interspersed with woodland meadows.

It felt like a dream as he rounded the bend of cedar trees and Mirosa came into view. The dacha's peaked roofline and wooden timbers were exactly as he remembered, nestled into this calm, timeless haven. The old waterwheel beside the cider mill rotated as always. Crates of apples were stacked beside the mill, ready to be made into cider.

He hadn't even dismounted when people came rushing out of the house. Old friends. Neighbors. People from all over the valley streamed toward him. Laughter came from deep inside as he vaulted off the horse, striding the last few yards to meet them.

He reached for his mother first. Others surrounded them to bombard him with back-pounding hugs and kisses on both cheeks. So many familiar faces! He came of age with these people. The Antonovichs from across the lake. Count Ulyanov had taught him how to hunt doves, and he used to fish with Baron Moroshkin. Olga, still as lovely as the moon. The local shopkeepers, the priest, and the tutor from the local school were all here.

After three years stationed in Siberia and then the year of exile, at long last Dimitri had come home. And for the first time in four years, he was utterly and entirely content.

The celebration to welcome him home lasted so long into the night that most of the guests remained at Mirosa and slept late the following morning.

Not Dimitri. Knowledge that he was back home awoke him before dawn. At four o'clock he stood on the front porch, watching the sun rise above the horizon in a dreamlike haze of amber light.

God, thank you for bringing me home, he silently prayed. *The glory of your everlasting kingdom is spread out before me, and everything inside me rejoices. I know I must continue to fight in your name. Please be with me as I carry out the final chapter of this quest.*

Dimitri stayed to feel the sun begin to warm the earth and until the chatter of sparrows in the cedar trees became lively. People were stirring inside the house, and it was time to join his guests, but he wanted to remember this moment for all time. His life came with no guarantees, and each golden sunrise could be his last.

By the time he headed back inside, Boris Antonovich was settled in the breakfast room, preparing a pipe. Mr. Antonovich was a lawyer from Saint Petersburg who rarely indulged in languid mornings of leisure. Already he had a law journal open before him, but he pushed it aside to welcome Dimitri to the table.

"Your mother is impatient to return to Saint Petersburg," Mr. Antonovich said, drawing on his pipe. "She knew you'd want to come straight to Mirosa, but she'll start nagging to go back to town soon."

Dimitri prepared himself a cup of tea. "My mother deserves to do whatever she wishes. I shall remain here."

"Olga has been waiting for you. She'll probably want to go back to town too."

Lovely Olga. When they were children, he and Olga used to catch frogs together, and in the evenings, they searched for fireflies. Now she was a widow with two children under the age of five. She had left her children in Moscow with their nanny, which was a sign that Olga might be here to rekindle their romance. There were all sorts of reasons he should welcome it . . . but he had not given up on luring Natalia here.

"What about you?" Dimitri asked, since lawyers like Mr. Antonovich rarely spent much time at their country estates.

"Saint Petersburg isn't what it used to be," Mr. Antonovich replied. "Even the czar has left. He now lives at Tsarskoye Selo and rarely ventures into the city except on state business."

Dimitri blinked in surprise. The town of Tsarskoye Selo was south of Saint Petersburg and where the czar had a summer home, but it was nowhere near as grand as the Winter Palace.

"Why has he left?" Dimitri asked.

"Baron Freedericksz insisted upon it."

Woldemar Freedericksz ruled over the imperial household with an iron fist. It was Baron Freedericksz who had refused to allow Dimitri access to the czar after the catastrophe at the Amur River. To this day, Dimitri didn't know if blame for what happened to him should lie with Baron Freedericksz or Czar Nicholas. Possibly both.

"So if I wish to see the czar, Baron Freedericksz is the man I must consult?"

Mr. Antonovich nodded. "Yes, but why jump into matters of state again so quickly? You have your freedom and your property back. Relax and regain your strength, because it looks like you have aged ten years in the past twelve months. Nothing in the world will heal you like a month at Mirosa."

A part of Dimitri agreed with Mr. Antonovich. The peaceful rhythm of life in this valley was a balm to his soul. He had everything he wanted or needed right here.

But within an hour, he had drafted a message to Baron Freedericksz, insisting on an audience with Czar Nicholas, because until he had an official recommitment to the 1858 treaty, he could never rest easy.

30

The best remedy for a broken heart was a daunting task, and Natalia found that challenge in learning all aspects of the budding music industry. The creation and distribution of records required equal parts musical insight and business acumen, along with a dash of chemistry, physics, and engineering.

She began educating herself in Jersey City, where the record factory looked more like a chemistry lab than a place that could mass-produce records. Henry Weisbaum was the production manager. The wiry man wore grease-stained coveralls, but he had the vocabulary of a physics professor as he explained how master copies of musical recordings were made. Sound caused vibrations to oscillate a stylus as it traveled across a waxy disc, cutting minuscule grooves in the surface. An acid bath fixed the grooves, allowing it to serve as a master copy from which additional records could be produced.

"This is aluminum oleate," Henry said as he pried the lid from a steel drum to show her the brown, jelly-like material. "Up until a year ago, we used it to coat our master discs before the recording, but lately we've been experimenting with a blend of montan wax and petroleum jelly. The musicians hate it, because we've got to keep the recording studio hot so the wax stays pliable, but the results sound better. We've got a team of chemists working on a modified version that will be soft enough to work at room temperature."

Henry kept filling her arms with discs as they toured the production floor. "This one was made with the electroplating technique," or "this one is the old stamp technique. It's cheaper but sounds a little tinny in the higher registers."

By the time Natalia finished her tour, she had ten sample recordings, each manufactured with slightly different techniques. She would listen to them all and then decide which sort of process would be best for Tachenko's recording. All the samples were of a soprano singing the same opera song to make the comparison easier.

Normally Natalia disliked opera, but not anymore! Now she felt like a scientist as she studied the recordings, listening for variations caused by the different chemicals and recording techniques.

She wanted additional opinions and took the records to the *Black Rose*, where she played the records for Liam and Darla.

Liam didn't like opera either. "You owe me a gourmet dinner for making me listen to that soprano bellow."

"Her name is Adelina Patti, and she is a very famous singer," Darla said. "I think it's marvelous that she's lending her talent to help advance the industry."

"She sounds like she's being tortured on the rack," Liam replied.

Natalia put on another record to listen to the same song recorded using a different blend of wax. "Close your eyes and tell me if this one has better sound quality."

Despite his disdain for opera, Liam dropped his pained expression and settled down to listen, closing his eyes in concentration as the different recordings filled the room with music.

"I don't mind a little of that background noise so long as the sound is good," he said. "What did you call that noise?"

"Clutter," Natalia replied. "That's what the production manager calls it, and it's going to be a challenge to get rid of it." Some of the discs had no clutter but sounded tinny. Others were perfect, but the music sounded as if it came from very far away. "My hunch is that it won't be so noticeable when an entire orchestra is playing a song instead of just a solo performer."

"Let's have the next one," Darla said, and Natalia swapped out the electroplated disc for one made with the new wax blend.

Once again, Liam settled in to listen with total concentration as he closed his eyes and turned his ear to the music, but this time he clasped Darla's hand. The way he traced his thumb across the back of her hand was sweet. They seemed such opposites: Liam a big tough man and Darla refined and smart as a whip, but they seemed to fit.

It made Natalia feel like a third wheel. Was there anything worse for a lonely person than to be lumped in with a happy couple? This time when the needle came to the end of the recording, the disc kept rotating, and the needle made a staticky clicking sound over and over. Neither Liam nor Darla noticed; they just kept staring at Liam's thumb tracing a pattern on the back of Darla's hand.

Natalia rose and lifted the needle. "I should head home."

Liam snapped back to attention. "Did you get what you needed?"

Mostly. She already knew which technique could make the most of Tachenko's talents. What she really wanted tonight was human companionship. She'd found it but somehow felt lonelier than ever.

It was late before Natalia arrived back home to begin preparing dinner in her newly remodeled kitchen. When she first bought this modest townhouse, she wanted to prove herself superior to Poppy by living humbly and doing everything herself. Even after the plumbing disaster, she tried to repair everything on her own to prove her independence to Poppy.

It had been nothing more than immature pride. She didn't need to prove herself against Poppy. Natalia paid a plumber to add a hot water heater and additional lines so that she now had decent plumbing throughout the house. The charming wood-land mantelpiece had been repaired with a series of tiny screws that were almost invisible. The house smelled like new plaster and fresh paint, and the water no longer gurgled in failing pipes.

Poppy never breathed a word about how Natalia hired out-siders to do the work. She probably neither knew nor cared. Natalia's life became much easier once she stopped competing in endless games of one-upmanship with Poppy.

A knock at the door interrupted her thoughts, and she opened it to see a young man from the Western Union holding a telegram.

"Miss Natalia Blackstone?" he asked, and she nodded. She shouldn't get too excited, because the message could be from anyone, but it had been three weeks since she'd said good-bye to Dimitri, and he should be home by now.

She signed for the message and tipped the man, then tore the message from its sleeve. The lengthy, rambling text was a dead giveaway that it was from Dimitri. She smiled at its length, because no one else on the planet wasted so much money on telegrams.

Dearest Natalia. I have returned to Mirosa. The valley is as I remem-ber, with amber sunlight that makes the air shimmer like spun gold. I like to imagine you beside me as I walk the hills of my estate. I would show you the apple groves and the profusion of lilacs that perfume the air. When we are tired from walking, we will lie on our backs and gaze at the clouds overhead and dream of the world to come. Natalia, I want you to join me in Russia. These days have been the happiest and saddest of my life. My spirit rejoices at being back home, but my soul aches for you. Come to Mirosa, Natalia! I will be waiting for you with open arms. If you wish to work in a bank, we shall find a way to make it happen. If you wish to relax and do nothing more stressful than watch the sun rise and set, there is a balcony from my house overlooking the valley where we can do this together.

I have not yet seen the czar or secured a reaffirmation of the treaty. The czar surrounds himself with people who shield him from distasteful

news, but I continue to work toward a meeting. Until then, I savor my
time at Mirosa and dream of the day you will join me.

Natalia leaned against the doorjamb, holding the telegram
to her heart. The world Dimitri painted seemed so perfect. She
could pack a trunk and be on the next steamship, but the logical
part of her mind overruled the wayward impulse.

She would turn into a shell of a woman if she lived at Mirosa.
She still didn't know exactly what God wanted her to do with
her abilities, but it wasn't to watch the sun rise and set in a
rural dacha.

She and Dimitri hadn't even been apart for a month, and it
was natural for the pain of separation to still be fierce. It might
not last. It was easy for Dimitri to ask her to join him in Russia,
but he wasn't the one who would leave his home, family, and
every familiar guidepost in his world.

But still, a part of her was tempted.

31

Once Dimitri began wiring Natalia, it was impossible to stop. Back when they corresponded during his work on the railroad, he hadn't truly known her. They liked and respected each other, but he didn't know the cadence of her voice, or the way she could sound serious even when she was teasing, or how comfortably her head fit beneath his jaw when he embraced her. Now he knew all those things and heard Natalia's real voice while reading her messages, which made them all the more meaningful.

In the mornings Dimitri worked in the old cider mill on his estate, but in the late afternoons he rode into town, since Natalia would be awake in New York and he could pester her for a little conversation. Lately she had been eager to tell him about her recording of "Waves of the Amur." Maxim Tachenko recorded the song perfectly on his first and only take, and she was currently shipping the discs across the United States.

Her success with "Waves of the Amur" had inspired her to commission additional recordings of other musicians, and he wanted to know more. From the moment she told him about her new venture, he had been cheering her on from afar.

Well, mostly cheering her on. He hectored her mercilessly over her regrettable fondness for German composers, but what vision! What chutzpah! Watching Natalia embark on this new line of business was almost as much fun as being a part of it himself.

The general store was two miles away, a sad little outpost with one wall of canned goods, a shelf of vodka and hard cider, and barrels of flour, barley, and oats filling most of the floorspace. In one corner behind the front counter was a telegraph machine, possibly the best invention of the past century for rural people because it was a lifeline to the rest of the world.

Natalia usually gave more interesting replies when he teased her, so he started with a modest jab.

Dearest Natalia. I await with bated breath to learn which musical interlude you have chosen for your next release. For the love of all humanity, I pray it is not another German composer. Sincerely, your devoted Dimitri.

He went outside to await her reply. It would take a while for the message to arrive at her townhouse and then for her to walk the two blocks to the nearest pharmacy, but he liked to imagine her receiving his note. The smile on her face. The way her clever eyes would flash with calculation while planning her reply.

A gust of wind carried a smattering of leaves through the air. The days were growing shorter, and soon the dark Russian winter would be upon them, but for today he looked with fondness on the worn country lane leading to this store. He was getting used to this view as his regular exchanges with Natalia filled his hours.

Twenty minutes after sending the telegram, mechanical tapping from inside the store brought him to his feet. He loitered impatiently as the clerk handwrote the message for him and put his hand out to read it as soon as it was done.

"Two rubles," the shopkeeper demanded, holding the telegram to his chest.

Dimitri paid the man, impatient to see what Natalia wrote.

He smiled as he read that she had commissioned a recording of Brahms's *Hungarian Dances*. The master copy was already complete, and she was headed to the factory in Jersey City to oversee the production of a thousand copies.

His heart swelled with pride. Natalia had made the bank the center of her world for too long. Now that she had been driven out of it, she was pursuing her love of moody, romantic music that she'd always kept carefully concealed.

He could not resist the temptation to advise her on upcoming recordings.

> No more German music, please. I humbly suggest one of the new Russian composers whose visionary style will lead us into the new century.

Her response wasn't long in coming. She insisted that Russian composers like Rimsky-Korsakov and Alexander Borodin were not well known in America and she wouldn't earn her investment back on the master copy. He replied they were famous in Europe and had attained near-sacred status in Russia.

Once again, her response came within a few minutes.

> I am not selling records in Russia. I need to sell them in America.

Dimitri set the message on the front counter, thrumming his fingers against it. Why couldn't she sell them in Russia? If she could ship railroad supplies to Siberia, why couldn't she send a few crates of record albums to Saint Petersburg? It was the most sophisticated city in all of Russia, and he could sell them for her. He and Natalia had been business partners on the Trans-Siberian, and they could be partners again.

He impulsively scribbled out his proposal and thrust it at the clerk.

> Commission five thousand copies of "Flight of the Bumblebee" by Rimsky-Korsakov and ship them to me. I will sell them for you here.

Her reaction was shocked, as he knew it would be, but Natalia was a woman of business and naturally cautious. In time, she would see the merit of his proposal. After only two more exchanges of messages, she agreed to the venture.

That day began their new business relationship. In the coming weeks she advised him on which types of retail shops sold musical recordings, and he sought them out to initiate an agreement to sell Natalia's records. Their new partnership wasn't as good as having her here, but it was satisfying.

And perhaps in time, he could figure out a way to bring her here in person, and for good.

32

*D*imitri had been back at Mirosa for two weeks but still had no response from Baron Freedericksz about an audience with the czar. Perhaps the baron thought Dimitri would be satisfied by the return of his title and property and would no longer stir up trouble regarding the massacre on the Amur.

If so, the baron thought wrong.

Tachenko's recording of "Waves of the Amur" was now selling all over America, and Dimitri was prepared to start selling them in Russia too. It would be dangerous to release the incendiary violinist's recording, but unless the czar renewed his commitment to the 1858 treaty, Dimitri intended to start the drumbeat here in Russia as well.

In the meantime, he sank back into work at Mirosa's cider mill, doing everything from making the apple mash to bottling the cider. It was exhausting work, but a good sort of exhaustion that came with a sense of accomplishment from a job well done. Things were exactly as he remembered, from the creak of the waterwheel to the sweet scent of autumn hay. All of it was a balm to his soul.

Yesterday he had worked with Pavel Golubev, the overseer of the mill, to repair the ancient waterwheel, which was beginning to wobble and show its age. This morning he helped unload a cartload of apples from a local farmer. The Sokolovs grew more than enough apples to supply the mill, but they always bought from local people too. Apples were an easy form of income for the poor, and buying from them helped ease tensions in the valley.

The afternoon was growing late, and Dimitri hoisted another bushel of classic reds onto his shoulder and dumped them into the vat of water. Pavel cranked the flywheel while Dimitri used a rake to nudge the apples toward the millstone, blinking as cold droplets splashed his face.

He and Pavel had worked in tandem for several minutes when Pavel abruptly stopped cranking the flywheel and swept the cap from his head. Dimitri followed his gaze, surprised to see his elegant mother picking her way across the lumpy yard outside the mill.

"Mama!" he greeted her affectionately. He had been upset when he first saw her upon his return to Mirosa. Her hair had turned mostly gray, and worry lines had been permanently carved onto her face. Her traumatized appearance eased following his return, but the past year of being turned out of her home had been difficult for her. Perhaps that was why she was doing her best to regain her former standing in the valley by always appearing immaculately dressed, with jewels on her hands and pearls around her neck.

"Come in out of the mud," he urged, leading her to the patio outside the mill.

"Why is the ground so sticky?" she asked as she eyed the slate pavers.

Dimitri had been too busy to notice the condition of the slate, but Pavel quickly answered. "Ilya Komarov was here last night. He never cleans up properly."

His mother's face stiffened. "If that ruffian can't be respectful of the privilege we grant him by allowing him to use our mill, he should be fined and banned from the property."

"Mama, please," Dimitri said soothingly, even though it looked like Pavel agreed. The last thing Dimitri wanted to do was stir up trouble in the valley, and Ilya was a hard worker. He lived in a ramshackle cabin with his wife and two sons down at the river's bend. Instead of selling his apples to Dimitri like others in the valley, Ilya paid a small fee to use the mill and produced his own cider. At least, that was what Ilya claimed to be doing. Dimitri suspected Ilya fermented his cider into applejack, which was almost as potent and profitable as vodka.

"He's using our best barrels too," Pavel said. "The older the barrel, the better the cider. Last night two of our best barrels went missing. He's been doing it every year since you left for Siberia."

"Does he bring them back?" Dimitri asked.

"Eventually."

Dimitri didn't want to discuss this in front of his mother. He turned to her with a smile. "What can I do for you, Mama?"

"I need help planning the house party, and you always have such clever ideas."

His mother loved hosting gatherings that lasted for days. Local landowners and aristocrats from the valley gathered for party games, walks in the woods, and singing long into the night.

"Come sit on the bench and let's discuss it," Dimitri said, eager to get his mother off the subject of the sticky mill floor. It was a working mill, which meant it was going to get dirty, but someone of his mother's station had little experience with the world of work.

He led her to the bench outside, but before they could begin the discussion, he spotted a familiar figure heading their way.

"Is that man back again?" his mother asked, displeasure plain in her voice.

Ilya Komarov had just rounded the bend by the cedar trees, walking alongside a wagon filled with apples and pulled by an aging nag. Dimitri pitied the old horse. At least Ilya had the decency to walk instead of riding in the wagon and making the nag work even harder.

"He pays to use the mill every evening after six o'clock," Dimitri said.

She frowned in disapproval. "We don't need the money, and I don't like him spattering apple juice on the floor."

"Then head indoors while I speak with him." Dimitri didn't care about the sticky floor, but he did mind the loss of the barrels. The milling season wasn't even halfway over, and he might need them.

His mother was gone by the time Ilya pulled the wagon up to the mill and unhooked the kerosene lantern attached to the buckboard. Ilya would need the lantern because he rarely finished before midnight. It couldn't be an easy life. During the day Ilya worked as a carpenter, and then he made cider long into the night.

"Is Pavel done for the day?" Ilya asked as he began unloading crates of apples. He had blond hair and pale blue eyes and was the sort of strong, brawny man whose features looked like they had been carved by an ax.

Dimitri nodded. "The mill is yours until dawn."

Ilya gave a brusque nod and lugged a crate of apples inside the mill. Dimitri followed a few steps behind, and Ilya looked at him curiously.

Dimitri glanced at the supply room. "Am I going to find two more barrels missing from the supply room by morning?"

"Maybe," Ilya said with a nonchalant shrug. "Why should you care? You've got plenty, and I always return them."

"You didn't ask, and I might need them."

Ilya's blue eyes turned flinty. "Those barrels were made by my father back when he was a serf for your family. Nobody ever paid him a kopek for those barrels, and your family took his labor for free all his life."

"Ilya, let's not refight the emancipation battles. All that happened decades ago."

Like hundreds of others in the valley, Ilya came from a family of serfs bonded on Sokolov land until they were liberated by Czar Alexander II in 1861. At that time, a third of the Russian population had been born into serfdom, which was little better than slavery. The czar wanted to liberate the serfs from above rather than wait for revolution from below. Czar Alexander successfully freed the serfs, but it didn't buy him goodwill. He was blown to pieces by an assassin's bomb twenty years later because the anarchists claimed he hadn't done enough. The aftermath of the czar's assassination put the Russian nobility on edge for years, but those times were long past. In the decades since liberation, many of the former serfs managed to earn a respectable standard of living.

Ilya Komarov was just such a man. He was hardworking and successful, but his pale, flinty eyes always seemed to be glaring in resentment. Perhaps liberation hadn't changed Ilya's world all that much. While Dimitri was sent off to elite schools in Moscow and Zurich, Ilya never went to school at all. Ilya grew up in his father's footsteps by becoming a carpenter. It wasn't fair, and ever since that horrible day at the Amur River, Russia's history of oppression weighed more heavily on Dimitri's conscience.

"Keep the barrels," he said impulsively.

"Keep them?" Ilya asked, surprise evident in his voice.

"Yes. Your father made them. They are yours."

Ilya's expression did not soften. If anything, a hint of suspicion took root, but he nodded and touched the brim of his cap as he turned away to unload the rest of his apples.

Dimitri was going to have to keep his eye on this one.

To Natalia's surprise, Liam's proposal to improve the wages for the workers at U.S. Steel was finally taking shape. The meeting of the board of directors was coming up, but despite how hard Liam had been working, it was doubtful his idealistic proposal would fly. It was too ambitious, and Liam refused to scale it back.

Natalia arranged for Liam to practice his presentation for her father on the *Black Rose*. When Oscar owned this yacht, he used to host regular parties for her entire family. She'd loved the afternoon sails as her aunts, uncles, and cousins gathered to play shuffleboard and dine al fresco on the deck. Now that Liam owned the yacht, she'd persuaded him to continue the periodic gatherings. Most of the family was up on deck while Liam and her father retreated to the cardroom downstairs to discuss his proposal.

Poppy didn't approve of Alexander being exposed to so much sunlight and wanted the nanny to take him downstairs, but Natalia volunteered to play with the child instead. It was the perfect excuse to remain in the cardroom and eavesdrop on Liam's presentation. She sat on the floor with Alexander, casually tossing blocks across the carpeted floor. She watched the baby scramble after them while listening to Liam and her father at the nearby table.

"The profit margin on steel has increased thirty percent because of the new furnaces," Liam said.

"So has the cost for iron ore and limestone," Oscar interrupted.

Liam shook his head. "Iron is only up twelve percent, and limestone has held steady. The profitability of steel has gone up thirty percent, and the men on the line should get the same raise."

"And if the price of steel falls?" Oscar asked. "Do the men absorb a pay cut each time the price dips?"

Liam answered the question perfectly, referencing a mathematical model she had written for him with a built-in floor for wages during economic downturns.

The baby crawled back to her, presenting a block to her with a radiant, drooling smile. Alexander had recently started saying his first words, and he called her Nala, which she loved. His attempts to say *mother* ended up as *mud*, which annoyed Poppy but made Natalia secretly smile.

She gave Alexander back his block, which promptly went into his mouth. Meanwhile, Liam continued outlining his plan for ensuring the labor force could be paid during economic downturns.

A knock on the door interrupted them, and Patrick stepped inside the cardroom, one of the ship's porters standing behind him.

"Excuse me," Patrick said. "I hate to spoil the afternoon sail, but Gwen is a little seasick. We'd like to return to port."

"Seasick?" Oscar growled. "Nonsense. Gwen has the constitution of a horse."

"A pregnant horse," Patrick said. "The chop on the water is getting to her, so please head back to port."

Natalia looked away. Gwen was four months along, and Natalia was happy for her. Of course she was. But it made her miss Dimitri. A tiny part of her had harbored hope that as soon as Dimitri arrived in Russia, he would quickly secure the necessary promises from the czar and rush back to America. Instead, she was treated to rapturous messages about the loveliness of his valley and the joy he took in being home.

Dimitri would never come back. He would probably marry Olga and raise her children while Natalia stayed in New York and watched other women have babies. She sighed and pulled Alexander onto her lap, hugging him tightly.

Oscar wasn't happy with Patrick's request. "My wife was looking forward to seeing the West Point cavalry on parade this afternoon."

"We're only half an hour into the sail," Patrick said. "You still have plenty of time to get there."

Her father glanced at the porter in annoyance. "Very well, order the helmsman to turn about as soon as lunch has been served."

Liam stood. "Go ahead and order him to turn around now. It's my yacht and my decision to make."

Natalia bit her tongue. Why did men have to beat their chests like that? Her father owned this yacht for years before Liam managed to finagle it out of his clutches, and the loss of it still smarted.

Patrick nodded and left to arrange for the ship to turn around, but the business negotiation suffered. Oscar started attacking Liam's numbers, and Liam got defensive. Then he confused depreciation with deflation, and Oscar pounced on the error. Liam was going to have to do better if he expected to win the confidence of the other board members on Friday.

Natalia had turned her attention back to Alexander and his uncomplicated love when the door opened so abruptly that it banged against the outside wall, and Poppy stormed inside.

"Patrick says you've turned the boat around," she accused Liam.

"That's right."

"Gwen shouldn't have come if she was going to get seasick. I never suffered a day of seasickness when I carried Alexander, and if I did, I wouldn't have made the rest of the world cater to my frailties. I want to see the horses at West Point."

Natalia shifted Alexander in her arms. "The cavalry practices every weekend," she pointed out. "We can always come back next Saturday."

"But I wanted to see them *today*. Alexander, don't put that block in your mouth. It's dirty."

Natalia said nothing, but she took the block away, causing a snivel from the boy. She sent him a reassuring smile to fend off a crying jag, and Alexander beamed back at her.

His adoring smile sent Poppy into a rage. "Alexander, come to Mama," she ordered, stepping forward to swoop the boy into her arms.

Alexander's face twisted as he started whimpering.

"Hush that nonsense right now," Poppy ordered, hefting him higher in her arms, which caused him to break into a wail.

"I think he's getting hungry," Natalia said.

"You don't know that," Poppy snapped. "And why did you let him put that dirty block in his mouth if you knew he was hungry?"

The harsh tone frightened Alexander, who tried to twist out of Poppy's arms and reach toward Natalia. Poppy grabbed the boy's hands and jerked them back.

"That's enough, young man," she said, shooting Natalia

a poisonous glance. "I think you're trying to win him away from me."

"Poppy, that's ridiculous."

"Is it?" she demanded. "You spoil him with attention every time you see him. I think it's time for a little more distance between the two of you."

Poppy left the cardroom, taking Alexander with her and leaving that ominous threat hanging in the air. With a sinking feeling, Natalia realized there was nothing she could do if Poppy decided to withhold her brother.

Natalia watched the moonlight glint on the water as she stood on the deck of the *Black Rose*, alone in the darkness. The day had been awful. After returning Gwen to port, they sailed up the Hudson for the two-hour journey to West Point, but the cavalry had just finished their afternoon parade when they arrived, and it put Poppy into a royal snit. Alexander had not reappeared from the stateroom where he had been banished to keep him away from Natalia.

The thought of returning to her empty townhouse was dispiriting, and she had gladly accepted Liam's offer to spend the night in one of the staterooms on the *Black Rose*. It was ten o'clock, which meant it was only five o'clock in the morning at Mirosa, too early to send a telegram to Dimitri and pour out her heart. Her greatest fear was beginning to happen. Poppy could take Alexander away from her, and Oscar wouldn't stand up to Poppy. He would make a few gestures, but when push came to shove, Poppy ruled the household and everyone in it.

She swiveled at the sound of a door opening and was relieved to see Liam heading her way with a small silver flask in one hand and a jug of milk in the other.

"Nightcap?" he asked, holding up the flask. She shook her head, and he held up the jug. "Milk?"

She shook her head again. Liam joined her at the railing and took a swig directly out of the milk jug. He used to drink plenty of hard liquor, but in recent months an ulcer had begun eating at his gut. The doctor said it was caused by stress, and now Liam drank only milk.

"Out with it," Liam said after he set the jug on the deck. "What's got you so glum?"

She shrugged. Only a perfectly horrible person would be jealous about Gwen's pregnancy, but there it was. Natalia would slip into a cold and lonely bed tonight. Tomorrow she would face a myriad of decisions with no one to lean on. And with each passing month, she grew a little older with no child in her life, just a brother Poppy might withhold from her whenever the mood struck.

"Sometimes I wonder if I should have followed him."

Liam immediately knew who she spoke about and sent her a pained smile.

"I miss him," she continued. "When we were together, it felt like we could fly. He was strong and funny and confident. No matter what, I always knew Dimitri would look out for me."

Liam snickered. "Every time I saw him, he was pestering you for a manicure."

She laughed because it was true, but what other people didn't understand was that she and Dimitri took care of each other. They were equals, leaning on each other when needed, but usually their combined energy and talent made them soar.

And she *liked* giving him manicures. After all he had been through, Dimitri deserved a little pampering, and she'd been happy to provide it. Knowing that she might never again have the chance to do so triggered a physical ache in her chest. She looked at the moonlight on the water, wishing she could see all the way across the ocean, Europe, and straight to Saint Petersburg.

"I still wonder if I should go. Between a steamship and a train, I could be there in three weeks."

"You don't want to go to Russia." Liam's voice was unaccountably serious.

"Why not?"

"There's trouble brewing in Russia. You won't read about it in the newspapers because it's simmering beneath the surface, but it's been building up for years, like a valve about to blow. I still have union friends, the sketchy type who mingle with bomb-throwers and rabble-rousers. They have their ear to the ground in Russia, and it's not going to be good for people like Count Sokolov."

She stiffened. "Thank you, Liam, but I don't need your advice about Russia."

He frowned. "You don't need to sound so snotty about it."

"I'm heading to bed," she said, reluctant to continue this conversation.

Because she feared Liam might be right.

33

imitri finally received an answer to his request for an audience with the czar, and the news wasn't good. The family's secretary personally delivered the message to Mirosa, and Dimitri went with Felix into his father's old study to read the message.

> *This is not a matter for the Imperial Majesty, but you will be allotted fifteen minutes to present your concerns to Baron Freedericksz's office on February 3rd at Tsarskoye Selo.*

Dimitri wasn't going to wait five months, especially since neither the baron nor the czar would be in Tsarskoye Selo in February. Everyone knew the entire royal family and its entourage would spend the winter in the Crimea.

Dimitri glanced up at his secretary. "They are hoping I have become seduced by my life of leisure here at Mirosa."

"Have you?" Felix asked.

It wasn't an irrational question. Dimitri looked around the careworn study brimming with old books, comfortable furniture, and a view over the valley. This was the only life he'd ever wanted, and if Natalia were here, it would be perfect.

"Yes," he admitted. "I am enchanted with my life here. Sadly for Baron Freedericksz, I also remain committed to forcing a public reaffirmation of the Treaty of Aigun from the czar, and I have a plan to force his hand."

He passed an old, battered volume filled with dry government reports to Felix. "I've always found that shining sunlight on inconvenient facts is the best ammunition," he said, and quickly conveyed his scheme to Felix. After a few hours fleshing out the details, he sent Felix to Saint Petersburg to continue gathering research.

Then Dimitri joined his guests. It was the fifth day of his mother's weeklong house party for their friends from the valley. The days were filled with card games, charades, and long hikes in the woods. They sang songs around the piano late into the evening. Tonight they planned a bonfire out back, and the local schoolmaster would recite a theatrical reading.

Dimitri loved the languid pace of life in the countryside. A few of the men had gone fishing, but most relaxed after a full luncheon in the gathering room. Dimitri settled into the corner table with a cup of tea. From here he could watch Olga by the fireplace as she chatted with his mother, because any man with a pulse found it easy to admire Olga Zaripova.

She no longer wore mourning clothes. Olga's dark emerald gown looked spectacular against her blond hair, which was perfectly styled, as always. Olga was Count Ulyanov's daughter, a good man who loved the valley as much as Dimitri did. They'd both been disappointed when the marriage was called off, but perhaps it was for the best. Olga had always preferred the city.

Count Ulyanov beckoned Dimitri over to join a game of dominoes with his wife and the young man who worked as the village tutor. While the tutor distributed the dominoes, Count Ulyanov used the break to retrieve a flask from his breast pocket and pour a splash of amber liquid into a tumbler.

"Applejack?" he offered. Dimitri declined with a slight shake of his head, but Count Ulyanov pressed. "Are you sure? It's the best in the valley. I paid ten rubles for it."

"Is it from Ilya Komarov?" the tutor asked.

"Indeed it is," the count affirmed, and the tutor eagerly proffered his own glass.

"Then you were cheated," the tutor said. "He only charged me four rubles, and I hear he sells it to the farmers for as low as two."

"I told you that man wasn't trustworthy," Dimitri's mother called from the other side of the room.

The tutor shrugged. "It seems like good business to me."

"But he's making it at our mill," his mother sputtered.

"He's only pressing the cider here," Dimitri said. "The work of growing the apples and fermenting them happens on his own property."

Why was he defending Ilya Komarov? The man was a surly hothead who never had a kind word for anyone. He hadn't even thanked Dimitri for the barrels, just walked away as though they were his due.

The dominoes were forgotten as a good-natured debate ensued about whether it was dishonest for Ilya to charge people different prices for the same applejack.

Olga approached, a hint of amusement in her eyes. Dimitri had never realized back when they were children prowling the woods together how lovely she would someday become. Now, with her elegant figure and white-blond hair, she looked like an ice princess . . . but a warm and friendly ice princess.

"When are you coming to Moscow?" she coaxed. "Princess Maria has begged me for an introduction to you. She says heroes are too rare in the world today, and she wants to hold a feast in your honor."

Heat gathered in Dimitri's face. It still felt odd to be considered a hero. No man who quaked in terror the way he had in the Siberian forest could claim hero status, and those anxieties were starting to take root again as he contemplated his coming battle with Baron Freedericksz.

"You know I don't care for Moscow," he said. "Too big. Too crowded."

"The princess lives in a palace surrounded by three hundred

acres. You won't feel crowded. I can introduce you to the princess, and then we can dine on caviar and champagne." Olga settled on the arm of his chair. She lowered her voice as she leaned down to whisper in his ear. "Then we can run out into her garden and search for frogs."

"You remember that, do you?" He smiled up into her eyes. She was so close that her lemony scent surrounded him.

She touched the back of his hand, her fingers soft as eiderdown. "Of course I remember."

The spot where her fingers touched tingled. It was only Friday, and they had a long weekend ahead of them. He needed to change the subject from thoughts of running into a moonlit garden with her.

"When am I going to hear you play the piano?" he asked. "My mother says your rendition of Chopin could make angels weep."

Olga squeezed his hand. "But will it make you weep, Dima?"

No one besides Olga called him Dima anymore, but his childhood nickname felt right on her lips.

"We won't know until you play," he said, wondering if it was wrong to flirt with Olga when his heart still belonged to Natalia.

Either way, he needed to escape from her. It was suffocating in here. He stood, causing Olga to shift off the armchair.

"Forgive me," he said. "I promised Pavel I would help at the mill this afternoon."

He gave a perfunctory bow to Olga, who looked stunned as he left, but he needed to get away. The prospect of working at the mill with Pavel suddenly seemed more appealing than another game of dominoes. Wasn't that odd? There was a time when he loved every moment of these long house parties from start to finish, but that was before he started work on the Trans-Siberian. Things were different now. Around-the-clock leisure no longer held quite the same allure.

He grabbed a rough canvas coat from a hook in the mill and nodded a greeting to Pavel, who had already begun a vat of apple cider vinegar. Dimitri pried the lid from a barrel of discarded apple cores needed for making vinegar. It was a sticky, smelly job, but he didn't mind.

He was scooping apple scraps into the hopper when he spotted Olga picking her way across the yard.

"Dima, please," she coaxed as she stepped up onto the old slate of the mill. "Let's talk."

He didn't want to have this conversation, but it was time. Pavel pretended not to notice as Dimitri brushed off his hands and gestured to the old stone wall bordering the creek that fed the waterwheel.

This wall of fieldstone rock was one of his favorite places on the estate. As a child he used to walk along the top of it even though his father forbade it because a loose stone could send him tumbling into the frigid water. Later he learned that his father had also walked atop the wall during his youth, and his grandfather before him. They had all been scolded about the danger, and should Dimitri ever raise a child here, he would do the same.

Dimitri gestured for Olga to join him on the bench beside the wall, and she started pressuring him to come to Moscow with her.

"You are a celebrity," she said. "Come to Moscow, where you will be the toast of the town. It won't last forever. You can come to the city and meet my children. They are adorable."

A fond ache bloomed in his chest. Olga would someday make a charming wife to a Moscow aristocrat who enjoyed city life as much as she did. Perhaps the curse of the illness he suffered at nineteen had been a blessing in disguise. Olga was not the right partner for him. He wanted Natalia. He wanted Natalia here in the valley, where they could adopt children and watch them grow up tramping through the apple orchards and fishing in the lake and making cider in the autumn. They could spend time at his townhouse in the city, where Natalia could commission the Saint Petersburg Philharmonic to make records to sell all over Russia and Europe. Their lives would be perfect.

"Dima?" Olga asked, her expression confused. "What's wrong? You seem very far away."

He wasn't. His heart was here at Mirosa as it had always been. Now he merely needed a way to bring Natalia to him.

He turned an affectionate gaze to Olga. "You are a rare gem, Olga. You are meant for champagne and caviar, not apple cider and country living. I belong here, not in the glittering world of the city."

Her pout was equal parts teasing and sorrowful. "And that will never change?"

"That will never change."

She kissed him softly on the lips. It was their first kiss since he was nineteen years old, and it would be their last. Affectionate, gentle, and a little bittersweet.

"Farewell, my friend," she said. "I will be off to Moscow in the morning."

Memories of Olga haunted Dimitri the rest of the afternoon while he made cider vinegar with Pavel. He didn't want to return to the house yet because things might still be awkward with Olga.

Just as the sun began to set, Ilya Komarov came down the path with his ancient nag pulling another cartload of apples. Dimitri didn't want Ilya's surly mood tainting one of the last fine evenings of the year, so he retreated back inside.

Even the awkwardness of dealing with Olga was easier than making peace with Ilya. It made Dimitri wonder if allowing the surly carpenter to use his mill had been a mistake.

It was time for Dimitri to confront Baron Freedericksz about the czar's continuing silence on the Treaty of Aigun. Thanks to Felix, Dimitri had everything he needed to make his point blindingly clear to the baron, and hopefully to Czar Nicholas as well. Since his request for a private audience with the czar had been blatantly disrespected, it was time to confront the baron in public.

Before his elevation to the czar's household, Baron Freeder-icksz had been commander of the Imperial Stables, a sprawl-ing complex of manicured fields and stable blocks built in the Gothic Revival style. The buildings all featured pointed arches, mullioned windows, and turrets with crenellated tow-ers. Perhaps Dimitri had spent too long with Maxim Tachenko and Liam Blackstone, but it seemed a shame that the czar's horses lived in better quarters than most of the Russian people.

Baron Freedericksz still attended the weekly cavalry drill, and as expected, he was in attendance today. A group of cavalry officers had gathered near the review stand, all wearing jodh-purs and riding boots, but the sixty-year-old baron was easy to spot. Baron Freedericksz had been growing his mustache for decades, and it was waxed, groomed, and twisted to extend several inches from each side of his face, making him the most recognizable man in court.

Dimitri smiled thinly as he approached. He would project an aura of relaxed charm, but he and the baron would both know the truth.

Dimitri paused a few paces away from the group of cavalry officers. "Baron Freedericksz, we met a number of years ago at the Nevsky Regatta. Count Dimitri Sokolov, at your service."

The officers paused their conversation, and the baron's eyes grew cold. "Yes?" he drawled.

"I would like to arrange an audience with the czar."

"My secretary already made arrangements for us to meet early next year," the baron said dismissively, turning back to the junior officers. On the far side of the field, soldiers walked their horses out of the stable blocks, preparing for review.

"The matter is of considerable importance," Dimitri said.

"Which is why I consented to meet with you early in the new year."

Icicles dripped from the baron's voice, but Dimitri had ex-pected this. Baron Freedericksz was going to stall, delay, and belittle Dimitri in an effort to sweep everything under the carpet and out of sight, but Dimitri was ready to begin firing his ammunition.

He reached into the deep pocket of his overcoat for the slim volume from his library at Mirosa and presented it to the baron. "Please," he said, pushing the book into the baron's hands, "I have marked the chapter on the Treaty of Aigun, and I hope you will review it ahead of our meeting."

"An old law book?" the baron asked.

"An old law book that is in four hundred libraries across the Russian Empire, two hundred in Europe, and seventy-five in the United States. The treaty is well known here, but I have sent copies to statesmen in the United States, Japan, and England to refresh their memories." He reached into his pocket again for a copy of Tachenko's album. "In case you prefer something more modern, here is a recording that has just been released in America. It's called the 'Waves of the Amur,' performed by Maxim Tachenko."

One of the junior officers scoffed. "Tachenko is a disgraced hothead of no consequence anywhere in Russia."

"You should see the standing ovations he receives on his concert tours," Dimitri said. "Nobody in America had even heard of the Amur River until Mr. Tachenko made the song famous. Now this album is being played in parlors across America. The people who commissioned the album would like to distribute them in Russia as well."

They were fighting words, and the baron recognized the threat for what it was. "I shall prohibit any such recordings from entering the country."

A junior officer gestured to the album. "At least one copy is already here."

"Hundreds are already here," Dimitri corrected, for Natalia had made good on her promise to have them shipped. "At the moment they are in a warehouse, but that might change."

"Don't push me," Baron Freedericksz said. "What has been given can be taken away."

It was a reference to Mirosa and his title. Dimitri bowed his head in acknowledgment. "No one understands that better than I do. I would be happy to allow those albums to molder in the warehouse, provided the right conditions are met. Perhaps we can meet after the parade to discuss matters?"

Baron Freedericksz narrowed his eyes. "We will discuss it now," he said, gesturing to the administrative building on the far side of the parade field.

Ten minutes later, Dimitri had agreed to delay the distribution of the albums in exchange for an audience with the czar the following week.

34

*I*t felt strange to listen to Christmas carols in September, but the album Natalia had commissioned needed to be recorded now in order to press enough copies for the Christmas season. Even though there had been no softening of her father's willingness to allow her back into the bank, he enthusiastically supported her music venture. He offered advice on contracts and let her take advantage of his shipping connections for her overseas exports. He'd even come to the studio to listen as a trio of brass musicians recorded her Christmas album.

The room was small, and the recording device looked similar to a phonograph, except the flaring bell was much larger to capture the sound. Instead of a shellac album, the rotating disc was coated with waxy chemicals onto which the needle would make tiny impressions of the sound vibrations. The two trumpeters and the trombone player stood close to the bell-shaped receiver, while Natalia and Oscar hugged the back wall and held their hands over their ears as "Good King Wenceslas" filled the room. "O Holy Night" came next. Someday deep in December, this recording would be heard in farmhouses, tenements, and homesteads across the nation. Someday it would be heard in Russia too.

Maybe it was the swelling emotion in the music that made

her teary-eyed. It was too late to ship the records overseas in time for Christmas, but she could press enough copies to sell them in Russia next year.

Would Dimitri still be a part of her life next Christmas? It had been four months since he left, and even though their lively exchange of telegrams continued, the messages weren't enough to ease her loneliness. Thinking of Dimitri hurt more than it made her happy.

The final passages of "O Holy Night" were coming to an end when a door slammed in the hallway outside.

The loud bang caused a trumpeter to jerk his instrument aside. "What was that?" he snapped.

The technician lifted the needle off the waxed disc. The recording was ruined, and they would have to start again. Waxed discs were expensive too. She cast a baleful eye at the intruder who stepped inside. It was a delivery boy from the Western Union.

"Telegram for Miss Natalia Blackstone," he announced, oblivious to the lovely recording he'd just ruined.

"Here," she said, handing the boy a coin before signing her name on the clipboard to acknowledge receipt of the wire.

"Can I have an extra tip?" the boy asked. "I tried to deliver it to the townhouse where it was addressed, but a construction worker told me you would be here, so it's almost like I made two deliveries."

Natalia scrounged in her purse for another coin. It was true that she had asked the carpenter installing her new kitchen cabinets to forward messages to her here at the studio. She'd failed to anticipate anyone would ignore the *Do Not Disturb* sign on the door.

She pushed her annoyance aside to read the telegram.

Dearest Natalia. Yesterday I cut myself while trimming my beard. My hands are blistered from work in the mill, and I don't have the recipe for your special salve. This morning I awoke with a crick in my neck. My life is full of pain, but then I remembered you, and my world brightened! Oh, Natalia, when are you going to come to Russia and put me out of my misery? I need you to rub salve on my hands. Your devoted servant awaits word from you.

A wave of sadness overcame her. It was one of Dimitri's pointless telegrams, obviously just an opening salvo in preparation for a morning of flirtation. There was a time when she would have been delighted to fritter away a few hours in such a distraction, because Dimitri was fun and charming and she adored him. She *loved* him.

Which was why his messages were becoming painful. She didn't belong in Russia, and it was becoming increasingly clear he would never come back to America.

"Well?" her father drawled, knowing full well who the telegram was from and not liking it.

She tucked it in her purse before he could read it. "It's nothing."

The musicians were ready to record "O Holy Night" again. As soon as they were finished, she could hurry to the Western Union station a few blocks away and reply to Dimitri's message so he wouldn't be kept waiting too long.

The brass trio began playing, and the reverent, hopeful music gradually swelled to fill the room. Would she ever spend a Christmas with Dimitri? Or would year after year go by as she sought emotional sustenance from whimsical telegrams? Other women would have a husband in their bed, children to hold and nurture and raise.

She would have a stack of telegrams.

The joy of "O Holy Night" felt jarring against her loneliness, and she clamped her palms over her ears. It was time either to go to Russia or to end things with Dimitri. As long as she kept escaping into his telegrams, it would be impossible to move forward and find another man to love.

She wouldn't reply to today's message. A clean break would be best. She lowered her head, embarrassed by the tear that splatted on the tile floor, but this music made everything ache.

The song ended, and she held her breath because it was essential to capture a few moments of silence at the conclusion of the recording. She counted five heartbeats.

"Cut," the technician announced. "Well done, gentlemen!"

The musicians laughed and congratulated each other. There was a bit of applause and shuffling feet as the musicians stretched their muscles. She kept her head down, unwilling to show her face until she could contain herself.

"Don't cry, Natalia." Her father's voice was kind, and she wished he couldn't read her so well, but she had to keep her head lowered.

"Sometimes it's just so hard," she whispered, but in her heart she knew she was doing the right thing.

Dimitri waited impatiently at the front counter of the general store. It had been an hour with no return message from Natalia. Sometimes it took a while for delivery, so he'd come prepared with a book of poetry from Mirosa's library to read while he waited.

But the days grew dark early now, and the shop owner wished to close the store. Dimitri didn't like leaving before he heard back from Natalia, but there was no hope for it.

Surely her reply would be waiting for him in the morning.

35

It had been five days since Dimitri had heard from Natalia, and he grew increasingly anxious. Had there been a technical problem that meant she no longer received his messages? Was she ill? It worried him because he could think of no other explanation for this prolonged silence.

He briefly considered contacting her father. Oscar Blackstone was an easy man to reach, but the best ally Dimitri had among the Blackstones was Poppy. She was eager to claim a close relationship to a real aristocrat, and he was happy to take advantage of the situation.

He kept his telegram to Poppy brief, simply offering a belated congratulations for Alexander's first birthday, then asking after Natalia.

She has not responded to my messages, and I have grown concerned for her health. Please send assurances that she is well.

The answer from Poppy came the next day.

Natalia is fine but absorbed in her silly music business. She has announced that she will never become a countess. Make of that what you will, but we all know Natalia has warped priorities.

A cascade of denials ricocheted in his head. Natalia wouldn't just stop talking to him. Poppy could get things wrong. Worse, she wasn't entirely trustworthy and might deliberately do something to hurt Natalia. He couldn't believe Natalia would cut him off so abruptly and sent another telegram to Natalia, demanding an answer.

He heard nothing until an actual letter from Natalia arrived. It was postmarked the day after his telegram when she abruptly stopped returning his messages. The letter was short and to the point.

> *Dear Dimitri,*
>
> *I will be seeking another business agent to distribute my recordings in Russia. It brings me great sadness, but I think it is time to end our association. Your friendship has been the deepest and most rewarding of my life. I have become a better person for having known you. I wish you all the best and pray for Mirosa's continued prosperity. Please remember me fondly, as I shall always treasure my memories of you.*

He sat on the old stone wall bordering the waterwheel, her letter held loosely in his hands. It felt odd to see her handwriting. In all their years of correspondence, he had never seen Natalia's handwriting, but it was neat and refined, just as he would have expected.

A squirrel darted across the loading area. The creek of the rickety wheel and the slosh of water dumping from the buckets was constant. The thump and grind of the millstones continued. All around him the world was proceeding as normal, but during the sixty seconds it took to read this letter, everything had changed.

Mirosa suddenly felt lonelier and more isolated. Sadder.

It took a few minutes for a change in the sound of the waterwheel to penetrate his fog of dejection. The scraping noise near the axle sounded bad. He moved closer for a better look, but a wooden plate covered most of the rotating mechanism. A blacksmith had replaced the metal gears less than ten years ago, so it probably wasn't a problem with the gears. The scrape sounded like wood against wood. This waterwheel had reliably turned for almost a hundred years, but it was now tired and old.

He sighed. Why was he getting so morose over a mill needing repair? He was rich. He could afford anything. If he wanted, he could tear this old waterwheel down and build a modern one powered by electricity.

The prospect made him cringe. He liked the age and heritage of this mill. The massive oak trees felled to make this cider mill came from right here in the valley. They would have been alive when Peter the Great hunted stag in these forests. Tradition was important, and he would save this old waterwheel no matter what the cost.

That meant he needed to stop its rotation lest more damage be done. He trudged up the steps that had been cut into the hillside to reach the sluice gate and jimmied the wooden board to shut the flume. The wheel would stop rotating as soon as the water in the sluice came to a trickle.

Ilya Komarov was the best carpenter in the valley, and Dimitri summoned him to diagnose the problem with the waterwheel. Perhaps a healthy commission would soften Ilya's curt demeanor.

It didn't work. Ilya arrived a few hours later and resented being called away from the fence he had been building. He even demanded payment before looking at the wheel. Dimitri paid, and Ilya took a cursory look.

"The wheel shaft is out of balance," Ilya said, but Pavel disagreed.

"It sounds like a loose bearing to me. It's not making proper contact with the iron band on the axle."

Ilya's face twisted in scorn. "Of course it's not making proper contact, because it's out of balance. You haven't been maintaining it properly."

Dimitri didn't want to listen to these two men squabble like cats in a knapsack. He was inclined to agree with Ilya but wanted to understand how to maintain the waterwheel so this wouldn't happen again.

"How do we get it properly balanced?" he asked.

"You're not going to like it," Ilya warned. "The western sun has been hitting this wheel for decades, causing it to warp. The best thing would be to take it apart, flip it around, maybe remove a few of the boards to help redistribute the water, and hope for the best."

"That's it?" Pavel scoffed.

The idea sounded far-fetched, but Dimitri needed a better idea of what taking the wheel apart would entail. Wearing waist-high waders, he climbed over the stone wall and into the flume. The water slowed his stride as he trudged toward the wheel. It had been motionless ever since he closed the sluice gate this morning, so he was able to get close enough to examine the axle and metal bearings in the center of the wheel. Ilya hunkered down on the wall beside him.

"You see how those boards are warped? That's your problem. Let's get this thing rotating again so you can see the problem in action."

Dimitri stepped back a few paces, and Pavel opened the sluice gate. Water poured down the flume, and the wheel groaned as it went back into motion. The internal thump seemed even louder. Dimitri stepped farther back, but his foot slid on the algae, shooting out from beneath him. He crashed into the water. A weight clamped down on his ankle, dragging him forward. The wheel! He yelled, but icy water flooded his mouth and throat, sucking into his lungs. He thrashed, craning upward for a breath of air, but couldn't reach the surface.

His ankle exploded in pain as the wheel dragged him deeper beneath its weight. Blue sky rippled above the surface of the water. So close, but he couldn't get to the air. Icy water seized his muscles, but he had to keep fighting. Pain was everywhere. Was this it? Why hadn't he known that dying would hurt this badly?

A hulking shadow blotted out the sunlight. Someone was

over him, a weight on his hips holding him down, hands around his ankle pulling. His ankle felt torn apart, but finally it slipped free.

Hands beneath his shoulders hauled him upright. He broke through the surface and gasped for air but coughed up water. Ilya was in the flume with him, hoisting him to the stone wall.

Behind them, the waterwheel slipped back into rotation, the familiar sound causing him to shudder in horror. Another minute, and he would have been dead.

He was freezing. Pavel helped him out of the sluice, and both Dimitri and Ilya collapsed on the ground. Dimitri puked up water and sputtered for air. There was no way he'd be able to stand. His ankle was surely broken.

Ilya looked shaken too. He'd risked his life by reaching under that wheel to pry Dimitri's foot free. A bloody scrape marred Ilya's face, and he shivered in his sopping clothes.

Pavel sounded panicked. "I'll send for a doctor," he said and raced toward the house, leaving the two of them alone in the dirt, shaking with cold. Pain radiated from Dimitri's broken ankle, but he got up onto an elbow to look Ilya in the eye.

"I owe you my life," he managed to gasp. "You saved me at great risk. What is it that you want? If it is in my power, I will grant it."

Ilya's eyes widened. He was no longer the surly, angry peasant. He was a shaken man, bloody and panting from what had happened. Then suddenly a fire lit in his pale eyes, and he said the last thing Dimitri expected.

"I want to go to America."

Dimitri knew even before Dr. Sopin arrived that his leg was broken. He was given a shot of vodka and a lungful of chloroform that put him in a painful daze while the doctor set his leg and wrapped it in a cast.

It was dark before Dimitri emerged from the drugged stupor. He lay beneath a mound of quilts in his bedroom, the cast-iron stove heating the room at full blast. His mother hovered over him, worried he would catch his death of pneumonia after being submerged in the icy water for so long.

He drew a breath. His throat hurt, but his lungs felt clear, and he would never take the blessing of a deep breath of air for granted again.

He relayed the entire story of what happened, and Anna was appalled—not so much by the danger Dimitri had endured but by Ilya's audacity.

"He can't go to America," she sputtered. "He's the only carpenter in the valley. What would we do if he leaves?"

Dimitri had to smother a laugh at the self-centered horror in his mother's voice. Before the freeing of the serfs in 1861, no worker could leave an estate without permission, but they lived in a new era, and Ilya was free to seek his fortune in America if he wished.

"We will find a way to survive," he assured his mother, but a part of him envied Ilya's ability to forge a new destiny for himself.

36

atalia loved watching Alexander totter around her home. In light of Poppy's jealousy, Oscar now brought the baby to her townhouse for a visit at least once a week. It let Natalia play with her brother while talking business with her father. This morning she sat on the floor with Alexander while Oscar watched them from the upholstered corner chair, looking like a king on his throne as he listened to her grim predictions about the disaster Liam was about to confront. His proposal for a drastic workers' pay raise would be presented to the board of U.S. Steel tomorrow, and it was too ambitious to succeed.

"He's determined to shove it down their throats no matter what they say," she told Oscar. "I've tried to suggest a more structured rollout, but he won't listen."

"Let him proceed," Oscar said. "Getting taken down a notch will teach him a lesson."

It sounded as if Oscar was secretly hoping for that to happen, but she hated watching Liam walk straight toward a buzz saw while doing nothing to intervene. Liam was a strong and charismatic man. His heart was in the right place, but he didn't respect the rules of Wall Street, and it was going to cost him.

"I don't want to see him be publicly humiliated," she said as Alexander tried to climb on top of her.

"That's his doing, not yours," Oscar replied. "Speaking of public humiliation, you should know that I have initiated a libel suit against Silas Conner for the rumors he spread about you."

Natalia sighed. An investigation at the bank confirmed that Silas had been the one feeding inside gossip about her to the Russian embassy. Her father wanted vengeance, but a lawsuit wasn't the right course of action. She scooped Alexander up and carried him to the sofa, where she settled him on her lap while parsing through her complicated feelings about what Silas Conner had done to destroy her career.

"I wish you wouldn't," she finally said. "The damage is already done, and getting a pound of flesh from him can't undo it."

Her father's expression was iron-hard. "It's not my way. When someone strikes at me or my family, I retaliate hard enough to ensure it will never happen again. I intend to make an example of Silas Conner. Do you really want to let him get away with it?"

Sometimes life wasn't fair. The Chinese villagers who lived along the Amur River could attest to that. She would probably never know why Silas was so resentful of her, but he obviously wasn't a happy man. Punishing him might bring a quick rush of satisfaction, but it would never bring her the lasting peace that forgiveness could provide. In the grand scheme of the huge, weighty issues of the universe, what had happened to her was no more than a mosquito bite.

"I will leave vengeance to God," she said simply. "Please don't pursue this. At least, not in my name. I want to move forward to create an honorable and productive life, not wallow in resentment of the past."

The baby grabbed something from the table to shove in his mouth. It was the firebird Dimitri had given her in San Francisco.

She pulled the cheap trinket away. "Don't eat that, sweetheart."

Dimitri had warned that the firebird was either a blessing or a harbinger of doom. It certainly wasn't suitable for a child's toy.

Natalia didn't mind walking toward uncertainty and danger, but she'd protect Alexander to the death.

He started fussing and reached for the firebird again, but she stood to pace the floor with him, hugging him tighter. How she loved this child! She and her father both probably spoiled him, but she didn't care. Oscar had gone decades waiting for a son to carry on his legacy, and now, in his middle age, he finally had one.

She turned to look at her father. "Before Alexander came along, did you and Mama ever think about adopting a son?"

"We never considered it."

"Why not?" Suddenly the answer was very important.

Oscar looked a little taken aback. "I'm not sure I could love a stranger's baby. One can never be sure what sort of people the parents are."

Natalia pondered the answer as she patted Alexander's back. She'd loved Alexander from the moment she saw him despite her dislike of Poppy. He was a blessing from God. All babies were.

All babies. She loved Alexander regardless of who his mother was, and she could do so for another child. Why had she been so obsessed with having a child from her own body? Dimitri would someday marry and adopt children, and those children would be lucky to have such a loving and generous father.

She patted Alexander's back and wondered what kind of fool she had been to let a man like Dimitri Sokolov slip away.

It was Friday afternoon, and the U.S. Steel board meeting should have concluded an hour ago, but something must be wrong. Natalia paced the lobby of the Waldorf-Astoria, the grandest hotel in the city, where the board members deliberated in a conference room down the hall. Powerful men from all over the nation had gathered for this meeting, and she prayed Liam could hold his own among the business tycoons who'd never wanted him on the board.

A toast was planned for the conclusion of the three-day meeting, and a cart loaded with buckets of iced champagne had been parked outside the room for over an hour. What on earth was taking so long? She battled the temptation to press her ear against the crack in the door to eavesdrop, desperate to learn if Liam had managed to present his proposal for raising the workers' wages without making a complete fool of himself.

At long last, a trio of waiters arrived to wheel the champagne into the conference room.

The meeting was over. For better or worse, all the decisions had been made and worrying wouldn't help. Now she just had to wait another twenty or thirty minutes until the toasts were concluded and the board members finally left the room. Liam wouldn't drink, of course. His ulcer had been so bad this morning that he could eat nothing except bread and milk, but good manners dictated he would stay for the toasts.

She began another lap around the marble lobby, but before she could get far, Liam came storming down the hall, his face a thundercloud.

"Liam?"

He ignored her and kept striding toward the front doors. She hurried after him. His entire body looked tense as he barged through the doors and onto the street. The sidewalk was thick with pedestrians, which slowed him down enough that she was able to catch up to him.

"Liam, what happened?"

He didn't answer, but they arrived at a busy intersection, forcing him to stop. He turned to a bench and braced his hands on the back of it, staring down at the concrete sidewalk.

"They voted a fifteen-percent raise," he bit out.

She gasped in surprise. "They did? But that's wonderful!"

"It's half of what I asked for. Half what the men deserve."

"It's more than I thought possible. Liam, this is a victory." Maybe there was something to be said for Liam's brash demeanor, because he had just accomplished the impossible.

A muscle ticked in Liam's jaw as he stared across the street, where a half-built skyscraper towered above. The fourteen-story building already had its elegant stone cladding on the lower floors, but higher up, the exposed steel frame crawled with construction workers.

Liam pointed up at the men welding beams into place. "*Those* are the guys who are building this city. Not men in suits who sit in fancy offices and drink champagne."

"And thanks to you, men like that will be enjoying a healthy raise because you fought for them. I still can't believe you pulled it off. Tell me what happened."

She took a seat on the bench and listened as Liam described the meeting. Just as Natalia predicted, Liam's chief rival on the board, Charles Morse, threw up arguments to block any increase in wages, but Liam pushed back hard. The two men almost came to blows before the chairman proposed a compromise.

"It took some doing, but the chairman helped me get a majority to agree to fifteen percent. He wanted the lawyers to write things up and have it printed on fancy paper before everyone signed it at the end of the month, but I said no. I scratched out the original numbers on my proposal, wrote in the new ones, and forced every man there to put his name to it."

"Even Charles Morse?"

Liam snorted. "The cheapskate refused to sign, but it doesn't matter. All it took was a majority vote, and that's what I got."

"Nobody thought you would get this much. You should be very proud."

All he did was grunt, and it was frustrating that Liam didn't understand just how big a victory he had won.

"Why don't we go find Darla?" she suggested. "Maybe she can help cheer you up."

If anything, Liam looked even gloomier. "I won't be seeing much of Darla anymore. It's over."

Oh dear. Perhaps this explained his dark mood. "What happened?" she asked gently, and his mouth twisted in bitterness.

Her heart sank as Liam relayed how he was supposed to

meet Darla last weekend at the art museum, where she had already gathered with a group of her arty friends. "I was heading toward them, and they didn't realize I could over-hear when one of them asked Darla when to expect the Swiss Guard."

Natalia blinked in confusion until Liam reminded her of the long-ago afternoon at her townhouse when he thought the pope lived in Switzerland because of his Swiss Guard. Darla had laughed at the time, but apparently she'd shared the story with her friends. Now she and all the others called him "the Swiss Guard" behind his back.

"One of them asked her what she saw in me," Liam contin-ued. "I hid behind a column to listen. Darla said she likes me because I'm big and strong like Hercules, but I've also got a fortune in the bank, and she doesn't care that I'm as dumb as a stump. Those were her exact words."

Natalia felt ill. Darla's careless remark had hit Liam where he was most vulnerable. Liam wasn't dumb, he just never had a chance to get an education beyond the eighth grade because he'd been yanked out of school to work in a steel mill.

"I already miss her," he continued. "I taught her how to weld, and she showed me how to sculpt with a blowtorch. We had fun together, you know? The only thing I do at work is bang my head against the books and wear these smothering collars, and I hate everything about it." He watched the welders working on the steel beams high above the city, his face filled with longing. "I liked being a welder. At the end of every day, I felt like I'd built something. I'd give anything to be up there with those guys and quit pretending to be someone I'm not." He looked tired, dispirited, and old, and Natalia didn't know how to comfort him.

"I'm sorry about Darla," she said. "Is there no hope you can forgive her?"

Liam shook his head. "She doesn't respect me. She wouldn't have talked to her friends like that if she did. And maybe she's right. I don't belong in the boardroom. I don't even *like* it."

"But you're good at it," she said. "Nobody thought you could cram that proposal through, but you brought insight and passion to the table. Enough to get through to those cold-hearted businessmen and make an important change."

Her words of comfort didn't seem to help. Liam continued to glower at the men across the street as he spoke.

"I'm not going to give up," he said. "I'll agree to that fifteen percent raise for now, but I'll keep fighting in the boardrooms and in the back alleys. In the courts or on the floors of a steel mill. If I start a mission and come up short, I'll only retreat long enough to lick my wounds, saddle up, and then ride back into battle. Nobody is going to stop me. Not the board, not your father, and certainly not Darla." His mouth twisted in irony. "It's good that I found out about her. Darla was a distraction. If I ever get married, it will be to a woman who isn't afraid to walk into a cauldron of fire with me."

Natalia nudged him a little, hoping to lighten his mood. "Most women don't want to walk into a cauldron of fire, Liam."

He shook off his melancholy and winked at her. "That should have been my clue that Darla wasn't the right woman for me."

Perhaps Liam was right. He and Darla had always seemed like an odd pairing, but his comment saddened her because Dimitri *had* been the right man for her. Why did she need a baby from her own body when there were countless needy children filling the orphanages in this city? Why did she assume his commitment to Mirosa was a fatal flaw? The world had telegraphs, steamships, and trains that could close the distance.

Liam had just said that if he ever came up short in a mission, he would retreat only long enough to lick his wounds, saddle up, and ride into battle again. She would do the same.

That night, she sat at her mother's dainty rolltop desk to write Dimitri a letter.

Dearest Dimitri,
    How does one apologize for a hasty decision? It occurs to me that although I have always relied on careful

research before making a business decision, I have not always been so circumspect in my personal life.

Perhaps it was arrogant, but I grew up assuming I could choose exactly the life I wanted, but sometimes God has other ideas for us. Nothing has been working out as I planned, but I am slowly learning to appreciate the strange curves in my path. There are many things I did not fairly consider until forced to do so. The music industry is one of those things, and it has been an unexpected delight. There could be more. Adopting a child? Exploring the possibility of living in Russia? I don't know, but I wanted to ask your opinion on these things.

Having read both Tolstoy and Napoleonic history, I have too much respect for the Russian winter to brave its ferocity, but I would like to visit Mirosa in the spring. What do you think?

I will understand if you do not find this letter welcome. Just say the word, and I won't raise the issue again, but I felt compelled to ask your opinion.

Sincerely, Natalia

Her fingers shook as she sealed the envelope.

She clutched Dimitri's firebird in her hand as she carried the letter to the post office the following morning. The Russians believed the firebird was either a harbinger of something wonderful or of a dark catastrophe. It was surely a fitting symbol for this letter, as she had no idea which fate loomed before them.

37

It was time for Dimitri to confront the czar. His mother feared he was walking into a trap, and she spent the night before the meeting begging Dimitri not to go. Sitting in the candlelit dining room at Mirosa, she looked as old and haggard as he'd ever seen her.

"It's over," she said. "Nothing you can do will bring those people back from the dead. Why must you lay your head on a chopping block for them again? Stay here in our lovely valley. What happened in that barren wasteland should not be our concern. Why can't you let sleeping dogs lie?"

He wished he could, but that day at the Amur had changed him forever, and it was impossible to return to the innocence of his past. "I have to go, Mama," he said, reaching for her hand.

Her shoulders sagged. "I know you do."

The anguish on her face haunted him the entire train ride to Tsarskoe Selo, a rural county dotted with imperial palaces south of Saint Petersburg. He didn't *think* it was a trap but couldn't be certain. That slim, niggling possibility that he was about to be betrayed put a sour feeling in his gut and made it hard to draw a complete breath.

Arriving before the czar on crutches was not ideal, but he had no choice, and he awkwardly shuffled out of the carriage and to the ground. The cast covered his entire foot, ankle, and lower leg. A chest cold had settled in his lungs from being dunked for so long in the icy water, but it couldn't be helped. Everything in his life had led up to this moment, and he couldn't permit an illness to interfere.

From a distance, the czar's palace looked serene, with soothing yellow walls and an arcade of white Corinthian columns. The two wings of the palace stretched open like welcoming arms, looking both grand and calm in front of the backdrop of a deep forest.

Navigating up the front stairs was difficult and painful, an ache shooting up from Dimitri's broken ankle with each difficult hop, but once on the landing, he fit the crutches beneath his arms and propelled himself toward the entrance.

Baron Freedericksz awaited him in the grand vestibule, wearing full military regalia. His voice was cold as he rapped out instructions.

"Do not make eye contact with his imperial majesty," the baron warned. "You will be shown into the courtyard where the czar is handling his morning appointments. You will wait silently until he acknowledges you, if he chooses to do so at all. You are not to sit in his presence. If he approaches, you are to bow and express your gratitude."

Dimitri nodded, his mouth dry. How many thousands of miles had he traveled to reach this time and place? Memories of the savage cold and brutal hunger crowded his mind. The scar on the back of his head tingled, and his ankle ached as he limped behind the baron through gilded staterooms and mirrored corridors. Every time they turned a corner there was another series of doors, each with servants stationed on either side who opened and closed them as they passed. Dimitri tried to memorize the maze of corridors should he need to escape, but soon put that effort aside. If he was walking into a trap, there would be no escape. Not in his crippled condition and with armed guards at every doorway throughout the palace.

At last he was shown into a courtyard. It was surrounded on two sides by the colonnaded wings of the palace, but straight ahead the land opened up to a lawn, then a small lake, and then forestland in the distance.

Dozens of people loitered in the courtyard. Men in cavalry uniforms mingled with army officers. Other men wore civilian garb and clustered in tight groups with attaché cases. Only one man seemed out of place and alone. The somber man looked like a college professor in his tweed jacket and scruffy beard.

And then there was the czar. With his trim form and neatly groomed beard, Nicholas II was easily recognizable, but today he was casually dressed, kneeling beside a young girl as he showed her how to aim a bow and arrow. She looked around five years old but wore the uniform of an archer. Half a dozen cavalry officers stood nearby, watching her take aim at a haystack target a few yards away.

"Everyone here is awaiting an audience with the czar," Baron Freedericksz said. "He has decided to visit with his daughter for a while and is not to be disturbed, but perhaps you will be recognized soon."

Dimitri blanched, trying not to show his surprise. How could the czar make the world wait while he frolicked with a child? And yet the men gathered in the courtyard pretended this was normal behavior as they stood in respectful groups, awaiting their turn.

On the far side of the courtyard, the czar positioned his daughter's elbow, then prompted the girl to draw back her arm and shoot. She did. The arrow missed the target but found the haystack, clinging to the straw for a moment before falling harmlessly to the grass.

"Well done, Tatiana," the czar boomed, and the officers and courtiers clapped. Dimitri followed suit. Only the bearded college professor remained stonily unmoved.

Dimitri relaxed a fraction. If he had walked into a trap, it was an odd one. Too many witnesses, including the czarina, who sat on the other side of the courtyard with a toddler crawling nearby.

A sense of unreality settled over Dimitri as he watched the

czar fuss over his daughter. He had three daughters, and the czarina was heavily pregnant with another child. Surely it would be a boy this time, but the way the czar doted on Tatiana as she nocked another arrow into position was charming.

Over the next hour, Dimitri watched as the czar alternated his attention between his children and appointments with people who loitered in the courtyard, hoping for a few moments of his time. Dimitri's good leg began to ache from standing on it so long, but he distracted himself by listening to the czar's meetings. A cavalry officer requested the relocation of a barracks, which the czar approved, and the minister of finance asked for authorization to put the Russian ruble on the gold standard, which the czar refused.

The minister looked annoyed as he left the courtyard, and the czar strolled over to his wife, who poured him a cup of tea. He seemed to be enjoying himself as a toddler pulled on his leg. Everyone else in the courtyard affected casual stances while hoping they would soon be recognized. Dimitri's discomfort from standing on one leg morphed into pain, but he dared not sit. Not when he was this close to his goal.

Baron Freedericksz finally approached. "His Imperial Majesty will see you now."

Dimitri nodded and positioned the crutches, his heart thudding as he crossed the smooth lawn to the shade of the tea table. Several officers and courtiers stood nearby, listening to everything. The czarina ignored him, but Czar Nicholas sent him a tepid nod.

"Count Sokolov," he said. "I have been informed of your efforts to call attention to the terrible business out east. What a dreadful affair. I understand there was some confusion about your title and assets, but that's all been cleared up, correct?"

Dimitri bowed. "Correct, your Imperial Majesty."

"Excellent. So what happened to your leg?"

His face heated. "An unfortunate accident at my family's cider mill."

The czarina tutted in sympathy, and the czar looked amused.

"Good heavens. Well, be sure to have some schnapps before you leave." He glanced up and sent a signal to Baron Freedericksz, indicating the transaction was over.

That was it? Dimitri straightened to meet the czar's gaze. "And who shall I see about the reaffirmation of the Treaty of Aigun?"

The czar quirked a brow, and Baron Freedericksz looked ready to implode. A few of the courtiers glanced nervously among themselves.

The czar's voice was cool. "Have we decided a reaffirmation is necessary?"

"No final decision has been made," Baron Freedericksz insisted, looking pointedly at some of the nearby courtiers, all of whom shook their heads in agreement.

"I didn't think so," Czar Nicolas said and proceeded to slather butter on a scone.

"We *have*, your Imperial Majesty," a strong voice called out from several yards away. It was the man who looked like a college professor.

The czar's manner cooled even more. "Count Witte," he said in a tight voice. "I gather you have an opinion on this, as you do so many things."

Dimitri straightened in surprised admiration. Count Sergei Witte had been a rising star under the previous czar and was the driving force behind the Trans-Siberian Railway. Ever since Nicholas ascended to the throne seven years earlier, there had been a concerted effort to diminish Count Witte's influence at court. The czar did not appreciate people who brought him bad news.

"Yes, we have," Count Witte said as he approached the table. "In two years, the Trans-Siberian will reach the Pacific. It will aggravate our relations with Japan and raise military concerns with our allies in the east. We don't need additional trouble from China. The existing Treaty of Aigun must be publicly reaffirmed."

The czar took a bite of scone, chewing slowly and deliberately as he pondered. Count Witte's forceful declaration hung in the air, and the courtiers shifted in discomfort as the czar dabbed his mouth and wiped his fingers.

"Very well," he finally said. "I shall alert the foreign minister that a public reaffirmation is to be issued. And then we shall speak no more of this, correct, Count Sokolov?"

A warning underlay the words. A dozen officers and courtiers had just heard the pronouncement, and with the momentum already underway in America, it would be hard for this matter to be ignored again. Dimitri had won.

"Correct, your Imperial Majesty," he murmured, taking care that his bow was low, obsequious, and long. His entire body ached, but he'd endured worse. He straightened, and Count Witte gave him a brief nod of approval.

Dimitri gripped his crutches and started toward the court-yard door, feeling hostile eyes on him the entire journey.

"You idiot," a gentleman wearing a peach satin waistcoat hissed. "You've made him angry when we need him to grant us concessions to avoid hereditary taxes."

Another man with a diamond cravat pin glared at him as well. "You have just taken food out of the mouths of my children."

Dimitri ignored them as he hobbled onward toward the pal-ace. A pair of servants opened the doors, and a footman led him through the twisting corridors.

"Please," Dimitri appealed to the footman. Exhaustion over-came him as tension from the past few hours drained away. Every muscle ached, his lungs wheezed, and he was dizzy with relief. He braced his hand on the silk wallpaper, trembling in fatigue. It was a struggle to catch his breath.

He had won.

He had won!

Natalia should be here. Relief cascaded over him, but instead of rejoicing, everything hurt because Natalia was not here to share this moment. The triumph was not complete without her.

After a moment, he regained his breath and repositioned the crutches. "Thank you," he said to the footman once he was ready to proceed, then continued following the man through the maze of corridors.

What sort of symphony would Tchaikovsky have composed to capture this past year of adventure? Natalia would be represented by the sweet tone of an oboe, soaring high above the music, while Dimitri would be the clarion call of the trumpet. The drumbeat of the percussion would represent Maxim Tachenko and Count Witte and Ilya Komarov, all of them a force driving toward a better world.

Dimitri smothered a laugh while battling tears. He could barely play the violin, and here he was, composing a symphony for Tchaikovsky to write. But he couldn't help it. Even now he heard the rush of the violins coming to the rescue.

It was over. The quest that began more than a year ago had just been completed. He had done well. He was a weepy, blubbery mess. *But oh, Natalia, we did it!*

He propelled himself faster. *Natalia, do you hear me? We did it. You should be here. What kind of symphony ends with lovers on the opposite side of the world?*

A bad one. He could not tolerate this ending to their story, and he pumped his crutches faster until he reached the carriage.

"Sir?" the carriage driver asked him. "Are you well?"

He wasn't but boarded the carriage anyway. "Take me back to Mirosa, please."

There were final details to manage to ensure the czar's public affirmation was printed in newspapers across the land, but then he would begin working on a way to correct this intolerable situation with Natalia.

The day after his triumph with the czar, Dimitri escorted Ilya Komarov and his family to the train station in Saint Petersburg. True to his promise, Dimitri was paying for the entire family to emigrate to America. It would begin with a three-day ride to the port of Hamburg, then a steamship bound for New York. All their belongings fit into a single trunk and two threadbare carpetbags. It occurred to Dimitri that Poppy Blackstone's hat boxes took up more space than all the Komarov family's worldly goods.

As they waited on the train station platform, Ilya's two adolescent boys sulked about leaving home, but Ilya and his wife brimmed with a combination of hope and nervous anxiety. Typical sounds of a train station surrounded them. Peddlers hawked goods, and the hiss of steam began building in the train. A loud-mouthed malcontent carping about revolution was trying to pass out leaflets, but most of the bystanders ignored him.

"That one won't last long," Ilya said with a nod to the rabble-rouser. "The authorities will get him before much longer."

Probably, but Dimitri paid no attention to the malcontent as he followed the Komarovs to the train. Just before boarding, Dimitri pressed an envelope into Ilya's hands.

"This is a letter of introduction to Maxim Tachenko," he said. "He has a dacha north of New York City that is in terrible shape. He could use a good carpenter."

At last he saw a smile from Ilya Komarov, who nodded in gratitude, touched the brim of his hat in genuine respect, and then ushered his family aboard. Ilya paused in the doorway to lift his hat in farewell, and Dimitri was inexplicably moved. It took courage to head off into the unknown with little but a few clothes and a letter of introduction, but Ilya would do well in America.

Why did he envy Ilya? The gray metropolis of New York was going to be a difficult transition for this rural family, but still, the envy persisted.

It would be a few more minutes until the train departed, and Dimitri limped to a bench, setting his crutches aside as he lowered himself to sit. His ankle hurt, his lungs were still congested, and the rest of his body seemed inexplicably old, but he would stay until the train left. He'd neglected to bring anything to read, so he looked for a newspaper boy but saw only the loudmouthed revolutionary handing out pamphlets and yammering about doom.

A peasant girl selling matches wandered through the crowd. Her arms and ankles were so thin that they looked birdlike, and on her feet she wore a pair of lapti shoes. His feet itched just looking at them. Lapti shoes were uncomfortable in the best of times and not warm enough for this time of year.

He summoned the girl, and she came over, offering a box of matches for ten kopeks. He shook his head and pressed fifty rubles into her hand. "Buy a pair of winter shoes."

Her eyes widened in stunned surprise, but she clutched the money and ran to the front of the station, where her mother was clustered with other children. Fifty rubles ought to buy them all new shoes, but he didn't feel good about the transaction. The station was filled with equally threadbare children. Why had he never noticed the poverty in this station before?

The stationmaster walked along the platform, closing train doors and making the final calls. The cylinders and pistons creaked as the wheels began moving. Dimitri stood to raise his hand in farewell to the Komarovs, wondering once again at this strange sense of longing that came from nowhere as he watched the train round the bend and disappear into the distance.

He adjusted his crutches and prepared to head back toward the stable yard. The matchgirl showed her mother the rubles from Dimitri. The malcontent revolutionary was louder than ever, but he wasn't passing out leaflets anymore. He had something dark and round in his hand. He threw it toward the station, then turned to run as if his life depended on it.

Understanding came quickly.

"No!" Dimitri bellowed, hobbling toward the matchgirl. Others started running the other way.

He didn't hear anything, only saw the explosion of flying wood, bricks, and metal. A flash of fire. The matchgirl was blown across the station, and a wall of wreckage came flying at him.

Then everything went black.

Dimitri's condition steadily worsened in the days after the explosion. The gashes on his face made speaking painful, and his concussion throbbed like a sledgehammer, but the worst was his lungs. The chest cold had morphed into a crippling case of pneumonia that made it impossible to draw a full breath. Sweat poured off his body, and he shivered with unending chills no matter how many blankets his mother piled on top of him.

Anna constantly hovered, her face white with grief ever since Dr. Sopin told them Dimitri was unlikely to survive the week. Anna tried to fend off visitors, but Dimitri insisted on seeing Sergei Antonovich, the only lawyer in the valley, to draft a new will. It needed to be completed today. He'd already done everything to ensure his mother would have Mirosa and its land, but he wanted Pavel to have the cider mill. His mother didn't need the mill's income, but it would mean the world to Pavel. Maybe Pavel wasn't the smartest man in the valley, but he'd always loved the mill and the orchard and would take care of them.

"Allot ten acres of the apple orchard to Pavel," he rasped to the lawyer. "Give him the mill in perpetuity." The scratching of Sergei's pencil sounded unnaturally loud as he scribbled the instruction. Dimitri was propped up in bed because it was easier on his lungs and his wheezing didn't sound so bubbly.

He was too tired to think clearly, but he still needed to do something for Temujin. The newspapers had just announced the affirmation of the Treaty of Aigun, and Temujin deserved to know that they'd succeeded in their quest. The treaty reaffirmation had been Dimitri's cause, but Temujin still cared and would want to know.

"Mama," he whispered. "The newspaper about the treaty . . . send it to Temujin. Along with a gold coin."

"That man is a thief and a heathen," she sputtered. "Why should you waste good money on such a man?"

His eyes drifted closed in exhaustion. "You're right. For a man of Temujin's worth . . . fifty gold coins. Put a bible in the package." His lips quivered a little in humor, because on long winter nights, Temujin's curious mind would probably crack it open.

Sergei and his mother both grumbled in disapproval. No one here in the valley understood him anymore. He missed Temujin. He missed Natalia. As difficult as Ilya Komarov had been, at least they understood each other. They were fighters. People who laid everything on the line day after day, year after year. This was a struggle Dimitri understood and appreciated. He rarely saw it among the wealthy aristocrats of the valley. He loved them all, but he respected the fighters more.

Sergei fussed over how to get the bequest to Temujin. "We don't even know where this man lives," he said. "We can't send a fortune in gold through the post and expect it to arrive at its destination. We don't even have an address."

It was a problem. Temujin planned to stay in Chita, but Dimitri had no idea if he'd bought a farm.

"Hire someone to take it to Chita," he said. "Ask for directions to a man named Temujin who is missing his right foot and has only two toes on the other. There will only be one such man."

Thinking of his unlikely friend coaxed a smile despite the searing pain on his cheek. He probably just split the scab open, but he'd suffered worse.

What to do for Natalia? She had no need of gold coins or apple orchards. He scanned the interior of his bedroom, looking for something special to send to her. An icon of a sad Madonna frowned on the wall, but Natalia already had plenty of icons. A piece of his jewelry? A book? A pile of books was stacked on the bureau, and she always liked books.

"Bring me the second book in that stack," he instructed Sergei. His lawyer put the pad of paper down and retrieved a leather-bound book embossed with gold.

"This one?"

"No . . . the little brown one beneath it. Bring a pencil too."

Sergei did as requested. Dimitri suppressed a weak laugh because the gurgling in his lungs upset his mother, but he managed to flip open the cover of *Little Women* and find a blank page. It was a Russian copy. The original one Natalia had sent was long gone, but he'd bought another copy once he arrived at Mirosa because it reminded him of her. Now she would have it.

Anna propped the book on a pillow so he could scribble a message.

Dearest Natalia. You were right.

The pencil stilled as a surge of memories came to the fore. He hadn't cared for this book when he first read it, but in hindsight, it was about the sort of family he wished he could have had. A case of the mumps at nineteen had robbed him of that, but he hoped Natalia would have such a family someday. He loved her enough to wish that for her. He blinked a sheen of tears away. Ridiculous self-pity would not be tolerated when he had work to do. He adjusted the page and continued to write.

Dearest Natalia. You were right. This book contains a wonderful family. Thank you for sharing it with me, but I still contend the best scene is when Beth dies . . . as all good heroes do.

He choked back a laugh, but it turned into a strangled cough, and his mother began to panic. Liquid in his lungs gurgled and bubbled up, strangling him. He couldn't breathe.

"Go get Dr. Sopin," his mother cried out to Sergei.

Pain banded across his chest and back. He was dizzy. Suffocating. The edges of his vision turned dark, but he forced himself to calm down. He waited until he had the strength to take a sip of air . . . only a sip. Any more could lay him low again, and he needed to finish the will and get it formally witnessed and signed.

He lay against the pillow, taking shallow breaths until his vision cleared, but then the chills set in again. The sad Madonna frowned down at him from the wall, but he smiled up at her.

God had been good. This life had been good. Too short and filled with pain and calamities, but joy and purpose too. Yes, God had been very good to him.

Sergei completed the will an hour later. Dr. Sopin and Count Ulyanov witnessed it, and Dimitri signed the document with a shaking hand.

His job was complete. He smiled and lay back, savoring a job well done . . . as all good heroes did.

38

Natalia's kitchen was delightfully warm as she fussed over a pot of simmering cranberry sauce on her new enamel stovetop. Her kitchen now had a new oven with two burners, new cabinets, and a new icebox. Today she would host her first Thanksgiving meal, and she was determined to do everything right. She may have once struggled to boil an egg, but in an hour a holiday feast would be served with great fanfare.

The chef on the *Black Rose* had provided the main course, since a roasted turkey was beyond her fledgling skills. Liam helped Natalia in the kitchen, but there was no room for Gwen, who was seven months pregnant and probably ought to be off her feet anyway. She sat in the parlor with Patrick, who was lazily skimming the newspaper before the meal.

By the time Natalia lit the candles, Liam was teasing Gwen about her choice of baby names because Gwen wanted to name her children after plants. The baby would be called Iris if it was a girl and Florian if it was a boy.

"You can't name a boy Florian," Liam insisted.

"Why not?" Gwen asked. "It's an ancient name going all the way back to Roman times, and it means flower."

"*That's* why you can't name him Florian," Liam said. "The

kid won't be able to hold his head up in school. Patrick, you can't be on board with this."

Patrick kept his nose buried in a newspaper. "I'm hoping for a girl."

"I'm hoping you grow a backbone and stand up to your wife if you have a son," Liam said.

The bickering continued, with Liam trying to think of other names from the botanical world that might work for a boy, but all Natalia could come up with was Basil, which wasn't much better than Florian.

Suddenly, Patrick looked at her over the rim of the newspaper. "Have you read today's news?"

"Just the headlines," Natalia said. After all, part of her efforts to broaden herself beyond the world of business meant that she no longer had to obsessively monitor stock prices and economic news. Still, Patrick looked concerned. "Why?" she asked.

"There was an explosion in a Saint Petersburg train station. Twenty-six people were killed."

She sucked in a quick breath but forced herself to remain calm. "I'm sure Dimitri is fine," she said. "His estate is two hours south of the city."

Thinking about Dimitri was worrisome. He still hadn't responded to the letter she sent him almost a month ago. All she had was a strange package containing a Russian translation of *Little Women* that had arrived last week. She hadn't even realized it had been translated, but she'd flipped open the cover, reading the odd message from Dimitri scribbled on the title page, reasserting his insistence that Beth's death scene was the best in the book.

What was she to make of it? There was no letter, no other message, just a copy of *Little Women*. Dimitri was rarely that succinct.

Actually, he was *never* that succinct. Something must be deeply wrong for him not to have sent along an effusive note either ripping into the entire American literary canon or at least commenting on the letter she sent him about her pending visit in the spring. Maybe he hadn't gotten her letter. It was the only explanation she could think of to explain his strange silence.

"What else does the newspaper say?" Liam asked, his voice grim.

"Not much," Patrick replied. "Most of the victims aren't listed, but the anarchist who threw the bomb was killed. So was a twelve-year-old girl who'd been selling matches."

Liam swiveled his gaze to her. "You see? Things are getting bad over there. You shouldn't go."

"Are you going to Russia?" Gwen asked in surprise.

Natalia was reluctant to answer. What if Dimitri finally responded to her letter by telling her not to come? It would be embarrassing to admit he was the main reason she wanted to go, so she scrambled for an excuse.

"My mother told such wonderful stories of Moscow," she said. "Now that I'm selling my records there, I ought to go and learn a little more."

Patrick sounded skeptical. "You're selling records in London and Berlin too, but I haven't heard any plans for you to visit those cities."

"Who would want to see Russia in winter?" Gwen asked.

Even her mother had nothing good to say about the Russian winter, and Natalia hastily assured them she would wait until the spring to go. Provided Dimitri was willing to see her.

But as November passed and the snows of December deepened with no additional word from him, her worries grew.

39

Natalia had always believed that Christmas in
Central Park was magical. Tiny electric lights
were strung through the trees, ice skaters glided
across the frozen pond, and vendors sold hot chocolate to the
throngs of people bundled in coats and cheerful red scarves.
And the music! What celebration would be complete without
festive Christmas carols serenading the crowd?

It was the perfect opportunity to sell her Christmas album.
The same brass trio she'd hired for the album played carols at
the music pavilion, while she and Liam set up a table to sell
copies of the recording. The stall next to them sold phonograph
players, which were an ideal Christmas gift. Naturally, people
who had just bought a phonograph needed albums, and sales
for her Christmas record were brisk.

She blew into her bare hands to warm them. It was impossible to make change while wearing gloves, and it was cold
tonight, with steadily falling snow and a hint of wind.

Liam was with her, but he was completely useless as a sales-
man. He kept wanting to give the records away for free.

"It's Christmas, Natalia," he nagged. "Show a little of the
giving spirit."

She pretended not to notice when he slipped an album to

a woman wearing a patched coat who had just purchased a phonograph for her children.

Natalia reached down to the crates beneath the table for more albums. This was the infancy of a new industry, and she hadn't anticipated how much fun it would be to share music with others.

Once, Dimitri was the only person who shared her taste in music. She had found others who loved discussing music, but Dimitri would always be who she thought of first whenever she heard a new symphony, a mournful sonata, or a lively Russian dance.

It still hurt to think of him. It had been two months since she wrote to him of her plans to visit Russia in the spring, and she hadn't heard a peep from him. On the day she read that the Treaty of Aigun had been reaffirmed, she went to her father's house, where her mother's Russian chapel had been undisturbed for months. She lit candles and knelt to give thanks to God for being allowed to play a tiny part in this adventure that might bring peace and security to a tiny corner of the world. But she desperately wished she could have been with Dimitri. It strengthened her resolve to seek him out and settle things once and for all. Natalia had stared at the gold icons flickering in the candlelight. "Mama, I'm going to Russia," she whispered, and in her imagination the icons seemed to approve.

She shook off the memories and loaded another crate of records onto the table.

"Tell me that isn't who I think it is," Liam said, squinting into the distance. The annoyance in his face caused her to straighten and peer through the fat clumps of falling snow.

Poppy was marching through the crowd, wearing her finest chinchilla furs, her expression triumphant. The evening had been so pleasant until now.

Poppy cut to the front of the line, ignoring the annoyed glances behind her.

"You'll never guess," Poppy gushed. "It baffles and amazes me, and I have no idea what Count Sokolov sees in you, but he showed up on our doorstep, looking like death itself, and claims that he wants to see you."

Natalia looked around, but Dimitri was nowhere in sight, and nothing made sense. "Poppy, I have no idea what you're talking about."

Poppy rolled her eyes. "I think he's being ridiculous and ought to stay home where I can host a proper celebration for him, but he insisted on coming to the park. That cane he uses makes him so slow, but he should be here any moment."

If this was a joke, Natalia was going to smash this stack of records over Poppy's head, but her heart was pounding so hard that she couldn't think straight. She came out from behind the table, scanning the crowds.

There he was.

Dimitri's tall, slender form was unmistakable. He looked as gaunt and sickly as he'd been in San Francisco, but he was gorgeously attired in a fine black overcoat with a red scarf wrapped around his neck. He was leaning on a gold-handled cane. Scars marred the side of his face, and he walked gingerly, as if each step hurt. But oh, that smile! It cut straight to her heart.

She closed the distance between them, heart pounding as she arrived to stand before him. "What happened to you?" she asked, taking in his ghastly pallor and a fresh scar running from the corner of his right eye down into his beard.

"A bomb in Saint Petersburg," he said, and she recoiled in horrified surprise. He was supposed to be in his country dacha, not mingling with crowds and anarchists.

She reached out to lay a hand, gentle as a butterfly, against the side of his face.

"Ouch!" he said and flinched back.

"I'm sorry," she gasped. "Is it still tender?"

"No, your hands are cold."

She choked off a laugh and wanted to berate him for being such a crybaby except that it was obvious he'd been through something terrible. Every ounce of longing for her sweet, heroic, and terribly dandified dearest friend came roaring back.

She wanted to embrace him but didn't dare, because he truly did look awful.

"Oh, Dimitri, I'm afraid I've missed you terribly."

"I was hoping so."

"You did?"

"I've come all this way to see you, and it would be a shame if you had not suffered at least a little on my behalf. And now here I am. Half-dead on my feet and nowhere to sit down."

She would fix that! She glanced over her shoulder at Liam. "Get Poppy to help you sell the records!" she called out. Poppy looked aghast, but it would do her stepmother good to stand on her feet in gainful employment for an hour or two.

Natalia led Dimitri to a bench, and he winced as he lowered himself to sit. The light from a nearby lamppost made the hollows on his face look even worse.

She held his hand as he told her of the explosion in Saint Petersburg, how time felt suspended as he watched the explosion unfold before his eyes, incapable of escaping the bricks and glass that came flying at him. He suffered a concussion from the blast, as well as cuts on his face and elsewhere on his body from the flying shrapnel. He fell sick with a wicked case of pneumonia, and his ankle had been broken during an accident at Mirosa.

"It is mending?" she asked, glancing down at his foot.

"Yes, but look—I have a blister on my palm because of the cane."

She kissed it.

"I have not had a decent manicure since I left New York."

"I'll take care of that," she assured him, already looking forward to the chance to start pampering him. Once again, he seemed to have suffered terribly over the past few months. He needed someone to look after him, and she desperately wanted to be the person to do it.

"Why did you come back?" she asked.

"I got your letter suggesting you would visit in the spring. It got me to thinking. . . ." The corners of his eyes darkened with grief. "Natalia, I do not think you belong in Russia. It is not the sort of open society where a woman like you can flourish. I came to tell you not to come."

She swallowed hard. "All right."

Did that mean they didn't have a future? If so, he could have told her in a letter.

"I realized that I must decide between you and Russia," he said. "I will always love Mirosa, but it has changed. Or perhaps it is I who have changed. A peasant from Mirosa emigrated to America, and I found myself envious that he could break away for a new life. A lady I cared for who once lived for nothing but her father's bank broke away from it to start a new company, and I was envious of her too."

"Even though she lives in New York City?"

His shoulders sagged, and he looked even more tired. "Even though," he acknowledged with a reluctant smile. "When I struggled with pneumonia, I feared I was about to die. I had so many regrets, mostly that I had found my dearest friend and the woman I wish to spend the rest of my life with, but I walked away from her because of my love for a family farm. A farm! Natalia, I don't know what the future holds, but we have conquered greater challenges in the past, correct?"

"You got the czar to recommit to the 1858 treaty," she said. "You moved a nation."

"Only because you helped," he said. "*Together* we moved a nation." His hands covered her chilly ones, warming them. "I came here so we can have some of those conversations you mentioned in your letter. I think we are destined to be together, and it must happen here in New York. Perhaps my fate is to be like one of your mundane domestic novels with a predictably happy ending. A shame, but I have survived this long, so perhaps I am not supposed to enjoy a heroic death quite yet. Dearest Natalia, if I stay here, would you be willing to marry me?"

A lump swelled in her throat. All her dreams were coming true at the same time, but it hurt because Dimitri was giving up Mirosa and so many other things he loved. She would spend her life making sure he did not regret it.

"I would be willing to marry you," she said. She reached up to cradle his face in her palms, touching her forehead to his. "I hope we will have mundane domestic bliss, but who knows?"

They lived in a world of corporate titans, scheming politicians, and a burgeoning music industry. None of it sounded like mundane domesticity to Natalia, but Dimitri's measuring stick had always been a little different than hers. It was one of the reasons she adored him, and together they would step out into this bold new world side by side.

Epilogue

*D*imitri leaned over a lilac bush, frowning at the brown splotches on the underside of the leaves. Their entire garden was a glorious, overgrown tangle of clematis, wisteria, and climbing roses. The Blackstones thought he was demented for refusing to trim the profusion, but this was how a proper dacha was supposed to look. He had bought the property next to Maxim Tachenko's land, and now their dachas shared a ridiculously overgrown garden.

"Natalia! The spots on my lilacs are back!" The windows were open, but he had to shout because she had the phonograph playing.

She eventually came outside in the red-and-yellow sarafan he had bought for her during their honeymoon. "Didn't you use the formula Gwen recommended?" she asked.

"Yes, but it's not working. Gwendolyn needs to come out and inspect these in person."

"She's not going to do that," Natalia said.

Gwen was in the city finishing her doctorate and had her hands full with a toddler. She rarely came out to the lake house. Likewise, Tachenko had gone overseas for a European tour, so it was up to Dimitri and Natalia to keep an eye on all three lake houses.

"We can take her a clipping when we are in town next month to record the Chopin sonata," Natalia said.

He quirked a brow at her. "Will I be allowed to accompany you?"

"Of course! Just please don't adopt another child while I'm not around."

They now had two children. Shortly after they adopted four-month-old Anna, he and Natalia were in town to commission another Brahms duet. While Natalia was at the studio, he went to the orphanage with no purpose other than to be sure the facility was well provided with everything they needed. That was his intention, but his heart was swiftly captured by three-year-old Mischa, a little boy who'd recently been orphaned and spoke only Russian. How abandoned and lonely he looked! None of the nurses could understand the toddler, and Mischa clung to Dimitri's leg while looking up at him with huge, soulful brown eyes. In that instant Dimitri knew this boy was destined to become his son.

He brought Mischa home to Natalia the same day. They had not expected to adopt again so soon, but how could he leave his son overnight at an orphanage where no one could under-stand him? Natalia had been taken aback but quickly agreed that Mischa belonged with them. They'd decided to hold off on adopting more children for at least two years, and for now their family was the perfect size.

"Let's take the children to the city so they may play with your little brother," he said impulsively, and Natalia flashed him a blinding smile.

He preferred their country home, but Natalia was always keen for a visit to town. He still mistrusted the city, but he liked indulging Natalia, so they went often. Besides, it would be another six years before the apple trees he planted would bear fruit. By then the mill Ilya Komarov was building him would be operational, and he would try to recreate a bit of the pastoral bliss he once had in Russia.

His homesickness wasn't as bad as he once feared. It still descended upon him occasionally, but Natalia could usually spot the signs and knew how to cure the ache in his soul. She'd beckon him inside, then make him a cup of spiced cider and rub his feet, begging for stories of the vast Russian steppe, or the palaces of Saint Petersburg, or of Temujin and their dangerous trek through the wilderness. Somehow, in recounting the stories for her, his memories of that faraway land became a shared recollection they both treasured, and that helped ease the wistful ache.

Someday he would take Natalia and their children to Russia so they could see the endless fields of autumn wheat, the wooden churches in the countryside, and the land where Natalia's mother had been raised. He would show Natalia the ring of birch trees that surrounded Mirosa and the creaking waterwheel where he almost died. Beneath the immense sky they would share the cider grown on his ancestral land and raise a toast to their shared heritage.

And then they would return to America, where they all belonged.

Historical Note

The Trans-Siberian Railway was completed in 1904. The railroad's chief proponent was Count Sergei Witte, who believed it was the key to transforming the Russian economy by gaining access to the rich natural resources of Siberia. Construction was challenging because the railroad crossed hundreds of rivers, swamps, forests, and permafrost. Extreme temperatures constantly interfered with the schedule, but the railway was completed on time and under budget.

The Boxer Rebellion (1899–1901) affected construction of the railroad when the uprising spread to the Russian border. When Chinese insurgents shelled the Russian town of Blagoveshchensk, the Russians used the incident to assert greater control over the region by expelling ethnic Chinese villagers. The expulsions took place at numerous towns along the Amur River, resulting in thousands of deaths from drowning, shooting, and stampedes. Estimates of the deaths range between three and nine thousand people. The name for this series of pogroms in rural Russia is not standardized but is generally referred to as either the Blagoveshchensk Massacre or the Sixty-Four Villages East of the River Massacre.

Count Arthur Cassini was the Russian ambassador to the United States from 1898–1905. He was as brilliant as described in the novel but is perhaps best known today for his famous relatives. His daughter, Countess Marguerite Cassini, was best friends with Alice Roosevelt, and the two teenaged girls were notorious for scandalizing Washington society. Fifty years after the events in this novel, Marguerite wrote of her relationship with Alice in her memoir, *Never a Dull Moment*: "Our friendship had the violence of a bomb. We were two badly spoiled girls set only on [our] own pleasure." By her own admission, she and Alice inflicted "a veritable reign of terror" on Washington society. Their friendship imploded when Alice's future husband became infatuated with Marguerite, who ultimately married and divorced a Russian count, moved to Italy, and founded a fashion house. Her son, Oleg Cassini, was Jacqueline Kennedy's favorite designer, and her seventeenth-century ancestor, Giovanni Cassini, was the astronomer for whom the Cassini spacecraft was named.

Today, the Trans-Siberian Railway remains the world's longest passenger railroad at 5,772 miles. Riding the Trans-Siberian from Moscow to Vladivostock takes seven days, crosses eight time zones, and is routinely cited as an adventure of a lifetime.

Discussion Questions

1. Dimitri reflects on his difficult years while working on the railroad in Siberia with the following: "*Sometimes our best memories are born during our harshest trials. They become happy only in hindsight.*" What did he mean by this?

2. During a weekend party at Mirosa, the wealthy landowners debate whether it was dishonest for Ilya Komarov to charge people different amounts for the same pint of applejack. What do you think?

3. Dimitri asks Natalia to say something positive about Poppy, which forces her to reassess Poppy's contribution in restoring Oscar's health. How might focusing on an admirable trait help you view an otherwise frustrating person in a more positive light?

4. Liam splits with Darla because she spoke disrespectfully about him to her friends. Is he too hasty in walking away from her?

5. Is Dimitri really a hypochondriac? Why do you think he dwells on his various aches and pains?

6. Oscar is willing to sue Silas Conner for his libel of Natalia, but she dissuades him. She reflects: *Punishing him might deliver a quick rush of satisfaction, but it would never bring her the lasting peace that forgiveness could*

provide. Is it possible to truly forgive someone if they have not expressed remorse?

7. Neither Dimitri nor Natalia needs to work for money, but they both undertake difficult jobs in order to prove themselves. Why do they do so?

8. Liam dislikes his job but does not feel he is able to quit, even though he does not personally need the money. Is he right to stick with a job he hates?

9. Much of Natalia's fascination with Russia comes from the stories her mother shared. Have you inherited a similar fascination for a different culture, profession, or experience from your own relatives? Have you tried to share something of your own culture or experiences with the younger people in your family?

10. Natalia believes an unhappy ending to a novel ruins the story, while Dimitri loves such endings. What do you think?

READ ON
FOR A SNEAK PEEK AT
Book Three of
THE BLACKSTONE LEGACY SERIES
by Elizabeth Camden

*T*he prospect of apologizing to the only enemy Liam
Blackstone had in the world was galling, but he had
to do it to keep Fletcher's respect. Liam strode down
the street alongside his mentor, listening to all the reasons he
should apologize to Charles Morse, possibly the biggest scoundrel in the city.

"The point of yesterday's outing was to have a cordial afternoon sailing in the harbor so you and Charles could bury the
hatchet, not to stir up new resentments," Fletcher said. "Kick-
ing him off your yacht opened up a whole new front in the war
between the two of you."

"He struck a seventeen-year-old deckhand," Liam bit out.

"Yes, and that was appalling, but there were better ways to
handle it than letting your temper fly off the handle."

Yesterday's fight had been a doozy. The afternoon sail on
Liam's private yacht had collapsed quickly after Morse slapped
a deckhand, a sweet kid named Caleb. Caleb was a little slow,
but once he understood a task, he carried it out doggedly and
never tired. The problem was that Caleb couldn't adjust. Any
change to his routine got Caleb flustered, which was what happened when Morse started banging out orders yesterday.

They had been two miles out at sea when Morse slapped
Caleb. As tempting as it had been to retaliate in kind, Liam
ordered Morse to be rowed ashore, and the incident cast a pall
over the rest of the afternoon. Several of the other businessmen
on board privately commended Liam for the way he protected

the deckhand, but no one approved of what he'd done in throwing Morse off the yacht.

Now Fletcher was dragging Liam to Morse's home like a disobedient child to apologize. The Morse estate squatted on a large plot on the richest part of Fifth Avenue. It was where robber barons flaunted their wealth in grandiose palaces towering five stories high with molded entablatures, spires, and turrets. So different than the slum where Liam grew up.

"I understand that you are still new in the world of Wall Street," Fletcher said. "Everyone appreciates the fresh perspective you have brought to the board of directors. You are the only one among us who has actually worked inside a steel mill or made anything with your own two hands. Against all odds, you persuaded the board of directors to authorize a huge pay raise for the men in the steel mills—"

"Against Morse's objections."

"Yes! Charles Morse is the shrewdest man on Wall Street, and you got the better of him. Be proud of that. You won. Why can't you simply get along with him?"

Because Charles Morse was a bully. He showed it in his brusque manner in dealing with waiters in restaurants and how he cheated at cards if he couldn't win honestly. If the rumors were true, even Morse's own wife didn't like him, and they were newlyweds.

Fletcher continued his litany. "I've spent the past year playing peacekeeper between the two of you, and my patience is wearing thin. You are an asset to the board, but if push comes to shove, we need Morse more than we need you. As chairman of the board, it is my job to create a strong and productive group of people dedicated to maintaining U.S. Steel's prominence in the industry. If the two of you can't manage to be in the same room without coming to blows, it won't be Morse I ask to leave."

The pronouncement landed like a fist in Liam's gut. He was the only person on the board committed to putting the welfare of the workers ahead of profits. U.S. Steel employed 160,000 frontline workers in steel mills all over the nation. They were in Pittsburgh, Scranton, Cleveland, and Chicago. Those men earned a living with their hands, their backs, and their brawn. They didn't get ahead by scheming, cheating, or smacking servants. They depended on Liam to represent their interests on the company's board of directors, and if he had to choke back his pride and kiss Morse's ring to keep his seat, he'd do it.

They marched up the flight of marble steps to the cool shade beneath the stone-arched portico of the mansion.

"This is where I leave you," Fletcher said, offering a good-natured handshake.

Liam was flabbergasted. "You're not coming inside?" This was going to be a disaster without Fletcher to play the peacekeeper. Morse usually pretended to be friendly in front of the chairman of the board, but when no one was watching, Morse's true colors emerged.

"You need to manage Charles Morse on your own," Fletcher said as he retreated down the steps. "Take my advice and apologize for what happened yesterday. Get the incident behind you, and we can begin this afternoon's board meeting with a clean slate."

Fletcher sauntered toward the street as though the matter were already settled, but Liam braced himself for the confrontation ahead. Maybe it was for the best. He didn't have to like Charles Morse, he merely needed to form a workable truce.

He drew a deep breath and rang the bell. Distant chimes tolled deep inside the mansion, sounding like gongs of doom. Everything about going down on bended knee before Charles Morse felt wrong, but it had to be done.

It was still early, which probably accounted for why the door was answered by a parlor maid instead of the butler. She looked about twenty, with freckled skin and a shock of red hair.

"Can I help you, sir?" she asked in a charming Irish lilt.

"Please let Mr. Morse know that Liam Blackstone is here. He'll understand why."

The maid led him to an opulent mess of a parlor while she delivered the message. It was no surprise that Morse made him wait. Ten minutes stretched into twenty as Liam paced, too anxious to sit as he scrutinized every object in the fussy, overly decorated room. Why did rich men feel so compelled to show off their fortune?

An ugly lump of rock looked out of place among the fancy knickknacks on the mantel. He tilted the granite lump, which appeared to have veins of fool's gold embedded inside.

"Copper," Morse announced from the doorway, his voice chilly.

Liam turned, the lump of rock still in his hand. Morse's growing dominance in the copper industry was one of the reasons Fletcher wanted to keep him on the board. Now the rock made sense. It gave Morse an opportunity to brag about his vast copper mines out west. Liam set the rock back on the mantel and faced Morse, a good-looking man with a strong build and a full head of black hair that matched his neatly groomed mustache.

"Thank you for seeing me," Liam said, striving for a polite tone.

Morse gave the slightest tip of his head but remained frosty. "Your ship's rowboat is dreadful. It doesn't have any ballast, and there were no cushions on the seats."

That was because it wasn't meant for ferry service. If Morse had simply shown remorse over slapping Caleb, Liam wouldn't have ordered him ashore.

"Charles, we are two men of business who only want the best for the company," Liam began, but Morse interrupted.

"Do we? It seems you care more about the men in the factories."

As if those men weren't part of the company, Liam silently thought, but he continued as though he hadn't heard. "We don't need to be the best of friends, but I am prepared to be cordial. You couldn't have known the challenges my deckhand has when he gets contradictory orders, and I shouldn't have lost my temper. I'm sorry."

He waited, hoping the older man might express remorse for striking Caleb. It didn't happen.

"Perhaps you should consider hiring a better quality of staff when entertaining guests," Morse said.

Liam resisted the urge to defend Caleb. "Whatever the cause of the incident, I'm sorry I got angry."

"Can't you even control your temper when you're in a business gathering?" Morse asked. "Perhaps that's how they handle things in the back alleys, but you are among men of quality now."

Liam itched to point out that slapping a servant wasn't a sterling example of gentility, but a ruckus in the hall distracted him. It sounded like two women squabbling. The Irish maid's voice was easily recognizable, but there was another woman in the mix, sounding equally adamant about demanding an audience.

The frazzled maid rushed inside. "I'm sorry, sir, but she insists on seeing you."

A pretty young woman pushed her way into the room. She was smartly dressed in a trim blue jacket and a straw boater hat, but obviously of the middle class. She was lovely, in a fierce, strong sort of way. Even the scar splitting one brow did not detract from her appeal.

The woman held an envelope aloft. "This bill is four months overdue," she stated. "I've sent invoice after invoice, and you have ignored them all, so I have no choice but to collect in person."

Morse flushed in outrage. "How dare you. If there has been a mix-up in the payment of a legitimate expense, you should submit the bill to my secretary, not interrupt a business meeting like a fishwife."

The woman didn't back down. "I have been hectoring your secretary for months. He has refused to pay, and I won't tolerate it. You owe me $135 for the ice cream we delivered for your wedding reception at the Belmont Hotel, and it's now four months overdue."

Morse's smile was oily. "Then of course I refuse to pay. Your complaint is with the Belmont Hotel, not me. If you haven't been paid, I suggest you take it up with the hotel."

"The Belmont told me you've stiffed them too," the woman said. "Perhaps they're willing to absorb the loss, but I won't. You owe me $95 for the ice cream, a twenty-dollar late fee, and three percent for interest."

"That doesn't add up to $135," Morse snapped.

"I added the court fee I just paid to file a lawsuit against you."

A momentary silence stretched in the room, and then Morse threw back his head and affected an amused laugh. "You're going to sue me over a $95 bill?"

The woman nodded. "I hate bullies. You have succeeded in bullying the hotel and the hardworking baker who has also been stiffed for the wedding cake he provided, but I'll sue you to kingdom come until I have been paid."

To Liam's surprise, Morse agreed to pay.

"Very well," he said tightly. "The cost of a nuisance lawsuit is not worth my time, and it's little enough to pacify an annoying gnat." He beckoned for the woman to follow him into his private study.

Liam followed. He didn't trust Morse alone with this woman, and he monitored the interaction from the open doorway of an elaborate, book-lined study.

"Please address the check to Molinaro Ice Cream," the woman said primly.

Morse affected an indulgent grin as he opened a desk drawer and removed a leather book of checks. The smile did not reach his eyes as he wrote out the check, the pen scratching in the silence of the heavily carpeted, silk-draped room.

Liam took the opportunity to study the young woman. She was slim but strong. They had the same coloring, with olive-toned complexions and glossy dark hair. Her pretty, gamine face was full of character, even with the faint white scar that bisected an eyebrow.

She must have felt his stare, because her gaze flicked to his face, and he flashed her a wink.

She flushed and looked back at the bank draft as Morse pulled it from the notebook, gently wafting the slip of paper to dry the ink. Several seconds passed in silence. If Liam wasn't a witness, he suspected Morse would make her beg for the check.

"Give it to her," Liam said.

Morse continued fanning a few more seconds before flicking the check toward the woman with a twist of his fingers. "Don't spend it all in one place," he said with a smirk.

The woman snatched it from his hand, then whirled to leave the room.

"Thank you, sir," she whispered as she passed Liam, trailing the soft scent of vanilla as she hurried down the hall.

Morse resumed his seat and looked up at Liam. "This whole apology nonsense is not going as swimmingly as Fletcher hoped, is it? But what a good little soldier you are to come across town and offer it."

Heat began gathering beneath his collar, but he wouldn't let Morse goad him. At this very moment there were 160,000 men showing up to work in sweltering steel mills. They had a long, grueling week of dangerous labor ahead of them, and Liam was their only voice. He wouldn't let Charles Morse run him off the board.

"Fletcher wants what's best for the company, and that means you and I need to get along," he said.

"Fletcher wants to make money," Morse corrected him. "He needs me on the board because he knows I can make it happen. What I can't understand is why he needs *you*."

Liam raised his chin a notch. "He needs me because the unions trust me. I can keep peace in the mills."

"You were appointed to the board because of family connections," Morse said dismissively.

Liam tried not to wince, but the charge was true. If Liam weren't a Blackstone, he wouldn't have had the leverage to demand a position on the board. Everyone knew it, and Morse gloated.

"You have nothing but an eighth-grade education and a history of rabble-rousing from your days in the union," Morse continued. "I could go into any steel mill in America and find

men who are more intelligent, more articulate, and better edu-
cated than you. You've still got calluses on your hands and a
chip on your shoulder."

Liam skewered Morse with a look of contempt. "I don't need
your approval. Any man who would stiff a woman over $95
worth of ice cream isn't someone whose good opinion I value."

"You'd better start valuing it," Morse said in a silky tone.
"No one on the board likes you. Everyone wants you off, and
I've decided to call for a vote of no confidence. I've wanted to
call it since the day your family forced us to accept you onto
the board, and after your stunt yesterday, I've got enough men
on my side to vote you off. I'm going to introduce a resolution
to oust you from the board. I expect it will pass with flying
colors."

An ache began in the pit of his belly. Liam had known since
his first board meeting that he was in over his head. All those
men had college educations and friendships that dated back to
when they were in short pants. While his fellow board members
grew up in New England boarding schools learning to play
polo and speak foreign languages, Liam was shoveling coal into
furnaces at a Pittsburgh steel mill.

"Hogwash," Liam said. "The only reason the unions didn't
go on strike was because they know I'm on the board and looking out for them."

Morse shrugged. "None of those men get to vote. This afternoon the board will discuss how to recapitalize the sinking
funds for our subsidiaries and whether we should renegotiate
the maturity dates. Each member will be expected to offer his
opinion. And yours is?"

Silence stretched in the room. Liam rarely spoke at board
meetings on anything besides worker compensation because he
lacked the qualifications to have an informed opinion. Everyone
knew it. He clenched his teeth, scrambling for a way to defend
himself, when Morse offered a surprisingly kind concession.

"Come, Liam. You accomplished your mission in getting
the steel workers a considerable pay raise last year, but now

it's time for you to go back home and enjoy the fruits of your accomplishments. Your father would be proud of you."

Liam stiffened at the mention of his father.

"Did I ever tell you that I knew your father?" Morse asked. "What a rare combination of academic brilliance and compassion. He was always so even-tempered and gentle. He founded a college, correct?"

"He did."

"It must be intimidating to walk in Theodore Blackstone's footsteps."

It was the first entirely true statement Liam had ever heard Morse say. Yes, it was intimidating to be such a great man's son, and Liam desperately wanted to be worthy of his father's legacy. The only way he could ensure his father's humanitarian interests would triumph over men like Charles Morse was to keep his seat on the board.

Everything else was secondary. Nothing and nobody was going to stop him. It didn't matter that he lacked an education and didn't have any friends on Wall Street; he had a seat on the board and would fight to keep it. He would force himself to get along with Charles Morse.

"Any man with a functioning brain would be honored to walk in Theodore Blackstone's footsteps, and that's what I intend to do." Liam smiled a little. "Brace yourself, Charles. I intend to ensure that my father's humanitarian sentiments are well represented on the board of U.S. Steel. You will *never* succeed in voting me out."

Liam turned on his heel and left Morse fuming in his study, but secretly he feared he wouldn't be able to live up to those bold words.

Elizabeth Camden is best known for her historical novels set in Gilded Age America, featuring clever heroines and richly layered story lines. Before she was a writer, she was an academic librarian at some of the largest and smallest libraries in America, but her favorite is the continually growing library in her own home. Her novels have won the RITA and Christy Awards and have appeared on the CBA bestsellers list. She lives in Orlando, Florida, with her husband, who graciously tolerates her intimidating stockpile of books. Learn more online at elizabethcamden.com.

Sign Up for Elizabeth's Newsletter

Keep up to date with Elizabeth's news on book releases and events by signing up for her email list at elizabethcamden.com.

More from Elizabeth Camden

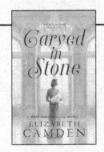

When lawyer Patrick O'Neill agrees to resurrect an old mystery and challenge the Blackstones' legacy of greed and corruption, he doesn't expect to be derailed by the kindhearted family heiress, Gwen Kellerman. She is tasked with getting him to drop the case, but when the mystery takes a shocking twist, he is the only ally she has.

Carved in Stone
THE BLACKSTONE LEGACY #1

You May Also Like . . .

Luke Delacroix's hidden past as a spy has him carrying out an ambitious agenda—thwarting the reelection of his only real enemy. But trouble begins when he falls for Marianne Magruder, the congressman's daughter. Can their newfound love survive a political firestorm, or will three generations of family rivalry drive them apart forever?

The Prince of Spies by Elizabeth Camden
HOPE AND GLORY #3
elizabethcamden.com

Secretary to the first lady of the United States, Caroline Delacroix is at the pinnacle of high society—but is hiding a terrible secret. Immediately suspicious of Caroline but also attracted to her, secret service agent Nathaniel Trask must battle his growing love for her as the threat to the president rises and they face adventure, heartbreak, and danger.

A Gilded Lady by Elizabeth Camden
HOPE AND GLORY #2
elizabethcamden.com

Libby has been given a powerful gift: to live one life in 1774 Colonial Williamsburg and the other in 1914 Gilded Age New York City. When she falls asleep in one life, she wakes up in the other without any time passing. On her twenty-first birthday, Libby must choose one path and forfeit the other—but how can she possibly decide when she has so much to lose?

When the Day Comes by Gabrielle Meyer
TIMELESS #1
gabriellemeyer.com

More from Bethany House

Allie Massey's dream to use her grandparents' estate for equine therapy is crushed when she discovers the property has been sold to a contractor. With only weeks until demolition, Allie unearths one of her Nana Dale's best-kept secrets—about her champion filly, a handsome young man, and one fateful night during WWII—and perhaps a clue to keep her dream alive.

By Way of the Moonlight by Elizabeth Musser
elizabethmusser.com

Within months, Isabelle Wardrop lost her parents, her fortune, and her home, and with no qualifications, is forced to accept help from Dr. Mark Henshaw—the very man she blames for her mother's death. Mark has hopes of earning Isabelle's forgiveness and affections, but an unexpected incident may derail any hope they have of being together.

A Feeling of Home by Susan Anne Mason
REDEMPTION'S LIGHT #3
susanannemason.net

After moving to Jerusalem, Aya expects to be bored in her role as wife to a Torah student but finds herself fascinated by her husband's studies. When her brother Sha'ul makes a life-altering decision, she is faced with a troubling question: How can she remain true to all she's been taught since infancy and still love her blasphemous brother?

The Apostle's Sister by Angela Hunt
JERUSALEM ROAD #4
angelahuntbooks.com

⊠ BETHANYHOUSE